Brown Water

Brown Water

Getting There is Half the Fun...

Samuel C. Crawford

Library of Congress Control Number: 2002091543

ISBN:	Hardcover	978-1-4010-5464-9
	Softcover	978-1-4010-5463-2
	eBook	978-1-4653-2723-9

Print information available on the last page.

Rev. date: 10/15/2021

To order additional copies of this book, contact:
Xlibris
844-714-8691
www.Xlibris.com
Orders@Xlibris.com
554607

TO MY LOVING WIFE OF 25 YEARS, PATRICIA AND OUR LOVELY DAUGHTER STEPHANIE. THANK YOU FOR YOUR LOVE AND PATIENCE.

Personal and deepest heartfelt thanks to Murray A. Armstrong, Mickey D. Burriss, James H. Crawford, U.S. Navy, Retired, Tony Maskello, Patrick J. Murphy II, and Randall K. Smith for their time, ideas, suggestions and words of encouragement.

Forward by Joni Bour

Now and then, I will read a book that leaves me wishing there were more pages to read, more story to follow. Sam Crawford has written such a book and I know I shall fail miserable in trying to describe his book, and why I think you should read it, but I am going to give it a shot anyway.

A story of two young men, both nearly the same age, and yet worlds apart. Charles Edwards has gone to war, knowing nothing about survival and nothing about life or death. He becomes a real soldier, a real man, and survivor in the short time he is there. Then he meets up with another young man, Petty Officer Dan, who takes him under his wing.

This story is comical, sad, and beautiful in its simplicity and one of the most charming books I have ever read about the Vietnam War. In reading this book, there were times when I laughed until my sides hurt. Other times when the story described something funny, I felt tears fun down my cheeks. Because in a real world, the world I live in, day to day warm meals, safe streets, happy kids, and a dog name Roy, things like those that happened to Dan and Charles, don't happen. Not knowing why everyone else leaned their sea bags against the window next to their seat on the bus-might have made me laugh if it hadn't been for the fact that it was because they were trying to keep bullets that went through the window from hitting them first.

It was a great adventure to follow along as Dan showed Charles the ropes, except for the cold hard reality that the ropes were not the way to do your job faster or easier, they were ways to simply stay alive.

What I enjoyed most about the story, was also the most difficult thing about the story, and that is that the author approached his life, (which do you think he is, Dan or Charles?) with humor and self-deprecation. He was so matter of fact about things like a Vietnamese boy selling his sister on the street corner the way an American boy might sell a newspaper. How could he be so casual about something so unbelievable? The answer of course is that he had to write the truth about the war that he survived—a war where the value of commodities you could trade or sell were the only things of value. You may find yourself just staring at the page as if you don't understand at all what he just said. You know it is true, you have heard those sorts of stories before, and yet, your heart really cannot fathom such lack of feeling or lack of concern for your own family or fellow human being. He brings to light many things few authors bother to write about. Things like day to day life that were probably quite ordinary after a while, but at first, they were shocking and terrifying to a young man in a war torn land, a zillion miles away from his peaceful homeland.

Sam Crawford will make you laugh and laugh, and feel sad all at the same time. He will make you wonder and worry about those two young men by the time you read the end of his book. I guess that is his plan so that you will go out and search for his second book. I know you will, and right you will be to want to do that. I can't imagine that you would be disappointed. To the contrary, by the time you get the end and get a change to look at the pictures and wonder about the young men you have grown to love, you will already know the secret. Maybe . . . .

Chapter 1

At 35,000 feet, Braniff flight 727 from Travis Air Force Base in California was one packed flight. This type of airplane normally carried about 160 passengers, but since this was a chartered military flight, I estimated over 190 service men sardined onboard. There were no women, children, or crying babies on this flight.

Almost everyone was in dress uniforms: Marines in dress blue, Army in olive green and a few Navy guys like me, in dress whites. A few guys—the officer seated next to me, for example—were ironically conspicuous in jungle utilities. There was no first class section or even coach, for that matter. There was just third class and that probably explained why I was sitting with an officer. He was sound asleep and had been since I got onboard. As if things were not strange enough, the airplane was painted orange.

The flight was not really so bad, it had been only twenty-four hours since I had left my home in Baltimore after a week of leave from boot camp. The flight from Hawaii alone had been eight hours and that was a long time to be in one seat. From sitting so long in one spot, it felt as if I no longer had the split in my butt. Furthermore, the seats were so close together that I had to step into the aisle just to change my mind.

My first set of orders out of boot camp directed me to report to the USS SUMMIT (ARR23). As far as I could tell, she was some type of repair ship now deployed somewhere near Saigon, Vietnam. It was my understanding that she pulled into port at Saigon every so often, which was why my orders had me reporting to Saigon. No one had explained to me just how to go about finding this ship, much less, how to get around once I arrived in Saigon. Who would I ask if she were there or not? What would I do if the SUMMIT were not in Saigon?

I naively hoped there would be an information desk at the airport. It would have been to my advantage, if I could have found a map at the airport, especially if that map had on it a little red "X" and the words, "YOU ARE HERE." It would have been great if the map also had a few little boats at one end with names on them . . . USS SUMMIT, to be specific. It would have been my luck that the vessel's location was some military secret. And that no one would be willing to inform me of anything. How would I even find out if she were still afloat? She could have sunk or been decommissioned after I received my orders.

Would I get a cab at the airport? If I did, would the driver communicate in English? Would he take American money for the fare? Hell, even if I did get an English-speaking cab driver and he did take American money, I would not have known where in the world to tell him to take me.

It was strange how things had changed in such a short time for me. When I left home and told my parents' good-bye, I felt like a man going off to war. On the plane, I knew I was just a kid who was a few days shy of his nineteen birthday and completely terrified. I had no idea what to do when my flight landed. I knew what my orders were; I just did not know how I was going to accomplish them. This was not the way to start a new job and possibly, a new career.

The pilot announced that we would be landing soon and instructed everyone to buckle-in. I thought about my predicament and slowly shook my head from side to side. "Damn, Damn, Damn," I said softly to myself.

At that moment, the officer next to me woke from his nap and said, "What do you want? Do I know you?"

"Sir. No, sir. Just thinking aloud. Sorry, sir," I answered with obvious apprehension.

He questioned me as he rubbed the sleep out of his eyes, "Weren't you calling my name? Dan, Dan, Dan?"

"Sir. No, sir. I just said 'Damn.' I didn't mean to wake you. Sorry about that, sir," I said with some embarrassment.

"No sweat my man," was his response that relaxed me a little. His friendly smile was most reassuring.

"No sweat," I sort of asked under my breath. I wonder what he meant by that?

"Yeah. No sweat. It just means that it don't mean nothin," he explained for my benefit.

"Cool," was the only response I could come up with for now.

"Well, I'm awake now. Who the hell are you?"

"Sir, I'm Charles Edward, Seaman Apprentice, from Baltimore Maryland, sir," I answered him as I tried to sound military and all that. I was sure that I was doing it correctly because I was saying, 'Sir' at the beginning and end of each statement.

He looked me over and said, "Let me guess. Fresh out of boot camp and on your way to, 'The-Nam.' Right?"

I responded smartly, "Sir. Yes, sir. Where are you going, sir?"

After a long flight without anyone to talk to, I was full of questions and wanted to hold a conversation with anybody, even if he was an officer. In boot camp, the only time I had a conversation with an officer was when he was yelling orders at me. Besides, I liked the way this guy called Vietnam, 'The-Nam.' Coming from a seasoned soldier, it sounded different than it had on the evening news.

"First off, boot, I'm not an officer. So, you can cut out the 'sir' shit. This is my third trip, 'The-Nam,' and I'm a Petty Officer Third Class," he said as he tried to stretch out his long legs in the little space between seats.

"But you have an officer's pin on your collar. An eagle. You're a captain, right?"

"Wrong my man. It's not an eagle. It's a crow. An enlisted man's run of the mill, petty officer's-crow. You'll learn soon enough that officers get the cool stuff."

"Cool stuff?" What was this guy saying?

"Yeah, Navy Captains wear eagle pins on their collars. You know . . . eagles . . . majestic, proud, symbol of America, excellent hunters. Us enlisted guys get the crow for our insignia. It's black, makes a lot of noise, and eats road kill."

"Besides," he continued, "with the way rank has its ups and downs here, in, 'The-Nam,' there's no telling how long anyone will keep his stripes. It's easier to just pin on a different set every now and then on your collar to keep things current. Sewing and re-sewing is such a pain, after a while you'll need a new shirt."

I did not know what he meant by all that, so I just ignored it. "You don't dress like you're in the Navy," I pointed out. "You look more like a Marine."

"Navy personnel serving in-country are authorized to wear greens. Once you get in-country, you don't want to be walking around in your dress whites. You will make a nice target in a place where everything is either brown or green. Even the water is brown. Everything over here stays green and brown, year round."

"I don't expect to be in Saigon very long. I'm trying to find a ship called the SUMMIT. It's an ARR and first, I've got to figure out a way to get to her and then I'll be out to serve my one-year tour. I'll be on a silver navy ship, sailing on the blue ocean. I'll get to wear my little white hat and bell-bottom pants. I really won't have to worry about anything being brown or green," I answered projecting that I was pretty sure of myself. I hoped he would have some suggestions on finding my ship.

"Oh really? First off, navy ships are Battleship gray and not silver."

"All right," I answered.

"So, what makes you think, Charles Edward, Seaman Apprentice from Baltimore, Maryland, that your ship is out at sea?"

"Well I'm not positive, but she is a ship and ships spend time at sea."

"Do you know what the ARR in ARR23 stands for?"

"Yes, some sort of repair ship."

"It stands for Auxiliary Repair River," Dan explained.

"So maybe she's tied up in the Saigon harbor somewhere," I responded, as if I almost knew what I was talking about this time.

"Well, when I left her two weeks ago, she was about 100 miles from Saigon. And not exactly in the easterly direction that you're thinking."

I could not believe my good fortune that he was stationed on my ship, or at the very least, knew where the SUMMIT was located. Now maybe I could find out, with his help of course, how to find her. "Well, I assume," I responded. "That she goes in and out of Saigon every so often to repair ships in the South China Sea. Then she probably goes back to Saigon for supplies and repairs."

"She's only been to Saigon once in two years," he answered. "She's a repair ship and can repair herself when she breaks down. Besides, an auxiliary repair ship doesn't repair ships at sea. So, what do you think?"

"Hey, I'm the new guy here. I'm not sure what to think." Now that I got him answering questions for me, I might as well continue. I had to ask the one question that I often heard civilians ask Vietnam veterans, "So what's it like being over here?"

He looked at me as if he had fielded this question a million times; "It's fear and fascination. Sometimes it's a little more of one than the other is. Other times, it's just the opposite, with everything else mixed in."

"Everything else?"

"Yeah, I can't leave out the mass confusion and death."

I wanted to know more about that, but I needed to check on other things, such as where he left her two weeks ago, whether he was going back to her, and anything else he could tell me about the ship. However, before I could ask even one more question, the pilot ordered everyone to take their seats, buckle up for landing and to put out all cigarettes.

Dan turned and stared out the window as if trying to find something; or maybe he just wanted to ignore me. He might even have been as scared as me, third time here or not.

My flight started out to be an adventure. It felt as if the pilot was gaining speed to land rather than slowing. The last few thousand feet it appeared to me that we were heading almost straight down, only to level off at the last moment before we touched down. I did not think this was normal and I commented to Dan, "That was some landing."

He responded with, "That was a great landing."

"Great?" I questioned. I didn't think that it was all that great.

"Yep. A good landing is one in which you can walk away from. A great landing is one after which they can use the plane again."

"I guess that a good or great landing is optional," I commented.

"That's not exactly accurate."

I questioned him, "What do you mean?"

"It's the take-offs that are optional. The landings are mandatory," he answered.

Thinking that he was joking with me, I asked in jest, "You have any more tidbits of airplane trivia?

"One more," he quickly responded. "You know that you've landed with the wheels up if it takes full power to taxi to the ramp."

Before I could respond, I found myself a little more interested in what I saw outside my window. All I could see was rows and rows of military aircraft of all types and sizes. I had never seen so many choppers in one place in my life. Just as Dan had explained to me earlier, everything was brown and green. Different shades of browns and greens, but brown and green just the same.

In spite of the pilot's orders to stay seated until the plane came to a complete stop, a few people got up and were moving around. They gathered their bags and made their way up front to the exit the aircraft. Some of them were officers, some were enlisted, and each of them were wearing utility greens, unlike the passengers who remained seated who wore dress uniforms. I assumed that these guys were returning to Vietnam by the way that they were dressed.

Dan was already up and getting his things together.

"We were just told to stay seated, weren't we?" I asked, trying not to sound confused.

"We need to get off the aircraft in a timely fashion," he stated matter-of-factly.

"Why? Is there something I don't know? I thought we were ordered to stay in our seats."

Looking at me as if my questions were a waste of his time, he answered, "First off, we don't take orders from a civilian. Second, why is it that at 35,000 feet and moving at 400+ miles an hour, we can walk all around the aircraft having a smoke and a drink? Then, while we're on the ground and moving at five miles an hour, we had to stay in our seats, buckled up without the relaxing affects of a good cigarette and drink? Third, you don't sweat the small stuff. You see, while you are over here, you need to learn that everything is small stuff."

Not wanting to lose this guy and, with him, any hope of finding my ship, I got up and started to gather my things.

The pilot announced, "Flag officers will depart the aircraft first after we have come to a complete stop."

When I heard that, I just knew that I was going to be the last person off the plane. I realized that I was probably the most junior person onboard because I was fresh out of boot camp. Still, those dozen or so guys were doing their best to be the first ones to vacate the aircraft. Amazingly, no one spoke a word of reprimand to any of these men.

I stopped for a moment to re-think this situation. All of the men who were still seated were watching those who were standing. Two guys coming from the back of the plane were about to trample me because I was standing in the middle of the aisle. The first guy said to me as he passed, "Make-a-hole, boot."

The second guy just said, "Ass-hole. You dinky-dau newbie."

I was unnerved and embarrassed by their rebukes. I must ask Dan what a dinky-dau newbie was when I get a minute.

Dan noticed that I had stopped what I was doing and that I was about to get back into my seat.

"And fourth," Dan added, "I know that a parked airplane filled to capacity with military personnel makes a grand target for snipers. So now you have a choice my new friend, you can get into gear; or, you can put it in park."

I looked at him and before I could say anything, he said, "As for me, I'm gonna di-di-mal myself out of here."

Those words drove home the realization that I was really in Vietnam, a war zone. So, I prepared myself for the scramble to get off the plane just like the other men. Assuming that di-di-mal meant to do it quick.

As I stepped back into the aisle, I made eye contact with a very young looking sailor sitting across from me. Other than looking extremely young to be in uniform, his face showed total confusion to see me moving around after we all were ordered to stay seated. I didn't say anything to him because I wasn't sure what I was doing.

I did feel a little strange ignoring orders, especially when I passed officers still seated and buckled in. I worried that each of those officers was taking a good look at me so later he could write me up for disobeying orders. For this little excursion of mine, I could expect one of my two stripes to be stripped away. Nevertheless, Dan had said that stripes were, 'easy on and easy off'. However, it was probably better to lose a stripe than to lose your life, but right now, I didn't want to lose him . . . or my life.

I wondered what would happen if you were reduced in rank and that you only had one stripe to start with. Would that mean that you had zero rank, an E-0? An even bigger question was what would happen to you if you did not have any stripes to take away and you had to lose me. I decided to save these questions for a later time because getting off the plane required my full attention. No need to be called an ass-hole a second time.

To my surprise, at least the first six guys made it off the aircraft before the door was even fully opened. The remaining six or so of us were close behind and moving fast. Even the stewardesses had known to step aside quickly to let us exit.

I jumped a short distance to the approaching stairway because it had yet to reach the plane. I assumed that the guys who had exited first had had to make quite a jump.

It required all of my concentration just to run down those stairs that were still moving toward the plane. The first groups of guys were charging down the stairs at full speed, making the entire stairway shake, rattle, and roll. Vietnam was beginning to be a very exciting place.

I dismounted the stairs and tried to catch my breath. Dan turned to me and said, "After I get my sea bag, I'll help you get yours. It's going to be a mad house when our bags are dumped on the tarmac."

Dumped on the tarmac I questioned. Somehow, I had imagined something a little more organized . . . perhaps finding my bag on the conveyor belts as I normally would at most airports. I kind of wanted to see my bags go passing by in an organized, single file military fashion.

Once everyone was off the plane and on the tarmac, we just stood around. We were a little ways from any buildings and I had no idea what to do next. How could I expect to find a ship if I could not even find the terminal. In addition to that issue, if they were going to dump my sea bag on the tarmac, I needed to find just where on the tarmac this was going to happen.

Just as I was about to ask Dan about our sea bags, he looked over past me and said, "Try to stay in the middle of the group."

"Why?" I figured that we could see our sea bags better if we were on the edge of the group of almost two hundred men.

"If someone wants to take a shot at the group, it's better to be in the middle," he told me as he made his way into the center of the crowd.

With little delay, I followed him to the middle of the pack. I was not surprised to see that the same guys that exited the plane first were also there. "I would have thought that we were safe from the VC here on base," I questioned.

"Not as easy as you may think," Dan responded.

"What do you mean?"

"Well, describe a North Vietnamese for me. Then describe a South Vietnamese."

"Yeah, I guess you're right," I nodded sheepishly. I had no idea what a South Vietnamese looked like, much less what one from the North. However, I did assume that they looked alike.

Just as I was about to ask yet another question, I noticed that a cargo door opened in the rear of the aircraft. Someone was launching all two hundred or so military issue green sea bags directly onto the tarmac, twenty feet out, and over fifteen feet down.

"Look at that! How in the world is anyone going to find their sea bag when they're all exactly alike?" I wondered aloud.

I was a little taken aback by the way our bags were treated. In a matter of minutes, the pile was eight feet high and twenty feet in diameter. I imagined that the flight crew was getting even with us for not staying buckled in our seats until the plane came to a complete stop.

"Don't sweat the small stuff. This is not a big deal. It's true that all of our bags look same-same. But I already told you, after I find my bag; I'll help you get yours."

I could not imagine what made him so sure that he would find his bag, even before I found mine considering, as he said, they were all same-same. Then I noticed that one bag being thrown off had a large 'X' on two sides made with two-inch masking tape. At that moment, Dan said, "There be mine."

With a cocky mannerism, he walked to the pile and climbed a few bags. He casually grabbed the marked sea bag and balanced it on his shoulder. He walked back and dropped his bag beside me as if it was a prized trophy.

This guy really seemed to have his act together and I was glad that he had decided to help me. I needed to find out more about my ship before he and I went our separate ways. Assuming we were going to part ways. However, I hoped we were reporting to the same place. I would like this to be a, 'no sweat' adventure for me. I noticed that the same guys that exited the plane so quickly were picking out their bags in the same manner. All had similar marking on their bags. One had a large red bow and another was sprayed with black paint in some weird design. This must be the bag of someone that had been a hippie in his early days. Still another had masking tape circling his bag. What a great idea this was. Everyone who had to scramble for his bag noticed how helpful the markings were. It appeared to me that each was thinking of doing the same thing to their bags on their next flight.

After a few minutes of waiting, I was getting rather hot and very inpatient. The heat of the sun was broiling my head and the heat off the tarmacs was cooking my feet. I decided to start with my search without him. I walked past Dan, toward the pile of sea bags, when he said to me, "Hang on a minute, my man. The officers will be in there making it tough for the enlisted guys to find their bags. Let them finish first."

"What do you mean?"

"The officers will be shouting and giving orders like, 'is that my bag soldier? What name do you read on that tag? Hand that bag to me, boy.' We'll just wait a few minutes. The pile will be easier to search when the officers are gone."

Just as he said, I could see officers yelling at enlisted men and enlisted men helping officers find their bags.

As Dan and I stood there watching the officers giving orders and being rude to the enlisted men, Dan said, "You see there are three types of officers that arrive in-country. The first type is the, 'General Washington.' He thinks he'll be a general someday and then become president. Not a bad style for an officer, because he'll take care of you, keeping you alive and well."

"Now what does that mean?"

"He wants you to live so you can vote for him in twenty or thirty years when he runs for public office."

I wonder how accurate he thinks he is. On the other hand, did he think he knew it all?

"Then there's the, 'General Custard'. He marches to his own drum. Not always using common sense and not listening to others who have more time and experience in-country. He tries out his own untested ideas and eventually gets himself and everybody else killed. He doesn't understand that good judgment comes from experience. Unfortunately, good experience usually comes from making bad judgments. This type I can spot a mile away and I try very hard to keep them, a mile away."

Now this was starting to sound like a lot of crap to me, but I'll listen to be polite. "And the third type?" I asked, wanting to stay on his good side until he could help me find my ship.

"Finally, 'General Bob.' These officers just report in-country not wanting to give or take orders. These guys aren't very smart, even though they have a college degree."

"What do you mean, they are not smart? They have a college degree?"

"These guys have a college degree, yes; however, they are not smart enough to avoid the draft. They just want to put in their 365 and stay out of combat. They blend in with the scenery and bring little attention to themselves. They're the ones that allow the enlisted men who know what they are doing, to do what needs to be done. These officers are well liked by the men who have been here for a couple of tours. They even get along with the unhappy enlisted draftees because they're in the same boat. We generally think of them as weird ass-holes, but acceptable weird ass-holes just the same."

"How can they be both?" I asked doubtfully.

"Ass-hole because he's an officer, but acceptable ass-hole because he was drafted."

None of this was what I learned in boot camp about officers. Officers were people to be obeyed. Whatever they demanded, I did it, and I did it quickly. I figured that he just had it all wrong. He may have known how to get off planes and find his luggage quickly, but he can't be right about officers . . . at least not all of them.

After about twenty minutes, the pile of bags was about half-gone. Dan and I began our search the still, massive pile. Fortunately, I found my bag after searching only a dozen or so.

With our sea bags slung on our shoulders, we headed toward the terminal. I felt as though something were missing, then I remembered the nightly news broadcasts back home showing soldiers marching smartly up the beach, four abreast. There was always a band playing, flags flying, and newsmen taking pictures. Here, there was nothing. Everyone headed toward the terminal by ones, twos, and threes, talking, joking, and smoking cigarettes . . . the perfect opposite of an orderly column of new arrived military personnel.

Dan noticed that I was looking all around and asked, "Looking for the band?"

"Yeah." Now how did he know that?

"No bands for us today."

"No, why not?"

"We are replacements, returnees, fresh meat, and spare parts. Bands are for whole units arriving and departing this lovely country."

Damn, I had expected-and even wanted-a band. There had been no hula girls handing out leis at the airport in Hawaii, either, and I was really expecting that. I hoped this wasn't a sign of things to come. I knew that Vietnam Vets returning home were finding themselves treated like shit. It appeared that I was getting the same treatment on my arrival. Not a good sign of things to come.

I was about ready to ask him what he meant by, 'spare parts,' when I noticed the sign above the door that read, 'Welcome to Tan San Nut Air Force Base, Saigon, Vietnam.' I had seen this place on the nightly news, full of coffins with American flags draped over them. Out of morbid interest, I looked around for some, but didn't see any. Then I felt shameful for thinking that. A flag-draped coffin was an awful thing to see. That would have meant that for every body inside, there would be a grieving family back home. Hope I never have that kind of thought again.

"So now what are you looking for?' Dan questioned.

"Nothing in particular. Just checking the place out."

With a smile he said, "I bet you're looking for someone with a sign above his head with your name on it. You know, a limo driver at an airport like they have back in the real world."

"That would make things easier, wouldn't it?" I answered. Naturally, there was no way I was going to tell him what I had really been looking for.

Still smiling, he teased, "I think that you are still expecting some kind of limo service. At least a military bus that reads, 'USS SUMMIT.'"

I responded by kidding with him with, "Well maybe not a limo and driver, but at least someone to give me directions."

"No sweat, we'll just have our orders stamped and follow the crowd. Stick with me. I know the routine."

"Stamped? You mean like S&H Green Stamps?"

"Yeah, two tours and four books will get you a grenade launcher that doubles as an umbrella stand," Dan quick wittily replied.

Next to the door, leading into the terminal was a mailbox. The kind you would find on any corner back home. Instead of being blue, it was red with the words; AMNESTY BOX stenciled on the side. "What's that?" I questioned Dan.

"A freebie. If you have something that you don't want to be caught with, place the item in the box and no one will say a thing about it," he explained.

"Like what kind of things?"

"Illegal things, you know what I am talking about," he responded, looking at me as if I was trying to act innocent.

Well, for me, I have nothing illegal on me, and I will just walk proudly on past it. I hoped that he would do the same and pass it by, and he did.

When we arrived inside the terminal, we found a counter with three lines of us new arrivals. The sign above each window read,

'Exchange.' A guy using a bullhorn herded us into a roped off area. I saw one guy; wearing jungle utilities like Dan, try to go under the rope. An MP appeared out of nowhere and shoved him back under the rope. I thought it was odd that neither one said anything to the other. It appeared that they have done this before, you know, I try to sneak out and you catch me. Whatever, he remained in line.

"What's this?" I asked.

Dan leaned close and whispered, "This is where we make the exchange from our green backs into MPC. Keep all your tens and twenties. Just turn in your fives, ones, and all your change."

"MPC?"

"Military Pay Certificates. Even our coins are changed over into paper. It's a real pain."

"So, why should I keep my tens and twenties?"

"Keep it down, man. Can't you whisper?" He snapped in a stage whisper. Clearly unnerved, he looked around to see if anyone had overheard us.

"Listen, my big mouth friend. When someone whispers to you, trying not to be heard by others, try to whisper your answer in the same way."

Great. I had just pissed off my one and only passport to my ship. Dan must have sensed that I was worried about angering him, because he immediately regained his cool. "You can sell a twenty for twenty-five dollars of MPC. American greenbacks are worth lots of money over here."

"Is that legal?"

"All I'm doing is selling something that's already mine. Granted it's not legal, but I'm not paid enough to get shot at," he answered, somewhat defensively.

"I can't do that," I said in a low voice because I didn't want anyone else to hear me. "I'm just going to turn it all in and do the right thing. Besides, no one is going to be shooting at an Auxiliary Repair Landing ship sitting in the middle of the South China Sea."

I was trying to be humorous, but he was obviously not in the mood.

"No sweat. Do what you think is best."

The line moved quickly and in a few minutes, we were at the counter. The officer behind the counter took Dan's orders, pulled off one of the copies, stamped it, and put it on a pile of about fifty others. He then stamped Dan's original copy of his orders and asked him, "How much are you going to exchange?"

"Nine dollars and twenty-five cents, sir."

The lieutenant behind the counter looked at him as if he knew he had more.

"Is that one hundred nine dollars and twenty-five cents? Or did you say two hundred nine dollars and twenty-five cents?"

Dan looked the officer right in the eye and politely said, "Sir, I just came off R&R. I ran out of money and I had to borrow this little bit that I have here to get back, sir."

"So where did you go?"

"Hawaii."

"Was it cool?" The officer asked, relaxing a little.

"No sir. No matter how much money you take, you will quickly run broke if you decide to spend your R&R there. Be sure to take lots of money."

The officer responded with a smile, as Dan continued with, "Just remember sir, if you don't spend all of your money, then you can count on not having as much fun."

The officer paid Dan little attention after that. With the money exchange completed, Dan stepped aside to allow me room to reach the counter.

The officer asked for my orders and I obliged. He then asked, "How much are you going to exchange?"

I knew he noticed that Dan and I were together and I assumed he was waiting for me to answer with an amount less than ten dollars. I spoke up and said, "I have two hundred and thirty five dollars and some change."

With a genuine confused look, the officer gave me a quick, 'once over,' as if I was somehow holding back something. With what Dan had said earlier, I could only imagine that I was the only person handing in to exchange more than ten dollars.

"Did you say two hundred and thirty five dollars and change?" He questioned.

"Yes sir I did."

The lieutenant made a face of surprise and then handed me my MPC replacement bills in five, tens, and twenties.

The money was a little smaller and had the same feel as regular money. I placed the bills in my wallet. I got a real surprise when he handed me a few bills in the five and ten cent denominations. These bills were smaller than the dollar value bills. (APPENDIX A) However, this made sense because it was of a lesser value. This made my wallet hard to close with the volume of bills that I now had.

The exchange completed quickly and we stepped away from the counter when Dan said in an amusing way, "Dumb shit, you could have made fifty dollars."

I tried to be cool and said, "No sweat."

"No sweat man. I was just trying to put some money in your pocket," Dan answered me apologetically.

"I know. I'm just being cautious. First time in Vietnam and all that."

"Hey, do me a favor. Guard my bag for a minute. I'll be right back," Dan asked me, as if all was fine now.

"Sure thing." I mumbled distractedly. I wondered if I had done the right thing by turning in all of my money the way I did. Maybe I didn't always have to be so, by-the-book. I could always use an extra fifty bucks. However, too late, what was done was done. I never liked getting into trouble before and there was no reason to start now with my new career ahead of me.

Dan dropped his bag and headed for the men's room. While he was gone, I had some time to check out my new surroundings. For such a small place, there was a surprising amount of activity. It seemed as though everyone but me knew where he was going. I was hit with a sudden wave of anxiety. I wanted to find my ship, not stand guard over a guy's sea bag while he made a head call.

A voice behind me said, "Excuse me." I turned and saw an Army private carrying a small cardboard box. The lid was closed and he was holding it with such care and secrecy that my interest was sparked. He probably had some puppies, kittens, or snakes in this box of his. Just what I needed. Anyway, I answered, "Can I help you?"

"No, I believe that I can help you," he smiled and handed me a small booklet from his box.

To be polite, I took it and saw that it was a book of Vietnamese courtesy phrases. He nodded knowingly. "You'll need this while you're here in-country. It's very helpful for your day-to-day dealings with the locals. Everybody has one."

The pamphlet was like a child's dictionary, full of useful pictures. (APPENDIX B) It hadn't occurred to me before that I would need to communicate with locals, but now I could see that this pamphlet was something I sorely needed.

"Only one dollar and it's yours," he said.

It seemed like a fair price to me and I wondered if I should buy Dan one. Yet, then I thought that he probably already had one since he had been here before.

"Okay man, just one," I responded, accepting his offer.

He took my dollar, thanked me, and immediately found another customer.

I skimmed my book and saw the value of what I just purchased when Dan returned, looking like the cat that ate the canary. "I just made a hundred bucks," he boasted but just loud enough for only me to hear.

Since he had just come from the men's bathroom, I was a little worried about how he'd made his hundred dollars. I hoped that he wasn't some kind of queer hooker, or something. No way was I going to hang around some fag, even if he was going to be my guide here in Saigon. Maybe he had sold some greenbacks.

Anyway, to share my good news, I said, "I just bought me a pamphlet on Vietnamese Phrases. Should I get you one? My treat." I held out my pamphlet as if it were the prize catch of the day.

"You bought it?" He sneered.

"Yeah."

"Why?"

"Well, he wasn't giving them away." I answered and wondered why he looked so amused.

"There are a couple of reasons why you shouldn't have bought that."

"And they are?" How could this purchase not have been a good deal?

"First off, they're free. If you're Navy and you're over here, it's free. Second, everyone here wants to learn to speak English. They don't want to teach you Vietnamese."

"So I got taken?"

"Yeah, twice. And we haven't even left the terminal yet."

"Twice?"

"Yeah, twice," Dan answered back quickly.

"How twice?"

"You paid one dollar for a free pamphlet and then you lost fifty dollars on the exchange," Dan explained.

"Give me a break. I'm the new guy here," I answered, feeling stupid.

"No sweat," Dan answered, finally showing me some mercy.

"You said that everyone wants to learn to speak English," I asked, hoping to change the subject.

"Not only that, the girls here want to have the surgery to make their eyes round and American looking. Everything over here will someday be Americanized and we might even make South Vietnam a state like we did with Hawaii and Alaska."

"No sweat. I mean, no shit."

"Yeah. No shit," he answered, as if this would someday come true.

The lines to the exchange windows had dwindled to about one or two people when someone with a clipboard began yelling orders. "Anyone just arriving in-country and needing a ride to the BOQ or BEQ, listen up. I have some instructions."

Guessing that I might be in need of this ride, I gave him my undivided attention. I wished I knew what a BOQ or BEQ was.

He continued, "The buses are outside, so get your asses onboard, now!"

Finally! Things were sounding like they had in boot camp. Everyone there was called an ass, too. It appeared that this enlisted guy, because of his clipboard, had some kind of magical authoritative power over everyone. Even the officers were taking his orders, and they didn't seem to mind being called, 'asses,' either. I didn't understand that at all.

The clipboard guy yelled, "Everyone outside, board the buses for your BOQ or BEQ!"

I looked over at Dan and asked, "Do we need one of these BOQ, or BEQ's that this guy is yelling about?"

"Yes we do, my new lost friend."

"And a BOQ or BEQ is a what?"

We followed the crowd outside, as he explained, "BOQ stands for 'Bachelor Officer Quarters' and BEQ for 'Bachelor Enlisted Quarters.'"

Outside, there were six military buses parked side by side, facing the front of the terminal. Three buses had, "ARMY," posted above the front windshield. Two others said, "MARINE," and the sixth said, "NAVY."

"What? No Air Force bus," I questioned.

"Why would you think there would be an Air Force bus out here?"

I quickly responded with, "Why not? Air Force personnel got to report to their base."

"Look around you my man. We're already on an Air Force Base. Didn't you read the sign on your way in?" He answered me with a chuckle.

"Oh yeah. Tan San Nut Air Force Base was the first sign I saw when I walked up to the terminal," I said in response.

At that moment, I heard the drivers that stood next to their buses, shouting to everyone to get onboard. I started toward the Navy bus, but saw that Dan was heading toward one of the Army buses, the wrong way I assumed. Dan looked back at me as if to suggest that I follow him. I followed him with some reservation, reasoning that if he was smart enough to come up with that sea bag trick, he probably knew what he was doing. Emphasis on 'probably.'

I boarded the bus and made my way down the aisle. Dan plopped down in an aisle seat and threw his sea bag in the window seat next to him. I thought that, if I was still worried about how me made that money in the bathroom and if he was a queer or not, with that, I didn't want to sit next to him. I took the two seats behind him, placed my sea bag in the aisle seat, and sat by the window. I thought to myself, 'Damn, I've been here in Vietnam for less than an hour now and already I found myself on the wrong bus, I was not sure where I was going, and I paid a dollar for a free pamphlet.

"My first day in-country friend," Dan said, turning around to look at me. "Who do you think has the better seat? You or me?"

Shit, now I was in the wrong seat. However, I suspected that I was about to be the butt of some joke, but I bit anyway, "You." I thought that maybe he wanted me to sit next to him. Regardless, I was fine sitting right where I was.

"Correct. Now why do you think I have the better seat?"

"No idea, but I'm sure you'll tell me."

"Yes. You see someone just might want to take a shot at the bus while it's driving through scenic downtown Saigon. My American made military issue sea bag that has a window seat just might stop the bullet; or, at least slow it down before it hits me."

Once again, I was surprised to find out that he said made sense. I started to change my seat around, but the bus jotted and backed up. I decided to sit tight and hope that, with a little luck, no one would shoot at me today. Besides, if they really needed to shoot at the bus, then maybe they would do it from the other side of the street. The bus rolled forward only to stop behind one of the other buses.

"How did you make that hundred dollars, anyway? Did you sell some American money in the men's room?" I asked to change the subject. No need to dwell on the subject of being shot at.

"That's right."

"So how does that work, you know, making money from selling money?" This seemed like something that I should know about.

Looking and sounding like an economic teacher, Dan explained, "You see, American money, or greenback, will always have its value and is traded anywhere in the world. If this country were to fall apart, its currency will be worthless. This way, if you have American greenbacks, then your money is always valuable. I know it doesn't make a lot of sense; but I do know that I can make some money this way. There's usually someone in the men's room exchanging money before and after each flight."

His explanation made sense. It was another tidbit to remember for the next time that I fly into Saigon. What was I thinking? I had just gotten here. Why was I even thinking about coming back? I joined the US Navy to see the world, not to see downtown Saigon more than once.

As the bus started up again, I noticed that the windows had metal screens in them. These screens were unusual because they were of one-inch spacing and appeared to be quite strong. I couldn't imagine how screens with such large holes could be useful. They did let the air flow through, a welcomed relief in this hot and humid climate. I looked behind the bus and noticed a jeep with a large machine gun mounted on a tripod in the back followed us closely. I assumed it was there for our protection, but I wasn't sure if it made me feel safe or not. The jeep reminded me of the TV show the, 'Rat Patrol.'

It was a short ride to the main gate. As we left the base and headed into town, I saw that almost everyone was riding around on small motorcycles and none were bigger than 100cc. The few cars that were around were small, and most of them were taxies along with a few buses. The only trucks were military and most of them were dump trucks. It was strange, but most, if not all of the trucks seemed to be occupied by an oriental driver and his entire family. The truck cabs were nearly large enough for the family to live in them. In fact, everyone I've seen so far over here seemed so little.

Some of the buses had so many people riding them that it reminded me of pictures on bus travel in India. I saw a number of people hanging on the sides with others standing on the bus steps. One bus had a little boy on top of the roof in the luggage rack holding onto a chicken.

There was a lot of traffic noise and the motorcycles were deafening. Everyone was blowing their horns, apparently just for the sake of blowing their horns. It sounded like New York City at rush hour. The only difference was that these horns sounded more like little toy horns

I noticed four people riding on a motor scooter alongside us. It seemed to be a mother and father with two children. It looked kind of cool to see so many people on one little moped. No one could do something like that back home and get away with it.

The trucks were driving crazy, trailing very close to the motorcycles, and laying on their horns to make them move out of the way. I looked over at Dan and asked, "Do the truck drivers always drive this way?"

"Yeah. The first thing the gooks do when they get a new truck is take away the brakes and add extra horns."

"Gooks," I questioned. I didn't know if he meant that gooks were truck drivers, or that they were the local people here.

"Gooks," he repeated. "You know, everyone that's from over here. If your eyes are round, then you are not a gook."

This guy was full of jokes. With that tidbit of information, I kept my eye on this one truck that passed us and his brake lights never did come on. Somehow, I could imagine that Dan just might be right about this.

I saw that we were passing the presidential palace. I recognized it from newspaper photos. Guards surrounded the palace and two tanks lurked inside the grounds. The palace was an attractive building, though it wasn't in keeping with the brown and green theme. It was sparkling white, and its cleanness contrasted drastically with the surroundings.

Each time we passed a good-looking girl, some of the guys on the bus would start to yell all kind of remarks at them. Some of the remarks were pretty foul and I wished that some guys would just shut up and leave those girls alone. Some of the girls looked back and smiled, while others ignored them. It was hard to tell if the local girls appreciated this busload of servicemen or not.

Dan turned toward me and said, "Some of these rednecks are enjoying themselves with all the women around."

"What do you mean?"

"See, for most rednecks, these are the first girls they have ever seen that they aren't related to." That was an interesting point and the more I thought about it, I realized that most rednecks did kind of look alike.

"Rednecks are a breed of people," Dan continued.

"What are you talking about?" Maybe he had all rednecks catalogued as he did with the officers.

"You know, you have the Irish, the English, the French . . . and you have Rednecks."

To change the subject, I asked, "So Dan, what's with the screens on the windows? Are they afraid we're going to jump out?"

"You see," he answered with a serious look, "the mosquitoes here are so large and strong, that it takes a screen like this to keep them off the bus."

This information did not strike me as good news at all. I couldn't imagine mosquitoes being that big. They could probably induce anemia in one sitting!

Dan smiled and said, "You look worried."

"I am! How many bites can anyone take before passing out? Do these things travel in groups, wolf packs, schools, herds, or flocks?"

"I don't know, but the mosquito is the national bird over here."

I gave him a look of being pissed and confused. He must have felt somewhat sorry for me because he came back with,

"Man, I'm just joking about that. You're going to make a good gullible friend."

I tried to hide my embarrassment, "I knew that, I just wanted to see how far you would take the joke."

Dan gave me a look as if thinking, "Yeah right."

"So what are the screens really for?" I asked again.

"It's to keep grenades from being thrown into the bus."

I was hit with a wave of panic. "No Shit. Come on, tell me for real."

"For real man. One of those answers is the real reason."

"I don't know which story I want to be true. Either way, I could loose a lot of blood."

"Well, my new and confused friend, the mosquitoes are large here in-country, but the screens don't really work all that well against them. As far as grenades go . . . well, the screens don't really work all that well against them, either."

I just needed some straight answers, not a lot of bullshit. "So, are you going to tell me straight this time why the screens don't really work for either one? Or are you going to give me a third scenario?"

I could tell that a few of the guys onboard were starting to enjoy my gullibility. They didn't have the guts to ask any of the same questions that I was asking, but they wanted to hear the answers just the same. I felt like telling all of them, who were chuckling at me to, 'Give me a break. You were fooled, too.'

"Okay, for real. The grenades the VC now use have hooks on them, so they will just attach themselves to the screen and cause more damage than if they came in. The mosquito stuff is just a bunch of bull. You almost fell for it."

I heard a few guys on the bus laughing and I felt like a real jerk. I swallowed the remainder of my pride and asked, "So what would you do if that were to happen?"

"If what were to happen, the mosquitoes or grenades?"

"The grenade thing. I don't care about the mosquitoes," I answered.

"Don't know. Just enjoy the ride."

He dropped his smile, turned, and stared out the window as if he really didn't want to talk about it anymore. It was just as well because I didn't like being the butt of the joke in front of a group of strangers.

Just then, about a hundred horns sounded. To my relief, the focus was no longer on me as everyone turned and looked outside. The commotion was just a group of motorcycles racing by in a hurry. Everyone was cutting everyone else off and no one did anything about it. Crazy driving seemed to be the norm around here. Maybe if there were some police around, the traffic would be more orderly.

Our bus driver was just as guilty as all the other drivers were. He would speed up, just so he could slam on the breaks, and then speed up again. When we were moving, we were cruising so fast that it was hard to really do any sightseeing. Whenever we stopped, though, I could see that some of the people were dressed in traditional Vietnamese clothes, while others wore American outfits: mini skirts or hot pants with Go-Go boots. Some sported flip-flops and a few wore no shoes at all.

Dan apparently taking note that I was looking at everyone's outfit said as he pointed off to a woman wearing a dress and straw hat, "Her dress is called, ao-dai. Non-la is what you would call her hat."

"Thanks," I responded, wondering how he knew what I was looking at.

Our bus driver came to a sudden, but controlled stop. I could not tell why we stopped, but I could clearly pick up that he was very nervous at having to do so. He looked all around in front of the bus, blew hard on the horn, and yelled at whoever was in his way. I looked behind us and noticed that the guys in the jeep that were following us also seemed concerned. Every time someone approached the bus, the gunner pointed his machine-gun at him and yelled, "Back off." Welcome to Vietnam, I thought.

The bus continued without incident. That little stop got everyone that was yelling at the girls to stop and quite down for a few minutes. I assumed that the gun pointing at some of the people brought a little reality to those guys. Now it appeared that they were looking for snipers and not for girls to yell at for the rest of our ride.

Dan looked back at me and asked, "Aren't you wondering why we are on an Army bus and not a Navy bus?"

I had almost forgotten about that. "Yeah, what's the story? And please, no jokes this time." I didn't know why I was asking him more questions; he was probably going to give me some more of his crazy answers.

"See, when Navy personnel arrive in-country, they have to check in with the Officer-of-the-day at the Navy barracks. He stamps your orders, takes a copy for himself, and notifies your unit that you have arrived in-country. They arrange for transportation to your unit, assign you a bed for as many nights as you need, and issue you some meal tickets."

"So what's wrong with that? I still don't understand why we're on an Army bus. Moreover, are we going to see the Army's Officer-of-the-day? Won't they just tell us to go check in at the Navy barracks?" I felt a scam coming my way.

"No, I'll explain to them that the Navy barracks is full and we were told to check in at the Army barracks. Now, the main reason for not checking into the Navy barracks is to avoid standing watches. Navy personnel staying at Army barracks don't stand watches."

"I've done watches before. What's the big deal?" I asked.

He said, sarcastically, "What you did was to stand, 'Fire Watches' in boot camp. A sissy watch, with no real danger. Here, you stand real watches. I'm talking about being issued a loaded weapon and then realizing that you're a sitting target."

Unfortunately, he was making sense. I didn't like the idea of being a target.

"Trust me on this. You will not enjoy being on watch. They'll have you pulling four-hour watches sometimes, two, three times a day. Snipers here shoot at military personnel at least twice a week. That means that a guard or two is hit every week in Saigon alone. Besides, when you reach your unit, you'll be pulling a lot of guard duty and the snipers will be shooting at you three or four times a week. Why start now?"

"I'll tell you this," Dan continued, "Let the guys that will never see action pull some guard duty while they are here in Saigon. With some luck, or bad luck, the Navy guys that pass through Saigon might see some action before being shipped out to sea."

A little confused, I asked, "But isn't that where we're going? Out to sea? Gray ship, blue water, white hat, and all that navy stuff?"

With a serious look, he asked, "You have no idea where our unit is, do you, my new lost friend?"

He said, 'our unit.' That meant that we were going to the same place after all. I was relieved. "No, not really. I know nothing about nothing. Where is our unit?"

As I waited for his response, the bus stopped, the door opened, and everyone started to unload. Just as the plane exodus earlier, only the ones dressed in utility greens knew to get off quickly, the guys in dress uniforms took their time. I decided to follow Dan and exited quickly.

As we left the bus, I noticed everyone was heading toward the building across the street. It was a small hotel with a squad of guards outside, standing guard behind sandbag bunkers. Each had a rifle and a few manned machine-guns. Just like the bus windows, a screen fence encased the two-story building and all its balconies from the ground to the roof. The guards were vigilant while everyone crossed the street to the front door.

As we crossed the street, Dan looked at me and said, "It will be best that we are at the end of the line, it'll be easier. Otherwise, we'll be told to get at the end of the line and wait until everyone has checked in to see if beds are available."

So, this was it. I was in Saigon, Vietnam, Southeast Asia.

Chapter 2

Of the three Army buses that were at the airport, ours must have been the first to arrive at the hotel because there was no line at the check-in counter. The lobby was not very big and the single line formed by our busload of men snaked its way outside the lobby door. Dan and I, along with two others, stood in the open doorway. One of the guards approached us and suggested that we get inside so he could close the doors. We tried to oblige, but there were too many guys in front of us. The guard yelled, "All right, nuts to butts. Make it tight." The line tightened up, we made it inside, and the door slammed behind us.

The check-in process was quick and very efficient. As each man approached the desk sergeant, his original orders were stamped and a copy retained. Next, each man received an orange pill along with a couple of meal tickets. The line moved left and another sergeant assigned each soldier a bed by its room and bunk number. Another move left and you would be issued a time and location for your first watch. At the next stop, you were asked if you had any firearms. If you said yes, you were able to go and find your bed. If you answered no, you were told to report to a room upstairs to be issued a weapon. I noticed that the ones in their dress uniforms needed rifles and the ones in utilities did not.

As I observed all of this, I thought to myself, "Wow, I am getting a gun!"

As the last man stepped up to the desk, we fell in behind him. After he moved over, Dan gave the man behind the counter his orders and said, "Navy BEQ is filled. We were told to report here to see if you have two extra beds."

"We do," he muttered and shook his head to indicate that it would be a real pain in the ass for him to check in two more guys who were not even Army.

Just as the others before us, our original orders were stamped, a copy taken, an orange pill issued, we moved left and assigned a bed. At our next stop, Dan told the sergeant, "We're Navy. Only going to be here a night or two."

Although Dan had already told me that we were not going to pull a watch, I was still surprised when we were not assigned one like the other guys. It didn't seem fair, but I wasn't going to complain.

Dan walked away without being asked about a weapon. I completed my part at the desk with the same results, no gun being issued. I caught up with Dan and asked, "What about getting us a gun?"

"No watch, no weapon. Just take your pill," he instructed.

Just then, the desk sergeant called out my name. I turned to see what he wanted.

"When you can, get out of your dress whites. I can't believe that you Navy guys always show up in a war zone wearing all white looking like you're going to be in a parade or something," he said gruffly.

I gave him a puzzled look because the only other things I could change into while traveling were my winter dress blues. No way was I going to wear my wool uniform in this hot and humid weather.

Dan spoke up, "Sergeant, he's fresh off the plane from boot camp. All he has are his dress whites and winter blues in his sea bag. Is there still the room upstairs where he can check out a set of jungle utilities?"

He nodded, in the affirm, and reminded me to change before dark.

"Follow me and I'll get you fixed up," Dan reassured me.

"Sounds okay with me. Now about these pills, what are they for?"

"It's no big deal. It's to fight off malaria. Just take it. We get one every Monday."

This made sense, however I just stuck it in my pocket after I noticed that Dan placed his in his pocket. I guessed that I would have yet another question for him later.

I followed Dan as he made his way down the hallway then up the stairs and into a small, dark, smelly room with no windows. On the floor was a large pile of clean, pressed uniforms. They might have been in a neat pile at one time, but it appeared that many people had rummaged through them since then. Off to my left were three rows of boots. All different sizes, some new, and others well worn. To the right was a pile of hats of all types and as expected, everything was brown or green.

Dan stood in front of the pile and said, "If you find a shirt your size and it's an officer's, grab it. You'll need one set of greens to hold you over until we get to our unit."

I started ransacking the pile looking for my size, thinking that these were new uniforms, unlike the used boots, until I noticed that some of them already had a nametag sewn above the right shirt pocket. There was also a nametag above the right rear pocket on each pair of pants.

"What gives with these uniforms? Am I supposed to find one in my size that had my name on it also?" I said jokingly.

"What we have here is . . . well . . . these belonged to someone who was killed, missing, wounded, or shipped home quickly. Somehow, these things were overlooked when their things were boxed up. Maybe they were in the laundry, or lent to someone. At any rate, they end up here for anyone reporting in-country without a set of jungle utilities. Don't sweat it, they are clean, and it's just temporary."

Struggling to comprehend what he just said, I stood up and stared at this pile of dead men's clothes. I almost expected to see bullet holes and bloodstains, but of course, there were none.

"Are you serious? This is not funny," I said, choking back my fear.

"There you go again sweating the small stuff. Look, this is not a big deal. You need a uniform, right? You know, other than white."

"Okay," I answered.

"With these, you will blend in and these are it for now, my fashion conscience friend."

"But these belonged to someone else."

"Right. Belonged, as in no longer his. And that someone else doesn't need them anymore. It's not that big a deal my man."

"Okay."

Looking a little pissed, Dan asked me, "Are you going to sweat over everything little thing over here?"

Apparently, dead soldiers were only a big deal to me.

He continued, "Look, you have a choice, my friend. You can wear your dress whites around here if you like. The only thing you'll be missing is a red bull's-eye on your back."

I was considering my options when he continued, "Look, just find a set and put them on and quit complaining. Besides, if you choose to wear your whites, then I choose not to walk anywhere near you."

"Okay, I get it. I just wasn't expecting things to start out this way."

I knelt by the pile and continued to look for my size while he looked for officers' rank on the collars. I questioned, "Why should we be looking for officers' uniforms?"

"I know, I know, you are not supposed to impersonate an officer; but, you are ordered to find a set of greens to wear in place of your whites. Right?"

"Well. Yeah. Right. But . . ."

"If you are unable to find a set of greens for an enlisted man with your rank and in your size, then you did the best you could. You found a set of greens that were your size that just happen to be that of an officer. You are obeying the last set of orders issued. You found a set of utilities that fit."

"Makes sense, but I'm worried that I'll get in trouble. You said not to sweat the small stuff, but this is not small stuff. This is big deal stuff."

"No sweat. I was only thinking about how much easier some things would be for us. You understand, between now and when we check in with our unit. No big deal."

I was curious. "Just what kind of things would be easier for us?"

"We would get in the front of some lines and not kicked out of others. We'd almost never be bumped off a flight and we'd get good seats. It's just an all around good deal for us."

"I still think that it's a bad idea. Maybe we can do this officer thing some other time."

"No sweat," Dan answered, and we continued with our search.

In a matter of a few minutes, we found a set of utilities that used to belong to an enlisted man, an Army private. I didn't really expect to find any Navy uniforms in this pile. I took off my dress whites and started to put on these, these used clothes. The pants and boots were a little big, but acceptable. My shirt was a perfect fit and I removed the nametag. Overall, my choices were rather slim because I was six three and 175 pounds, but I had managed to find jungle utilities. Not exactly boot camp issue, but military issue just the same. At least I am brown and green like everything else around here.

I quickly made the change and I felt like I was in the Army now. I neatly folded my well-worn dress whites and placed them in my bag. I asked, "What's next?"

"We'll find our beds and stow our stuff. Then we can take a walk to the Navy BEQ and check on the location of our unit and work out transportation."

"Answer this question for me," I asked sarcastically. "You suggest that we don't report to the Navy BEQ and that we check into the Army's BEQ. Okay, we did that and now you want to go to the Navy BEQ. Won't they ask questions? Like 'Where are you staying?' Or maybe, 'what watch are you standing?'"

"Relax. We'll only have to visit for a minute or two. Just long enough to read the board showing the current status of most of the Navy unit's in-country, and those that are out-at-sea."

I wanted a complete answer on the ship's location. "Will the SUMMIT be on the out-at-sea list?"

"I doubt it, but we'll see," he responded with his shoulders up and hands out.

"How can you doubt that the ship will not be on the out-at-sea list? Won't a ship be on a list that lists ships?" I asked.

"Let's just wait until we get there and see how things line up."

"Okay," I answered and we headed out. No need for too many questions right now. He did seem to have his act together. At least, it appeared that he did.

The hallways were poorly lit and very dirty. I kept stepping on clumps of mud that were all over the floor.

"Dan, what's with all this mud?"

"Well, the entire building here is being used as a floor mat."

"Now what is that supposed to mean?"

"Think about it. Here we are, in a country where it rains almost every day and only a few streets have sidewalks."

"Yeah, but why is all this mud inside?"

Dan stared at me, clearly wishing I would quit asking all these stupid questions. "Look at the soles of your new boots. They have deep grooves in them and they'll get packed full of mud when you walk in the mud. And this country has plenty of mud."

"And?"

"And, when you finally get to walk on solid ground, the mud just falls out in clumps."

"Okay, I got that part. But why is all this mud inside? I mean we are on the second floor."

Dan spoke to me as if answering a two-year-old. "You didn't see a 'Welcome Friend' floor mat out front did you?"

"No, of course not."

"I'd even bet that you didn't look for one, right?"

"Right."

"And I bet you didn't wipe your feet when you came in, right?"

"Right." I thought a bit, and then asked, "Yeah. So why are you right?"

"I think that everyone is just happy to get inside where it's safe and wiping ones' feet just isn't a main concern."

I was very grateful to have gotten all this new information about life. I was beginning to think this guy had an answer for everything. I noticed that, by the time we reached the end of the hallway, there wasn't as much mud as before. I just followed and asked nothing more.

We reached our assigned room and what a room this was. I promised myself that I would never speak badly about the sleeping conditions in boot camp again. In boot camp, we had sixty-five guys in one long room with bunk beds about every four feet. That meant that the smell and noise of sixty-five guys sleeping at the same time in one place filled the room all night long. We had to go to sleep and get up all at the same time, and with such little room between racks . . . well . . . it just wasn't a pleasant experience.

Our room was the size of a very small hotel room. However, we didn't have a private bathroom, dressers, or even a chair. Just ten bunk beds. To make it worse, there was only three feet of space between each of the bunk beds. The entire room was lit with just one twenty-five watt bulb in the ceiling fan that made a loud humming noise. Apparently, it could not tolerate high speed; for it swayed and shook so much that I thought that it just might fall at any minute.

Looking out the window and through the wired screen that encased the building, I noticed the arrival of one of the buses from the airport. Behind the bus was another jeep riding shotgun. I assumed this the norm over here. Before I could ask about the jeep, Dan told me, "Now this is a decent room, plenty of space."

"Are you kidding? This is the pits. Are things better at the Navy's BEQ?"

"Better? Nah, it's about the same. Look, it's not a big deal because we aren't going to move in or anything. It's just for a night or two."

"I know, I know. Don't sweat the small stuff. This room is definitely small stuff." I joked.

"Right," Dan said, "Just a night or two."

"What do you mean, a night or two? I was hoping that we'd stay here for just one night."

"What's your hurry?"

"I'm not in a hurry or anything. I just want to get to our ship. Besides, why would we have to stay more than one night?"

"It just depends on the location of our unit, which way it's heading, and how we plan to get there. If we need a flight out, we might get one that leaves today, or tomorrow or even the next day."

"How do we find that out?"

"That's why we need to take a trip down to the Navy BEQ and check out the green chalk board. The sooner the better."

"Have you done this before," I questioned.

"All the time."

"What do we do with our bags? Do we unpack now or what?" I asked.

"No, don't unpack. You want to keep your things packed in case we need to make a fast getaway. Now, take the lock off your sea bag and follow my lead."

"What do you mean, a fast getaway? We just got here." I couldn't keep up with this guy. I was thinking that if we are here for a few night, then why the need for a quick exit?

"If we have a ride out, we might not have time to get back and to pack up. Besides, where do you want to put your things, anyway?"

I looked around the room; there was definitely no place to unpack even a toothbrush. "Yeah, you're right. I'll just follow your lead."

I watched as he took the strap from his sea bag and wrapped it tightly around the bars at the head of his assigned bed, and then he locked it. "You see, no one can walk off with your bag or even open it." The strap was wrapped so tight, that it made it difficult to even try, to cut the strap.

"Would people steal things out of a sea bag?" I asked.

"I don't know about anyone else's. I just know about mine and to date, using my method, no one has taken anything."

I followed his lead and did the same with my sea bag.

I asked, "Will there be time to eat today, now that I have a meal ticket?"

"Yeah. I'm hungry, too. We'll fit that into our schedule today."

"So where do we go to eat around here? Do you know a nice place?"

"There are no nice places here, just places to eat for volume."

"So when or where do you want to eat for volume?" I asked, as my stomach gave a low rumble in the body language of, feed me.

"Soon, my man. After we check the board, we'll see how busy the chow line is at the Navy BEQ and what they're serving for dinner. If it's too busy or it's a shitty meal, then we'll just have dinner at the Army's expense."

There I was, my first day in Vietnam, and my new career had really taken off in a new and adventurous direction. I was hungry, tired, and wearing clothes that belonged to a dead man, well, maybe not. I had shoes on that were too big and hurt my feet and pants that would fall down unless I held them up. As if that weren't enough, I had locked my sea bag to a bedpost in a dimly lit room for ten men. In addition, I was following a man that reminded me of, Colonel Hogan from Hogan's' Heroes and all the while being treated like Ensign Parker on McHales Navy.

As we worked our way down the hall and out of the building, I couldn't help but notice that everyone except Dan and I had a rifle. I wouldn't have known what to do if I had one anyway, but it seemed like a good idea to be carrying a rifle around like everyone else.

"How far to the Navy BEQ?" I asked.

"Just two blocks," he answered, pointing in the direction we were headed.

As we approached the Navy BEQ, I noticed that it was the same type of building as the Army BEQ, but a little smaller and enclosed by the same heavy screen. We entered through the front door and walked down the hall. Just as Dan had predicted, we found a green chalkboard. We gave the chalkboard a once over and somehow I was not surprised that our ship was not listed.

"What do we do now? It's not even listed," I asked.

"Well, one of two things has happened. Either she has been sunk or no one knows where she is."

"Yeah, right," I answered, not wanting to be suckered into one of his jokes.

"Just to make sure, we'll take a quick stroll to the Comm-Center and ask."

"To the what, and do a what?"

"It just a communications center and, nine times out of ten, someone there will have an idea where most of the mobile units are at any given time."

"A quick stroll you say?"

"Not far. Only a few blocks from here."

"Is it safe to be walking around without a rifle? I see that everyone else is carrying one," I questioned with concern.

"It's not so bad between here and the Comm-Center. Every corner has someone on watch. Some guys are perched up high and some are just squaring the block."

"What? Squaring?"

"Yeah, someone will just continually walk around the block for two hours like a roving patrol."

"What about the VC?"

"They don't have guard duty here in Saigon."

"No, not that. Are we okay?"

"If Charlie is going to try something, I don't think that it will happen in this neighborhood," Dan explained.

"What about the TET Offensives that took place a few months ago? That was big time news back home. Wasn't that a big deal?

"That was a big deal back then, but more people are on guard now and it's okay for us to travel to the Comm-Center and back."

"If you say so," I responded as we headed toward the front door with me hoping he knew what all he was saying.

Next to the door was a small corner table and on top, in a neat pile, were some pamphlets. (APPENDIX C) Dan grabbed one, handed it to me, and suggested that I read it along with a remark that it was free and certainly not worth a dollar.

Taking his suggestion, I took the pamphlet, 'Welcome to The Republic of Vietnam.'

Looking inside I came across a set of instructions about sitting around in your underwear between 11am and 1pm. It would figure that the Navy would have something to say about that. As expected, a paragraph about standing watches in the, event of enemy attack along with a few Do's and Don'ts. One of the Do's, number three for example, Pay all bills. One of the Don'ts, don't become involved in political discussions. That should be easy for me, because I didn't exactly understand the political reasons anyway. Hell, I could not even vote.

I told Dan, "Thanks," as I placed the pamphlet in my pocket, and out the door, we went.

A block away, I saw a guard-post up on eight-foot tall stilts surrounded by sandbags. The guard in the tower looked like one of the guys that were on our plane.

"Dan, isn't that one of the guys from our flight today? Didn't he sit right across from us?" This was that kid that looked totally confused as I made my way off the plane earlier. He looked more confused now and that was hard to believe.

"Yeah, I think so. See, what did I tell you? This poor sap has only been here for less than an hour and already he's doing a watch," Dan proudly announced to me.

"Won't these guys get mad at us when they notice that we aren't standing watches?" I asked with concern.

"By the time anyone takes note, we'll be gone and on our way up the river. A laugh a minute, a walk in the park."

Whatever that meant, however, I was thinking how bad I felt for him when Dan spoke up and said, "Don't worry about this guy. He has a gun and we don't."

Dan's reasoning sounded good, but was not reassuring. I wondered what he meant by, 'up the river.'

"What's happening? How are you doing up there?" Dan asked as we passed by the kid on guard duty. I caught myself thinking about this guy as a kid and remembered that I was only a kid myself. I bet that we were the same age, teenagers.

"Okay I guess. At least I have a good view," he responded with a touch of false bravado.

I was relieved not to be standing a watch after being in-country for only a few hours; however, I didn't think it was completely fair that I was not doing my part.

Dan looked at me as if he knew what I was thinking, he then told me, "Don't feel bad, you'll get your turn soon enough."

As we continued on, we passed a few street vendors and I marveled at how dirty everything was. Even the people selling the stuff were dirty. The methods of food storage and preparation seemed like something from the Middle Ages, complete with open fires and live animals. The smell was so strong that I could taste it as it saturated the entire area. I couldn't tell if it was rotten food or animal shit. "Is this food safe to eat?" I asked.

"Yeah, no sweat. But you're better off eating Army chow while you're in town."

"Aren't there any health inspectors or anything like that around?" I couldn't believe that anyone could find these conditions acceptable.

"No, not really," Dan responded indifferently.

"I don't know exactly what they could be cited for, but at first glance, I figure they can probably be cited for almost everything."

We passed a few more food stalls and I wondered aloud, "Why do you think that things are the way they are here? You know, no health inspectors and stuff?"

Dan rolled his eyes at me and said, "This country spends money on helping people in the south, to kill people in the north. The people in the north are also trying to kill the people in the south so more money is spend on protecting the people in the south from the people in the North. Health inspectors are a luxury nobody here thinks about or could afford."

"That makes sense," I responded, believing what he said.

"Besides," he continued, "the body count for those dying by food poisoning is far too insignificant to worry about when compared to those dying by bombs and bullets. You know what I mean?"

Despite his insensitive answer, I pose still another question. "Why don't they put up some signs telling these people how dirty things are? Besides, if they all die from food poisoning then, the people from the north won't have anyone in the south to kill."

Dan thought for a moment and answered, "I guess that the people in the south spend money on bombs and bullets instead of health signs. If they're going to spend money on health signs, then the signs should say things like, 'Mine Field, Stay Out,' or 'Free Fire Zone, Stay Away.'"

"I guess so," I answered reluctantly to what he just said. "I've just never seen a place where everything was so dirty. No wonder everyone here was so little and frail. I guess it's kind of hard to grow up big and strong with eating conditions like this."

Dan agreed and we didn't say anything else for the next few blocks. I just followed him and took in all the sights.

"I need to make one quick stop to pick up my laundry," Dan said.

"Your laundry?"

"Yeah. This may be a dirty, unhealthy town, but that's not a good enough reason to walk around and wear dirty clothes." Dan glanced at me, laughed, and continued with, "Who in the world is your tailor, my new fashion statement friend?"

"Not amusing. Not amusing at all. Actually, you are my tailor. Besides, these would be a perfect fit if I were to gain about 40 pounds and drop two inches in height."

"Okay, you got one on me."

"Do you always have your laundry done in Saigon?"

"Nah, only when I leave country for a few days."

"Why is that?" I braced myself for another of his ridiculous explanations.

"Easy. This way I'll have clean clothes when I return and since I didn't have to take them with me, I saved some space in my bag. On top of that, they won't get all wrinkled up."

"Great idea. At least you have a change of clothes. That's something I might need if we are going to be here a couple of days."

"No problem," Dan grinned. "You can always visit the second hand clothing room again for another set. Maybe a set that fits."

"No, thanks. One set from there is enough for me. I don't expect to be in them all that long."

As we continued walking, I looked around to see if I could pick out a sign that would indicate where one would take clothes to be laundered. Nothing was in English and almost every letter had a dot or little squiggle mark above it. I gave up. "So where is this place?"

"We're here. Can't you read the sign?"

I could not believe it. In the middle of a thousand signs, all of them written in what appeared to be Greek or Chinese, there was one clearly marked 'Tailors.'

We stepped into this little shop, which looked as if a tornado had ripped thought it. There was a huge pile of dirty clothes on one side of the room and another pile of what appeared to be folded and clean clothes on the other. In the middle of all this organized confusion, was a small table with a pencil and a small pad of plain, white paper. A little old man with no teeth grinned at us and inquired in broken English, "Joe, I help you?"

Before Dan could answer, the old man looked at me and said, "You need numba-one tailor. I fix you like movie star. Numba-one job. You like."

At first, I didn't know what he was talking about. He kept talking, while apparently trying not to laugh at me, and saying,

"Leave uniform here. I fix. I fix numba-one. You like. Two days. I fix for you two days."

Before I could respond, Dan handed him a slip of paper and told him, "He no need fix today. Maybe tomorrow you fix."

The little old tailor read the paper and peered at the pile of clean, folded clothes. I had visions of the old man spending the next fifteen minutes searching for Dan's stuff, hopefully in the clean pile. Maybe it would have an 'X' taped to it, like his sea bag. Instead, he just reached right into the middle of the pile and pulled out a shirt, a pair of pants, and a pair of socks. He read the name above the shirt pocket and compared it to the slip.

He smiled at Dan, as he said, "Okay Joe."

"Okay. I'll change into them now, okay Charlie?" Dan nodded at the little man.

"Okay, you pay first," agreed the old man. "How you pay?"

Dan thought for a moment and asked, "How much?"

I wondered what they were talking about this time. I'd never heard the term, 'how you pay.' I knew that this shopkeeper could not be asking if Dan was going to pay by American Express or Diners Club.

Dan looked at me, smiled, turned toward the shopkeeper, and offered, "Two green back or three MPC?"

The man quickly responded, "Two green back or four MPC."

Dan handed the man two American dollars and they smiled conspiratorially at each other. With the exchange completed, Dan changed his clothes, right down to his green underwear, in the middle of the shop.

"This might be a dirty place to walk around, but no need to walk around dirty," he said with feigned innocence.

I nodded helplessly.

Dan handed the tailor his dirty clothes and the man asked hopefully, "Okay Joe, you want clean for you? I clean one day. You like."

"No, thank you. Not today. Please wrap them up and I'll take them with me this time."

The old man placed Dan's clothes on a pile of brown paper and skillfully wrapped them like fish fresh from the market, tied with a string.

"Dan, is it normal to pay in American money?" I was getting nervous about money again.

"No, not a good idea. However, I've been here before and it's okay. Don't you try it yourself, unless you know what you are doing. It could have been a set up or trap."

"Remember, I don't have any American dollars."

"That's right." Dan picked up his package, and out the door, we went. I would never have thought that picking up laundry could be such an experience.

We walked about half a block, turned a corner, and approached two guards standing in front of the door of an office building. Dan nodded at them and walked inside. I followed and saw two more guards inside. One very tall and the other very short. The two of them reminded me of a basketball player standing next to a gymnast.

Dan told the tall guard, "We've just arrived in-country and we need to locate our unit. I've been on R&R and this is his first time in-country. I need to verify its location before I can arrange a flight out for the two of us. I think it might be at Dong-Tam."

I thought, "What is a Dong-Tam?"

Dan sensed their hesitation and added impatiently, "I've been here a number of times before, and I know where to go and who to see. This will only take us a minute or two."

"I need to see your orders and ID," asked the taller of the two guards.

"No sweat," mumbled Dan as he took out his orders from his shirt pocket and his military ID from his wallet.

Both men gave the orders and ID the once over and the tall guard nodded, "Okay, if you know the way, go ahead."

"Thanks. Come on, Charles."

"Stand fast," snapped the little guard. "I need to see your orders and ID, too." "No sweat, John Wayne. It's not that big a deal, little man," retorted Dan, sounding pissed at this little guy. Dan turned to the tall guard and pointed to me, "He definitely looks Oriental and not American to me. I can truly understand why you need to check him out."

I didn't want to cause any trouble, so I quickly produced my orders and ID. "Here, sir. Is everything in order?"

The little guy looked pleased with me because I called him sir.

Dan butted in and snapped, "Don't 'sir' this guy. It'll just make him feel like a big man." After a pause for effect, he added, "Nah, never mind. You'd have to 'sir' him a lot more than once before he could feel like a big man."

I was taken aback by the way Dan was talking to these guards. I expected that all hell would break loose at any moment, but the little guard just gave Dan a dirty look and me back my orders and ID.

"Is this your only ID?" The little guard demanded of me.

"No, I have my driver's license too, and . . . ," I started to respond as Dan interrupted.

"No need to show him all that shit. We're not here to cash a check. We're only here to check on the location of our unit. When we get that, we can get back into this man's war. You know, what all happens outside this building."

"I'm not talking to you, sailor boy," barked the little guard. "No additional ID, no admission to communications."

The other guard broke in and said to short guard, "Man, don't sweat these guys. Just let them go on in."

The short guard, apparently of lower rank, glared at Dan and me as he stepped aside whimsically to let us pass.

As we walked by them, Dan grumbled to the little guard, "Little shit. A little shit in a little uniform with little authority. Hell, Shirley Temple, and Howdy Dowdy were taller than you."

Fortunately, I was the only one who heard that, I thought.

Once down the hall, I looked back and saw the two guards arguing with each other. I asked Dan, "What was that all about? Was there a problem? Or were you trying to create one?"

"I've met that little guy once before. I didn't like him then and I don't like any little guys that act like that. Sometimes they need to be put in their place. Even if it's a small place."

"What do you mean?"

"Little men with little authority trying to make themselves big men by making what they do a big authority thing. Don't like it. Don't like it at all." He was visibly upset.

"Okay," I said, as if I could have answered any other way.

"Did you see how the little guard was standing?"

"No, I didn't pay him all that much attention."

"He is so little that the sidearm he has holstered made him lean to one side."

"I'll check-it-out on our way out. At least his uniform fits better than mine."

"Yeah, he must have gotten it at the Boy Scouts store." We burst into laughter just as we approached another door with another guard-not too tall and not too short.

"We need to have someone check on the location of our ship. We need to find out where she will be tomorrow so we can arrange a flight out," Dan said to the guard.

"Wait one," the guard answered calmly as he stepped inside, closing the door behind him.

After a few moments, the guard returned, accompanied by an officer. The officer inquired, "So what's the name of your unit, and where do you think she is now?"

"USS SUMMIT, ARR 23. She's attached to the Mobile Riverine Task Force 117. I believe that the task force is either at Dong-Tam now or is due to arrive there tomorrow, sir," Dan responded in his business like tone.

"Give me a copy of your orders and ID and I'll check your story. I'm going to call the ship and see if you two guys are for real," said the officer, studying our faces.

After the officer examined our orders and ID, he shot Dan a piercing look and demanded, "Do you boys have any additional ID?"

I hoisted up my loose pants and said, in a clear voice, "No need to show him all that. We're not here to cash a check. We're only here to check on our unit so we can get back into this man's war."

All in one motion, Dan stepped back and the officer thrust his face directly in mine. I had no idea what I had done wrong. I had only repeated what Dan had said to the other guard. I swallowed and waited for all hell to break loose.

The officer shouted, "Say again, mister!"

I stood dumbfounded. I knew I was in real trouble and I felt totally helpless.

After what seemed like an eternity, Dan rose to my defense. "Sir, he's new in-country. It doesn't help that he's from California, either, sir."

The officer withdrew a little. Seeing that he was making progress, Dan continued, "Sir, I believe what he is trying to say is that the other guards have already validated our orders, ID, and other independent identification, sir."

"Is that so?" The officer glowered not releasing his look on me.

"Sir. Yes sir. You see, sir; we know how busy you must be and how important your duties are. We only want to get the information about the location of our unit and we'll be on our way, sir."

The officer's scowl relaxed into what was almost a look of pity; though his face remained close enough for me to see every pore on his nose. I didn't know whether he pitied me for what I had done or for the fact that I was from California. What ever that meant.

"All right then. You might want to explain to your California friend here that everyone is helping in, 'this man's war,' and that he's not alone," he told Dan without taking his eyes off of me for even a second.

"Yes, sir. Right away, sir," answered Dan, relieved.

The officer shifted his eyes to the guard, "If I find these orders to be fake or in any way not in order, you can shoot them both when I get back."

"Yes, sir! No problem sir." The guard grinned as if someone had just given him a million dollars.

The officer's eyes were again fixed on my face. "The big-mouthed guy from California, shoot him twice."

"Yes sir!" Blurted the guard with far too much enthusiasm for my comfort.

"This is not California, young man," the officer said sternly.

I could do nothing except look as pitiful as possible. The officer finally backed out of my face, turned crisply, and walked into the communications room. He turned to me and said, "Welcome to 'The-Nam,' California Man."

He chuckled and walked away. As he entered the communications room and before he closed the door behind him, we heard him laugh even louder.

The guard smiled at me and patted the 45 in his holster.

"What's the story?" I asked. "Are we going to be shot by our own side? What do you mean, I am from California?"

"Listen to me, my gonna get us shot friend. If you keep talking to officers that way, we just might be shot. You might deserve it, but I sure the hell don't."

I relaxed a little and tried to take in all that was going on around me. At least my heart was still beating.

Dan continued, "I used the California bit hoping that he would think you were a drafted flower child and give you a little slack. At least he walked away laughing."

"How did you know he would give me a break if he believed that I was from California?"

"He has a Boston accent and looks a little high strung. High strung people from Boston don't generally like free loving people from California."

"Okay," was the only response that I could give.

"Forget that for now. Why did you talk to him that way?"

"I only did what you did a minute ago to the guards," I explained in my defense.

"I did it to an enlisted man, a little short enlisted man. You did it to an officer and talking back to an officer in a war zone can get you killed," Dan informed me indicating that I should not forget any of this that he was telling me.

"Killed?"

"Or at least assigned to do something dangerous."

"Okay, I got that part. So, what's going to happen to us right now? This guy was given orders to shoot us. Can that really happen?" I asked with genuine fear.

"No sweat, I think he was just joking."

"You think? You think! Don't you know for sure?"

"Well, we'll find out in a minute or two. Besides, if that happened, at least I can have the pleasure of watching you get shot twice."

"Not funny man."

"I didn't say it to be funny."

Now the only thing I could focus on was the smile on the guard's face as he practiced his quick draw. I got the feeling that he really would shoot us and that he would enjoy it. If this was a dream, I wished someone would wake me.

It was a long two minutes before the officer returned and stood smiling at us. I wondered why he was smiling. Was it because he was going to see us get shot, or because he had found our ship and everything was okay?

"Can I shoot them, sir?" The guard asked with a snicker.

"No, there's no one for you to shoot right now, Marine. But hell, man, we still have the rest of the day. Maybe you'll get a second chance. The California Man here might have something else to say."

The guard nodded sadly, "Yes sir, understood sir."

Somehow, I was not surprised that the guard was disappointed.

"Your unit will be in Dong-Tam tomorrow for two days. Anything else I can check for you?" he asked as he returned our ID.

"No, nothing else needed, sir. Thanks for checking on our unit," Dan answered dutifully.

As we walked away, I tried not to have any eye contact with the officer because I didn't want to upset him twice in one day.

As we passed the two guards on our way out, Dan whispered tauntingly to the little guard, "Ass-hole, little ass-hole."

"Hold fast," snapped the little guard.

I halted, but Dan, who was walking behind me, pushed me toward the door. "Keep going. John Wayne has a hard-on and he needs someone to yell at."

I obliged and as soon as we were outside, we broke into laughter. Yet, in the back of my mind, I was wondering if the little man would get pissed enough that he would to take a shot at us. Well, maybe not us, but at least Dan.

Still laughing, Dan said, "The little man even has a little job."

"What do you mean?"

"He's just a guard standing watch inside a building. A real job is standing watch outside."

Just as I was about to respond, I heard gunfire from around the corner. Two shots. Two shots, for sure.

The two guards outside now held their M-16s at the ready. One of them stepped inside and the other peered around the corner. I froze in place. I didn't know whether to go inside the building or to head in the direction opposite of the shooting. If I stayed in place, I might be shot by whoever was shooting. If I went inside, the little guard might decide to shoot me and use the confusion as a cover story.

Dan grabbed my arm. "Come on, we'll just go this way. It'll take a little longer, but it'll be all right. We aren't in that much of a hurry."

He was so calm that I got the sense that the shooting was no big deal to him. With that reassurance, I followed as if nothing had happened.

"What do you think the shooting was about?" I asked after we had walked a short distance.

"Don't know. It was just a couple of shots. It could have been a sniper; maybe two guys got into an argument and shot each other. There is the possibility that someone was robbed. I don't really know."

"Robbed?"

"Yeah, why not?" Dan was matter-of-fact as if robbery was an option that everyone would consider.

I never would have thought that a country with an on-going war would have crime.

"You seemed surprised by that," Dan noted.

"No, not really. Now that I gave it a little thought, it does make sense, since everyone was armed. If someone over here got into trouble, you know, like with the police, are they sent to the front as punishment?"

"I don't know. Besides, this is, 'The-Nam.' Where is the front?"

I didn't have an answer for that. I started to think that with everyone carrying guns; maybe it wasn't such a good idea for Dan to give that little guard a hard time. What if he decided to shoot us and just say, "Oops, sorry about that." I wondered if someone could be awarded the Purple Heart for being shot in an argument in downtown Saigon. I could be shot by accident by someone on my own side. Wasn't that called, "friendly fire?" Somehow, it didn't seem very friendly to me.

As we continued on our way toward the BEQ, I started to ask Dan, "Dan, can you get a Purple Heart if . . ."

I noticed that he wasn't paying me any attention. He stopped abruptly, pointed toward the corner that we passed earlier where the guy from our flight was on watch and groaned, "Shit. The new guy is down. I think he's been shot."

I didn't know how to respond. I didn't know this kid, but somehow, I felt a connection with him. We came in on the same flight and all that. I was hit with the realization that, if I had checked into the Navy BEQ, I could have been on guard duty in his place. I could have been the one lying there. I imagined my parents being notified that I was shot my first day in-country. First day . . . hell, this guy was hit in just the first few hours! It was going to be a long year.

We walked over to check-it-out and saw that he was hit in the neck, just above his flack jacket. He was still alive, moaning. Someone was already treating his wound and another guy was climbing up the ladder to take his place on guard duty. I found it interesting that someone was already replacing him.

Dan shook his head, pointed to the new guy on guard duty, and commented, "I wouldn't want this guard duty right now."

"Why not?"

"Whoever shot him already has this location zeroed-in. He probably got shot from one of those balconies across the street."

"Do you think the sniper got away?"

"Yeah, he's gone. Take a look. Everyone on that side of the street is gone."

I looked across the street and saw that the sidewalk was completely vacant. Minutes ago, the streets were crammed with people and traffic. Now, there was not a single person over there.

"Where did everyone go?" I asked, expressing fear in my voice that I could not hide.

Dan stared at the empty sidewalk and explained, "Think about this. You are on the side of the street from where a shot has been fired and someone is down."

"Yeah?" I didn't know where he was taking this line of reasoning.

"And almost everyone on this side of the street has one type of rifle or another and is able, willing, and hoping to find a target over there. Now, would you want to be on that side of the street?"

"I guess not," I answered as I looked again across the street.

"Well, the people on that side of the street didn't guess, they just got the hell off the streets. It appeared that they didn't want to be used as target practice."

It did not seem real to me that there was no one on that side of the street, even if his reasoning was accurate. I could not understand how that many people could have disappeared so completely.

"This is not a cool place to hang around. I'm ready to move on," I said to Dan.

I looked up at the new guy on guard duty and recognized him as someone else from our flight. He didn't look happy about replacing the guy that was just shot.

The kid on the ground was now very still. Even his breathing appeared to have stopped. I'd never seen anyone so near death before. Not up close, anyway.

Dan took note of the number of people attending this situation and remarked, "Now is a good time to get a bite to eat."

I looked at him not sure what he was saying.

"The chow line won't be so long since everyone is here."

He could he be so cold. How could anyone think about food when this kid was down and dying here on the concrete? I could only imagine that after two tours here that death was no longer a big deal to him. It was still a big deal to me. However, I had to admit that I would feel better if we left the area. I gave our fallen compatriot one last look, then left to catch up with Dan, who was already a few paces ahead of me.

As I fell into step alongside him, Dan muttered, "This is why I didn't want to stand guard duty in Saigon. Here it's just target practice for the VC. They just look out a window and shoot. Then, they just walk away and there is no way to counter the attack. Besides that, they'll never find the shooter."

I glanced back at the balconies, looking for snipers training their sight on us. I didn't see anyone and if I did, I wouldn't have known what to do. I guess I would have ducked.

"I thought you said this was a nice, safe neighborhood."

"Well, I've been gone for awhile. Things must have changed."

Chapter 3

We arrived at the Navy BEQ and walked past the guards out front. I saw two guys inside still wearing dress whites and Dan was right, they would have made terrific targets. I felt a little better about the fatigues I was wearing, even if they were a bad fit.

"Let's get our flight taken care of before we eat," he suggested.

"No sweat." I didn't know what he was talking about, but it sounded like he had things under control.

Dan asked me for my orders and I handed them over. He approached a chief petty officer sitting behind a desk on the other side of the check-in counter. The middle-aged petty officer was reading a pocket book that he balanced on his huge beer belly while drinking coffee with a lit cigarette hanging from the side of his mouth. Not exactly a picture of respectability, or to be used as a recruitment poster I thought quietly to myself.

"Two for Dong-Tam. Tomorrow morning will be fine, if available, chief," Dan said politely as he handed the chief our orders. I noted that he didn't 'sir' the chief. In boot camp, all chiefs were sir'd.

The chief stamped our original orders and took a copy of each for himself. He didn't read them or even look up at us. He phoned someone and said, "Dong-Tam, tomorrow, AM, two seats." He looked up at us for the first time and told the person on the phone, "Enlisted. Two enlisted."

He sipped his coffee and went back to reading his book while waiting for an answer. He was not a real neat guy because the ashes from his cigarette flaked off onto the desk, unnoticed by him.

His eyes then focused on the top of his desk as he was apparently listening to someone on the phone. He received whatever it was and then responded, "Okay," before he hung up the phone. He scribbled a few remarks on the copies of our orders and stuffed them in his top drawer on top of other copies of orders. Definitely a dis-orderly filing system.

"Tan San Nut Air Force Base to Dong-Tam. Two seats. Tomorrow. 0900 hours," he informed us between sips of coffee.

He returned to his reading and added, "Hangar six, C-130."

"Two for Dong-Tam, tomorrow at 0900 hours. Thank you, chief," said Dan and we started to walk away.

"Hangar six, C-130. Got it?" The petty officer asked as he turned a page still avoiding eye contact with us.

"Yes, chief. Hangar 6, C-130. Got it."

"Was that it? Don't we get tickets or anything? He doesn't care where we want to go after we get to Dong-Tam?" It all seemed too easy. Not very military at all.

"See? No big deal. He just calls ahead and sets aside two seats on a flight that's heading to Dong-Tam. He doesn't care where we want to go after we get there or where we have been to get here," Dan shrugged.

"But the guards gave us a hard time just for asking directions. Hell, that one officer wanted us shot if we had anything out of order. This chief is willing to send us on a military flight, without any verification at all. He barely even looked at us."

"Yeah, but he's a chief. What's your point?"

"Yeah, okay. He did seem a little preoccupied," I said

"Oh yeah," Dan answered sarcastically. "We interrupted him at a very crucial point in his book reading. That must explain his friendly nature."

"Crucial point?"

"Yeah, the first crucial point was that he had to figure out the proper time to turn to the next page."

"And the second crucial point?"

"He had to remember which way to turn the page. You know, left to right or right to left."

"Come-on, he wasn't all that bad. I meant, we did get our flight out without any hassle and all that."

"But that's his only job. He just sits there, collects a copy of your orders, makes a phone call, tells you the flight information, makes a note on your orders, and files it. He only has two other major decisions to make each day."

"And they are?" This had to be good.

"One, he has to decide which book to read next."

"And two."

"He has to remember when it's time for him to go off duty."

"If you say so. Now, can we see about getting something to eat?"

"We'll try here first. If it looks decent and the line isn't too long, we'll eat Navy chow," Dan responded.

"No sweat," I answered starting to sound military and all that.

After a short walk down a hallway and up a flight of stairs, we came into a small room crowded with tables and chairs. To one side was a small window with a ledge into the next room. On the other side of this ledge was the kitchen.

Next to where we were standing was a seaman seated behind a table. "Please sign in and let me see your ID," he instructed as he motioned toward the clipboard in front of him.

I questioned, "What's this, we need reservations?"

Dan explained, "They keep a record of the number of meals a day between the Army, Navy, Air Force, and Marines, along with our Vietnamese allies. Sometimes the VC will try to slip in and get a free meal."

"I didn't need to hear that. Is it true?"

"I've only heard stories about that. I don't know for sure. I mean hell; you know how they all look alike anyway. How could anyone tell?"

I let that one go because that just couldn't be true. We walked to a window and found a pile of metal trays. We each took a tray, and a local Vietnamese boy appeared from behind the counter to ask, "What you want, Joe?"

Dan answered, "A little of each. Is this food numba-one or numba-ten?"

"Numba-one, Joe, everything numba-one today. Try, you like, okay Joe?"

Dan placed his tray in front of the cook. The cook used the same large spoon to serve a little of each of every kind of food that he had.

"Numba-one," the cook kept repeating with each spoon full. "You like, you have more, okay Joe?"

"The same for me," I said and placed my tray on the ledge.

I was amazed at how each serving of corn, peas, and mashed potatoes was dished out in exactly the same portions. The cook then dropped two pork chops in my tray, still using the same spoon.

Holding the full tray with two hands, I followed Dan to a table when my pants started to fall down. I tried to balance my tray and keep my pants up by closing my legs together, but my tray fell from my hands. The sound of the metal tray on the tiled floor was quite loud and the food made a disgusting mess.

To my surprise, two guys came running in to see what caused the noise. Each pointed a rifle at me. From my point of view looking up, they meant business.

"Wait! Wait! I just dropped a tray! I'll clean it up." Was I going to get shot for just dropping a tray? They both just looked at me and I couldn't tell if they wanted to laugh at me or shoot me. Maybe they would do both. At least it wasn't the little guard from the Comm-Center, as he would have shot me.

The little Vietnamese cook was immediately on the scene to assist me. "You okay, Joe? I fix. I give you new tray. No sweat Joe."

With a smile, he added, "I see you have numba-ten pants. You eat numba-one meal and get more weight. Pants no more fall down."

All I could say was, "Thanks." I didn't see any reason to explain my problem here. I just wanted to eat my meal and avoid bringing any more attention to myself.

He continued with, "I know numba-one tailor. He fix pants. Good job, numba-one good job. You like, okay? I tell you him."

I could only smile in return as he continued to help me clean the mess. The two guys that came running in were already gone when I looked up a second time. I got another tray, got back in line, and with my second helping, tried again to find my seat while keeping my pants up.

I took my seat and noticed that Dan was almost finished with his meal. He hadn't skipped a beat. Hell, I didn't think he even missed me at all.

"It's about time you got here," he told me.

"You didn't see what I did?"

"Yeah, but I was hungry and my food was hot. Besides, you already had enough people around you," he explained with a mouth of food.

"Well, I've learned that I have numba-ten pants and a numba-one meal. Whatever a numba-one and numba-ten are."

Dan didn't say anything. He just kept eating as if this kind of thing happened all the time.

I took a bite, and asked, "Why did I get such a major response for just dropping a tray?"

"Numba-one is good and numba-ten is bad," responded Dan, lagging one question behind.

"Okay," I answered.

"As for your second question, my numba-one friend doing a numba-ten-thousand stunt, any unusual sounds will cause an immediate response from anyone on guard duty inside this building."

"Okay, I understand that part. But with their guns drawn?"

"Because of the TET offensives, as you bought up earlier, confusion in a place like this is a serious manner. Remember that we just had a shooting outside. That could have been staged as a diversion from a more serious situation in here."

"Well, that makes sense," I agreed looking around the room. I didn't know why I was looking around the room; or what for; it just felt like the natural thing to do.

"Consider this. Would you want the guards to come in first and then decide if they should have their weapons drawn?"

"Excellent point."

"You're off to a good start, my almost got us shot twice in one day friend," nodded Dan.

"Yeah, almost got myself shot earlier for being a smart ass to an officer and now for making too much noise in a dining room. In high school, this kind of stuff would have only gotten me a few days in detention and a note home to my parents."

Dan smiled and continued to eat. After a few minutes, he looked up. "I'll hate to be with you when you get around the VC."

I decided to ignore that comment as my mind raced through the events from my short life. Well, maybe just the events of the last couple of hours and I concluded that I deserved a few more years to live. At least the time to complete my one-year tour.

I looked down at my food and it was almost gone. I didn't realize that I ate that fast. I couldn't even remember if it was good or not. Whether it was a numba-one or a numba-ten meal.

Dan got in line for seconds, but I couldn't decide if I wanted more or not. When he returned I asked, "Is it that good?"

"Don't know."

"You don't know?"

"No, I just eat for volume. Besides, we might not eat tomorrow."

"Speaking of tomorrow, where on the coast is this Dong-Tam place?"

"Well, Dong-Tam is not exactly a city with an ocean view. It's about 100 miles inland on the Mekong Delta. We'll land at the air base near the town that's next to the river where our unit should be anchored."

"How long do to think we will be inland?"

"What?"

"I mean, is she there to get supplies or something?"

"No, she's patrolling the rivers. She just goes up and down the river following the patrol boats."

"How is it that a repair ship does patrol in the rivers?"

"She follows the patrol boats providing repair, food, and shelter. In addition, she sometimes provides entertainment for the troops."

"So that's the function?"

Dan thought for a moment and said, "In simple terms, the patrol boats are there to guard and protect the supply and repair ships. And the supply and repair ships are there to supply and repair the patrol boats that are there to guard and protect the supply and repair ships."

"Like a Catch-22?"

"Yeah, that's about it."

I was about to ask another question when the cook came over, and asked, "Numba-one or numba-ten?" He asked hopefully for a good report.

"Numba-one," answered Dan, giving him the thumbs-up as the cook walked away with a smile on his face.

Dan ducked his head down and whispered, "It was an, all-right meal. Not quite a numba-one, but better than a numba-ten meal. While you are here in-country, you will have the misfortune of eating a numba-ten meal."

I could only look at him confused; I didn't completely know what he was talking about again this time.

Dan continued after making a face as if he was in heavy thought, "Now that I think about it, once you have eaten a numba-ten meal, every meal thereafter will be a numba-one."

"Here is some advice my friend," he continued in his conspiratorial voice, "You should always keep the cooks happy, and say that it's a numba-one meal."

"Why?"

"Think about it. You piss off a cook and he might piss in your food."

"You got to be kidding."

"Nope, I am not kidding."

"But we signed in and everything."

"That was for a head count, not a poison count."

"But this is a military chow hall!"

"Yeah, this is true. However, was the cook an American?"

"Damn man, I've only been here a few hours and already I'm afraid to talk to officers, stand guard duty, and eat the food. Hell, I probably won't even die with my boots on. They might just fall off because they are way too big for me."

Dan smiled at me as I continued, "The only person that doesn't want to harm me is the tailor and he only wants to make me look good. I guess to look good for those who want to hurt me."

Dan laughed at that one. "Don't sweat the small stuff, my man. Just wait until you are working on some real issues. Then you can complain."

I decided to change the subject. "Where are we off to now?"

"Why? Is there something else you need to do right now?"

He could be so sarcastic sometimes.

"No, not really. I'm just curious about what we'll being doing next."

"Let's head out for a short walk while it's still daylight and check out the sights," he answered, perking up a little.

We polished off our food, returned our trays, and headed outside. On the way out, Dan gave the cook another thumbs-up; I'd figured that I'd better follow his example and I did the same.

At least I got a smile back from the cook.

Once outside, we walked toward the Army BEQ in the opposite direction from the scene of the shooting that happened earlier. A few blocks from the mess hall, I noticed two Army guys doing business with a group of little kids. They were buying and selling something.

One little boy approached us and I heard him try to sell Dan a kid. Dan cut him off. "Not now. Maybe some other time."

We walked on and I asked, "A kid? What does he think you're going to do with a goat?"

"No, he wants to sell me a kid. You know, a little person type kid."

Thinking that he was joking, I ignored him. I wasn't going to fall for any more of his tricks.

A moment later, a few other kids stopped us and asked if we wanted to buy some Christmas cards. One little boy, I guessed to be about ten years old, tried to hand me his wares. I took one to be polite. I thought that if they were halfway decent then I might want to send some home.

They had 'Merry Christmas,' printed on the front, in English, and were very appealing. (APPENDIX D) Above the lettering was an oriental woman in a sampan, wearing one of those oriental outfits. Another card just had a sampan floating down the river and both cards had nothing to do with Christmas. Anyway, part of the card was made of silk and that made it somewhat elegant. Well, maybe not real silk.

"How much?"

"For you, Joe, two dollar four cards."

Not bad English for this little kid. I figured he'd probably been to a Catholic school.

"For a good deal, you must know the rules," Dan whispered not wanting the kid to hear him. "You only want to pay half of the asking value. So start low and work your way to one dollar."

Although I felt that two dollars was a fair price for the four cards, I took his advice. I thought it might be fun to bargain with this kid.

"These cards are all right. I'll give you fifty cents for all four."

"Okay, Joe. I see you have no taste, but for you, I sell you numba-one deal on one card. One card for fifty cents, or four for two dollar."

His response surprised me. I didn't think that a kid of his age was clever enough to try to outwit me. Besides, I'd been to high school, after all.

"I can give you seventy-five cents, no more." I answered.

"Seventy-five cents for one card?" The little boy asked, grinning widely.

Now this smart little kid is starting to be a smart-ass little kid.

"No, seventy-five cents for all four."

"Look Joe, I have a mother and three sisters to feed. Give me one-fifty for four." He was practically ordering me to buy the cards now.

I sensed that Dan was standing behind me snickering at all this. I decided to just ignore him and work on closing the deal at one dollar. "Okay, for your mother and three sisters I will give you one dollar," boldly I spoke as if I was a super salesman.

"Okay, Joe, my mother break my arm because I give you numba-one deal."

I paid the money and felt pleased. I was proud of having bargained so well, even if it was with a little kid. The longer I am over here, the better I'll get at this bargaining ritual. I smiled at Dan because I did something right today.

"I feel very good about this," I boasted.

"You did a fair job." He did not look nearly as impressed with my bargaining as I was.

"What do you mean, 'fair?' I got it to half the asking price, just like you suggested."

He smiled and said, "Check out the little kid again. I believe he has something to sell you."

I thought, "What now? Am I about to buy Easter Cards?"

"Hey, Joe," the little boy called to me.

"What?" I responded eager to make another good deal.

He looked over at Dan and smiled conspiratorially, "You want buy envelopes for cards? I give numba-one deal," he offered.

My good feeling had only lasted a short time . . . not even a minute. Disappointed and slightly pissed, I asked, "How much for envelopes?"

"Two dollars, numba-one envelopes. They perfect fit for Christmas cards. I even sell you numba-one lick'em, stick'em, American stamps."

Dan laughed very loud at my predicament. Apparently, I had made a complete ass out of myself. I couldn't believe that I hadn't seen this coming. The little kid took me for a ride. Nevertheless, I had no choice, I needed the envelopes, and he had them.

Cautiously, I started out again with the same routine. I said fifty, he said one-fifty, I said seventy-five, he said one-twenty-five, and then we agreed on one dollar. I again paid the little shit one-dollar and after I got my envelopes, the kid asked me, "You need stamps for cards, right? I make you good deal."

"How much for stamps?"

Dan grabbed my arm and said; "Hold on a minute, my numba-one sales executive, you don't need any stamps today."

He pulled me away; laughing at me all the while, I was dazed and confused.

"So what am I going to do about stamps? Do I buy them from another kid?"

"No sweat. While you're in-country, you only need to write the word 'free' on the envelope in place of a stamp." He could barely speak; he was laughing so hard.

"Say what?"

"That's right, no need for stamps while you are over here. We get fifty dollars extra each month for being shot at and our outgoing mail is free," he said between giggles.

"I'm glad you're having a good laugh at my expense. Any other ideas for a good time today?" I asked, embarrassed once again.

He began to calm down. "Not . . . not now, maybe later."

I couldn't believe it. Another group of kids right in front of us, trying to sell all sorts of items. Dan looked at me and started to laugh all over again.

"What's so amusing now?" I asked. "Where did all these kids come from?"

Still laughing, Dan said, "I guess the word is out on the streets that an FNG is in town and is willing to pay top dollar for anything."

"FNG?"

"Yeah, 'Fucking New Guy.' Once they heard that you're paying full price for cards and that you're still willing to buy stamps, well, they'll try to sell you some waterfront property next. I can see it now. Waterfront property with a great view of the Mekong Delta from your front porch. With an exciting view of the Ho Chi Minh Trail out from the back deck. Pre-laid mines in your yard to keep out the neighbors' kids and their pet water buffalo."

Even I had to laugh at the image. It was rather humorous that I had just spent two dollars on four Christmas cards. Not forgetting that they came with the accompanying mailing envelopes.

As the crowd of kids gathered around us, I noticed each one had something different to sell. Apparently, I could get a great deal on cigarettes, cigarette lighters, hats, and candy bars. There was another kid trying to sell me his little sister. That made two kids for sale in the same block.

I followed close behind Dan, repeating what he was telling the kids. "Not now, buy later."

"Care for a change of pace?" Dan asked.

"Yes, anyplace but here. I don't need to buy anything else right now. Okay?"

"I know an interesting bar we can visit for a good time. It's called The Saigon Bar. It's just around the next corner."

"I could use a good, cold beer right now. I'll agree to almost anything, just to get away from all these kids. By the way, any other rules that I need to be aware of? You know, bar rules."

"There are some different rules for venturing into bars while in-country," Dan answered apparently giving my question some serious thought.

I braced myself for another round of his bullshit. "What kind of rules are there and why do we need them?" Vietnam had many rules and none of them had any military value. There were rules to follow thanking a cook for a poor meal, getting off planes in a quick manner, how to ride a bus, exchange money, what to wear in-country and, now, some rules for going to a bar just for a cold beer.

"Rule number one; do not fall in love with any bargirl. I do not care how good-looking she is or what she tells you. Two, do not kiss any girl on the lips and don't let any girl kiss you."

"I wasn't expecting to walk in and get a little lip today," I answered, jokingly suggesting that I was not an idiot.

"Listen up. Three, do not buy any girl a Saigon Tea."

"Saigon Tea? I thought we were going for a beer. I have no desire to visit a tea shop."

"Listen up my man. A Saigon Tea costs three times as much as any other drink. Way too much for a drink, that has no alcohol. It's a way the girls make their money."

"Got it," I think.

"Four. Never, ever, be alone with one of the bargirls. Keep an American near you at all times. Five, remember: this is not back home America. We are in the middle of a nightmare and you have 365 days until a wake-up."

"That's a lot of rules," I complained, but still taking mental notes.

"You'll never get a chance to experience this kind of stuff again in your lifetime," Dan went on as if he was telling me a story.

"For real? I mean, it's just a bar. I know I'm not twenty-one yet, but I do have some ideas about how to act in a bar."

"One more thing. You only need two things to pick up a girl. One, an empty seat next to you, and two, money. The more money you have, the better your choices." Dan paused, and then continued, "Ah, take away one. You do not need the empty seat. Just leave enough room for a girl to talk to you." Another pause, "Nah, take that one away also. These girls will talk to you from across the room if they know that you have money. They really don't even have to talk to you. Eye contact will be sufficient in most cases."

"If this is such a bad place with so many rules, then why go? Why not just go back to the barracks and kill some time until our flight tomorrow?"

"You go to these places so you can have a good time, even if it's not totally real. It'll help you appreciate what you have back home. You're still new in-country and a lot of this will be educational for you."

"Okay, I guess."

"These little pockets of cool times are needed to offset the bad times. You will definitely have your share of bad times," Dan explained, apparently thinking about some of his, bad times.

"I've been to bars back home, it can't be that different. I mean, come on, a bar is a bar."

"True. But over here, everyone acts a little different than if they were back home. See, no one here knows anybody that you know back home. No one will tell your parents or friends what you are doing. My attitude is, 'It don't mean nothin, what's the worst thing that could happen to me.' Just try to enjoy yourself."

"Can't we get into trouble? You know, kicked out of the military or something. A dishonorable discharge?"

"Okay, sure. You get a dishonorable discharge. The only people who want to see your discharge papers are potential employers. With the way people treat us vets back home, the last thing you want to let anyone know is that you were in the military. And no way should you volunteer that you have served in Vietnam."

"Good point, but yeah, I am the FNG. I don't want to get into any kind of trouble my first day here."

Ignoring me, Dan pointed to an open door. "After you."

I wasn't totally sure what to expect, but thought I could at least check-it-out. Besides, I had nothing else to do. I entered the small doorway, walked in, and found it very dark inside. I stopped to ask Dan what kind of money would they take, when, to my total surprise, someone yanked my zipper down, grabbed me where no one should be grabbing me, unless of course we were properly introduced, and started to walk away.

"Stop! Stop!" I yelled at the back of this woman's head and with no other options, I just followed behind her, real close-like. She paid me no attention, aside from the death grip she had on me. It felt as if I had grown a few inches and it wasn't even that hard to do.

Once more, Dan was laughing hysterically. "Ride'em Cowboy! Don't make any sudden stops or turns! I'll be coming in just a minute!"

What I had was a young girl with my family jewel in her hand, walking me between tables, and past other customers. I was doing a kind of shuffle walk, taking very small, deliberate steps behind her, making extremely sure that I followed her every move. She sped up and I had to lean back to maintain my balance. It didn't seem like now was the time to fall down. At least, with the hold on me she had on me, I knew that my pants weren't going to fall down as long as my button stayed buttoned.

The three of us arrived at an empty table. "Sit Joe," she commanded.

I quickly obliged and she took the seat beside me. She had yet to relax her grip and the pain was bringing tears to my eyes.

"You very handsome man. You buy me drink. I show you good time. Okay Joe?"

There I was with my mouth open, zipper down, and my little-fellow sticking out in a room full of people. This was definitely not a turn on. Maybe for her, but for sure not for me. I was mortified by the idea that the other people in the bar were watching, but I cared less about that than about getting away from this woman. I didn't know how to extract myself from the situation without causing myself even more pain. I assumed this was the normal way to enter such a place. I was afraid to think what would happen when it was time to leave! No way would I want to stop here twice in the same day. Hell, once a year would have been plenty for me.

"A drink, Joe. Buy me drink. Buy me drink now," she said with a smile that revealed her ability to torture me, if she wanted to.

Just then, Dan and his girl came to the table. He took his family jewel out of her hand and said firmly, "Me no buy you drink now. Later I call you."

Again, my girl demanded, "Come on, Joe, you buy me drink. You buy me drink now!" And as her voice became more demanding, her grip became tighter. Tears were streaming down my face now. I looked to Dan for help and he was shaking his head no.

"Just tell her no," he said to me.

I tried, but what came out instead was, "Wh.. Wh.. What do you want?"

"You buy me now drink, Joe. I love you. I show you good time. We boom-boom all day. You got money?"

Again, I looked over at Dan through my tears and he was still shaking his head no. I needed to make a decision soon. I couldn't allow her grip to tighten any more.

Dan spoke sternly to her, "No, not now. Go away. We call you later."

"No, no thank you," I squeaked.

At that point, I knew first hand that a man's voice does go up in such a situation.

As if a switch had been switched, she let go quickly, got up, and walked away. I wiped the tears from my face, placed 'stretch' back in my pants, pulled up my zipper, and got myself composed. I was utterly amazed that all of the so-called excitement took place in only a few seconds. In fact, it happened so quickly that I didn't remember anything about her other than how she looked from behind, and that she had a strong handshake. Hell, she could have been blue-eyed or blind for all I knew. Well, not blind. I mean, she did make it across the room without hitting anything or anyone even with the room being very dark and crowded with people. This was a feat in itself for anyone with good eyesight that had someone in tow.

Examining the room though tearing eyes, I could see why they kept the room so dark. Everything was dirty. The floor was full of trash and empty beer bottles, the non-working ceiling fans had spider webs all over them, about half the lights in the ceiling were off or burned out, and the main source of lighting came from the beer neon lights at the bar. This was the kind of place that you would always hear stories about, but you never believed them to be true.

Getting back to my girl with the strong handshake, she took a seat on the couch by the door and waited for the next GI to walk in so that she could execute the same trick on him. I watched and noticed that each time someone came in, he too, had the ride of his life and followed his girl to a table of her choosing. If a girl stayed with the GI, she would continue to hold onto him and he would buy her a drink. Dan was right about this place. I would never see this kind of stuff back home.

Before I could formulate a response to what had happened, a waitress showed up to take our order. The waitress looked as if she were about sixty years old and her outfit was made for anyone but her. There was just something wrong with anyone her age wearing hot pants, a tube top, and go-go boots. "You no want girl. You order drink. You order drink now. What drink you want?"

She sounded like one very unhappy old person, who clearly did not like her job. Maybe she had to try to get me to buy a drink from her instead since I did not buy the other girl a drink. I was more than willing to buy her a beer or a Saigon Tea, just to get a guarantee that she would not touch me!

"Two beers. Fallstaff." Dan told her and she walked away.

"Some friend you are. Why didn't you tell me about this place? I had no idea that my little pride and joy was going to be stretched across the bar in front of everyone. I could have been hurt, you know. Really hurt."

Dan laughed and had nothing to say.

"What's so amusing this time?"

"Like I said earlier, things here are different. This is not the real world. Besides, it's not like this will be the last time Little Charles will be dragged out and paraded in front of people." He laughed again. Maybe he could see that I was a little pissed because he tried to smooth things over with, "Come on man. Relax. Today, the beer is on me, my friend."

Dan snickered to himself and it appeared that he had told himself a joke. Well, I might as well be in this. I asked, "What's so funny?"

"I called your little guy, 'Little Charles.'"

"And."

"For me, I call my little guy, my 'Love mussel.'"

"Yeah, well, when the waitress comes back, order me another cold beer to dip my damaged goods into. That should help with the swelling," I joked. "You know, I should have turned my head and coughed twice, since I already had it out."

"No sweat my man."

The pain faded after a few minutes and I felt a little better, both physically and emotionally. I was really looking forward to a cold beer after what I had just been through, but not for a dipping or anything like that. It didn't seem like a good idea to stick it out a second time. A guy could lose more than his virginity in a place this rough. "Are all the bars in town like this?" I asked.

"No. The ones that aren't as cool as this place, well, no one goes there. On the other hand, pardon the reference; some bars are more exciting than this place. We'll hit them the next time we're in town."

"More exciting than this?" I couldn't imagine.

"Yeah, I'll show you some other time. If you get this excited about this place, you might just pass out at some of the other bars."

"You're not serious? Better than this?"

"Yeah, there are some places that even the Green Berets and Navy Seals stay out of."

Just then, our two beers were slammed down in front of us. No glasses, coasters, or napkins. Our drinks weren't even opened. I was expecting our waitress to open the beers and leave us with glasses; however, she turned and walked away.

"Damn," I said, "They can open your pants and yank out your crank, but they can't open your beer for you."

"Man, don't sweat it. Just enjoy your beer."

"Now she was one unhappy waitress," I continued. "One girl wants to make my day and this one wants to ruin it."

"It's tough to be old in a place where all the young girls make the good money," Dan explained.

"Say what?"

"Yeah. The young girls get all the guys to buy them a Saigon Tea while they talk and dance with you. This old woman, on the other hand, must run back and forth and is probably making less than half what the young ones do. But don't feel sorry for her."

"I wasn't. But why not?" I questioned.

"Don't sweat it."

"Okay, no sweat, but why not feel sorry for this old lady?" I persisted.

"She probably made all her money from the French troops that were here years ago, before they lost the war."

"Well, now. I know that you don't like little men or old ladies."

"That's not exactly true. I don't like little men that act like big men," Dan clarified.

"All right."

"Now, as for this old lady, if she's so unhappy with her job in a bar like this, either she should not show up, or she should demand better. I mean, as long as us Americans are here spending money, there should be work for everyone. A good war keeps everyone working."

I figured that was about enough of an attempt at intellectual conversation with Dan that I could handle in one sitting. With that, I decided to keep my legs crossed and try to enjoy my beer . . . if I could get it open. Back home, I could open beer bottles with the seat belt buckle in my car.

I looked to Dan for instruction. He placed the bottle cap on the table's edge and hit the neck of the bottle with a hard downward motion. The cap flew off and he tilted his head back and took a long swig. Dan glanced at me and offered, "Let me open that for you. Watch."

He did, and I was grateful.

"It's no sweat. You don't want to drink out of a glass that they filled anyway. You may not always get what you ordered. Your drink might be watered down or spiked with rat poison."

I didn't know what he was talking about, once more. We were in South Vietnam, not North Vietnam. I downed nearly half my beer in one swallow. It was good and cold, and since it came unopened, I didn't need to think that it could have been filled with rat poison.

Dan held up his beer as if to toast my new experience. "Cheers," he said to me with a huge smile on his face. He finished off his beer and asked, "Ready for another cold one from Miss Congeniality?"

"Yeah. The beers here are as cold as she is," I said, feeling better now about being here.

As she walked by, Dan told her to bring two more beers. She didn't acknowledge him or anything. She just kept on walking away. I guessed it would be a while now before we got our drinks.

To my surprise, she brought the two drinks, and relatively quickly. The second time around, I was able to open my own beer.

Every three or four minutes, a different girl would come over and ask us to buy them a drink. Dan always answered, "No, not now."

"How long will they keep coming over and asking us to buy them a drink?" I asked.

"They wouldn't come as often if the place were crowded. They'd just make the rounds. Unless of course it was payday and then it would go on the entire time we were here."

"Is there any way to make them stop?" Their demands started to get on my nerves. Even though, some of them were quite pretty, I was afraid to say, 'yes' to any of them. One of them just might grab me and go running across the room to another table. Not letting me go until I bought her a drink.

"There's one thing I do that usually works," Dan informed me.

"And that is," I questioned. I would have thought that he would have just told me instead of me having to ask.

"I sometimes scratch my crotch for awhile," Dan explained as he made an obvious gesture to scratch his crotch and made a facial expression as if he was in pain doing so.

"I was hoping that a simple, 'Go away, leave me alone' would work."

"Think about it, this is their job. Their other job options could be out in the rice fields, walking around in the mud behind some water buffalo, trying not to step in buffalo shit in their bare feet."

"I guess you're right. I never would have thought about it that way."

We finished our beers and ordered another round. Dan was right again. As soon as I started to scratch myself on a regular basis, the girls didn't stop by as often. Still, I noticed that a few girls continued to approach us.

"Why doesn't the scratching work on all the girls?" I wondered aloud.

"Simple. They can't catch what they already have. Your itch, their itch, everybody itch-itch. It doesn't really matter."

"Okay, what? Say again." Now I was really confused.

"If you both have the same reason to scratch, then she has no reason not to spend time with you. These girls, they still have to work. Gives new meaning to the saying, 'Itchy palms.'"

"I see," I answered as I continued to scratch myself. At the very least, it did cut down on the number of visits. I made it a point to watch one of the girls that just asked me for a drink as she walked away. Sure enough, she made it back to the front door and started to scratch herself. Good thing to know and definitely something for me to remember.

A few minutes passed in silence. Dan asked me what I was thinking.

"I'm thinking about my new uniform, the guy that was shot, my new Christmas cards, how sore I am and that I keep scratching myself, and how tired I am. I'd like to call home and let my parents know that I have at least arrived."

Dan finished his beer. "Drink up and we'll head on back. A good night's sleep will do us both good. Phones are hard to come by; but, we'll find you one while we're here in town."

We enjoyed another beer and paid our tab. As we rose to leave, I made it a point of holding onto my crotch, just in case one of the girls decided to lead me in another direction. Our departure was uneventful, to my relief.

Just as we stepped outside, two guys walked in behind us. A second later, I heard them yelling. One was yelling out of excitement, the other had fear in his scream. I could tell by the scream, which one was in there for the first time.

We started to cross the street, but had to wait because of heavy traffic. Crossing the street over here in the middle of the block was tricky. We were faced with a four-lane road with eight lanes of traffic. There were fast moving bikes and trucks, along with slow-moving carts pulled by men, horses, and or buffaloes. The speeds ranged from four miles an hour to forty. In the middle of all this, there were several people trying to cross. The noise was overwhelming and with all the horns that were beeping; there was no way to tell who was beeping at whom. The traffic here was just awful.

"Is crossing the street always like this?" I asked.

"No, not really. You should see how busy it gets during rush hour or bomb time."

Rush hour I understood, but what was bomb time? I had to ask. "Okay, what are you talking about?"

"Rush hour. A time when traffic is full of drivers going to or from work."

"No. I know what rush hour is. I'm asking about the, 'bomb time' part."

"Okay. People hear a bomb go off and they expect that another might go off nearby. Anyone driving will put the pedal to the medal. Anyone crossing the street will do so very quickly to try to get into a doorway. Not a very pretty sight."

"What if it's just a gun shot like we heard earlier?"

"No, nothing like a bomb going off. A gunshot sounds like any good old-fashioned backfire from a car, truck, or motorcycle. Unless you see that someone is down, then no one pays that any attention."

"So I guess we'll ignore all sounds and only focus on crossing the street," I said.

Dan was too busy looking for an opening in the traffic to answer me. Behind every taxi or truck were a couple of motorcycles trying to pass on both sides. A person waiting to cross couldn't see them until they floored it and saw that they were aiming for pedestrians crossing the street. In addition to all of that, not everyone was heading in the same direction in the same lane.

In spite of all the activity surrounding us, crossing was uneventful until about halfway across the street, when a motorcycle crossed closely in front of us and ran over a huge pile of buffalo shit. It splattered all over my new oversized pants and boots. None got on Dan, just me.

Dan looked at me and remarked coolly, "No big deal. It's just your turn to get shit on."

"Yeah, yeah. I know, welcome to, 'The-Nam.' This is a shitty deal," I said choking back sadness, anger, and embarrassment.

"No, that's not it. You just got, 'shit on.' That's not a shitty-deal."

"What do you mean?" I don't know why I asked. I wasn't in the mood for any of his ridiculous philosophizing, especially in the middle of the street, with the potential of having buffalo waste splattered on me again.

Fortunately, I was spared. Dan had spotted someone that he knew. He spotted a guy just in front of us on the sidewalk and shouted, "Billy Bob Joe Jim!"

What? Was he yelling at four people?

A strange-looking guy yelled back, "Mr. Dan! When did you get back?"

Saying that this guy was strange looking was being very kind to him. He had the appearance that would cause a parent to warn their children about getting to close to him. As for me, I wouldn't want to share a cab with him.

"A few hours ago. How about you?"

I wondered if we were going to stand there and hold a conversation in the middle of the street with the chance of having shit splashed on me again. At that moment, the traffic opened enough for us to cross the street.

"I've been here for two days, just lying low before reporting back. No way am I going to report back early," he explained to Dan.

Dan questioned, "Oh yeah. You're back early are you?"

"The local police asked me to leave Sydney early. I'm not sure what all I did this time; but I had to leave just the same." Billy Bob Joe Jim looked to be puzzled about what he just said.

"The last time you were on R&R, you were sent home early," Dan reminded him, as they approached each other and shook hands.

"Yeah, that was Bangkok."

"What ever happened with that?"

"Remember? I had to go to Captain's Mast for that one. I still don't know why it was wrong. I just said I was sorry and that I wouldn't do it again."

"Yeah, until you went on another R&R," Dan laughed.

"Now you see why I can't go back early," he said, as if he really had no other choice.

Looking at this guy, I couldn't figure out why he was holding onto a little kid that he had. Another kid was also hanging onto him as if he were made of gold.

"So, who's the guy with shit all over him? First time crossing the street?" Billy Bob Joe Jim asked.

"My new friend Charles."

"You need to give him some OJT on crossing streets."

"No problem, he picks up on things quickly," Dan answered, looking at me as if I was disgusting.

"Yeah, I can see that. Soon he'll be picking up some flies."

We exchanged greetings and he suggested that I just call him Billy-Bob. I came back with, "Glad to meet you, Billy-Bob."

"So what did you buy this time?" Dan inquired leaving me out of his conversation.

"This little girl," he said as he gave her a hug. "I got her for the cost of only two cartons of cigarettes. And I got them for

$1.10 on the base. Not the $4.50 a carton here on the street. Good deal, what do you think Mr. Dan?"

Damn! This guy bought the little girl the kids were trying to sell to us earlier! This had to be a joke. No way, no way could this be true.

"Not a good deal, Billy-Bob. Sorry my man. What are you going to do with this kid?" Dan asked him, looking as if he was a teacher asking a school kid why he had lost his homework.

"I don't know. I just knew a good deal when I saw one. I can always sell her to a Marine for five cartons of cigarettes."

"No man, you can't do that. Just return her. You don't need this kid and the kind of trouble that you will get into," Dan instructed.

Billy-Bob didn't say anything. He just hung his head low as if being scolded by a parent.

"Remember," Dan continued, "the time you bought a wife, and the Navy didn't let you ship her home?"

Dan had taken on the role of a big brother with this guy. Billy-Bob was thinking over the situation and the more he thought, the sadder he looked.

Dan stretched out his arms and took the kid from Billy-Bob. With a tear in his eye, he let go of the kid and Dan placed her on the ground. She walked toward the group of kids we saw earlier with the other child trailing closely behind her. These kids seemed pleased that she was being returned, maybe because they missed her or maybe because they could sell her again.

The strange guy just looked at Dan, and then at me. He shook his head from side to side and walked away.

"I'll see you back at the unit, okay Billy Bob?" Dan announced.

Billy-Bob didn't answer as he walked away. He just raised one arm halfway, giving us a pitiful wave back with all these kids following him. Some kids were teasing him and others were trying to sell him some more stuff.

"Dan, just who is this guy, and did he really buy this kid?"

"Yeah. Most assuredly, he did buy that little kid."

"But why? That can't be legal. Even over here, that just can't be legal."

"Look, Billy-Bob may be a little odd but he does have one good talent. He's able to buy and sell anything at the best deal ever."

"Okay, but so what?"

"Yeah, I bet this little kid had an asking price of five cartons of cigarettes. In a matter of minutes, he got it down to two cartons. He's able to do that for almost anything. He would have gotten your Christmas cards and envelopes for one dollar, total. And, he would have had them throw in the postage stamps."

"Okay, but what was he planning to do with a kid over here?"

"I don't think he has thought it out that far. He saw a good deal to make and he made it. Not a bad deal when you think about it. Five cartons down to two."

"Yeah, good deal; but, you are talking about a person that he purchased."

Dan paid me no attention. However, I asked, "Did you say earlier that he had bought a wife?"

"Yep, but he only kept her for a few days, and then he had to sell her. The Navy wasn't too happy with him on that one."

What had I gotten myself into in this place? This was a crazy place to be. Lucky for me I only had to last twelve months.

"He's in our unit?" I asked, trying to find out more about this guy.

"Yeah, he's a cool guy, but a little strange. Try to stay on his good side. Don't get him angry with you. If you do get him angry, it'll be to your advantage to ask for a transfer."

"Do I need to ask for details?"

"I'll tell you the details on this guy some other time. It'll give us something to talk about during the long days when there is nothing to do."

I didn't want to hear anything about long days; I only wanted short ones, 365 short ones to be exact. With it starting to be dark now, I could at least count off one day.

Whatever. We moved on and as we approached a small group of old men under a tree, we could hear all kinds of excitement. Wanting to check-it-out, I said to Dan, "What's that all about?"

"Don't know, let's see."

What we found was some kind of fight, like a cock or dogfight. Except, it was with bugs. I couldn't tell if it was crickets, roaches, or water bugs. Whatever, they were having a good time and 'bettin' money' was a flying everywhere.

I found this to be cool and quite a learning experience until one of the men ate the losing bug. I couldn't tell if he did this because his bug lost, or if he just liked eating them. Well, enough of this, we were out of here.

After a short walk and without having to cross in the middle of the block, we arrived at the BEQ. I noticed there were a few more guards on duty than before. Most of them had a rifle and some had shot guns.

"Is this a shift change or something?" I asked because of all the additional guards.

"No. It's going to be dark soon and there are always more people on guard duty at night. Look on the roof. See the guys up there?"

"Yeah."

"He has a night vision scope. The guards probably have orders that if they see anything that seems dangerous, they can shoot it and explain their reasoning later."

"Don't they give the standard challenge or anything? You know, 'halt, who goes there?'"

"Okay, say they do shout 'Halt, who goes there?' How do you think the bad guy will respond?" Dan questioned me.

"Hell, I don't know. It just seems odd that they can just shoot anybody."

"Look, everyone in town knows that it's not safe just to hang around an Army BEQ at night. So, it's very possible that one or two people will get shot by mistake. They should have known better. Anyway, you need to have a shooting or two every month to set examples for others to understand."

"I guess that sounds right." I couldn't believe that I just agreed to that.

We passed the guards and headed toward our room. Once inside the room, I noticed that three beds were occupied with guys that were already sound asleep. I tried quietly to get into my sea bag to get my things without waking anyone. I wanted to wash my face and brush my teeth before I turned in tonight.

I noticed that the traffic sounds outside were so loud that it would had drown out any noise that I could ever make. Besides the traffic noise, I could hear a group of guys next door playing cards and each was trying to, 'out talk' the other.

Dan looked at me and said, "So how was your first day?"

"Not exactly what I expected. Somehow, I thought that all the war action took place in the jungles. You know, first you take a chopper ride out away from your base and then with luck, you will run into a firefight. Or, if you are stationed on a ship, like I thought I would be, you just watch as the big guns are fired towards the shore."

As I continued to open my sea bag, I added, "I guess that I'm just thinking about going up and down the rivers of Vietnam, a hundred miles from the ocean. This is not what the Navy recruiter promised me."

"So, does this mean you are disappointed with your first day in-country?"

"I didn't like seeing that guy get shot. I didn't like having my dick pulled out and dragged across a bar, I didn't like having buffalo shit splashed all over me, and I don't like having to sleep in a place like this. I didn't like the thought of being shot at for talking rude to an officer and for dropping a tray of food. To top it all off, my clothes don't even fit."

"Look at the bright side," Dan suggested as he got into his sea bag. "You have me as your personal guide to beautiful, in-country Vietnam. I found us these luxurious living quarters, a delicious dinner at a good price, and a nightclub experience that you'll never forget. And, I did the best I could with your new summer outfit."

"Yeah, you're right." I said feeling that Dan was not the one to be complaining. What I really wanted to do was to call home. To at least let my parents know that I had made it this far, safe and sound.

"One more thing," Dan injected. "Because of my knowledge of where in downtown Saigon to stay, I kept you from being on watch and possibly from being the guy that was shot earlier today."

"I didn't think of that, and I owe you my thanks," I answered sincerely.

"Not a problem my man," he said, as if he expected that answer from me.

I told Dan, "I'm gonna take a walk to find the head and try to hose down my pants."

"Now that'll be much appreciated."

I made my way down the hall to the head. To my surprise, there was only one sink and the mirror above it was stainless steel. Shaving was not going to be easy for me tomorrow morning. Also, only one toilet and the shower stall had a garden hose attached to the wall with a garden hose nozzle. It was the same kind used to water your lawn or wash a car.

I was not very amused at all with this situation. I had always enjoyed taking a hot shower in the morning and it appeared that for my, big second day in-country, that it would be off to a bad start.

I walked over and squeezed the nozzle for a quick test. As expected, the water was very cold and the pressure was low. It was so low that I checked out the hose to see if it had a kink or two in it. It didn't.

Well, I was here now and I might as well try to spray this shit off my clothes. With luck, it would be dry by morning. I took my pants off and hosed them down. Not exactly clean as new, but clean.

Back at my room, I meant dungeon; I placed my pants on the side of my bunk to dry.

I looked at Dan and said, "The water was cold, real cold. Does this mean that we only have one temperature of water?"

"No, we have two different degrees of temperature. We have very cold in the afternoon and extremely cold first thing in the morning."

"What about the Navy BEQ? Does it have hot and cold water?"

Dan ignored that question and started talking to me about what might happen at night. "If you, I mean, when you hear any type of shooting tonight, it's best that you just stay in bed. There are plenty of guys on duty and all of them know what to do."

"What about the guy that got shot earlier, did he know what to do?"

"Good question, apparently not."

That was it, which was his answer, 'apparently not.' "What if this place becomes attacked or something? How will we know?" I asked, because this was the kind of shit I wanted to know about ahead of time.

"No sweat my man. There will be someone running down the halls yelling, 'The VC are coming, the VC are coming,'" Dan said with some laughter in his voice that was not very convincing.

"Come-on man, I'm serious about this. What do we do?" I asked wanting to put aside his joking.

"For real, if we must do anything, there will be someone yelling at us. Instructions will be issued and you won't be left out. Because you see, this place houses a lot of personnel that are in transit and we are all in the same boat. New in-country and not familiar with the area."

Feeling a little better with his answer, I said, "Well that does sound a little more reassuring. I'm okay with that. So, what time do we get up?"

"It'll be early and there will be enough people waking up all round you that you'll find yourself unable to keep sleeping."

"I hope that the water flow for the shower is better than it was tonight," I said.

"I wouldn't worry about how cold the water will be tomorrow. You might want to worry about how long the line, will be just to take a shower."

I didn't think about that because I was thinking about how good it would feel just to get a good night sleep. Traveling for two days and trying to sleep on the plane had made me sore in places that I didn't think would ever be sore.

After I made my bed, using the sheets that were left folded at the foot of my bed, I got myself settled and told Dan, "good night."

"No sweat, catch yaw at, 'zero six early.'"

"What's a, 'zero six early?'" I knew what a, 'zero six thirty' was.

"Nothing big, just early in the AM," he responded and I gave it no more thought. After that, I fell asleep quickly.

After a couple of hours, a loud noise from outside and the sound of someone crying in one of the beds near by woke me. Not much crying, but just enough to be heard. Is this that, 'zero six early' thing that he talked about earlier?

I whispered toward Dan's bunk in the dark and asked, "Dan, are you awake?"

"Yeah, I was awakened by a, 'sissy boy.' He started crying as soon as he heard a little gunfire outside. Hell, it wasn't even close."

I didn't think that was such a kind thing to say, because this guy could really be scared.

"So what do we do?"

"Nothing, just try to get back to sleep."

"Easy for you to say."

"Why? Is 'sissy boy' keeping you awake also with his crying?"

"No, that's not it. I was just wondering if there is something we should or should not be doing?"

"Yeah, we should be sleeping and not crying," came his quick response.

That did sound like good advice to me. Besides, what did I know? I was the FNG here.

A moment later Dan said to me, "Look, there happens to be a couple of dozen guys out there on watch and they're not crying. They're out there making sure that we don't get hurt, and most importantly that we get a good night sleep. So with that thought, good night."

His response seemed cold. The one guy that was crying did stop, and I guess he was glad that. With the room being so dark, that no one would be able to tell who he was. I did wonder why Dan was so mean in calling him a, 'sissy boy.' I would just ask him tomorrow about that. For now, I was ready to get a good night's sleep as suggested.

There continued to be some noise from outside our building. I could hear somebody shouting and giving orders and the only thing I could clearly make out was the response of, 'yes sir' and 'no sir.' It didn't appear to me that there was any type of excitement or confusion out there, but every now and then, I could hear a single shot. No return fire or anything and it did seem to be far away.

I could now hear what appeared to be two guys running down the hall and then down the steps. Yet, with all this going on, no one in our room seemed to care, except for the, 'sissy-boy.'

Oh well, with nothing to do about all of this, I would call it a night.

Again, I fell asleep quickly and the rest of the night was uneventful.

Chapter 4

Dan, who was already up and dressed, woke me with a jolt.

"Let's get it in gear, my man. I believe we have enough time to enjoy a quick breakfast before the bus leaves for the airport."

Taking a quick inventory of myself, I realized that I needed to take a shower, even if it meant taking a cold one. I would just take it like a man . . . an Eskimo man maybe, but a man just the same. "No problem. Give me a few minutes to shave and shower," I said, getting out of bed.

"Just remember, no matter how cold the water is here, at least it isn't brown," Dan explained without details.

"And what does that mean?" I asked.

With a serious look, Dan said, "Sometimes the fresh water and toilet water pipes are crossed on our ship, and taking a shower is not a good idea."

I refused to believe this one, but went along with him anyway. "No problem. I'll rough it for now."

"I'll meet you downstairs, right outside the front door," Dan said over his shoulder as he and his sea bag headed down the hall.

I looked around the room at the men still in their beds and the men who were getting ready to leave. I tried to figure out which one was crying last night, but I couldn't tell. I guessed I was looking for some young kid who might have been a momma's boy, or whose eyes were red from crying. Everyone appeared normal to me. Maybe I didn't know what a momma's boy would look like. I hoped the other guys didn't think that it had been me crying. No way was I a momma's boy.

Unable to think of anything clever to say to anyone about last night, I left for the shower. Besides, with my luck, if I had made a joke about last night, the guy that was crying would be a big dude who would get angry and crush in my face. Not a pleasant way to start my second day here in 'The-Nam.'

There was no line at the showers. I checked the water—as if I really expected to find hot water—and, of course, it was freezing. Freezing cold, and that explained the absence of a line. I knew I had to take a shower in spite of the freezing water because I would feel better if I were clean.

Taking a shower using a garden hose and nozzle was truly an entertaining experience. I had to master the use of the nozzle with one hand and hold the soap with the other, all the while wishing that I could soap myself up with a third hand. Shaving using this stainless mirror was something I desired never to do again, even with hot water.

After my shower, I dressed in my new set of old greens, and, just like the day before, my pants were still too big. At least they were dry and free of shit stains.

I made my way downstairs with my sea bag and found Dan just outside, talking to a couple of guys that were on guard duty.

"That was quick," Dan commented.

"Yeah. There's something about freezing water that cuts down the time I desire to spend in the shower. Besides that, there was no line for the arctic shower."

"Don't mean nothing. Be grateful, my man, that you were able to take a shower today."

"You're right," I said. "Did you take one this morning?"

"Sure did and I had plenty of hot water and only a short line ahead of me."

"How did you get hot water to come out of that garden hose?" I asked, incredulously.

"Garden hose? What are you talking about, man?"

"You know, in that little shower room with the terrible mirror," I questioned him.

The guard that Dan had been talking to asked, "Was it just one shower next to one big sink with a sad excuse for a mirror?"

"Yeah, why?" I questioned looking at the two of them.

"Damn man, that wasn't a shower, that's the maintenance room," he explained as he and Dan laughed at me.

Confused, I asked Dan, "Where did you take a shower?"

"Out the door, to the right, and then down the hall there's a big shower room with a bunch of showers and sinks. With real mirrors."

"Damn, I went to the left and then down the hall. Oh well, welcome to, 'The-Nam,'" I shrugged wanting to get off this subject.

"No, man," Dan shook his head. "This was not a, welcome to, 'The-Nam,' thing. You're just a dumb shit." Everyone laughed, even guys who were just standing nearby and had overheard my calamity.

"Fine, let's eat breakfast if you don't mind. At least I'm clean," I suggested, moving this conversation along and off of me.

"Okay my friend. We still have time for a quick breakfast." It seemed as though Dan was actually going to pass up this opportunity to make additional fun of me.

I questioned, "Do we take our sea bags with us?"

"Nah, these guys here will watch them for us. I knew them from the last time I stayed here. It's okay to trust them with our bags," Dan smiled broadly at the guards, then turned to me and whispered, "We'll just lock them together for extra security anyway, know what I mean?"

We locked our bags together and Dan said, "Just throw them over there by the outline, wouldja?"

I lifted the bags and turned in the direction he had just motioned. To my astonishment, the outline that he was talking about was the outline of a dead body, chalked on the sidewalk. Dan saw me frozen in place, just like the outline, and said, "Man, don't sweat that. It's not what you think."

I tried to regain my composure as I commented, "Look. I may be the FNG here and all that, but I do recognize a dead body outline when I see one. This is not some hopscotch chalked out by the local school kids, you know."

Looking more closely at the outline, I saw red stains near the head and butt. I wondered if it was the outline of an American or a VC. Yet, for some sick, unknown reason, Dan and the guards were laughing at me as if I was doing some kind of stand-up comedy routine.

"Is this from the shooting last night?" I asked, hoping that if I changed the subject, they would stop laughing.

"No, man," said one of the guards. "Last night was just target practice. We do that every now and then just to keep the neighbors up at night thinking we'll shoot at anything we feel is a threat."

The other guard spoke up. "If you notice, there aren't any dogs, cats, or rats anywhere around here. See, at night we use them to keep ourselves sharp and test our shooting skills."

Naturally, Dan had to contribute a sarcastic comment. "Yeah, when you hear too many shots being fired at night, that means that these guys have lousy aim and they do, indeed, need the practice."

"Not true man. Look, it's because we had more than one rat to shoot at last night, that's all that was."

I was missing something here. They were talking about target practice with family pets and rats while I was wondering about the man who died on the sidewalk last night. "No, man," I said, trying to direct their attention back to the outline on the sidewalk. "What about this?"

As I pointed to the outline, Dan stepped over and scuffed the line with his shoe to show that it was painted, not chalked. After closer examination, I could tell that the blood wasn't real. It was just red paint. I could not fully comprehend what all I was seeing. I could only stand there looking like a deer caught in headlights.

"Look," the second guard said, apparently noticing my confusion, "it's just painted there. For our protection."

"I can see that, but why? Protection?"

"If you thought it was real—and you did—then anyone walking by will think the same thing."

"Okay," I responded.

He continued, "So if you add in the shootings that we have at night, well, we have created our very own, 'safe area' where the locals know not to venture into in the middle of the night."

Dan looked at me as if I should have learned this in boot camp. "You understand?"

"All right, that makes sense now," I said, starting to feel a little better about the whole thing. I just wanted to go to breakfast.

"You aren't curious about the blood stains?" Dan prodded.

"I wasn't gonna ask, but now that you've brought it up, I guess you're gonna tell me." I braced myself for some stupid story he wanted me to fall for, so he could make more fun of me.

"Not me, I never knew myself the reason for the blood stains," Dan admitted.

The first guard was happy to fill us in and said, "The blood near the head means that we blew your head wide open and the other one shows that we blew you a new ass-hole."

The second guard chimed in with, "Yeah, we wanted to show that when we kick ass around here, we really kick ass in a serious way."

I thought over about everything that happened since I woke up. First, I took a cold shower while everyone else took a hot one. Then, I got all upset over a pretend killing in the middle of a war zone. I wasn't very happy about the shooting of the neighborhood pets for target practice, either. Well, I didn't care about the rats. Oh well, welcome to Vietnam.

The first guard boasted, "You should see the outline around back. This one is nothing."

The second guard pointed to his left, "Yeah, that one is cool, we had to paint two outlines for that one."

The first guard added, "It's great. We painted in the head about three feet from the body. Now that one is a tourist attraction for all the Japs that come over here, and you should hear all the Nikons clicking away. I mean shit; these guys are carrying two and three cameras each."

This was not Vietnam; this was the Twilight Zone, I thought to myself. Over here, you could pretend that you killed someone in the morning and then buy a wife or child to ship home in the afternoon.

Deciding that we had spent enough time there, Dan spoke to the two guards. "Listen up, we'll be back in a few, because breakfast awaits us. We got to get back in time to catch the first bus to the airport. You guys want us to bring you anything back?"

"No thank you," they responded at the same time.

Dan walked away, and I guessed he expected me to follow. "See ya," I told the guards, and off I went trying to catch up with him.

We had a quick, uneventful breakfast and were back within thirty minutes. As we approached the BEQ to retrieve our sea bags, I noticed a bus parked by the front door. Just like our ride yesterday, there was a jeep behind the bus with a driver and a machine-gunner.

"Just in time. That's our bus," I said.

"It depends."

"Depends on what?" Wondering how I could have messed up such a simple task.

"Depends on where it's going. It might be going to the airport and maybe not. There is also the possibility that it's broken down."

"I didn't think about that," I answered.

"No sweat, my new and confused friend. I'll just ask the driver and you can get our bags."

Dan approached the driver and said a few words to him. They talked for a few minutes, but I couldn't hear what they were saying. The two of them started to laugh about something and I could only assume that it had something to do with me.

Dan stepped off the bus and motioned to me that this was our ride to the airport. I unlocked our bags, thanked the two guards, and climbed onto the bus dragging the sea bags behind me.

This time, my sea bag took the window seat. At least I remembered not to make the same mistake twice. "How long before we pull . . . ," I started to ask, when the driver closed the door and pulled away from the curb. I noticed that we were the only two people on the bus.

"This is great," I said to Dan.

"Why do you say that?"

"We have a driver and couple of armed guards just for the two of us. I feel pretty important!"

"That's not all that great, especially for the two of us."

Damn, what had I said wrong this time? "All right," I asked, "why is it not a good deal or us?"

"If anyone is going to shoot at the bus, they'll only have two targets and that'll be you and me, my friend."

"Thanks for the sobering information. I didn't really want that kind of news this early in the morning."

"Not a problem, just maintain a 'low profile, low visibility' and make yourself look unimportant."

"Okay, that makes sense, I think." I didn't know what he meant by keeping a 'low profile' or 'low visibility,' but I could look unimportant easy enough. Now, this low profile thing, was he saying that we should sit low in our seats? Whatever, I decided to just keep an eye on him and do whatever he did. He didn't seem to be doing anything unusual. He was sitting straight up like a normal person. Not wanting to appear like an idiot, I just sat in my seat normal like and tried to enjoy the ride.

We made a stop at the Navy's BEQ where about a dozen or so guys got onboard. I guessed that half of them came in on the same flight as we did yesterday. There were two guys still in dress whites and they really stood out. Some of them were talking about the shooting the previous day and from what I could tell, the guy didn't die. I was relieved.

I found myself more interested in what they were saying than the sights that we were passing. Besides, we took the same route in from the airport yesterday and it was all the same traffic noise and confusion. Based on what I could pick up from their conversation, it sounded like the guy who had been shot was being sent home.

"Can you hear what they're saying about the guy who was shot yesterday?" I asked Dan.

"Yeah, I guess he's a very lucky guy."

"Lucky that he's heading home or because he didn't get killed yesterday?"

"Both," Dan responded. "No need for him to wait and put in a whole 365 to find out how he's going home."

I didn't need to hear that in such blunt terms. Was I to wonder how I was going to leave this place? Was I to think about it every day for the next twelve months? I hoped not.

The bus made another stop and two officers got onboard. I was about to yell, 'officer on deck,' but someone else beat me to it. When he yelled, he shot straight up and banged his head on the ceiling of the bus. I burst out laughing, thrilled to see someone besides me making an ass of himself.

To my surprise, one of the officers screamed, "Not on a bus ass-hole! Sit down."

The poor sap, rubbed his head, sank into his seat and said with his head lowered, "Yes, sir. I mean, no, sir."

Everyone laughed at this guy, but not loud enough to be heard by either one of the two officers. No need to tick them off again.

We soon arrived at the main gate of the Tan San Nut Air Force Base where an MP got onboard. He gave everyone a quick once over and took a seat. I started to ask Dan about the MP that got onboard, but the bus lurched into motion again and I found myself more interested in just looking around at the base.

"What hangar?" the driver yelled over his shoulder.

"Six, hangar six," Dan answered. A few others answered the same.

About three minutes later, the bus came to a halt near a hangar with two C-130 cargo planes parked outside on the tarmac. I assumed one of these was to be our ride to Dong-Tam, and I was looking forward to the flight. I'd never been in a military aircraft before, and it was going to be a real treat for me.

Departing the bus, I noticed that the driver was directing everyone toward the hangar. At the hangar, there was an Air Force sergeant with a clipboard separating everyone into two groups, one for enlisted and one for officers.

"Officers to the right and enlisted men to the left," he instructed.

Dan tapped me on the shoulder and motioned that we head in another direction. He didn't look back to see if I was following him, he just kept a fast pace toward the rear of the bus. I had to race just to catch up to him. It wasn't easy, carrying my sea bag and wearing boots that didn't fit, all the while holding up my pants with my free hand. Furthermore, I had no idea why I was following him against orders.

Finally, I caught up with him. I tapped his shoulder to get his attention and pointed back to the hangar. Gasping for breath, I asked, "Are we going to be assigned a watch or something back there? Why are we going this way?"

He responded, "Do not look back or point. Just stay close and act as if we know where we're going."

"But he was already telling us where to go," I explained.

"If you didn't make eye contact with him, then you don't know for sure that he was talking to you. Understand?"

"But he was about to give us some orders."

"You need to obey your last set of orders. We are to report to Dong-Tam, and that's what we're attempting to accomplish." Dan explained, as he continued to put some distance between us, and the guy with the clipboard.

I wondered what his brilliant plan was this time. I meant, we didn't ride the right bus, we didn't stay at the right place, and now we are not going to fly the right plane. Oh well, I would go along with him for now. It had worked out so far.

It was extremely hot walking across the tarmac. I could see the heat rising off everything in sight. There was an amazing quantity of equipment, planes, choppers, and personnel all around. Everything was buzzing with activity.

No one seemed to take notice of two guys walking around with their sea bags on their shoulders with no particular place to go. I guessed that no one thought that we were out of place, but I sure did. I would have thought that security on an air base would be a little better than this. I understand more clearly now why we had to exit yesterday's plane so quickly.

"Hold on a minute, that guy has the right-of-way," Dan informed me as he put out his hand for me to stop.

Damn, we were walking on an active taxiway. How did we get way out here? Whatever, we waited for a TWA commercial airliner to taxi past us. All the shades were down and I couldn't tell whether the plane was full of people or empty. I was about to ask where we were going when Dan pointed to a row of choppers and said excitedly, "That's what I'm looking for. Come on, and I'll get us a cool ride."

I had no idea what he meant by a, 'cool ride.' I was pretty sure that military choppers didn't have air-conditioning or even comfortable seating as part of their equipment package.

As we approached the choppers, I was thinking how they looked just like the ones I'd seen on the news back home. These were the 'hueys.' The ones used to carry troops to and from the jungles. They had machine guns and rocket launchers on each side and I couldn't tell if they were loaded or not. I still didn't see anything, 'cool' about this kind of ride.

There were about eight choppers lined up in single file. Each was enclosed on three sides by sandbag revetments about four feet high. No one was around the first two choppers we walked past. Dan saw and approached a colored airman that was doing some work near the motor on the third chopper.

Dan said, "Hang loose and watch the bags," as he headed toward this guy.

As Dan approached him, each put out their hands as if to do a normal handshake. Then both of them started an odd type of handshaking, knuckle-knocking, and finger-grabbing.

This seemed somewhat odd to me, but there was a smile on this airman's face and they both began to talk. After a few words, Dan left the airman to continue with his work.

Dan said to me, "That chopper is not going anywhere for a while."

"What's he fixing?"

"Oh, nothing much, it's just the, 'Jesus nut.'"

"Now what in the world is that?"

"From what I've been told, it's the nut that holds the rotor blades on."

"So for that, they call it a, 'Jesus nut?'"

"Yeah. If it comes off, only Jesus can save you."

Dan then motioned me to, 'stand fast,' and with that, I just waited patiently while the heat from the tarmac, that must be 115°, started to cook my feet. At least I had plenty of room to wiggle my toes.

He approached the fourth chopper and started to talk with another airman sitting in the doorway reading a book. Their conversation went on a little longer than the first. After their short talk, Dan returned with a smile on his face. He picked up his sea bag and said, "We have a ride to Dong-Tam. Let's secure our bags onboard and we'll have some free time for a cold beer or two."

A little confused and after we stowed our bags onboard with the help of this airman, we again headed down the tarmac. Naturally, we locked them together, but not to the helo itself.

"So early in the morning for beers?" I responded to his last comment.

"What? Is it the cold beer that you don't want; or, is it the fear that some girl will try to grab you?"

I came back with, "That's not what I meant, and yes, I don't need any girl grabbing me this early in the morning."

"No problem my, 'sissy friend,' and if you don't want a cold beer right now, then I'll order you some milk."

"Give a guy a break," I suggested.

"Not a big deal my man," he responded.

"Thanks."

What the hell was I thinking, I might as well join in because this was, 'The-Nam,' and all that and I was away from home.

"Maybe I'll join you anyway. You see it's just that I've never had one this early in the morning before."

"What, a girl?"

"No. A beer this early in the morning," I answered quickly.

"You must understand one thing about the military. There is no such thing as, 'early in the morning.' That's why they don't use the AM and PM thing. They'll just give us numbers to go by such as 0700 or 1400."

"All right, now I know."

"Do you know what the AM and PM stand for my friend?"

"I have no idea." I didn't really care. I just wanted to find my unit and get checked-in, but I guessed he was going to tell me anyway.

"'AM' means, 'before noon,' and the 'PM' thing means, 'after noon,'" he explained to me.

"Yeah right," and that certainly happened to be a stupid answer. I didn't know what it stood for, but I knew that he couldn't be right about that one. I would just play along with this.

I added, "Okay, like you have 12 AM. And 12 PM., right?"

"You can't have 12 AM, you will have midnight, and 12 PM. is just noon."

I came back with, "So what about the Zulu time I was told about in boot camp? Is that just for the African tribe, the Zulu's?"

He said in response, "You know what? If you can't comprehend the AM and PM thing, you'll never get the Zulu time."

I didn't say anything to that, I would let that one go, and apparently, Dan was thinking the same thing. He said to me, "Let me ask you this, are you hot right now?"

"Yeah, I am from all this walking around in the hot sun, on this hot tarmac, and not knowing where we are going."

"By the time we get to the bar, you will appreciate a cold beer. Early in the morning or not," Dan explained.

Again, he was right. The more we walked and talked about cold beers, the more I wanted one. Even this early in the AM.

"So just what's the drinking age here on the base?" I asked, because I was only eighteen. Soon to be nineteen, but eighteen just the same.

Dan looked over at me and said, "No one gets, 'carded' over here. Besides, don't you remember that you didn't get carded yesterday?"

"That's right, but at the time I had other issues to worry about and being carded was not top on my list. I was making sure that I kept all my body parts attached to my body."

Dan continued, "You see, Uncle Sam doesn't want you to get, 'shot at' and, 'carded' at the same time. It's a good morale thing for the troops."

"That sounds reasonable, now what I really want to understand from you is why we are walking all around this air base. I mean, here we are in the heat, looking for a ride and we already had ride to Dong-Tam."

He responded by saying, "Two reasons. First, a helo ride can be most exciting. And two, I noticed that the sergeant was separating enlisted men from officers."

"So?"

"So, that means only one thing to me."

"Was he separating officers for first class and enlisted to ride coach?" I questioned.

"Good guess; but, no cigar my friend. My military guess is that he's separating everyone for a working party."

"What about our flight to Dong-Tam? We can't be part of a working party when we have a flight to catch."

"Well, a C-130 is a cargo plane, and it be people and cargo that she'll be carrying. I saw that he was separating enlisted men from the officers, and I believe that he was arranging a working party. To me, cargo needs to be loaded or unloaded, and that requires a working party," Dan informed me.

"Aren't there people already here on base that do that kind of stuff with cargo? You know what I'm talking about? What do you call them, load masters or something like that?"

"True," Dan answered. "But why haul in these, 'load master' to load a plane when you have enlisted guys all ready there standing around with nothing to do."

"Okay, but that doesn't seem fair," I responded trying not to complain.

"What fair? You arrive early with nothing to do anyway. The military has an obligation to keep you active. To me, that will always equal loading and unloading cargo as part of a working party, and that will help us pass the time away."

Granted, I had only been in the service a few months, but I knew that a working party was something to avoid whenever possible. Therefore, for the moment, that sounded like a good reason. I was still a little puzzled as to why we had to find another ride to Dong-Tam.

"Okay, I'm fine with your reasoning to avoid a working party. Now, what is this, 'cool ride' thing you mentioned to me?"

"Let that be a surprise for now. So after we land, then you can give me your opinion as to what kind of ride we had to Dong-Tam. Deal?"

"Deal."

A few minutes later, he pointed toward a small shack just off the main runway, that was not far from where the bus dropped us off earlier. We must have walked in a circle, a large circle.

Inside was a bar with some tables and chairs under what appeared to be a parachute for a patio roof. We ordered two beers and took a seat in the shade, I was dry as a bone, and this cold beer would really hit the spot, even at 0800, 'At Morning.'

I looked around when I noticed that the two officers that were on our bus were sitting in the officer's section enjoying a cold beer. I said to Dan, "Won't they see us here, and make us get back to the working party?"

"We can't be, 'back' at the working party, because we were never 'there,' to start with. Don't sweat it my, 'worry-wart' friend."

Sounded like good advice and it seemed even better now that they had noticed us sitting here, and had said nothing.

Our two beers arrived and they sure did taste good this early in the morning. After my long walk in the hot sun, I believed I deserved a cold beer.

I looked over and saw Dan smiling, as he placed his empty beer can down on the table. Then he brought his hand down hard and crushed the can flat as a pancake. He tried to be cool with this can trick of his, and it did look rather cool. However, I would not attempt this trick back home on my mom's kitchen table, because she would crush me as if I was the beer can for trying a trick like that.

"Let's see if you can, 'crush a can, like a man,'" Dan teased me.

"I got to finish it first," I answered.

In a sarcastic tone he replied, "You're only here for a year man, so try and finish your beer before your tour is over, 'boot.'"

"Give me a break, okay, because it's early in the AM, and the time is still in the hundreds."

"That's a good one, and I like it."

After I finished my beer, I figured that I might as well try this, 'can crushing' thing of his. It looked easy enough, and I must remember to bang it down hard on my first try. Damn, I might get hurt with this stupid trick. I must figure a way to ask if there was a trick to this without making me look dumb. "So, what's the angle or trick to crushing this can?"

"Just hit the can evenly on top and aim for the table, not the top of the can."

"The table?"

"Yeah, the table. If you aim for the top of the can, you might not flatten the can. Just aim for the table," Dan instructed.

Seemed easy enough to me, I assumed. I went ahead with this trick, and as I raised my hand, and before my 'smashing the can,' I thought to myself, 'this is going to hurt.' However, too late now, I'll just try it.

Well, I did it, and it did hurt. I almost broke my hand doing this, 'cheap trick.' I was only able to half crush the can. I'll never try this again.

"Nice try, however you might have done better if you were using an empty milk carton."

With a little anger in my voice and pain in my hand, I said, "At least I tried."

"Relax," he said in a calm voice. "You have a whole year to get it right."

Whatever, we ordered another round of beers.

He leaned back in his seat, looked at me, and said, "Isn't this great?"

"What?"

"This is the life, because here we sit having a cold beer, in the shade. Those poor guys that were on our bus earlier are loading cargo onto those two C-130's."

As I looked toward the direction that he pointed, sure enough, I could see these men were unloading cargo off a truck and onto the tarmac. Others were loading that cargo into the plane. I could tell that by the way they were moving about, that most of them were ready to pass out because of the heat. Even their uniforms had turned to a dark green because of their body sweat. The ones in crisp clean dress whites were no longer in crisp clean dress whites. They were now wrinkled dirty and sweaty dress black.

I looked over at Dan with concern and asked, "Aren't we going to get into trouble for not helping out and doing our part?"

He leaned forward in his chair, ordered another beer, and said with calm assurance, "That don't mean nothin. What's the worst thing that can happen to us? Kick us out of the service? Send us back to the states?"

"I don't know about that, but still, shouldn't we be following orders?" I asked.

"Were we given orders to help with the working party? No. Were we told, not to fly to Dong-Tam on the helo of our choice? No. Were we ordered, not to have a cold beer and sit in the shade? No. Then don't sweat the small stuff, my worry wart friend," Dan informed me as he took a long swig from his beer.

Somehow, this made sense, but this just couldn't be right. However, I did finally sit back and started to enjoy my cold beer, in the shade, while not working in the hot sun, sweating my ass off loading cargo. Well, there was still a little pain in my hand from that trick. Generally speaking, this was not a bad a deal after all.

After about twenty minutes, Dan got up, checked his watch, and suggested that we get moving. We paid the tab and headed toward the chopper. I took one last look back at the working party that was still working very hard. I was wondering if they would ever make it to Dong-Tam anytime soon and if anyone would notice us walking away.

Part of me was thinking about the training I had in boot camp dealing with teamwork and how I should be back there doing my part helping with the working party. I was telling Dan about what I was thinking when he said in response, "I agree with the teamwork concept; however, not everyone can take part in every working party. Besides, we have a flight to take this morning and we may need to be rested for the next part of our journey."

For some reason, I didn't like the way he said that, 'needed to be rested' part.

I must ask, "So what do you mean, 'being rested?' It's not as if we were exhausted from working on the working party you know."

"Let's see how the rest of our day goes before I answer that question," he responded.

"Does this have anything to do with what you said earlier?"

"What did I say earlier?"

"Something about a, 'cool ride,'" I answered.

"Oh yeah. I remember that part. Again, let's just see how the rest of our day goes first."

I kind of wanted an answer, but I would just put that one on hold for now.

I was thinking that walking around in this hot sun after a few beers might not have been such a good idea. I didn't feel so good right now and at my young age of 18; I haven't had too many occasions where I downed a couple of cold beers before lunch. I couldn't recall even one time I had a beer, even one beer, so early in the morning. This was going to be a long day, and maybe I might want another beer, early this morning.

After our short walk, I tried to get in yet another question when we arrived at the chopper. Two officers were standing next to an airman as we approached; we both saluted the officers. One officer returned our salute while the other didn't, because his hands were full with maps and stuff.

Somehow, when Dan arranged this ride to Dong-Tam, I had in mind that this chopper was no more than a taxi. It just might be a little more interesting than being onboard a C-130, but a taxi ride just the same.

As I circled the chopper with interest, I noticed 50-caliber machine-guns mounted on both sides of the aircraft along with two rocket launchers with seven rockets each. Both loaded, and I assumed, armed. This was no taxi ride.

As the two pilots boarded the aircraft, the airman instructed us to get onboard. Dan pointed for me to sit between our two sea bags that were secured earlier, and to buckle-up.

I head Dan ask the airman, "Do you have an extra Chicken Plate?"

The airman just shook his head, 'no' and it seemed to bother Dan a little.

I had to ask, "Dan, are you ordering something for us to eat, or are we taking some chickens onboard as cargo?"

What I got from Dan was another look, as if, I just asked, yet another stupid question. Whatever. It was a good question for someone like me that didn't know what was going on.

"No on both counts my inquisitive friend," Dan explained. "Just a chest protector worn by helicopter gunners."

I appreciated the answer, but didn't like the wording of gunner. I hoped we didn't have to do any shooting while were up here.

Dan and the airman both took a seat at each door, with our sea bags between them and me. I wanted to sit in one of the two seats forward, so I could get a good view as we flew to Dong-Tam. At the very least, place one of the two sea bags up front and give me some additional room. Not only was I missing out on a good seat with a great view, the two of them were placing on a set of headphones, and now I couldn't even hear what was going on. Whatever. I just kept quite and remain seated.

After I settled in, the engine started to run, and I could see the shadow of the blades starting to circle the aircraft. The blades started to pick up speed quickly, and the whole aircraft began to shake a little. I was a little excited about this, and eagerly waiting for us to take off, when I noticed that Dan and the airman seemed a little bored of having to wait with nothing to do. I could only assume that they must have done this a thousand times. But so what. This happened to be my first helicopter ride, and I was going to enjoy it. Come to think about it, we didn't show our ID or anything. I hoped that it was okay, that we were going for a ride, and that we weren't going to get into trouble. Oh well, I will just drop it for now.

After a few minutes, the aircraft lifted a few feet off the ground. As it hovered, there was a little sway to it, the same sensation you would experience when getting on a Ferris wheel. The feeling you get after getting seated and then being moved up one slot, while the next seats filled in behind you. At that point, you rocked forward and backward a little, hoping you didn't tip over and fall out.

I was expecting, because we were above the revetment, that we would just go forward and then up, up and away. Instead, we moved backwards slowly for about twenty feet. That was just enough distance for our helo to clear the revetments.

I noticed there was an airman on the tarmac giving directions to the pilot. You know, 'okay, come on back, plenty of room, come on back, okay, hold it.' You would have thought were backing out of someone's driveway.

After a 90° left turn, we headed down the taxiway, about ten miles an hour, then another 90° left turn. We must have passed twenty or thirty choppers, another dozen or so cargo planes, and two parked jet fighters. This was quite an exciting experience and there was plenty to see. This was a 'cool' ride.

The slow and easy speed of our ride, and all the sights, made this appear to me to be some kind of tour of the base. This base definitely had a lot to show, and I would have paid money for this tour.

Dan looked over at me and yelled, "Don't worry. We'll be going faster than this once we take off and get airborne."

"I figured that," I responded.

"How do you like it so far," Dan questioned.

"Great. No problem," I answered, as if I could have said something different.

At this point, we passed an F-4 Phantom fighter jet with an open parachute trailing behind it. I assumed that it had just landed, and was not ready to take off again. I looked for its bombs under the wing when I thought, you 'dumb ass.' If it just landed, then there shouldn't be any bombs left. Besides, it would be rather hard to take off with an open parachute trailing behind it.

We taxied next to the main runway and just hovered until a cargo plane landed. The pilot then moved onto the main runway and after the nose dipped a little, we headed quickly down the runway gaining speed.

We began to gain altitude, and I now had quite a view of the air base. Saigon was passing below us now, and I could see mostly, 'greens, and browns.' The further away from the city we flew, the greener everything became.

Roads, rivers, and houses were all brown. Everything else was green.

This was truly a great view. It was rather pleasant not to be looking through the little airplane windows. You know the ones that never seemed to align up to your seat.

With the doors opened, the cool breeze felt great, and this might keep me from getting airsick.

I was again thinking how these two sea bags were really in my way when I noticed Dan and the airman doing something to the two 50-caliber machine-guns. Somehow, I thought that being between these two bags, that it might have been the safest place to be.

The airman attached his ammo belt to his machine-gun and then he reached under the forward seat and grabbed two helmets. He handed Dan one, and sat on the other. I looked over at Dan and watched as he also sat on his helmet.

I said to Dan, trying to be funny, "Isn't that a little uncomfortable? Doesn't that thing belong on the other end?"

He leaned toward me and said, "When we get shot at, the bullets will be coming up through the floor. These steel pots don't work for shit on your head in a helicopter, unless of course, you're flying upside down." He pointed down at the helmet and added; "This is the true meaning of, 'saving your ass.'"

I gave a smile showing that I enjoyed his comeback, when I realized what he said. He said, 'When we get shot at,' and not, 'if we get shot at,' and why were we even discussing the, 'shot' word? As my smile turned into a worried look, I asked, "What about Dong-Tam?"

Dan answered, "This flight is going to Dong-Tam; however, on its way, it's going to fly low and slow."

"Other than flying high and fast, as in a C-130, why is this better?" I questioned.

"It's faster in one way because we aren't spending time on a working party. The, 'cool' part comes to play for us as we try to draw enemy fire."

"What?" I didn't think he meant, 'draw' as in, draw with pencil and paper.

"We didn't spend time in the working party. Remember?"

"No, not the working party part, the part about drawing enemy fire."

"When we draw enemy fire?"

"What? When?" I couldn't believe I was having this conversation after we had already taken off and were already on our way.

"When we do, we'll fire back, until they are no longer firing at us; or, until we run out of bullets." After a short pause he continued, "We have lots of bullets."

"Damn man, you're not serious, tell me you're not serious." I said, trying not to appear as scared as I was.

"Like I've told you before, welcome to, 'The-Nam.' This is not real, it's a nightmare, and you'll have a wake-up in 363 days when your year's tour is completed. Sit back and enjoy the flight, nothing to sweat, this is a short flight."

I added that, "I didn't like the way you said, 'this is a short flight.'"

"Relax my, 'scared-as-shit' friend. With some luck, maybe nothing will happen to us today, and you can enjoy the ride."

My mind was running wild with thoughts. I was thinking about what happened yesterday and what was happening to me so far today. I had already downed a couple of beers early in the AM and now I had a good chance of getting shot at, on my first ride in a helo. With all that, I was to relax, not sweat it, and it was not even lunchtime.

Dan and the other guy were busy now looking around, mostly straight down and little forward. The flight continued for about thirty minutes, mostly following this river, and definitely flying low and slow.

We slowed a little and as I looked out, I found it amazing that I was really looking at grass houses. They were quite big and sturdy looking. We slowed to almost a hover and I noticed that everyone in the village was staring at us, while we stared back at them.

Dan leaned over to me and said, "Check out the girl in the boat wearing all white. Hope she's not a Co-cong."

"I see her. Co-Cong?"

"Yeah, a female VC. She'll screw you in more ways that one," Dan explained as he continued with, "She's giving you the, 'finger.' Do you want us to shoot her?"

Quickly I responded with, "No. Don't do that!"

"Relax, just joking."

I couldn't believe that. Was he joking? Was my response of, 'no, don't do that' going to save this girl's life? VC or not? He wasn't sure. Was he? I must have been looking at him in an odd way because he then told me, "Just joking my man. We'll need a little more than one finger, my new friend, to start a fire fight."

"Dan," I said, trying to talk louder than the helo. "I got a request to make."

"You can always make a request."

"No man, this is for real. No more jokes like that, okay. I'm busy looking for anyone that wants to shoot at us and you want blow away some girl because she gave us the 'finger.' That just isn't funny."

"She didn't give us the 'finger.' She was giving the 'finger' to you."

I almost took him serious on that one, "Cut that out man."

"Yeah, you're right, sorry."

"Thanks." Somehow, I felt a little better now.

"It'll take you a few weeks, and your sense of humor will surely change about these little people," he said in a mysterious way.

He continued, "Some locals want us here because of our protection, some want us here, because of our money. Others don't care that we're here, and still others don't know even why we're here."

I was trying to take all this in when he continued with, "Everyone else wants to kill us."

I would just put that thought aside for now. With this much noise from the helo, and wanting not to distract them from their duties, I could ask more questions about that some other time.

We moved on up a few hundred feet and I noticed that the houses were starting to be a little more spread apart. Sort of like going from the city to the suburbs. It appeared that each family had a little more property, the further from Saigon we flew. Even their boats were a little bigger. I guessed these boats were the same to them as us having a Winnebago. I figured that small boats equaled small pick-up trucks.

Without warning, the pilot yanked the controls, and we made a hard right turn. This caught me off guard but apparently not the door gunner because he was firing away at something down below us.

We flew around in a circle, and as we approached where we made that sudden turn, the door gunner fired again. It appeared to me he was firing thousands and thousands of rounds, but I guess in reality that it might have been just a few hundred.

"What's up?" I asked Dan, because he was holding his hands over his headset to hear better. He looked at me and made a facial expression, as if he would rather me be quiet, so he could hear what was being said.

A few seconds later Dan said to me, "The pilot saw someone take a shot at us, and told the gunner to take him out. The gunner believed that he got him on the first go-round, but we were doing a fly-by to visually verify that he got the kill."

Now that was exciting, and the whole thing took less than a minute. I was thinking that wasn't much of a firefight and how, 'that's all that there is,' when Dan said to me, "Check-it-out, your second day in-country and already someone tried to kill you."

After a short pause, and with humor in his voice, Dan joked, "At least this time it was the enemy."

I returned him a grin that suggested that I didn't find that funny. Not funny at all.

Dan noticed my response and said, "Relax man. You're too uptight."

He was right, I should relax. However, I gave some thought to what he just said, someone just now tried to kill me, and now he was dead. Well, that took the smile right off my face, and now I could not get relaxed.

Right then, the door gunner took out his camera and took a few pictures, and I assumed it was of this dead man. Without anything else happening, we continued up the river, and apparently, the crew treated this situation as if we ran over a squirrel, and now it was road kill.

After another ten minutes of flying, 'low and slow,' I happened to be looking at Dan as he was looking through binoculars, just as a huge grin showed up on his face.

"Jersey Joe!" He said to himself showing some excitement.

Quickly he crossed over to the opening between the two pilots. He leaned forward and started talking and pointing down at the river below. With that, I leaned forward to look in the direction he was pointing.

I saw a small green boat in the middle of this brown river. Dan was continuing to talk to the one pilot, while the other was talking on his radio, and looking down towards this boat.

After a few minutes of this, Dan leaned back and said, "We'll be getting off now,

I've made other arrangements for transportation. Besides, you might as well get used to the rivers, and now is as good a time as any to start."

"No sweat," I said as I was trying to figure out what he had in store for us this time. I was quite content to continue with the ride we had. It was not as if we would have a lot of cargo to unload or anything.

Our chopper made a slow 360° turn, and came up behind, and to the left, of this little green boat below us. It was about the size of a small cabin cruiser with an inboard motor. As we got closer, it appeared to be some type of gun or patrol boat and not something to go fishing on; however, it was going fast enough that I thought it could pull a skier or two.

I could see two flags flying from the mast. One was the American flag and the other appeared to be a state flag. I guessed it to be the state flag of New Jersey, because I remembered Dan saying something about Jersey. I was expecting the patrol boat to head toward shore so we could land near by and board her, but I noticed she was just maintaining the same speed and direction as before.

We were getting closer and I noticed, to my surprise, that a few guys on the boat were getting a few rays of sun, as sun tanning.

One guy was even sitting in a green lawn chair as if he were at the beach.

While Dan was unbuckling our sea bags, I figured that he was unaware that the patrol boat had not turned toward shore. I pointed to the boat and asked, "How are we going to get aboard? Does she know we're coming? Isn't she going to pull over for us or something?"

"Jump, yes, no," answered Dan to my three questions at the same time as he continued to fool with his sea bag.

"Give me a break. How about you giving me a straight answer and one answer at a time please," I asked him, because I wasn't completely sure what was going to happen.

"Okay, we'll jump onboard. Jersey Joe is a good boat captain, and jumping onboard will be no problem at all. He does know that we're coming, and no, he's not going to pull over for us. Come on and let's get our bags ready to throw out," he explained as if everything was normal.

It took a moment for the words, 'jump' and, 'to throw out' hit me, but when it did, I was not sure on how to respond. Damn, damn, damn. The last time we departed an aircraft, we had to jump without our bags, and this time, we'll be jumping with them. Was this going to be the norm for traveling in 'The-Nam,' I questioned myself.

"So Dan," I said, "please fill me in with some details with what we'll be doing in, say, the next few minutes?" I really didn't want to hear his answer, but I had to ask.

"No sweat. We'll just fly along side, throw our bags onboard, and then jump, trying not to miss. It's not that big a deal and besides, you might even find this to be fun."

"Not exciting? 'Just fun?'" I asked trying to be a little funny and an attempt to hide just how scared I was about all this.

"Yeah, 'just fun,' as long as you don't miss when you jump."

"Then we might have some excitement?" I asked, thinking that this is suicidal.

"It'll be like this," Dan added. "If everything makes it onboard safe and sound with nothing broken, then it will be fun."

"Okay?"

"If we miss with one of our bags and it falls in the river, it'll be exciting. If one of us misses the boat, well, then it will be, most exciting. So for now, let's just try to make it fun and we can work on exciting stuff some other time."

Well, this just might be cool. I guessed I was just going to have to agree and go along with the program. This was definitely a, 'write home about' type adventure. Sure, as if anyone was ever going to believe any of this anyway. I don't believe it, and here I am.

Both sea bags were by the door, and the airman was out of the aircraft standing on the landing skid. The sound of the patrol boat was increasing and we were now about twenty feet off the water, and I continued to think this to be a very stupid idea.

As we got closer, I could tell that the patrol boat was still moving. I was able to see some of the guys that were onboard and not one of them watched our approach. The chopper now tried to match speed and direction with the boat. The airman grabbed one bag from Dan. It was the dropped, and caught, by one of the men onboard the patrol boat. A few seconds later, the second bag was onboard and set aside. That seemed easy enough.

"Okay, let's do it," Dan said as he lowered himself down and stood on the skid. Only now did I realize that this was for real. Now is not a good time to get air, and or, seasick.

Dan hung on by one hand as he leaned out. After about three or four seconds, he then simply jumped onboard. He did make it look easy, and I must get off now, because my bag and guide, were onboard, waiting for me.

"Damn, damn, damn," I said to myself as I worked my way onto the landing skid. I could not believe I was about to step off a moving chopper and jump onto a moving patrol boat. Although we were flying low and slow, it was still too fast for me. I would be happy if we would just land, turn everything off, and then make this transfer.

I could envision the telegram to my parents now. Your son was killed when he jumped out of a speeding helicopter. You see

Mr. and Mrs. Edwards. Your son missed jumping onto a speeding patrol boat on his second day in Vietnam. He didn't get a medal for bravery, just one for being stupid.

Outside on the skids, I could really hear the sounds and feel the vibrations of the chopper that was very loud as well as severe. The wind, smell of jet and diesel fuel from the chopper, and the patrol boat were enough to taste. I could even smell and taste the river. Add to that, the beers that I had earlier, I was about to puke.

I happened to take a quick look at the door gunner and I noticed that he was not paying any attention to me at all. What I noticed was that he was looking all around the shoreline. I guessed this made sense, because there was still the possibility of me being shot.

"Damn," I said aloud. I didn't realize there was still the possibility of me being killed by Charlie, and at the same time, that jumping out of this thing might kill me. Oh well, for now I must make a move. The wind was so strong that it felt as if it is going in one ear and out the other. I guessed one reason for this easy clearance was that I must have no brains between my ears at all to be doing this shit.

I timed my jump and with total fear, I jumped. He was right and this was not that big a deal. With nothing broken, I felt rather good about what I just did. In fact, that really was rather cool.

Chapter 5

Onboard the patrol boat, I quickly stood up at the same time the boat started to take off, up the river, or maybe it was down the river. Whatever. With all that going on, I did not realize that the patrol boat and chopper too had come to a complete stop. I had in my mind that we were traveling at 30 or so miles an hour, and here I thought that this stunt of mine was a bigger deal than it actually was. Oh well, I was here now with nothing broken, and my sea bag was with me.

By the time I regained my footing, the chopper had climbed and headed away with the airman already back inside. I wanted to wave bye to the airman; or at least, to acknowledge to him that I made it safely onboard, but that just was not going to happen. Then I looked around expecting everyone, or at least someone, to give me a high-five for making such a jump; however, no one seemed to care. I assumed this kind of stuff happened all the time.

I told Dan, "Now that was a cool ride and an even cooler departure. I like the way we make connections over here."

Dan finally said an encouraging comment to me, "Nice jump my friend. See, I told you it was going to be a cool ride. Come on, I want you to meet a friend of mine, Jersey Joe. Now, he's a guy that truly knows the ropes. No way is anyone going to skate, or goof off, under his command."

As I made my way down the few feet toward the helm, I was aware of the way I was walking. After being onboard the chopper, with all of its vibrations, I found myself a little unsteady moving around on this fast moving patrol boat, especially while we were hitting the wakes. I thought that I was going to be seasick. I had never been seasick before, and I guessed that this was what it felt like. However, this was not the time nor place to be sick. I held it in the best I could. The worst thing was that I could start to taste it. Having those beers earlier was not a very good idea. AM or PM, it was still a bad idea.

It was kind of strange to be both, air and seasick, at the same time. Well, I best suck it up before I throw it up. I noticed that Dan did not have any trouble getting around and I intended not to complain. No need to give him any reason to start calling me a sissy or anything like that. What I really wanted to do was to sit down and talk about the jump I just made, and to discuss the firefight we just had. Somehow, I was still a little surprised that no one gathered around to ask me about the jump. Maybe if I wanted any attention over this, I should have fallen in river and made things, 'most exciting.'

"I want you to meet Boat Captain, Gunner's Mate, First Class Jersey Joe from New Jersey," Dan said as he stepped aside to let me shake his hand.

Jersey Joe was not what I expected a boat captain to look like. First off, he was an enlisted man and not an officer. Then his appearance seemed odd, but somehow it seemed to blend in with the surroundings.

"You can call me Charlie, I mean, Charles," I said, introducing myself.

As with everything else around here, he was wearing different shades of greens and browns. He was thin, of medium height, wearing an old green T-shirt, camouflage utility pants, and untied boots. He also needed a shave and a haircut. With all that, he seemed like a very likable kind of guy with a very friendly and relaxing smile.

I said to Joe, "Pleased to meet you Jersey Joe. Cool boat. What kind is it?" Now that was a dumb statement to make, cool boat. I wondered how dumb that made me look.

"First time in-country?"

"Yes," I said, as if he could not tell. I hoped that he would answer my questions, but it might be too much to expect of him, because he was driving and drinking a beer at the same time. He took a swig from his Pabst Blue Ribbon beer and gave me a smile.

In a very authoritative way and in a deep voice that did not seem to fit him, he said, "What we have here is a $90,000 Navy issue PBR, Patrol Boat River. She's powered by a General Motors 220hp diesel engine. She provides 2800 ROMs, direct drive, for a Jacuzzi water jet propulsion pump. She can deliver up to 30 knots and carries a draft of only nine inches. This gives me great speed and maintainability on these shallow rivers and that's not bad stats for a craft weighing about seven tons."

All that was a little more than I had asked for, but I will let him finish, to be polite.

"Forward turret," he continued as if he was a tour guide, "carries a pair of 50-caliber machine-guns with search light for night operations, not that we really use them that much. Up top, we have the Raytheon 1900 radar unit. In the rear, we have a rapid-fire, 40mm, grenade launcher and a pair of M-60 machine-guns mounted on either side."

A short pause to catch his breath and Joe continued, "The other day, I added a flame-thrower and that's very cool. Right now, I have a crew of four and each man has an M-16 rifle along with their personal M-79 grenade launcher. My little Thump-gun."

"Nice," I answered. Now that was another stupid response. I just could not think of anything else to say. I meant, I was using words like, nice and, cool to describe a patrol boat filled with guns, bullets, grenades, and flame-throwers. I should not be talking as if this was a 57 Chevy or a new girl at school.

"And one more thing," he continued, as he pointed toward the forward gun turret. "Where you see fresh paint, well, that's where Charlie had a couple of lucky hits the other day."

"Lucky hits, six lucky hits!" Dan exclaimed excitingly, as he counted the six spots on the one bulkhead near where we stood. "If I had known this, I would have stayed on the chopper and taken my chances flying low and slow."

"No sweat asshole. Do you want me to call the chopper back?" Joe responded in a deep angry voice that definitely indicated to me that he was most serious. As Jersey Joe fired this response back to Dan, I was not sure if he was joking or not. However, both men just shrugged their shoulders, smiled at each other and all seemed fine.

Joe motioned for one of the crew to take the wheel. He and Dan moved to a seat in the rear on two folding lawn chairs, and naturally, they were green folding lawn chairs. You know, the kind you find in everyone's back yard; but no way on a patrol boat in the middle of a river.

Joe opened a cooler near the port machine gun, pulled out a beer, and offered me one. "You want a PBR?"

I didn't know what he was talking about because I knew that he wasn't offering me his boat. Joe, apparently noticing my confused expression, explained, "PBR. That stands for Pabst Blue Ribbon Beer. Would you like a PBR?"

"No thank you," I responded. The last thing I needed right now was another beer.

Dan opened his sea bag and searched for something inside while Jersey Joe sat next to him showing much interest in whatever was in the bag. Dan pulled out what appeared to be a newspaper. A Sunday newspaper, complete with comics, classified ads, TV guide, Parade magazine, and coupons. There was a bright smile on Jersey Joe's face as he unfolded the paper and started to page through it. This was not an easy task with the amount of wind that blew across the back of the boat and water that sprayed them as we hit the occasional wake.

What a sight. The two of them were here in the middle of a war zone, with Dan and Joe sitting in lawn chairs, enjoying their cold beers, and reading the Sunday newspaper. I must buy a camera to catch all this because no one would ever believe what I was seeing right now. In my opinion, this would have made a great cover photo for National Geographic or Life magazine.

I kept thinking, shouldn't we be on the lookout for the VC instead of reading the comics?

After a few minutes with little success in reading the paper, Jersey Joe folded it up, headed toward the wheel, and placed the paper inside a small compartment. I took a seat next to Dan and asked, "So what's the big deal about a newspaper? Will he get to redeem his coupons over here, or was he just checking out the movie schedule for Saturday night?"

"You see, he's down to less than thirty days before he's out of here. He needs the newspaper to get a head start with his job search, and to check out prices for apartments in New Jersey. Also, he'll need to buy a car and this gives him a better idea about the costs."

"So, his year is up and he is on his way out of here?"

"No, not really. Jersey Joe has been in-country for three years now and he would much rather stay longer and finish out the war; or at least, see how it turns out before he leaves. However, a few weeks ago he was made aware of a wanted poster with his name on it."

I was a little puzzled, "A wanted poster? Like the ones in the Post Office?"

"Yeah, the VC are not impressed with the body count that Joe has totaled up in the last year or so. The VC passed out wanted posters, with a reward for anyone in the area, hoping that someone would get him."

"Are you serious about finding wanted posters?" I inquired. "We are not the days of the Wild West you know."

"No, but we are here, in 'The-Nam,' where everything is possible," Dan said, in a serious tone.

Just then, Jersey Joe came over and stood next to us. "You'll never guess what offer I received as a possible next assignment."

"Next assignment, I thought you wanted out of the Navy? Now, does this mean that you're going to turn yourself into a lifer?" Dan asked.

"I do want out of the Navy; however, I believe the Navy thought I might like doing something a little new and different after my tour."

"So tell me already," asked Dan. I wanted to know also.

"They want me to be a FAM."

"That is wonderful, my man is gonna be a FAM. Jersey Joe the FAM man," Dan said with much excitement. After a brief pause and with his facial expression turning serious, he questioned, "What is a FAM?"

"Shut up. FAM stands for Federal Air Marshall. The Feds are looking for guys to fly shotgun on international and US airlines. They need guys like me with my experience to volunteer to foil any high-jacking attempts."

"No shit," Dan said with surprise. "They asked you?"

"Yeah, I tell ya what. That doesn't sound like a bad assignment to me. Besides, if things do happen on my flight, I can be the one to blow the bad guys away," responded Jersey Joe with a smile on his face, as if he would really enjoy blowing away somebody bad.

"Do you travel in uniform?" I asked.

"Hell no, I'll be a regular passenger. I believe that I can let my hair grow a little too," was his response as he ran his hand through his short hair.

"So how did you find out about this?" Dan asked, with some desirability, as if he wanted someone to offer him that type of job.

"The last time I was in Dong-Tam, this officer came up to me and asked if I was Jersey Joe. I told him that I was, figuring that I was in trouble or something. With that, he asked me to join him for a drink, and I did."

"Things sure have changed around here if you're drinking with the officers now," came Dan's smart remark, that Joe didn't appreciate.

"Shut up and listen up ass-hole. I'm being serious here," Joe said, with a little anger in his voice.

"All right, all right, you have the deck," responded Dan.

"With all the high-jacking and shit going on these days, the government and airline people want some type of police force onboard certain civilian flight. You know, to try to protect passengers, crew, and aircraft. Nobody wants to go and visit Cuba on purpose these days."

Joe explained all this as if he was trying to persuade us to approve his possible decision to re-enlist and take this next assignment. Well, maybe not my personal approval, but at least Dan's approval.

"You know," Dan responded, "you will still be in the military and how much longer must you re-enlist to get this dream position?"

"They are asking for a two year commitment," Joe answered as if he didn't want to respond to that question.

"Two years! Are you crazy?" Laughed Dan as he continued with, "Just add in another ten years or so to that, and you can retire."

"Yeah, two years. Look, I'm getting out very soon and I don't have a job to go to, a car to drive, or a place to live. You know, there aren't many jobs out there for a guy with my talents. I can pilot a small boat, handle a flame-thrower in one hand, and throw hand grenades with the other."

After a short pause, he continued with, "Damn man, now that I think about it, I can do all that well, and with style. Hell, it might even be hard just to get an apartment, if, on my application I put down that I can handle small arms and a flame-thrower. Can you imagine me getting my drivers license? I'll just tell the examiner that I can drive with one hand and fire my M-16 with the other. You already know that half the people back home believes that we kill old people, women and babies. I can see how happy the neighbors will be to have me move in next door to them."

"Good points," answered Dan.

Even I had to agree to that statement. Besides, the nightly news back home had already made up my mind about guys returning home from this war.

"I have a week before I must give my decision and a lot will depend on what jobs and apartments are available in the classified you brought me."

"So you have some major decisions to make. Any ideas on what you want to do?" Dan asked, with genuine concern.

"Don't know," Joe said holding firm with a serious look, and that was followed by a good swig from his beer.

"Well, you do have a week and a lot can happen in a week to help with your decision," I spoke up wanting to be part of the conversion.

Shaking his head yes, Joe came back with, "Yeah, that's true. Then guess what happened to me the following day?"

"Well, tell us my man," Dan quickly responded.

"Another guy approached me, and he was interested in when I was being rotated out."

"Is this another drink with another officer?" Dan questioned, wanting Joe to move along with his story.

"Don't think he was an officer," Joe explained. "A foreigner, possibly not even in the military."

"Don't tell me. He wanted to hire you to high-jack the planes, right?" Came another, un-called for smart remark from Dan.

"Give me a break ass-hole. This is important to me," Joe responded quickly.

Dan motioned with his hands that he was submitting to Joe, and for him to continue without his interference.

"I thought he was a reporter or something because he didn't dress military style. Yet somehow, I knew that he was at one time or another in the military by his mannerism. He even had a slight English accent, like the old Queen's English. I would have bet that he came from South Africa or some place like that."

"So what did he want you for?" I asked.

"Believe this or not; he was looking for some mercenaries to travel to Angola, for another war that they have going on over there."

"Africa?" Dan repeated.

"Yeah man, Africa."

Dan pondered this for a minute before he added, "I've heard something about that before. They're paying guys that have finished their tour, to be part of an Army someone is creating over there. I believe the pay is quite good."

"Yeah, it's good pay. It's real good pay. I'm not sure what I should do," Joe responded as if looking for our opinion.

"So how legal is this Army crap in Angola? Are you guys gonna get a bonus for confirmed kills, and are they looking for anybody else for this assignment?" Dan asked eagerly as if he also wanted part of this action.

"We didn't get into those kinds of details. He mostly wanted to know when my tour was up, and for me to attend a meeting with some of his people. These people of his are in New York, and he was most willing to send me a round trip ticket."

"So what do you think you should do?" I asked, hoping that Dan didn't want to join him. He must still show me how to find my unit first.

"As always, I have to first make it out of here alive. Now is not the time to get killed, wounded, or worse. I must be careful not to do anything stupid," he responded.

"Worse?" I asked. I would of thought that being killed or wounded would have been a big deal to me. FNG or not.

Dan looked at me as if I asked another stupid question while Joe looked down at the deck and said, "Worse, like in being captured. You know, POW, a guest at the Hanoi Hilton. Hoa-Loa Prison is not a place to spend any time in."

I never thought that being captured could be worse than death.

Joe looked up finally and said to change the subject; "They had another requirement that I found strange until it was explained to me."

"Like what?" Dan asked turning towards Joe.

"Can I drive a manual transmission?"

Dan said, "I heard that was one of their requirements, to drive a stick, I never knew why."

I knew that I should just keep quiet; but I just had to ask, "Why is that?"

"Because they want you to be able to drive a Datson pick up truck over ruff terrain," answered Joe.

Dan added, "Now I think I remember. Don't they have some kind of big gun mounted in the bed on those small pickup trucks?"

"Sure thing, yeah, the guns are mounted in the truck bed as you said. The driving part was important from what he was telling me. He explained that if you can drive fast, then you could run over, trip a mine, and get past it before she blew up. Anything that is slow, like a tank, is easily blown apart into a million pieces."

I was enjoying this interesting conversation I was hearing when Dan said, "I guess there's a high turnover with drivers over there."

"That part never came up in our conversation," Joe answered, as if he was giving this whole thing a second thought.

Dan said, "Well, you know that no one is in charge on the outside and the world needs a good war every now and then to keep things in order."

"Yeah, and this one guy was very serious about it. He never even cracked a smile. To him, this was all business," Joe said, adding additional information about his conversation.

"I bet," Dan responded, in agreement. "I heard these guys will put $15,000 into your bank account, as up front money, and they promise to take care of all your expenses while you're over there."

"Yeah, that's what I was told. They will even do the money thing before I leave and allow for verification. All I am required to do in return is to give them a twelve month obligation and that can be handled with just a verbal agreement."

"They'll accept a verbal agreement from you? That doesn't sound right," Dan advised.

"I thought about that one also," Joe responded, giving the impression of serious thought. "But then I considered just whom I was talking to and dealing with. With these guys hiring a small private army, I believed this was not a group to mess with. And I highly doubt that they would want to put anything in writing."

"That's true. I bet these guys would get even in ways that we could never imagine, if you broke your word with them," Dan added, with Joe in agreement.

Now I didn't want to miss any of this conversation, but I had to relieve myself. Time for the beer to go and all that. "So what's a guy got to do to make a head call around here?" I asked not wanting to change the conversation. I just had to go and take five.

"It depends on what you need to do," Joe asked. "If you need to piss, just aim it over the side remembering not to face the wind. Otherwise, it's best to hold it until we hit land."

Dan added, "That's right."

"Well, I'll just wait on part two, but I will take you up on your suggestion for part one."

Now this nature's call of mine had never been a big deal to me until this moment. I had been used to doing this kind of thing, in private, all my life. I was not embarrassed or anything about any of this, but I just found it uncomfortable to piss here at the back of the boat, while standing just inches away from two guys holding a conversation. I wanted to go to one of the sides and relieve myself, but the wind was blowing across the deck. I could not believe that pissing out in the middle of nowhere could be such a big deal.

Well, luck was going my way, because one of the crewmembers came down and started to piss standing in the little space behind Dan, Joe, and me. I guessed this was as good a time to piss in the wind as any. I meant, with the wind. I took care of myself, buttoned up, and without embarrassment. I was grateful that the wind didn't change direction on me. Feeling relieved, I asked Dan, "So how long before we get to, well . . . where are we going this time?" I had no idea where we were, and even less of an idea as to where we were headed. I hoped that we were still headed toward that Dong-Tam place.

"We're still heading towards Dong-Tam and I believe it's about an hour or so from here," Dan responded, looking at Joe for verification.

"Yeah, about an hour," added Jersey Joe.

Even with my recent relief, my stomach was still a little upset, partially from all the excitement of yesterday, last night, and today. Not to mention my drinking of a few beers earlier and now this rough boat ride. I hoped I could hold off on number two until Dong-Tam.

Joe looked at me and told me to, "Enjoy the ride," as he headed back to the wheel and relieved the crewmember that was driving.

"So what do you think he'll decide?" I asked Dan.

"Don't know, but at least he does have a few weeks to decide one of four choices."

"Four, how do you figure four?"

"He can ride shotgun for an airline or get out and go home. He can decide to join the African Army, and there's still the slight possibility of him staying in the U.S., Navy doing the same thing he's doing right now."

I added, "That's true, and right now he must also decide how to keep himself alive and out of harm's way."

"Yeah, at least for now you have eleven months, before you must decide, what you're going to do next," Dan informed me.

"What do you mean? Decide what?" I asked, thinking this to be a trick question.

"You may even want to stay for another tour."

"No, not me. I don't think so, Dan. A second tour? No way in the world. Why would I? I'm not even going to consider that scenario. Remember, I didn't pick this for my first tour."

Dan smiled, sat back, closed his eyes, and said, "We'll see my man, we'll see."

I was not even going to entertain that kind of thought. I figured that I might as well get comfortable for the remainder of the ride, so I took a seat in the lawn chair next to Dan. I was becoming used to the ride now, and after a few adjustments to my seat, I got myself rather comfortable.

The engines had a continuous, smooth, and rather pleasant hum to them. The wakes were not too big and that made the ride even more enjoyable with a little rock'in and a roll'in. The occasional spray was a welcome relief while the sun baked my face. The combination of all of the above was very comfortable, and I no longer felt seasick or airsick.

"Here comes something to check out," yelled one of the crew from the front of the boat.

"What's up?" I asked Dan.

"Don't know; but, I bet it's got something to do with that boat coming our way," Dan responded, and pointed toward the sampan coming our way.

Joe yelled instructions to, "Let'em pass, let'em check us out, and we'll check'em again."

As the boat passed, Joe informed me as to what he was thinking, "If everyone is facing away from us, then that's reason enough to check'em out."

Not knowing what was going on or what to say, I just kept silent and watched them go by like everyone else. They appeared to me to be a bunch of women going on a trip, maybe even to the mall or something.

Sure enough, as Joe explained it, everyone but the driver faced the other way. I was not up to speed with why, or where, but Joe gave the order to turn around and catch up with them. We made the 180° and were soon along side them. I got the neatest feeling that I was a cop going to pull over someone for a moving violation. Now this felt both cool and scary. Cool because we were on a gunboat, and I assumed we had them out-gunned. Scary because they just might shoot back at us.

Once along side, Jersey Joe directed one of his crew to, "Check'em out."

Because there wasn't enough room for a crewmember to board their little sampan, he used the barrel of his M-16 to pick around at the items that were there. If that had been me being searched, I would have been scared to death. However, these ladies seemed more pissed that they were stopped, than about the actual search itself.

The only things that we found were six women and no military supplies of any kind onboard. After a detailed search of the little boat, they were on their way. We made another 180°, and we were again headed for Dong-Tam.

Initially, it appeared to me, that things were not so bad on patrol boats. The duty didn't seem all that bad. With our little spot-check out of the way, I took my seat again next to Dan and was so comfortable that I slowly fell asleep.

Moments later, the crewmember that spotted the last boat we stopped, started to yell something back and pointed in the direction we were headed. Jersey Joe was already talking on the radio calling somebody. Dan sat up and said, "So much for a peaceful ride."

"What's up?" I asked.

"Don't know yet. It's probably a firefight nearby. Don't worry," Dan suggested.

"Yeah, yeah I know. Don't sweat the small stuff because everything over here is small stuff, right?"

With some reservation, Dan answered, "Yeah, I hope this one is just small stuff."

"What do you mean?" I asked thinking that maybe I didn't want to hear his answer.

"I mean, here we are, in the middle of nowhere, and it's just us and one helo nearby." After some thought, he added, "Assuming that the helo we were on was still nearby. Now, with some luck on our side, it'll just be small stuff."

Looking up ahead, I was able to see the chopper that we were on earlier firing on three sampans about a mile or two ahead of us. I hoped that they had plenty of ammo.

Jersey Joe yelled at his crew, "Okay, you know what I want. Let's kill some VC!"

I noticed that each man was already in motion before Joe even opened his mouth.

Dan headed toward Jersey Joe and without a word, Joe pointed to a locker near his left foot. Dan reached inside and grabbed two M-16 rifles. He again reached down, grabbed a green pouch, headed back towards me, and handed me one of the M-16s.

I took it not knowing just what to do. In boot camp, we only fired an M-1 rifle a few times, and before boot camp, I had never even held a gun. I had only seen the M-16 on TV and a couple of real ones yesterday.

"Thanks," I said after taking the M-16. I just stared at it hoping, that I could figure it out, by just looking at it. I was giving the rifle the same look you would give a car engine when the hood was up, because you were broken down on the side of a highway. It was then that you were hoping for some kind of blinking light, or an obvious broken part, to indicate clearly, whatever was broken, with a suggestion as, what to do next.

"You wanted a gun the other day and now you have one," Dan said to me.

Under my breath I said, "I only wanted to carry one around so I would look cool."

Having heard me, Dan said to me, "Now you will look, hot!"

"Thanks," I answered, having nothing else to say. I didn't want to be hot; I wanted to go home. Oh well, I got to do what I was being paid to do.

I watched everything that Dan was doing as he reached into the pouch that Joe gave him. He handed me a magazine, took one for himself, and snapped it in place. He placed two additional clips in his pocket and again reached in the pouch and handed me two clips that I placed in my pocket. So far, this part was easy.

I was not paying much attention to anyone else, and when I did look around, I noticed that all the crewmembers were already at their posts. In some ways, I was kind of hoping to hear the PA system go off saying, "General Quarters, General Quarters, this is not a drill, all hands, General Quarters." Not that it was needed or anything, that was just the way I remembered it from old war movies.

The whole scenario was giving me the sensation that I was riding along with John F. Kennedy on the PT109. If we were hit and sunk, I didn't think that the little boat captain, Jersey Joe was big enough to pull me safely to shore.

Dan said, waking me from my trance, "Here, you got to put on this flack jacket."

I took it not knowing exactly what it was that he was giving me. I was looking to put on a jacket, and this thing was only a vest. Of all things to be thinking about right now, I was thinking why not just call this a bulletproof vest instead of a flack jacket. As I was putting this on, I noticed that the guy on the stern was looking in every direction other than forward. Then it dawned on me that this did make sense because this could be a trap or something. Someone had to be checking our rear. I did not pick up that combat knowledge in boot camp; I got it from watching old war movies. I had to forget thinking about old war movies for now and focus on the current circumstances at hand.

The engine sounds were not as smooth and pleasant to listen to as they were before; they were much louder now, and it drowned out the sounds of the firefight ahead of us. The wakes seemed a lot larger, and hitting them made it difficult to stand steady and straight. The spray that was once a welcomed relief from the hot sun, now sprayed into my eyes, impairing my vision, and it was down right irritating.

I didn't know why I was complaining so much. I meant this was Vietnam and there was a war going on, and I was an active player. I hoped that I was on the winning team.

As we got closer, I could see and hear the gunfire from the chopper. There was another, very different sound of gunfire, and I assumed this was coming from the VC fighting back. Somehow, I felt it would be safer on a chopper than onboard Joe's boat. The chopper had a much better escape route, just up-up and away, in any direction, and here on the boat; we could only escape up or down the river.

The only thing positive about this situation for me was that I had already experienced a firefight. The only difference was that I did not have a gun before, and now I did. Dan set me up with a gun, bullets, and a flack vest, I mean flack jacket, and now I was going to take an active part. 'Lions and tigers and bears, oh my,' I started to repeat to myself.

"Damn, damn, damn, this sure was turning out to be one interesting day," I said to Dan.

"True, and thank you for noticing. Tell you what," Dan added, "after this, we'll do lunch and it'll be my treat."

"Yeah, if we ever make it to Dong-Tam. Remember that I'm only here for 363 more days, and I want to get checked into my ship. You know, before it's time for me to check out."

Dan, looking extremely serious, said to me, "Your immediate concern right now should not be checking into your unit. For now, what do you say we just try to stay alive and kill some VC? This is not the time to check-out anything else."

"No sweat," I answered trying not to sound as frightened as I was. I was VERY frightened and it sure was different watching this on TV or at the movies.

"And one more thing my man, this is not the proper time to say anything with the word, 'checking out' in a sentence, know what I mean?"

I saw that now, and I responded with, "No sweat, sorry about that. I got to be more aware of what I say."

All of a sudden, I heard this 'tap, tap, tap,' followed by 'pop, pop, pop.'

"Fuckin VC," yelled one of the crew.

I detected a little touch of fear in his tone and a lot of anger in his voice. I realized that that noise caught everyone off guard and that the fear part was normal, well, normal for me. But what was he angrily screaming about?

Another crewmember looking back yelled, "Damn it, it got hit again. I bet those little shits-slope-heads, did that on purpose."

On purpose? What's on purpose? I turned my head toward the new sounds of fizzing, and could see that the beer cooler had apparently taken a few direct hits. I could see why these guys were so upset; they knew that there would be no more cold beer to drink today. I pondered; could Jersey Joe still drive this thing without a beer in his hand? Would he get a ticket from the river police for driving with an open beer can in his boat?

Dan looked at me and yelled, "Look out man. We're being shot at!"

It only took me a second to get back to reality and I was face down on the deck. No one should be firing at us because we had a few beers onboard; then I remembered that we're in Vietnam. I had made it to another firefight, and being face down on the deck seemed like the place to be.

Melted ice water was draining from the injured cooler. One hole was about an inch or two from the bottom, and it was spilling on me. Damn. Cooler water was very cold, especially if you were laying in it. I glanced over to the top of the beer cooler and saw that another hole was near the top, and that it had beer-foam spewing out of it. I would have thought that being in range of the VC would have been more of a concern for the crew than a wounded beer cooler. Oh well, as Dan had said on many occasions, this was, 'The-Nam,' and certainly not an old war movie.

Jersey Joe looked back at the bleeding water cooler and yelled to his crew, "Revenge, we need to afflict revenge. Let's get those little commie bastards."

Such a monumental statement from the boat captain, Jersey Joe created, a strange, but uplifting, patriotic, feeling in me. I had a vision of Roosevelt yelling, "Remember Pearl Harbor," and Davy Crockett shouting, "Remember the Alamo," before he was killed. I did not know if this was my imagination or not, but I believed that the crew observed a moment of silence in reverence for this bleeding and dying beer cooler. Then, as if on cue, everyone started firing back at the same time. I must find the time and write a book about all this, but the only thing was, no one would believe me on half of what had happened to me since I arrived in-country.

Oh well, I figured it was about time I joined in with the action. I meant, I was a soldier and all that, even if I was just a FNG soldier. I stood and fired away aiming for the shoreline in the general direction where I saw Dan shooting.

Right in the middle of all this excitement, I had to stop and pull up my pants that were starting to fall down. I must get myself a belt sometime soon. Not having one might get me killed; and if I was going to die, I want to die wearing my pants properly and not having them hanging down at my ankles. Besides, I might get shot right in the ass while bending over to pull up my pants. This would not be a good war story, nor would I want to repeat it to anyone, not that anyone would believe me anyway.

Moving on, and pulling up, I loaded another magazine and fired away. I started to feel as if I was a madman with a mission, and it felt rather good. I started to sing the song, Ballad of the Green Beret. (Not loud of course, just enough for me to hear.)

I would have bet that our firefight went on for hours. In reality it was probably only for a few minutes. Well, at least three or four minutes at the most. I stopped firing because everyone else had already stopped. Apparently, either we were out of range from the VC, or everyone ran out of ammo. As for me, I wanted to, at the very least, empty out my magazine. However, I followed their example and stopped firing. It would have been neater and military like if someone would have yelled, "stop firing, stop firing," or "cease fire, cease fire." Not a big deal, just something I would have expected to hear over here, especially at the end of a firefight or battle.

Of all things to crop up now, a new issue had come to a head making things a little more interesting for me during this time of war; I had to pee again. Beer in the morning was definitely something I should try to avoid in the future, assuming I got out of this alive.

With a lull in the fighting, or it might be that everyone was reloading at the same time, I held my rifle in one hand. I loaded a magazine with my other hand and wished that I had two additional hands, one hand to hold up my pants and another to hold myself; I still had to pee and I had to pee now more than ever.

Joe yelled something to Dan. Dan then instructed me to, "Hang on a minute. Let's wait and see what happens next."

Yeah, my pants will fall down and I'll pee myself. That's what would happen next. Whatever, I would hang loose for now, but not too loose. If my pants did fall down, I would be hanging out and not hanging on. At least I had the time to pull up my pants, and get them straightened out.

With no shooting going on right now, Jersey Joe and another guy were looking through binoculars as if trying to acquire a target, or at the very least, make sure that we weren't a target.

I questioned Dan, "Is it over? Did we win?"

He replied without looking at me. He apparently was keeping an eye out for trouble, "It's never over, and I don't think that anyone won this round."

Before I could ask another question, our boat made a hard, right hand turn. Now it appeared that we would be heading up this little river or canal thing, or whatever you called it over here.

Just as I was about to ask another question, without warning, a helo flew a few feet over our heads, as if leading the way for us. Even from down here, I could taste the jet fuel and feel the exhaust heat from the chopper's engines.

"It's a Cobra," Dan explained as it flew right over our heads. "Built for killing the VC."

Wow, this was sure getting to be an exciting day, and I assumed that we had the upper hand now. We got to have the upper hand, because we were chasing the VC and not retreating. We did have the superior force and all that. I commented to Dan, "This is great."

He responded to my positive attitude with a negative comment, "This is bad."

I might as well listen to his reasoning. If things were bad, I wanted to know about just how bad it was ahead of time. I had the feeling that I was off track somehow with my thinking, and this was not the time or place to be off track. I questioned Dan and tried not to appear scared or worried, "What's bad?"

"A small river like this puts the VC very close to us on both sides," Dan answered looking around.

Oh shit, I figured that we were winning and chasing after them as they retreated. Now they just might be setting up an ambush or something, and that would give them the upper hand, and our little beer cooler problem was no longer that important.

"What do we do?" I asked, trying unsuccessfully not to sound scared this time.

"We'll do nothing about it right now. It's not as if we must maintain the Three-mile limit or anything. Joe's the boat captain, and he's been in tight spots before," Dan assured me. But I didn't think that he was all that convinced.

This didn't sound too encouraging, especially with Jersey Joe on the VC's top ten-wanted list. Dan looked around and continued as if he did not want anyone to hear what he was telling me, "Remember my man, you're new at this and just along for the ride. Keep your eyes opened, profile low and your gun loaded."

I squatted down a little to create my own little 'low profile.' Of course, holding the railing for stability with one hand and my rifle with the other . . . well . . . so much for my pants staying up for now. Yet, if I stay squatted, they would not fall, I thought.

Chuckling at me, Dan said, "And keep your pants up. You're embarrassing me."

"I'm trying."

"I know you don't want to show them the whites of your eyes, but that did not mean that you could show them the whites from your, Fruit of the Looms," Dan joked.

I didn't have time to laugh just then because two shots landed very close to us. I assumed with the cooler hit and dying, that the VC were now trying for us. I wanted to get down so low and into a fetal position, so that no one would be able to see me, much less hit me.

Joe made another radical turn followed by another. After a few of these moves, I could not tell if we were headed into, or out of, this little river. Hell, I did not know if we were even chasing the VC or running away from them.

I got brave, or stupid, because I raised my head up to see what was going on. No one was shooting right then and maybe, it was all over. I could see a little ways in front of us, that a small sampan was being fired on from the chopper that just flew over us. Now, I had quite a view of this action and I found this amazing to witness. It was not hard to miss the rocket attack on the sampan because we were right under the chopper. I remembered from the nightly news, that the photo shots from the helo were taken from the chopper's point of view, and from far away. My view this time was new, exciting, and remarkable, much better than 3D.

I could see and smell the rockets as they left the chopper and fashioned their way down to the sampan. One made a direct hit and after the smoke and water spray cleared, there was nothing left at all, not even debris. Only some mud that was churned up after the explosion. It appeared that the rocket shoved the sampan and its crew right into the mud. That was where it stayed, almost as if they and their boat were vaporized. I didn't remember how many VC there were on the sampan, but it had to have been at least two, maybe three.

An explosion behind me caught me off guard. It was not strong enough to knock me down or anything, but close enough. Not that this was unusual or anything, I mean, I knew we were currently involved in a combat situation. It was just that it sounded different, like it was muffled or something.

I turned just in time to see a large tree fall in the river. Not until Jersey Joe shouted, "They got us trapped," did I understand the full significance of what just took place.

"Not good. Not good at all," Dan informed me as if I could not figure this out myself.

Joe then made one hell-of-a U-turn and floored it toward the fallen tree that was now blocking our way. I could imagine now that the tree would rip away at the hull as Joe continued, fast forward, on with our collision course, and imminent sinking.

"Hang on. It's gonna be close!" Joe screamed at everyone.

I grabbed onto the railing and prepared myself to be a crash dummy. Now, part of me wanted to close my eyes and not see our upcoming destruction, another part didn't want to miss anything; so, I decided to keep both eyes opened. I got to see how flooring the boat and crashing into a fallen tree was going to save us.

I maintained a tight grip on the railing, and was not worried about losing my pants this time. For some unknown reason, at the last second, Joe quickly threw his boat in reverse and kept it floored. I assumed that he chickened-out with this escape trick of his. The bow dipped down, and the stern rose up high out of the water. Then Joe cut the engine. To my surprise, apparently not to Joe, this wake that we created caught up with us. The stern lowered, the bow rose, and we coasted up and over the downed tree! I did not believe that we even scratched a branch or leaf with our exquisite escape. I definitely did not hear the hull scrape the tree, as we floated over.

Joe yelled, "All right. We didn't even nick the paint." Before we could gather around to pat him on the back for getting us over this tree trap safely, Joe threw it back in forward and floored it. In no time at all, we were quickly out of range.

I looked over at Dan and he said to me, "That was called 'Proposing.' I never knew what it was good for, but Joe had created one for the books. In no time at all, we were far enough away from the VC that even I was able to relax.

I asked Dan, "Did we just do a retreat back then?" I did not want Jersey Joe to overhear me on that one. No way did I want to hurt his feeling, especially with him saving our lives and all that. However, Joe did overhear me, because I was still unable to whisper properly.

Joe responded in his defense, "Yes, I did retreat. You got a problem with that?"

"No. No problem with me," I answered quickly showing that I knew right away that I should have just kept my mouth shut.

Joe continued, "I retreated to save our lives today. I will be available to kill more VC in the future and in my time frame."

Dan spoke up and added, "When Joe calls the shots, he really calls the shots."

Dan then told Joe, "You did good my man. You did damn good."

Before I could add anything positive to exalt Joe, I was alarmed to see that someone was still shooting at us. I saw what appeared to be machine-gun blast from the shoreline. Poops of white [illegible] caught my attention on that one. The rounds were [illegible] in a straight line toward us. Each round created a [illegible]spout about four or five feet high. It would have been som[illegible]at neat to watch, if it wasn't for the fact that someone was trying to kill us.

Joe noticed this and did nothing. In a frightened voice, I said, "We're being shot at."

Joe calmly told me, "No sweat boot, we're out of range. Relax."

I was not sure just what to say to that. I came back with, "It's your call Joe. Like Dan just said, you did good." As soon as I said that, I hoped that I didn't give them an impression that I was scared or something.

With both hands on his hips and showing some irritation with me, he asked, "If I keep on my present course, are you going to consider me a chicken?"

Damn, I got him upset with me. Well, I didn't think he would shoot me or anything like that. At any rate, I answered, "You the man, Joe. Like you said a minute ago, you will be available to kill more VC in the future, and in your time frame. You have a good body count, and it's apparent to me that you know what your are doing."

"Good," Joe responded. He then said to Dan, "Where did you find this guy?"

I took that as a joke and wanted to give it no more attention than he apparently sought. Wanting to change the subject away from me, I asked, "Did we win anything?"

"Like what?" Dan questioned me.

"A little piece of river, this canal, or maybe we could insert a little American flag on the map representing this place, anything at all?" I inquired.

"Nope. The only thing gained was a few notes in someone's log book, and a few numbers added to the body count."

What was he talking about? What was our reason for fighting here? "So how do we win? How does either side win? And if one does win, does the other side know about it?"

Joe added his two cents into our conversation, "Simple. We kill all of them before they kill all of us, then we will have a winner."

After a short pause as if everyone was thinking, Dan commented, "Or, we can do what the French did a few years ago."

Dan seemed very serious on this one, so, I asked, "And what did the French do?"

Joe answered for Dan by saying, "Yeah. The French got tired of not winning and dying; and with those results, they simply packed up and left town."

Joe wiped the sweat from his brow and continued, "Too bad our little Ensign buddy was not here for this little firefight. Every time he's onboard, it's a boring patrol and nothing happens."

"He needed his points," Dan said.

"Yeah. Very true. Now Tony, on the other hand, we had to transfer him out because he had gotten too many points, if you know what I mean?"

I decided that instead of asking Dan about this points system, that I would ask Joe. He seemed like someone that would give me a straight answer. "So Joe, what are these points you guys are talking about?"

Joe quickly responded with, "Shake-n-bake officers that are straight out of OCS, that have seen no combat experience. Officers that want to do well and advance in the system, will need to have combat leadership experience. Points are earned for this. The more points, the better the odds of him advancing. Army officers were expected to be involved in combat, and for them it's the norm. Now, on the other hand, Naval officers don't really get that many shots, to be involved in combat situations, leading a small group like this one."

I was not sure what he was talking about, but at least I got a straight answer from him. "What about this Tony person. Is he an Army or Navy officer? How can you earn too many points? Hell, did I earn any points for my little part here?"

Joe looked pissed, as if I was asking too many questions, or that I had asked a question that he did not want to respond. At any rate, Joe apparently tolerated me and responded with, "I don't want to talk about Tony; and, no, you did not earn any points."

No problem with ignoring the information about Tony, but I wanted to ask him about my points. If I did not earn any points, was it because of my little part, or was it because I was an enlisted type and not an officer. Whatever, I figured it best that I just keep quiet on that one for now.

Joe walked away and Dan told me, "Someday, I'll tell you about Tony. Hell, you might even get to meet him one day."

I did not know how to respond to what Dan just told me, so I just kept to myself. However, with Jersey Joe not in hearing range, I asked Dan a second time about this guy named Tony. "Dan, what's the big deal about this Tony person?"

Dan looked over to make sure Jersey Joe was not close by. He then proceeded to inform me, "Tony, Tony, Tony, now this guy loved to kill. He would kill anyone and anything that had a pulse. If a tree were in his way during a firefight, he would level it with gunfire. If a hooch was in his way, he would level it with grenades, flame-thrower, or just pump enough lead into it that it would just fall down from the weight. He was not a very delightful person to have as part of your crew."

I was curious, "Isn't that why we're here?"

"True, but we have rules to go by. There is even a policy in place that regulates the size ammo that we could lob into a village."

It must have looked to Dan as if I were a student that was asked a question while daydreaming and not paying attention. He continued to explain to me as if I was in class and he was the teacher. "If your weapon is too powerful for the conditions or place, any rounds that you fire may enter the town on one side and exit out the other. What that means in simple terms is that you might be killing the wrong people on the other side of town. What's more important, our guys might be coming in from that direction."

Joe came over, so Dan stopped explaining, and I stopped asking. No good reason to upset Joe, especially after he asked me to drop it.

The whole day had been some experience. It appeared that everyone had something to do. Jersey Joe opened his logbook and started making notes. Two crewmembers were cleaning up by throwing the spent casings over the side, and looking for damage. One crewmember was at the wheel, and the fourth checking the guns that had been used. Dan was cleaning up the mess created by the beers that exploded. I felt out of place because everyone had something to do but me. I did not know how to drive the boat or clean weapons, so I started to give Dan a hand with cleaning the spilled beer.

As Dan and I were cleaning, he said to me, "So, how has your day gone so far?"

"Is this the norm?" I asked.

"No, not really, because it's more like 95% routine and boredom, and 5% madness."

After a minute, Dan stopped cleaning, looked up, and said, "No, let me rephrase that last statement. It's really like 50% routine and boredom, 45% being on watch with 5% madness and excitement, with a little touch of fascination."

As we continued to clean, I thought how no one would ever believe this. Here I was on my second day in 'The-Nam,' and I was cleaning up beer after a firefight. I might even have sometime later to read the Sunday paper while sunbathing in a lawn chair, drinking a cold beer.

"So what's happens now?" I asked.

"We need to finish cleaning up this mess."

"No, I mean after this." Damn, this guy needed explicit questions.

"Like I said earlier, we'll get to Dong-Tam and have lunch. Remember, I'm buying. And then after lunch, you and I can work on getting a ride to our ship."

"No, I mean like right now, you know, the VC and everything."

"Well, because everyone got away, there's no reason to hang around. I guess for now we'll just keep heading toward Dong-Tam. Joe will need to get refills on bullets and stuff, and at the same time, get a replacement cooler."

"We must have hit at least one VC with all that shooting and everything, right?" I asked.

"Even if we did, we're just one boat. There's no way this crew and two extra guys are going to go into that jungle and find them. Jersey Joe will make his report and call it in. If the guys in charge want anything else done here, they'll decide what to do and then tell us. They might assign someone else to go and clean things up."

Having nothing else to ask, I responded by saying, "Okay with me."

After a few minutes Dan added, "Hopefully they'll send someone else in to complete the job."

"We'll get help with cleaning up all this beer?"

"No. The VC cleanup, dummy."

"Sounds good," I answered, and realized that I answered a question the same way he usually did.

"Besides," Dan continued, "with the possibility of one or more of them being wounded, they can get real nasty. We also just blew away their trap, and that one alone can make them very unhappy. You will soon learn that the VC are tough to kill, and they are even harder to kill when they are mad or wounded."

Nothing more was said until we finished cleaning the mess caused by the beer and cooler injuries. The beer cooler was a complete loss. There were six holes, not very big, but still she was hit three times. I believed the damage to be three holes in-coming and three holes out-going.

"The cooler has cooled its last beer and cold beer isn't that easy to find around here," Dan explained.

I came back with, "I'm rather glad I decided not to hide behind the cooler."

"Good move my friend," Dan congratulated me.

"What should we do with the cooler?" I asked.

"Nothing. It's Joe's cooler, he'll take care of it. Besides, Joe will have it replaced in a matter of days."

"Even if he's getting out soon?" I questioned.

"My man still loves his cold beer, short or not."

I didn't think that Jersey Joe was short, and I looked at Dan, as if suggesting, that what he said wasn't very nice. Dan looked at me and said, "Short. As in a, 'short time,' to go before going back to the real world. Not short as in, 'little person.'"

Joe came over to inspect the cooler and said, "I bet they did that on purpose just to piss me off, and it worked."

"Burial at sea?" Dan questioned.

"Yeah, you can do the honors," Joe told Dan.

I figured that as long as those two were working out the details on how to dispose of the cooler, that I would go ahead and relieve myself. Halfway through, I looked over and noticed that everyone was saluting the cooler as Dan threw it over the side.

I freed up my right hand and joined in along with Joe, Dan, and one other crewmember with a salute of my own. I felt kind of dumb doing that, but these guys were serious, and I made a point not to say anything negative about it. Although I was quite relieved when all this was done, I had to get back to my personal deed that was almost completed.

Joe turned to Dan and said, "As far as you guys are concerned, there were no, and I repeat, no confirmed kills. As in body count equals zero."

Figuring that Joe could not have seen that sampan that was incinerated, I spoke up and said, "I know that we had at least two kills from that sampan that got blown out of the water."

For the first time, he was speaking like a boat captain with all the authority that goes with the title and position. "I say again, there were no confirmed kills to be credited to this boat. Any kills can and will be credited to the chopper and its crew."

He said that without any facial expression or emotion as he turned and walked away.

Dan said, "Like the man said, no confirmed kills, and no confirmed kills it is."

I was a little confused and I asked, "I thought that everyone wanted to get credit for kills over here. What's up with Joe?"

"Have you forgotten already?"

"Forgotten what?"

"He's trying to get out of here alive, remember?"

"Yeah, I remember, but isn't it to his advantage to kill as many VC as possible, at the very least cut down the number of VC in the area that are looking for him?"

"True. But he doesn't need to have his confirmed kill count go higher than it already is."

"Oh, I get it now. A higher kill count for him with his getting out soon, might raise the bounty on his head."

"You got it."

Wanting to change the subject, I said to Dan, "With all the excitement and everything going on, I almost forgot that I still need to go to the bathroom. I don't believe that I can wait until I get to Dong-Tam."

"I thought you just took care of that problem a few minutes ago?"

"Well I did, but this is a little more than that, because I only took care of the front end before, and now it's the back end that needs my immediate attention."

"Okay, here's what you do," Dan said as he reached over and picked up some rope that was sitting near the cooler.

"Say what?"

"You must stand on the back rail and hold onto this line," Dan told me as he tied one end to a rail at the back of the boat. "Do not wrap the line around your hand. Just hold on tight."

"Are you sure about this? Is this some kind of trick that you're playing on me?"

Looking at me as if I was wasting his time, Dan asked, "Do you have to go or not?"

"I do, but not if I'm going to make an ass out of myself."

"Don't worry about that. You don't have to spend any time on making yourself look like an ass."

I did not know how to take that comment, but for the moment, I had to go, and I had to go now. Dan did make it sound as if he were serious. Besides, what other choice did I have?

"If I slip, then what?" I asked, looking out at the river and seeing how pretty and calm it was over here.

"If you slip, you fall in the river."

Not a good idea, and maybe I should reconsider this whole thing. I still thought this was a trick or something. "What if I fall into the river?"

"In case you fall in, you'll get wet and drink a lot of water and that, my friend, is not a very pleasant experience for anyone to endure."

"This rope, I just hang onto it?" I said thinking that I had figured out what was going on here, but I must be mistaken. No way was this for real.

"Get up on the rail, hang your ass over the side, and take care of business."

"What? You mean that I must stand on the rail, hold onto this piece of rope, and hang my ass over the side, and all the while we are moving down the river?"

"That's right. We can't stop here in the middle of the river every time someone needs to take a crap," Dan said, as he handed me the rope and insisted that I take it.

I could only give Dan a dumb, sad look in return.

"You must also remember to do this quickly, because you make a good target with your ass swaying in the wind. You'll be giving the phrase, 'shoot the bulls eye,' a new meaning," Dan continued.

"A real shot in the ass," I answered him trying to be funny, and not to let him know how scared I was about doing this stupid trick.

Dan laughed at me and said, "I like that one, and I must remember to use that on the next FNG."

Under my breath, I said to myself, "Nothing like having a whole boat crew watching me do this crap thing."

Overhearing what I just said, Dan responded with, "And one more thing, if you fall in, remember to yell loud enough to be heard, because no one will be watching you take your crap."

"I thought guys in the military always looked out for each other. You know, you watch my back and I'll watch yours. Isn't that true?"

"They do, and that's true, but you can take a crap by yourself and look after your own six."

I was not sure what that meant. Anyway, I asked, "Should I keep my flack jacket on or not?"

"No, you want to take it off before you do your thing. You must understand this one thing about flack jackets. If you do fall in the river, it's almost impossible to swim wearing one."

Dan continued, "If you're lucky, Joe may have some toilet paper. If not, just squat down a little and let the rooster-tail spray clean you."

"Then I'll be all wet," I answered.

"Not a problem," Dan replied. "Joe did say that he has a flame-thrower and that will certainly dry you off quickly and completely."

"No thanks, being a little damp doesn't seem to be an issue to me any more."

I was not totally convinced that this was not a trick or something, but I still had to go, and with the way things had been happening today, I should get started. I doubted that I could hold it in, through another firefight.

Dan held the rope for me as I took off my pants. I remembered Dan had said that everyone was looking elsewhere. If I did fall in, I planned to start yelling very loud, long before I hit the water. I made one quick look around to see if anyone else might be looking. Like someone on the shore or even another boat. Then I thought, why should I care about that?

I noticed we were about to pass a small sampan with five people, and one person in the water that appeared to me to be a little kid swimming. I waited until we got well past them before I made my way to the railing.

With great appreciation, Dan handed me some toilet paper. To my surprise, the roll was white and not green or brown. Even with the roll being a little damp from the humidity, it was quite acceptable considering my situation.

"It's one ply. Is that okay," Dan asked.

This was not the time to be selective. "One ply is fine with me," I answered, grateful that I had toilet paper.

Up on the rail I go, my business was completed quickly, and down and in the boat I returned. My ordeal only took a minute. I did my required clean up, and I was again thinking that someday I might write a book about all this, maybe not. No one would ever believe that this kind of stuff really happened.

As I noticed that Dan was now laughing and pointing at something, I had to look because he wasn't pointing at me.

He said, "Take a bow my friend. I believe they enjoyed the show."

To my surprise and embarrassment, there was a family of four with all smiles waving at me. I could hardly hear them, but I knew they were making fun of me. I could guess that if one of them wrote a book, they would surely include this show of mine.

"Oh well, too late now to change anything," I said feeling like crap. Naturally, I did not mean for that family to see me doing my thing. What a day this had started out to be. My mother would be so proud.

Still laughing at me, Dan said, "Check-it-out, I believe they loved you and want an encore."

That was not what I wanted to hear right now. The only thing I wanted to hear was that we were nearing Dong-Tam. Oh well, I just gave a wave and smiled back at them.

Dan asked, "Want a cup of Joe?"

"No more to drink right now," I answered, and besides, more beer, no way.

Dan came back with, "It's not beer. A cup of Joe is coffee. You want a cup of coffee?"

"Sorry."

"I know you are sorry, but, do you want a cup of coffee?"

"No thank you," I said, and hoped that I answered in the right way this time.

For now, I just wanted to take in the sights. Every time we passed a grass house, it reminded me of going through a National Graphic Magazine where they did a photo spread of places like this. Nothing here seemed real to me right now, because it was so quiet, so very quiet.

I was going to ask Dan some questions about this area when he looked at me, pointed, and said, "There's Dong-Tam, and we'll be there shortly."

Go figure; I should had guessed that we were only a few minutes away after I finished my, crap thing.

"What about our unit? Is our ship there?" I asked.

"I don't see her yet. She might be up river a little ways, or she hasn't arrived," Dan answered.

The only thing I saw on the river was this little kid making his way toward us. I didn't know what he wanted with us, and I had nothing to give him anyway. Joe floored the boat, and we blew right on by him. The wake from the boat almost turned him over. He was all smiles approaching us, now he looked all pissed off. Whatever. We were almost there and that's good news for me.

Chapter 6

After about twenty minutes, we finally docked along side ten other PBRs, and an assortment of other patrol boats. As our boat tied up, Dan and Joe started saying their good byes. With that, I picked up my sea bag and worked my way off this luxury cruise. I take that back; I should not be making fun of Joe's boat. I had a very educational experience and I earned the right to say that I was in combat. I wish I could have kept the rifle I used, because it was my first time and all that.

Joe shouted, "Peace."

"No sweat," I answered thinking that I was using that phrase correctly. I continued with, "Thanks for the exciting ride and I hope you make a good decision for yourself this week."

Dan grabbed his bag, made his way along side me, and said, "Let's find the air terminal and check for our unit."

I asked, "Why do we need to check at an air terminal for the location of a ship?"

"Simple, there's no harbor master here on an air base," Dan explained.

I did not have a problem with that and I just followed Dan since I still had no idea of how to get around. Besides, he was my tour guide. I made one last look back at Joe and his boat. Behind him, I could see a large ship in the middle of the river and that had a number of patrol boats tied along side. I asked

Dan, "What's that out there? Could that be our unit in the middle of the river?"

Dan looked back said, "Nope, not her, that's the Benewah."

Now the ship looked out of place because it was so big and on such a small river. She towered over all the patrol boats.

Dan said to me, "If you're wondering, it's about the same size and color as our ship."

"Looks like a big sitting target out there, don't you agree," I asked.

"That's most correct my friend. Remember, I told you before that we'll be standing a lot of watches mostly because it's just that, a very big sitting target," Dan answered as we continued on our way to the air terminal.

As we approached the terminal, Dan smiled, pointed toward a parked C-130, and said, "Doesn't that C-130 look familiar to you?"

"No, why would it? It's just my second day here. How many C-130's do you think I've seen in two days?"

"She's the one that we were scheduled to fly out on earlier this morning. Remember, the working party?"

I looked again and said, "Yes. It does look familiar."

To my surprise, the same guys were now unloading the C-130. "Look at them working so hard in the hot sun," I said with some selfish pride.

Dan looked over and said, "Yeah, and you think you had a bad day."

I added trying to fit in with the way Dan talked, "Well, this gives me the urge to down a couple of cold beers. What do you say about you and I finding a place in the shade and downing a few cold beers before we continue with our mission?"

Dan responded approvingly, "You catch on fast. You are going to work out just fine my, new friend."

With that good fortune, I continued with, "Cold beer in the shade is just what we need. We've done our fare share to help in the war effort today."

"Let's see if we can find an EM's club," Dan said as he looked around for whatever it was that he was talking about.

"What's an EM club?" I asked curiously.

"An Enlisted Men's club is a club where we can drink and socialize. Once we advance to second or first class petty officer, then we can go to the Acey-Deucey Club. After that, if you are still in the military, there is a club just for the chiefs," Dan explained.

"Okay, I get it. You're saying that based on our rank, we have different places just to drink a beer?"

"Yes, even on our off-time, we are still segregated into our ranks. Even officers have their own clubs based on their rank."

"So much for being treated equally in a democratic way," I remarked.

Dan enlightened me and said, "Hey, this is the military, not the civilian world and we are what we are. That's why they put our rank on our uniforms. That way everyone can tell where everyone belongs. You see we have our own class system."

I came back with; "It's funny how Americans try very hard to make everyone equal. Then it's the military that protects those rights."

Dan added, sounding like a schoolteacher, "We protect the rights that we don't have for ourselves. It's the only way a military can work properly. One guy is always giving the orders and others are following."

As luck would have it, and with a good view of the working party, the EM club was nearby. We headed that way and Dan told me to, "Take a seat, enjoy a cold beer, and watch my bag," and that he would be back in a minute, because he was going to check on our unit at the air terminal.

I took his advice and took a seat. I ordered a cold beer and glanced down to double check and see that our bags were no blocking the aisle. Now that was much better than guarding his bag outside a men's room at a busy airport. I did not know if he had ordered me to sit here and wait for him or that, he just helped out and saved me the walk. He was higher than me in rank; but

I thought that he just did not want to walk around carrying his bag. I wondered if he would, or could order me to carry his bag as well as mine. Nah, he did not seem like the type. I guessed I should be appreciative that I was not a short person.

I looked around the bar and to my surprise, just outside on a patio area, were the same two officers from earlier this morning that were on our bus and are now drinking a beer. I believed that one of them had recognized me and was probably wondering why I was not at the working party.

The two of them continued to talk to each other as they stared at me. After a minute or two of staring, one of them decided to walk over toward me. I thought, damn, was I in trouble?

He said to me, "Young man, shouldn't you be in that working party?"

"Sir. No sir," I answered. "I was not on that flight. I came in on a PBR a few minutes ago, sir."

He said, "Very well, my mistake," as he turned and walked away.

"Not a problem sir. However, I was on the bus with you this morning in Saigon. Maybe that's where you remember me from, sir," I answered.

He took two steps, turned around, and said, "Right. So how did you end up here if you weren't on our flight? Did you say you arrived by boat? A PBR?"

"Sir. Yes sir. My buddy and I took a helo flight out of Tan-San-Nut and then transferred to a PBR just a few miles down river from here, sir."

He made a face as if he was thinking about what I just said. I still doubted that he believed me.

"Thanks," he said as he turned and walked back to his partner. The two of them talked some for a few minutes and they kept looking at me. Not a good and fuzzy feeling. I hoped Dan would return soon in case they had additional questions. A few minutes later, the two officers just upped and left without giving me a second look. I hoped I would not see them again anytime soon.

Dan had been gone about thirty minutes and I wondered if I should try to find him. Since I did not know where he was and he told me, or ordered me to stay put, I just ordered my second beer and waited. I figured Dan knew where I was with his luggage. Besides, I did not feel like walking all around the base lost and carrying two sea bags.

The cargo plane was finally unloaded and the working party finished. I noticed that everyone now headed toward me and I assumed for a cold beer. I didn't know if they would remember me from this morning, I worried that if they did, one of those tired guys might ask me why I was not helping them. Great, I thought, what a fine time to be here without Dan to help me talk my way out of this. No one would believe that I had already been in two firefights today. As I came to my senses, I reminded myself that it didn't matter what I thought, I was not on the flight with them.

About ten seconds before the first man took his seat; Dan sat down beside me and quietly said, "With any luck, they won't remember us."

It was a relief to realize that Dan had the same thoughts as me. I said to Dan in a low voice, "No sweat, remember we weren't on their flight. However; the two officers that were on our bus this morning remembered me."

Dan asked, "Did they say anything?"

"One of them, the tall one, wanted to know why I wasn't on the working party and I explained how I wasn't on that flight."

"That was it?"

"Yeah. Don't sweat the small stuff, right."

I questioned Dan, "So why were the officers drinking at our EM Club?"

Dan looked over to where I was pointing and said, "See where they were sitting?"

"Yeah?"

"Did you notice the nicer chairs and table cloths?"

I looked over and responded, "I do now."

"That's officers' seating. It's always better for officers."

"Damn, they had it nicer than me and he still had to come over and mess with me," I explained and then realized that I might be speaking out of turn. There was no reason for me to knock officers who were just doing their job.

"Why are you whispering? They aren't here."

"Sorry. It seemed like the right thing to do."

"No sweat. I need a beer," Dan said.

"What about these guys?" I asked, and made a motion towards the guys coming our way. "Will there be a problem?"

"No sweat. Like you said to the officer, we weren't on the plane with them and they know that."

No one said anything to us and each man ordered a cold beer or soda and relaxed. They were so hot and sweaty that you could hear the sweat that dropped off them and splashed on the floor.

"What about our unit?" I asked, because he should have found out something.

"Good news and bad news. Which one do you want first?"

"Good news."

"Well, the good news is that I found a place for us to stay for the night."

"Now that can only be good news if our unit is here and we'll be staying there for the night, right?" I asked.

"Just a point of view. A wrong point of view, but a point of view just the same," continued Dan.

"Is this an, in 'The-Nam,' point of view?" I asked, hoping that the bad news was not real bad news.

"Now, the bad news," he stopped for effect, "is that our unit is not here and is not coming."

"Like, where is it?"

"She's now located near a small town called My-Tho," he said as he quickly finished off his first beer.

"Will this ever end?" I asked.

"Why all the worry? You've only been here two days. Relax, be cool man," snickered Dan as he ordered his second beer.

"Look," Dan continued, "we'll drop off our things, get some lunch, see if a movie is showing here on base and just take it easy. Think about it. You've had quite an exciting day."

"You can say that again."

"You'd be surprised how many guys do a full years tour and never once fire their weapon. For your information, not everyone in-country is even issued a weapon."

"Yeah man, like us," I reminded him.

"Yeah, like us," Dan said as he finished his beer.

A few minutes passed before Dan said, "After we finish these beers, we'll need to find the quarters we've been assigned for tonight."

"Will we need to stand watch or anything?"

"Usually not, but if we're told to do so, just do it. Don't bring up the fact that we didn't stand any watches while we were in Saigon at the Army BEQ. Okay?"

"Also, I won't bring up the part about missing out on the two working parties," I said, trying to fit in and be funny.

"Be careful of your choice of wording."

"What," I asked.

"We didn't miss out on two working parties, we were never assigned to a working party."

"Got it," I answered in agreement.

I paid the tab this time and after asking directions from a few people, we found our home for the night.

Dan said to me, "Nice quarters they have here for us transient enlisted type guys."

Everything looked okay to me. I was not expecting this to be a hotel with any kind of a star rating. Anyway, if it were to compete for a star rating, it would have gotten five stars, minus five stars. There was one big room with screens on three sides and there must be a dozen or so fans hanging from the ceiling.

Dan commented, "Not a bad place for the money, don't you think?"

I then gave a look of disappointment.

"Man ole man, you got to look at the bright side."

"Like what?" I asked knowing that he was going to tell me anyway.

"We have clean sheets and pillow cases, cross ventilation and the best part is that we have guards watching over us so we can enjoy a good night's sleep."

"Your right and I guess I should be grateful. I assume that if we were unable to stay here, that we would have been spending the night on Joe's boat."

"That's right my man, and that's no picnic. Believe you me."

Like the day before, we locked our bags to the bed frame. Dan suggested that we stop by and see who was on watch. I questioned, "Why do you want to do that?"

Dan wanted to avoid standing a watch, and yet he wanted to say, "Hello," to whoever was on watch? This made no sense to me at all.

"Couple of reasons. I'm going to ask if he wants anything brought back from the chow hall, like a soda, coffee, or a sandwich. Then I'll ask his name and where he's from."

"And what do you want to do with all that information?" If there was a scam here, it must be a self-serving scam I thought.

"Easy my friend. You see he now knows that I know that he is the one on watch. Now if anything of mine is stolen, he knows that I know that maybe he did it."

"Okay," I answered understanding what he said as well as what he meant.

"Besides," he continued, "He just might be hungry or thirsty and I can be a good guy." And after a pause, "It's a good thing to be a good guy."

"Good point, good guy."

"Right. You got it. You see, there might be a million or so Americans over here, but with the way I get around, I will always meet up with someone a couple of times. This way, I kind of have friends all over the place."

"Like the little guard at the Comm-Center," I questioned.

"Okay, good point. Not everyone will be my friend, but most will."

We locked our sea bags in a neat and orderly manner to our own bunks. To my surprise, I finished before Dan and I asked if he needed any help.

"No thank you," he replied with confidence. "Do you want me to check to see if you did it right?"

Damn, he always had an answer. "Nah, I got it." I replied with confidence.

"Ready for lunch?" Dan asked.

"Yeah. Do you know where the chow hall is?"

"Not a big deal, no sweat. Let's just head out and ask for directions."

Near the doorway on our way out, we came across the guy that was on watch. He sort of reminded me of the chief we saw yesterday when we got our time and flight out of Saigon. There he was with a cigarette in his mouth, coffee cup in one hand and reading a Mad Magazine. All you had to do to make him a twenty-year chief was to add about fifty pounds and swap his Mad magazine for a western pocket book. Naturally, the additional fifty pounds would be assigned to his stomach and you would have the chief's twin.

Dan said to me, "This guy looks like a born lifer."

I could definitely agree with that comment and I wondered if all chiefs started out this way.

"How's it going?" Dan asked him.

No verbal response, he just shrugged his shoulders and said, "All right I guess."

Again, like the chief, he did not look up and he kept reading his magazine.

To my surprise, Dan said nothing more and we went past him and headed outside.

I did not know why Dan did not ask the guard anything else and I questioned. "So, I gather that the guard and you won't become friends anytime soon?"

Shaking his head side to side, Dan responded with, "He just seemed so engrossed in his reading that I felt bad just asking how he's doing."

"He looks like a chief in the making to me," I commented.

Dan snickered at that comment, and said, "Yeah, you saw that too, huh?"

"Sure enough. That wasn't too hard to miss, even for me."

We came up to a Marine and I asked him if he knew the location of the chow hall.

"Head that way, turn left and it's the third building on the right," he answered.

"Thanks, that sounds easy enough," I replied.

The Marine added, "And if you can't tell your right from your left, or if you can't count to three, just follow the smell of rotten food."

"That's cool, thanks," I answered.

The chow hall was easy to find, and yes, there was an odor and vapor trail hovering over the building. Lunch consisted of well-done cheeseburgers with cold fries and a warm soda. There was no ice for our sodas because the ice machines were out of order. Even with all that, we finished everything. Thinking about home as we head out, I asked, "Any place around here to make a phone call?"

"I don't know about this base as far as phones go, but sometime the Benewah has a facility to call home."

"You mean that ship out in the middle of the river? It would seem to me that making a call home would be easier from here than from onboard a ship." I questioned, because I didn't see any phone lines going out to her.

As if he knew what I was thinking, Dan responded with, "You would think so with no phone lines attached to her, but you need to start remembering where you are."

I knew where I was. Oh yeah, I was in, 'The-Nam.' I get it now, or did I? "Okay. Now that I know where I am and I have an idea where I can make a phone call, how do we get there and back? Do we just go and ask Jersey Joe to give us a ride?"

"Nah, because we're at an air base, we can go and get a flight out, and a flight back."

"Another low and slow helo ride?"

"Does it matter? It's only a ride out and back."

"No sweat, I'll walk on water to get there if I can make a call home," I said. I had never been this far away before. My parents were just as worried about me as I was.

Apparently thinking aloud, Dan responded, "We need to find a ride going there and back; or, we need to create a reason for someone to take us."

I did not know what he was thinking about because you just could not use military transportation as your own personal taxi. Or could he? Whatever, I was just going to follow him and see what he came up with as if I had a choice. After all, it was my idea.

After a brief walk, we came up to a building and headed inside. We passed a few doorways and stopped at the one that read, 'Flight Operations' above the door. The only person inside was some kid in his dress whites. I did not know for sure, but it was a good guess that he was new here, and man ole man, he really stood out in his whites. He gave the appearance that he was the only thing around here that was clean. Naturally, everything was still brown and green, but in this room, it was dirty brown and filthy green.

Dan started to ask him if he knew anything about flights out to the Benewah that was anchored in the river. He told Dan, "Hang on" and that he would, check-it-out for us.

He got up from his seat and made his way to a chart on the wall that was behind him. The only thing that I was able to focus on was the back of his uniform. It was very obvious he had been sitting and leaning up against something dirty. It looked as if someone used a paint roller to roll dirt on this poor guy's uniform from his butt to his neck, and that included his shoulders and both arms. Apparently, the chair that he had been sitting in was never cleaned, until this kid sat down. Sure enough, looking at his chair, it was wiped clean where he was sitting.

Moving along, he told Dan and I that there were flights that go there and back about every two hours or so.

Dan asked, "What time is the last flight out?"

He turned around to check the board again; Dan looked at me and pointed at this guy's uniform.

I said to him in a low voice as not to be heard, "Should we tell him?"

"Why? At least for now, half of his uniform is camouflaged."

I felt that what he said was true and probably to this guy's advantage, so I left it alone.

"The last flight will be around sunset. Anything else you guys want to know?"

Dan questioned, "Is that the last flight out to the Benewah. Or is that the last flight from the Benewah?"

"Uh? I'll check." He walked back to the board and after a minute of searching, he returned and answered, "Last one from."

Dan questioned him again, "From here or from there?"

"From there. I'm pretty sure," he answered giving the impression that he was done checking up on anything else for us.

"You've been very helpful and that's all we need for now. Thanks," Dan told him and we headed toward the door.

I asked Dan, "Would he know about the phones? You know, are they doing the phone thing over there today?"

"Good question," he answered. "I forgot that part. Wait one, I'll ask if he knows anything."

Dan turned around and asked, "Do you know if the MARs is up and working on the Benewah today?"

"Yes, it's there now. That's why there are so many flights today. Don't know what a MARs is, so please don't ask."

I figured that I would tell him because he had been helpful to us. "It's a way of calling home."

He gave me a look as if I teased him. With that, I would just let it go.

Dan asked, "When is the next flight out?"

Most likely being a smart-ass, he answered Dan with, "Next flight out from here or the next flight out from there?"

"Here to there," was Dan's response.

"It's leaving right about now and I don't think you can make it in time. You might have to wait two hours for the next flight."

"Thanks. You've been real helpful," Dan told him again, as we headed out.

"What now?" I asked once we got outside.

"Let's check out the boats and see if anyone is going there anytime soon. If not, we can always catch a flight out in two hours."

"Sounds like a good plan to me," and off we go to make a phone call.

We made it down to the pier and Dan started doing the same thing he did for our helo ride out of Saigon. He was visiting each boat and asking if anyone was heading out anytime soon and if we could bum a ride.

While he was asking around, I saw an unusual boat headed our way and it was very fast. Besides going very fast on the water, she sat extremely low in the water. In no time at all, it pulled up to where I was standing and I noticed that there was no place for anyone to sit.

Two gooks got off leaving the driver onboard. I thought that this was some kind of Navy of speedboat until I saw that it was an Army boat. Easy for me to tell because it was green and had the word ARMY stenciled on it.

Dan stepped up beside me and said, "You checking out the mine sweeper?"

"Mine Sweeper?"

"Yeah, it's the Army's way of doing things."

"What do you mean?"

"Well if you notice, there isn't much for creature comfort onboard. She operates by remote control. You know, like those remote control model airplanes."

"Now that's kind of cool and a safe way of doing that job. I bet it's fun to operate," I said, sounding like a kid in a hobby store looking to buy a remote airplane or boat.

Dan ignored me, walked over to the guy that drove this thing and started to talk to him. I assumed that he was just asking about his boat when he returned to me and said with excitement, "We have a ride to the Benewah."

"On that thing?" I questioned.

"Sure, yeah, why not?"

Now I was thinking, sure, yeah, and why not. Might as well.

Dan told me that the driver would be back in a few minutes and we would leave then.

"Quick question for you before we go for this ride," I asked, because something about this thing scared me a little.

"What's your problem?"

"Our helo ride was to fly low and slow to attract attention. Now is this trip being used to attract mines?"

"Good question, but I don't think so."

"You don't think so! Isn't that a question you should ask?"

"No sweat, we'll see. Besides we'll be able to tell as soon as we leave."

"How is that?" I felt this to be a good question; I just did not want a bad answer.

"Look, if he rides with us, it's just a taxi ride. If he operates this by remote control with just us two onboard, then we'll just skip this ride."

Now that was a good answer, but not very reassuring. Whatever, as he said, if he rode with us, I would have no problem riding this thing.

After a few minutes, this guy returned and started the motor. He told us to get on and that we would be on our way. Because he stayed onboard after the engine started, I figured that this would be most acceptable.

We slowly pulled away from the pier and after we had gone about fifty feet, our driver floored it. This little boat seemed like a racing boat and this was fun. I had to hang on really tight so not to fall off. At this speed, it would not take long to get out there.

Just as we were passing by a patrol boat with a flat top, a bomb went off between us and it scared the hell out of me. I was about to yell something, I didn't know what, but before I did, Dan told me to, "Relax. That kind of thing happens all the time."

Not knowing exactly what to say, I didn't say anything. For my benefit, Dan informed me that the explosion was nothing more than a concussion grenade going off. A member of the boat crew that we just passed threw it, the grenade, in the water. The purpose was to keep swimmers away and that the explosion normally killed a number of fish, which the local fisherman seemed to enjoy. Because the ride was fast and loud, it would have been too difficult to hold a normal conversation with him so I just placed that incident in the back of my mind to bring up later.

Even with the Benewah a few miles away, we made it there in a few minutes without any additional explosions. I had quite an exciting ride and I was sorry it was over so quick. It was neat to be going that fast and low in the water.

We made our way onboard without difficulty; however, I assumed that we had to check in with somebody. I thought we needed to ask for permission to report onboard and then salute the flag or something. Oh well, I just followed Dan and he apparently knew the way to the radio room. Inside we were handed a pencil and asked to fill out a Telephone Request chit. The information requested was naturally our name, rank, unit, and the number and name of the person we wished to call.

Dan and I took a seat and started to complete the form.

"So how does this work?" I asked.

"You hold the little yellow stick in your hand and rub the pointed end on the paper."

"I know that part; I'm not from California you know," I answered feeling a little insulted.

"Okay, what happens is this. A radio call from here is transmitted to a HAM radio operator somewhere in the states. He will in turn, call your number and be the go between guy."

"So who pays for the call?"

"I have no idea. I've never been charged a dime for any of my calls before."

"So what does the HAM operator do as the go between guy?"

"You'll get instruction when it's your turn. The workings are simple. Whenever you finish what you're saying, you must say, 'over.'"

"You got to take turns?"

"Yes, you see it's because you both can't speak at the same time. It's a one way, one person at a time call, sort of like using a CB radio."

"Will the people back home receive the same instructions?"

"Of course, but they never get it right. Sometimes the HAM operator will just 'click' it anyway. With some people, it gets all messed up and it can be frustrating for them. However, it's very entertaining for those of us that can listen in on their calls."

"We listen in on their calls?" That does not seem right. I mean, I know that I was in the military and all that, but I would have thought that I could make a phone call home, in private. However, I should not complain, because I was getting a free call home and I only hoped that someone would answer.

Dan asked, "So who are you going to call?"

"I told my parents that I was going to try to call them as soon as I got here. What about you?"

"A girl that I've dated part time back home. Her parents never did think too much of me, but at least she does" he answered.

"A part time girl friend?"

"Yeah, this is something we agreed to do before I left. I see no justification for a full time girl friend as long as I'm over here. This way, if we should break up, then it's only half as bad. You know, being over here and all that with no way to personally fix anything."

I did not ask him any other questions and we both completed our chits at the same time. Dan took mine and along with his, returned them to the guy at the desk.

After Dan sat back down, I asked, "How long do we wait?"

"Don't know. Sometimes it's only a few minutes and then some days you'll never get called and that will depend on many things that are beyond our control. Besides, your odds are one in four."

"Why is that, one in four?" I questioned.

"Well, either you call goes through or it doesn't. That makes the odds 50-50."

"Isn't that one in two?"

"That's right. Then it's 50-50 if anyone answers the phone, now you have one in four odds."

I never would have given it a second thought that my call would not connect. Sometimes I kept forgetting that over here things that I had always considered normal were turning out not to be the norm.

"So do you want to place a bet," Dan asked.

"On what?"

"On who is called, or, are we both called, or, are we both out of luck today."

"Nah, I only want us both to get our calls today."

"Yeah, me too."

With that out of the way, I checked out my new surroundings. Our room had six guys sitting around waiting for their names to be called. Five out of six of them were asleep and I guess this made sense because we could be here all day.

Dan, apparently thinking of something funny, laughed to himself.

I asked, "What's up with you?"

Still laughing, Dan turned to me and smiled. I asked again, "Come on. You might as well let me in on what's making you so happy."

"Highlights magazine. We need some magazines around here."

"I was just thinking the same thing," I answered. "Not necessary the same magazine, but magazines just the same."

"What I want is a copy of Highlights. You know the section where they give you a picture and you are to find a dozen or so items hidden in the picture."

"Yeah. I remember that page. Lots of fun to do. I never liked it when the someone before you would circle the items prior to when you had a chance to find them on your own."

"They need one here. Only, instead of finding a bird, candle, or a man's hat, let the search be for the VC. You know what I mean. Show a jungle area and concealed Charlie's in the bushes and with weapons and stuff."

"I like it," I said to appease him. At times, I think he had too much military on his mind. However, that may be the norm over here. Now that I gave it some more thought, we were in the military and this was a war zone. I figured for now, just to let that one go. Changing the subject, I asked, "Dan?"

"What now?"

"Where are the phone rooms?"

He responded with, "We're in the phone room. You'll see how it goes when the next person is called."

Looking around at everyone, it appeared that I was the only one excited about calling home. Was it because no one else had anything exciting to say or was it because they were all asleep?

Five minutes go by and the guy behind the desk called out a name. One of the six guys shot up like a bullet and raced to the seat at the desk. Everyone else that wasn't called seemed unhappy.

The guy behind the desk moved over a large microphone in front of him and I could hear the instructions given out. "When you finish talking, say 'over,' and flip this switch."

"Okay."

"Listen up here. When you hear them say, 'over,' flip the switch again, and then wait a second or two before you respond. Got it?"

"Yeah, no sweat, got it. I've been here before," came the response from the lucky guy making a phone call home.

Those instructions seemed simple enough. The instructions continued, "You are not to mention where you are, what ship you are calling from and don't mention anyone's full name or rank."

"No problem."

"No unit ID's, don't mention your full name and rank. And don't be a smart-ass and try and use code. If I detect anything that resembles code, I will 'over' your ass right out of here."

"I said no problem," he answered expressing that he had had enough instructions already.

Everyone that was not called, returned to their sleeping. I was apparently the only one that paid any attention to what was going on here. I guessed they had all been here before and none of this was new to them or exciting. Well, it was new and exciting to me.

To my surprise, a voice came in loud and clear from a large speaker behind the desk. "This is KAFW0799. Go ahead, 'over.'"

"Hello baby. This is Ben. Who's on the line? Is that you Eva? 'Over.'"

The switch flipped and then silence.

Then as clear as day, I could hear, "Muffin butt, is that you?"

I could tell that everyone was in anticipation to hear the word, 'over' which did not come. Just then, I could hear, 'click' from the speaker and that must have been the sound of the HAM operator flipping the switch anyway without her saying, 'over.'

The guy behind the desk motioned for him to flip the switch, and talk.

"I love you baby. I'm okay. Nothing is wrong. Please say, 'over' when you're done speaking. 'Over.'"

'Click,' and then silence.

"I don't want to say, 'over', I want to talk to you as long as I can. I love you."

Like before, because she did not say the 'over' part, nothing happened but silence.

I assumed by this time the HAM operator had figured this woman out. We heard the 'click.'

"How are you doing? I really miss you. 'Over.'"

'Click.'

When she came back on, it appeared that we caught her in mid sentence, " . . . . home and we can do the wild thing again a thousand times. I got some new handcuffs, a Polaroid camera, and a few great ideas for us to try out. Do you want me to tell you all about it now? I can always describe them in my next letter, with pictures. I even have an instruction booklet."

Now everyone here had one eye open and both ears tuned in anticipation of what she would say next. She apparently had no idea that this was not a private line, but a party line with some half dozen guys listening in on her every word. In addition, there was the HAM operator and anyone that might be sitting with him. Let's not forget the VC who were presumably listening in to furnish Hanoi Hanna with something to talk about on her show.

I could tell that this poor guy would give anything right now for her to say, 'over' or that the HAM operator would throw the switch.

We never did hear, 'over' and there was a long pause before we heard, 'click.' I guessed along with everyone here, the HAM operator, and I wanted very much to hear all the details. I believe this might prove to be entertaining.

To our disappointment and to this guy's relief, he was able to continue, "Honey, please listen to me. A lot of guys are able to hear us talk. If you must say anything, just tell me how much you miss me. 'Over.'"

'Click.'

" . . . . with both feet straight up and it'll be fun. Only this time we will make sure that the ceiling fan is turned off. Remember the last time I almost lost my big toe. Honey, did you hear me? 'Over.'"

Damn, she said 'over.' I wondered what all we missed.

'Click.'

"Yes baby. We ALL heard you. Can you just tell me how everyone is? 'Over.'"

'Click.'

"You mean you're not alone? Do you have a woman with you? God damn you! I knew you couldn't be faithful to me for even one lousy year. 'Over' to you, you, you ass-hole."

'Click.'

"No honey, I'm in a radio room with a group of guys. I don't have any other woman here with me. You're all that I need baby. I'm being faithful to you. I love you baby. 'Over.'"

'Click.'

"So are you and your buddies having a good time listening in on our love life? Are you passing out our pictures? You are a sick bastard to do this to me. 'Over' to you again, creep."

'Click.'

"No honey. This is the only way I can call you. You don't understand. I can explain this a little better in my next letter. For now, just tell me that you miss me, and how you are doing. 'Over.'"

'Click.'

Silence and then all we could hear was static. The poor guy lowered his head on the desk and was almost in tears. All we could hear now was his moaning.

The guy behind the desk retrieved the microphone and said, "We've been cut off. I won't be able to make a second call for you today until everyone else had had a turn. Sorry man."

Like animals in heat, everyone started suggesting to puts this guy call though again to her. One guy, two seats down from me shouted, "He can have my turn. I want to hear some more about this new thing of hers."

Like a cheering squad, everyone suggested that he should get a second call.

The guy behind the desk seemed most military like and was apparently unwilling to change the rules. I would have changed them for this poor guy, however, nothing was done, and things quickly got back to normal.

As if on cue, everyone closed their eyes and went back to sleep. I guessed our entertainment was 'over' until the next call. He left sad, disappointed, and in trouble. He stood up and said,

"Thanks," to the guy behind the desk. He walked out the door not even taking the time to sign up to make a second call.

"Now that was cool, don't you think?" Dan asked.

"I feel somewhat sorry for the guy. He got a rotten deal."

"You want to hear about a rotten deal. The last time I was here, some guy answered the phone and the caller's wife was supposed to have been living alone. You know, MWOK."

"MWOK what?" I asked.

"Married without kids," Dan responded in a humorous way because this apparently was still very amusing to him.

"Yeah, that's a rotten deal. So what happened with the rest of that call?"

"He started to ask who he was and what he was doing there. Now this guy on the other end was asking him the same questions at the same time."

"For real?"

"Yeah. Now the wife gets on another phone to say who he was by explaining that he's some kind of repairman or something. Now this guy at the house is asking her if she's married because he apparently thought she was single."

Dan paused for a minute as if he needed to catch his breath, "And this guy is in here with everyone listening in to all this crap. The HAM operator is just clicking away trying to get in all this cool stuff."

"All the while this marriage is starting to fall apart," I asked that with a little more feeling for this guy than Dan showed.

He ignored me and continued, "Now this goes on for few minutes, you know, both men are continuing to ask her who the other man is. The caller is asking if she's fooling around and the guy at the house is asking her when she got married. Everyone is pissed at everyone and then the line goes dead. End of story."

"Does this kind of conversation go on all the time?" I asked.

"I've gotten to hear at least one good entertaining call each time I was here. The one we got today was mild. With luck, we might get a wild one before we leave today."

I did not know if I wanted to hear a wild one or not. I believed that it was rather sad to hear this happen to someone, or anyone for that matter. I meant, what could anyone do 10,000 miles from home? "Have you ever experienced a bad call from here before?" I asked.

"Never, but that can always change. Hopefully it won't happen to me, but we'll see."

"Brown. Who is Brown? You are next," announced the guy from behind the desk. A tall skinny guy jumped up and landed in the chair. He answered with excitement, "Brown. That's me. Let me talk."

We could hear his call ringing busy. His face went from all smiles to just short of crying. The guy behind the desk said, "Sorry man. We'll try again, but not right now. Can you wait?"

"Yeah," he answered sadly and he returned to his seat about ready to cry.

I asked Dan, "Busy, did they dial the right number?"

"Damn straight. Wrong numbers are never busy," he answered me as if I should have known that.

Before I could respond to that comment, "Edwards, Edwards your turn," was announced to everyone but I knew that it was meant for me, just me.

"You lucky dog, you're up," Dan said to me showing sadness that he was not called and yet, a smile that it was me instead of someone else.

I was a little nervous and scared. I could not believe that I was nervous and there was certainly no reason to be scared. I meant, I was only calling home.

I took a seat and the microphone was moved toward me. He instructed, "When you're done talking, say 'over' and press the button. At the other end, they will be getting the same instructions. There's nothing for them to switch or do, but they must say, 'over' just the same."

"How much time will I have to talk?"

"Usually it'll last for three or more minutes," I was assured.

Immediately, I could hear the sound of a phone ringing in the speakers. I was excited with that, but the phone kept on ringing. My smile slowly dropped to one of sadness as it ranged about twenty or so times before the line was disconnected. The response from the guy behind the desk was only, "Sorry man, better luck the next time."

With that unsatisfactory news, he moved the microphone away from me and made a few notes in his logbook. With nothing more to do or say, I got up and took my seat next to Dan.

Almost in tears, I told Dan, "I've never been so heart broken over a simple phone call before. I only wanted to say 'hi' to my parents and my little sister."

"There's always the next time," Dan reassured me.

"I don't really care about, the next time. I kind of wanted to talk to them now and I'm really disappointed about this."

"Get used to disappointment my man. You're in the Navy and you're in 'The-Nam.' There are lots of disappointments over here."

Wow, that was an odd thing to tell me. Did Dan care or not care? "Yeah, but this was personal."

"I know. Most all disappointments over here are personal."

"But this was a, 'back home' type personal disappointment. Not an, in 'The-Nam,' type of personal disappointment."

Looking at the floor, Dan said sadly, "My last, as you say, 'back home personal disappointment' was with an old girl friend named Kathy. Not a, dating kind of girl friend, just a friend that's a girl."

He was being serious here and I did not see a joke or scam coming. I asked, "What happened?"

"I found out in a letter from another friend that she was in the hospital because she tried to commit suicide with an overdose of pills."

"Is she okay?"

"Yeah, she's okay. It only made her real sick and I was told that they kept her in the hospital for a few days to check her out."

"What were you able to do?" Good question dummy. I just asked a stupid question considering that he was over here, as if there was something he could do.

"I wrote her a mean meaningful letter."

"A mean letter or a meaningful letter?"

"It was mean. Meaningful to me . . . but mean to her. I didn't say anything about how sorry I was about her or anything like that. I told her that she pissed me off with that stupid stunt of hers."

I could not believe how upset he was over this. "Did she answer you back or anything?"

"Not yet, it's been a few weeks. That's who I'm trying to call today."

"Hope you get to talk to her."

"Thanks," Dan replied as he kept staring at the floor.

For the next thirty minutes or so, we just waited for his turn. In the mean time, two guys did get their calls to connect with someone back home. Nothing exciting to mention other than it made them happy to talk with a family member back in the real world.

Dan was called up to the desk and I assumed that his call had gotten through. Instead, they only talked for a minute and he quickly returned looking rather sad. "Ready to go?"

"Yeah, what happen to your call?" I didn't hear the phone ring or anything.

"That number has been disconnected with no forwarding number. Oh well, another personal, back home disappointment."

"What do you think happened?"

"Simple my inquisitive friend," Dan answered. "She either disconnected the phone, moved or died."

Without waiting for me to respond, he headed out looking sadder than before. I followed him up to the flight deck for our return flight and I didn't ask anything more.

On the flight deck, I was expecting to see a chopper, not necessarily waiting for me, but at least one already there. The only thing there now was a group of guys laying on the flight deck tanning. I looked over at Dan and asked, "Are we too early or too late?"

"Don't know. I'll check. Wait one," he said to me as he made his way toward this one guy standing near by wearing a yellow vest and headset. I did not know why; but he just looked like someone that might know what was going on around here.

After a few minutes with this guy, Dan returned and said, "We have about an hour to wait, not a big deal."

"Do you think we'll have enough time to try another call back home?"

Dan thought for a minute, "Nah," he said. "We don't want to miss our ride if it comes early."

"How about you check with one of your friends back home. You know, someone that might know about that girl you tried to call?"

Showing no emotions about this, he simply repeated, "Nah, we don't want to miss our ride if it comes early."

"I didn't think you were in a hurry to get back." I only said this to help him out, trying to be a buddy and all that.

"Drop it my friend. Maybe I don't want to know what happened to her," Dan responded with a mixture of anger and sadness.

Okay, I got the hint on that one and I did as suggested, for now anyway. "So what do you want to do now?" I asked to change the subject.

"Nothing. Just want to get a ride back." Looking out towards Dong-Tam, Dan told me, "I see a helo coming in."

Sure enough, here comes a helo. I had no idea if it was our ride back or not, but it was going to be interesting to watch it land because I was so close to the flight deck.

There was a mad scramble going on now with everyone getting out of the way. Sun tan time was over. After everyone cleared the flight deck, two guys in yellow shirts looked over the flight deck as if checking for anything left behind by the guys tanning. Within a few seconds with direction from one of the guys in the yellow shirt, the helo landed. I found it interesting to see how the one guy in a yellow shirt stood on an angle to direct the landing.

After landing, a few officers got off and quickly left the flight deck. Dan said, "I bet that's our ride, let's check-it-out and see."

I first figured that I would just wait for him right where I was. Dan jumped onboard and I thought that he just might leave me here. I took off, caught up with him, and saw that he was buckling himself in. I just jumped in next to him and quickly buckled up. "This the right helo?"

Dan answered, "Yeah, I think so."

It would have been nice if above the pilot's windshield that there would be a sign indicating where it was going. Like the signs you see on buses. Not a big deal, but an idea that would be helpful.

Before I could ask for a little more clarification, I could see the yellow shirt guy giving directions for us to take off and head out. In a matter of seconds, we were already up and away and I asked Dan, "Do you know where we are going?"

"Yeah, I think he said Dong-Tam, or maybe it was Dong-Am. Whatever, if we don't land in a few minutes then he did say Dong-Am."

"You don't seem to care. You know, our things are at Dong-Tam," I asked because this might be a bad move.

"No sweat, we'll get back," Dan answered as if I needed to be comforted.

Lucky for us, we did land back at Dong-Tam and our ride only took about five minutes.

After we landed and got off, Dan said, "What do you say we get us some dinner and see if a movie is playing tonight."

"We had lunch not too long ago, you hungry already?" I asked.

"It's not a question if I'm hungry or not, it's just that it's dinner time and I never liked to skip a meal."

"I'm not that hungry but I'll join you," I said.

"Cool. Now you must remember that if you get hungry later that you just can't go out and find something to eat at the mall or hamburger stand. McDonalds may have, 75 million served, but none of them have been served over here. Burger King may do it your way, but no way over here."

"You know, I never would have thought about it in those terms. Yeah, I'll join you for dinner."

Having been here before, finding the chow hall was easy and this time the place was crowded. Pork chops, baked potatoes, and string beans for dinner and it was a good meal at that. We must have had three or four glasses of what Dan called, bug juice. I believed that it was just Kool-Aid of some type, and other than being too sweet, it was all right. We had ice this time and our drinks were cold.

After our meal and while walking back to our bunks, I asked, "What do we do for the rest of the evening?"

"We'll get back, check on our things, and see if and where a movie is playing."

"Aren't you curious what's playing?"

"No, you shouldn't be that particular around here."

I did not know why he thought I should not care because I did care. I asked, "How do you know what's playing so you can choose?"

"First off, there are no choices or selections. There is only one show place and that shows only one show a night. So, you can see that it doesn't make a difference what's showing. After it starts, if you've seen it before or you don't like it, then leave and head back to your bunk and do nothing. Unless of course you have something else to do."

"No sweat, just asking; any movie will be fine with me."

We found our things secured and after Dan asked for directions for tonight's show, we headed out. The theater was in a small corner of a warehouse and there were only about two-dozen guys there. There was a 16mm movie projector in the back of the room and next to it were four cans of film. We walked over to the projectionist and Dan asked the guy setting up the projector, "What playing tonight."

"Four episodes of Laredo."

Dan told him, "Thanks."

I questioned, "Laredo?"

"We have four, shit-kicking westerns tonight."

I questioned, "I've never heard of the movie, Laredo, and there are four of them?"

"These are not movies, these are four shows from TV, and they are not too bad. We don't have any commercials to sit through."

Like he said earlier, I had nothing else to do and this was the only show in town, so I might as well enjoy myself.

Just then, I heard a truck horn outside and Dan asked me, "You want a snack or soda while you watch the show?"

"I thought you said there are no snacks over here."

"Sorry, I forgot about the, Roach Coach.

"And that is?"

"Sort of like an adult ice cream truck. She sells stuff like sodas, and chips, cookies and crackers. She drives around the base all day long and apparently, it stops here just before show time. I just haven't seen one for a while. Come on, my treat."

I walked out with him and said, "I only want a soda." The Roach coach reminded me of those lunch wagons that I had seen around construction work sights.

We made it back inside just as the first of the four shows started. He was right, these were just TV shows, and seeing four in a row was enough for me. After four hours, heading back for a good night's sleep will be the highlight of the evening for me. After making my bed and settling down, I was ready to call it a night. I was thinking how I should keep a log or something and record the things I did today. Otherwise, I would get back home and what I did remember would not be believed by anyone. I was still having trouble believing that myself and I did it, and that I had done it all in one day.

I asked Dan, "Do you have an alarm?"

"No, we won't need it."

"We won't?"

"No, because when it's time to get up, you'll hear everyone else getting up and you won't be able to sleep in."

"Well, take care and I'll see you in the morning."

"Good night," Dan replied and I fell sound asleep.

Chapter 7

Two quick, loud, and earsplitting explosions woke me from a sound sleep. I sat up in my cot and found myself in total bewilderment, because this was happening in the middle of the night. Hearing explosions, people yelling at one another, waking up in a strange bed, and being in the dark was not my idea of a wake-up call. Setting all that aside, what was I to do about all this?

"Charles, let's get it in gear!"

Hearing Dan's voice did make me feel a little better. I had never been one to get right out of bed, but I knew this habit had to change soon, if this was an example of how wake-up calls were normally done over here.

"We need to get to a bunker, and we need to get there, like right now. Follow me!" Dan insisted as he yelled at me, as he was getting himself together.

My pants and boots were easy to put on because they were still too big. I felt like a firefighter that was getting ready for a fire, that all I needed to do was to step into my clothes.

Heading out behind Dan, I was very appreciative about having someone to follow at a time like this. Just outside the doorway, Dan came to a halt as if deciding which way to go. He looked right and then left, then right again. I thought, great, he had no idea where to go. Everyone else appeared to have a place to go as they all ran on past us.

Just then, Dan took off to his right and headed on down the street. I figured that going right was as good a direction as any. To make things just a little more interesting, it just happened to be a very dark night and it was difficult to see where I was running.

About every few seconds or so, an explosion would occur. It was then that I could see a little better. Nothing was hitting close to me, yet the flashes were still very bright and were lighting up the area.

I saw a puddle of water in front of me and I decided to jump over it. (Not that jumping over this little puddle was any big deal; I just don't like getting wet.) With my jump up, my pants went down, and me right along with them. I landed and slid right on my stomach, a real belly flop of a landing. The fall would have been softer if I would have just landed in the puddle. However, I made it over the puddle and landed hard on the gravel.

Dan looked back and yelled, "You okay? You hurt?"

"I'm all right."

In a soft, hard tone he said, "Then get it up, and let's go!"

I got up quickly and adjusted my pants. Again, I was off and running, trying to keep up so that I would not to lose him. When I fell and skidded down the road, some gravel scooped right into my pants. With each step, a few stones would make their way down a pant leg. Some would fall out and away but most of them just made it right into one of my boots. If I had known all of this before my jump, getting a little wet would have been completely acceptable considering my present situation.

With no socks on my feet, these stones started to cause some pain. They were being knocked all around my boots like pinballs in a pinball machine. I thought about slowing down, until another mortar round would go off somewhere near by. This quickly rekindled my fear, and I set aside my little foot problem. I must keep up with Dan, even if he didn't know where he was leading me.

Just to make things a little more interesting, a guy ran around and past us with no clothes on at all. All I could see were two bouncing white cheeks heading down the road, and he was making better time than I was. I could only guess that he got his pants at the Army BEQ as I did. He must have figured it to be easier to leave them behind, literally, or maybe he just ran right out of them as I might do with mine at any minute now. If I was not wearing my pants, I just knew that I would easily make better time; and probably could not have fallen and picked up an extra pound of stones.

What a night this started out to be. This was not what I expected a mortar attack to be like. In the movies, every time something got hit, it always went up in a huge ball of fire. Probably just a gasoline fire for show. Here, it was just a lot of noise, and I really felt the explosions. It was hard to explain, but it felt like sound waves hitting me from a set of very large base speakers.

From what I could tell, most of the hits were just hitting the ground, and not a building or anything. I also could not hear any secondary explosions. What was I saying, secondary explosions? I did not even know what a secondary explosion was, much less what one sounded like. I could only hear, feel, and see the bright flashes from the explosions. First, second, or third explosions, they all sounded the same to me: frightening.

One of the first things Dan mentioned to me about Vietnam was the fear and fascination of being over here. I felt both fear and fascination right now. I kind of wanted to be near the action and yet far enough away that I didn't get myself hurt.

After running a few hundred feet behind Dan, I followed him down this hole in the ground. We made our way down into the bunker, and worked our way to the next available seat beside the people that arrived moments before us. The explosion sounds were muffled now because we had a few feet of dirt between the outside and us. It was a little dark in here, except for a red light in the ceiling. I was still nervous about what had just happened and I wanted to talk to anyone about it when I noticed that I was totally out of breath.

After I caught my breath, I realized that I was more scared now than when I was outside running for my life. I did not think that I would be able to hold a conversation until I had at least calmed down a little bit, and right now, I was scared shitless. I best just sit still and pull myself together before I tried to start up a conversation. Besides, I was too embarrassed to let anyone see how scared I was right now. I would just sit here, get my breath back, and think about what I had just experienced. This was not as cool as I thought it would be, because it looked different in the movies.

Looking around at everyone, I noticed that no one was talking about what was happening outside because everyone was talking about other things. You know, like what plans they had for tomorrow or how their day has been so far. Even how upset they were that they were losing a good night sleep.

I could see the guy that passed me with no clothes on was seated two seats down from us. He did not seem to mind that he was completely out of uniform and no one else paid him any attention.

Dan must have made a good guess on which way to go when we left the barracks, I surmised. I must find out if he was guessing, or if he really knew which way to go.

"Dan," I said to get his attention, now that I had calmed down a little. "So how did you know which way to go? Was this a lucky guess for you, or did you have an idea on where to go?"

I was waiting for him to say it was a good guess; otherwise, how was he going to explain this one?

"It was an easy choice, not even a big deal," he responded with confidence.

"Yeah, apparently you made a guess, but a good choice."

"If you didn't like my choice, or my guess, then why did you follow me?"

Wanting to take my foot out of my mouth for what I just said, I answered, "I had nothing else planned for tonight, and I thought I would just accompany you."

"No problem, then the next time I'll follow you."

Damn, I just pissed him off and that was not my intention. Not a very good move on my part considering I did not know where in Vietnam I was, and I did not know where I was headed.

Hoping to change the focus on what I had said, I came back with, "Just joking, my man, just joking. How did you decide on this place? Besides, I might find myself in this type of situation one day. I might be the first one out the door, and I wanted to know in advance how I should decide on things like this." Now that came out making him look good.

"I just watched everyone as they ran by," he said as if I should have known this.

"And exactly what does that mean?"

"Their direction was import to me," Dan explained."

"And why is that?"

"I assumed that the ones with guns were going to take up a position; you know, to get into the action or guard something."

"Yeah, and the ones without guns?"

"I thought that the ones without guns were either heading for a bunker for protection or to a location to get a gun, and at the time, it seemed as good a direction as any for me to pick."

Again, he made it sound so simple, and yes, that was a good guess.

"So how long do we sit here?" I asked.

"Don't know."

"Then how will we know when it's okay to go?"

"We'll just follow everyone else as they leave."

"How will we know that they're leaving at the right time?"

"If it's the wrong time, then once outside, they'll hear explosions or gunfire. Then they, you and I, will return."

"That makes sense to me. So, what's next, you know, after we leave here?"

"We'll just head back and hope that our bed and things are all right. If so, we'll just get some sleep and hope for a quite night. If not, then we'll gather our things, if we can find them, and we'll find another place to sleep tonight."

I thought what he said was most interesting.

Dan continued, "However, if our things are blown up, well, that will ruin our night."

"What?"

"What? What do you mean, what?"

"What, I mean blown up, what," I assumed that I made this question clear and I really wanted an answer, a straight one.

"Bombs are to blow things up and that means that things are blown-up."

"I never thought about it in that way," I answered, and I guessed that I looked odd with that comment.

"What is it that you think bombs do?" Dan inquired, looking at me as if I were a child.

"This is my first bombing. What do I know? Remember, the FNG and all that."

"If our shit is blown up, this will only create a small problem. The Navy will issue us new shit that can be blown up at a later date."

I never realized that when things were blown up in war that some of those things could be my things. I always thought that the only things that were destroyed were jeeps, tanks, ammo dumps, bridges, planes, and not personal stuff like my bed and clothes. "You mean that there's a possibility that all I have left are these pants and boots that I'm wearing?" I asked, hoping this would not be true.

"Yes, my new, fashion statement friend."

I did not find this amusing at all, and I asked, "Have you ever lost any of your things? You know, like were you in a situation like this before?"

"Yeah, one time I lost some of my extra stuff."

"What do you mean, extra stuff?" I didn't know why I even wanted to hear this right now. I was trying to be serious and learn something. This might be one of his simple tricks.

"Think about this. When you left home, you only took some of your stuff with you because you believed that you'd be returning someday for the rest of your stuff, right?"

"Yeah, so?"

"So, you have some of your stuff in your sea bag, not all of your stuff. Your personal important stuff, okay?"

"Okay."

"And now this is when it gets important, and I want you to please pay attention."

"Is this like the mosquitoes on the bus the other day?" I asked.

"No man, just listen to this."

"Okay, okay."

"First, you become settled in after you unpack. If you must get away for a few days, you only take parts of your stuff with you, right?"

"Right."

"So this stuff that you leave behind is extra stuff. You didn't leave it back home and you didn't take it with you because you only took the good stuff. Are you following me so far on this?"

"Yeah?"

"Now it was this, extra stuff that was blown up and sunk along with a PBR about a year ago."

"For real?"

"Yeah, for real."

"What did you lose?"

"Nothing very important and as I said, it was only, extra stuff. I don't even remember all the stuff that I lost."

For a moment, he looked sad and I could only assume that he was thinking about what he really did lose. I believed that he was telling me the truth on this one and I did not believe that he wanted to talk about it by the way he was looking down at the deck. Maybe he lost more than stuff. Maybe he lost a friend or something. So, for now, I will just leave that one alone.

With nothing to do, and Dan not talking right now, I might as well do an inventory in my head about what I had in my sea bag. I was trying to classify my things into two groups, stuff, and extra stuff. With everything in my sea bag being Navy issue, I could only assume that it was all-important stuff; otherwise, the Navy would not have issued it to me. Maybe after a few months, I might start to collect some additional stuff. Giving this some thought, I did leave a lot of stuff home.

An hour passed, and we started to hear some people outside talking. It appeared to me, anyway, that it would be okay to leave or those people were very brave to be out there talking.

People were now starting to head out one at a time and Dan and I just followed the crowd. Even the guy with no pants on made his way out with the rest of us.

Once outside, I saw one small fire a few hundred yards away. I suggested, "Lets go see what's on fire"

"There's really nothing to see. Our best bet is to check on our stuff and to get some more sleep. Remember, our stuff might have been blown up and be on fire."

He was right about that, and we should check on our stuff first. If this were back home, everyone would be heading toward the fire to see what was happening. Here, no one seemed to care because most guys were talking about going back to sleep. Although I was wide-awake, I did agree that it would be in my best interest to get some additional rest. I had no conception what might be in store for me tomorrow and I really hoped that my stuff was not on fire.

I could see my first letter home to my parents now. "Please send underwear, shoes, and socks. I need to replace my stuff that got blown up."

We found our barracks untouched and I headed straight to sleep along with everyone else. Lying in bed for a few moments, I found myself thinking about what had just happened. I kind of wanted to talk about it because all this was really something to experience. I also wanted to write a letter, but I realized that I needed to get some sleep. Besides, as I looked around I noticed that I was the only one that was awake, and with little trouble, I fell asleep too.

We had an uneventful night and I was up at 0700 with everyone else. Dan was across from me sitting up in bed, and he said, "Ready for breakfast? Come on, Uncle Sam is treating."

"Yeah, I'm ready. By the way Dan, did I have a nightmare last night, or did we get shelled?"

I knew what his answer was going to be, but I hoped that he would tell me that I did have a nightmare and that our little trip to the bunker was just a dream. If the last few days were any indication of the next twelve months, I was in for a world of shit.

With a smile he said, "We had a little of both last night. We did get shelled, and I guess you can consider that a nightmare."

"Thanks, and yeah, I'll join you for breakfast."

For the next few minutes, we both did the trick with our sea bags and locked them to our beds. We finished about the same time and I followed him out the door.

After breakfast, we returned and got our things together to take a shower. We headed around to the next building to our left where the showers were and stepped inside.

Inside was a small room with a few clean towels on a table. There were two doors against the back wall, and there were no signs above them such as, "In," "Out," "Enter," "Exit," or "Men" and "Women." As I was deciding which door to use, an oriental woman walked out the door on the right. She appeared to be a cleaning woman because she was dressed and was carrying a spray bottle with a roll of paper towels.

I would wait for her to leave before I took off my clothes. Dan, on the other hand, wasted no time in getting undressed. The presence of the cleaning lady was of no apparent concern to him, so I followed his example. We both finished and laid our clothes out on the bench.

Walking in first, I used the door on the left and Dan used the door on the right. Once inside I noticed that this was just one big shower and both doors led in and out. Depending on which way you were going. I stepped up to one of the showerheads and turned on the water. To my surprise, there were two knobs, and I was able to adjust the hot and cold water to my liking.

"Hot water?" Dan asked.

"Yeah, good and hot."

Just as I started to enjoy the hot water, Dan started to adjust his shower. To my surprise, every time he made an adjustment, it caused my water to respond in the opposite manner. His additional hot water gave me additional cold water. So naturally, I adjusted mine causing him to again adjust his. It only took us a few attempts before we got it all worked out.

As luck would have it, and before we had any time to enjoy a well-calibrated shower, two guys came in and turned on the water for their showers. Just as I was expecting, my water got very hot then very cold. So here we were, four guys trying to adjust the water to keep all of us happy. It took almost a minute for everyone to come up with the desired water temperature.

As I soaped up, I could hear more people outside talking and apparently getting ready to shower. I realized that I had to hurry if I expected to finish sometime today with the water temperature of my choice. Lucky for me, the guys outside were still talking and had not come in yet.

After I finish with my washing and scrubbing, I just wanted to stand under the water for a little while and enjoy letting the soap rinse away. This shower was nice and hot and I deserved it, especially after what I went through yesterday morning.

However, my best-laid plan just dried up. Dan finished his shower and turned off his water. So for now, these other two guys and I were re-adjusting our water before the others came in, and we had to start the process all over again. At least I didn't have to spend time washing my hair like I did when I had very long hair. No sooner did I get the water adjusted, one guy left and two others came in to shower. Normally, this would have been no big deal, but the water went from extremely hot to extremely cold. All I could do now was to ignore the heat, and, or cold, and just rinse off quickly. It was amazing how some things over here were no big deal and other things, such as a shower, could be such a big deal.

I headed toward the one door and noticed that there were no obstacles in front of me. So I felt free to dry my face with my towel covering my eyes while walking. I did not think this would be a problem until I bumped into and then ran over something small, like a person, a very little person. Before I hit the ground, I could clearly hear a woman screaming right into my ear. I immediately knew, without even looking, that I must have run over that little cleaning woman.

This was not starting out to be a good day for me, now that I was on the floor with my arms around this little old lady. She continued to scream and I spent more time trying to say that I was sorry than I should have. I should have just gotten up, stepped away and let her go.

Dan showed up, placed his hands on her shoulder, and said, "It's okay."

She looked at him and started to scream even more. He backed off with his hands out to his sides as if saying, "No problem bitch, you can help yourself. I'm gonna go back to whatever it was that I was doing."

I stepped back quickly, placed my towel around me, and kept repeating, "I'm sorry, I'm sorry."

The two guys in the shower continued to give more attention to getting their water temperature right than to what was happening to me in the middle of the room. The guys outside the shower were looking in through the one door and laughing.

The old lady did finally stop yelling and was now giving me a mean look. I quickly stepped around her and followed Dan into the next room. We reached down, grabbed our clothes, and headed back to our bunks dripping wet wearing just our towels. I could dry off later. I just needed to get out of there.

Once we got back and while we were dressing, Dan looked over at me and said, "You are one amusing guy."

"Glad you think so."

"Not only can you piss off officers and enlisted alike, you can do the same to little old ladies."

I was a little upset with this and added, "A woman has no business in a man's shower room. If she didn't come in, I wouldn't have run over her."

"That excuse doesn't wash. Pardon the expression. Besides, don't sweat it."

"Still, that was very bad."

"Would you have felt better if you had run over a guy?" Asked Dan, as he continued to laugh at my current situation.

"Shut up."

"I can just see it all now," Dan said, "You and some other guy just rolling around on the floor in the shower with nothing on but a smile."

"Shut up," I repeated.

"Look. There's always a bright side."

"Yeah, like what kind of bright side?" I asked.

"You have the option to be sent home early."

"And how's that?"

"If that had been a guy, you could have said that you're queer, and then the Navy would send you home. On the other hand, you could have said that you liked little old ladies instead. Even with that, they'd send you home."

"I don't see anything amusing in what you're saying, and I would appreciate it if you would just drop the subject."

"Drop it? As in the way you dropped that old lady?"

"Shut up."

With a small chuckle, he said, "No sweat, at least she wasn't armed."

I was just going to ignore that for now. If were to write a book about Vietnam, I would most definitely leave that part out. Or at the very least, make it happen to someone else.

After I was dressed, I started to see the humor in what had happened to me and I said to Dan. "That was more exciting than last night, don't you agree?"

"Yeah, you are certainly Mr. Excitement."

"Thanks. Now what do you say we find out where our unit is today," I asked excitingly.

Taking a minute to respond, as if thinking of an answer, Dan finally said, "We'll just report to the Comm-Center and see if anyone there knows anything."

With that, we both headed out the door. Dan stopped just outside, looked in both directions and I thought, great, he had no idea which way to go again.

He said to me, "If you had to find the Comm-Center on your own, where would you look, and which way would you go?"

Good question for me and I gave it some thought before I answered, "Comm-Centers have radios, and radios have radio towers. It would seem reasonable to locate a radio tower first, and the Comm-Center should be close by."

"Damn, you be catching on just fine. So with that, lead on, my tour guide friend."

Now I felt rather good about what he just said until I looked around and could see radio towers all over the place. I said to Dan, "So how about a hint on how to narrow down my search."

"Tell you what. Because you're in such a hurry to report to our unit, I'll issue you a hint. It's really, really close by."

Sure enough, I looked around and just across the street was a building next to a radio tower with a sign above the door that read, Communications. I said, "Lets try that building and see what the story is this time."

We crossed the street and this time, without incident. Apparently, there weren't many water buffalos pulling carts around here on the base. At the front door, I was expecting to find guards outside, but there were none. We made our way inside and again, no guards. We went in and found ourselves right in the middle of the radio room. The room was filled with radios, wires from floor to ceiling, static noise, and radio operators with headsets on. There were no windows and it was kind of dark inside with maps on all the walls. We stood there for a few minutes before anyone took notice of us. Finally, one guy approached us and asked us what we wanted.

I answered, "Can you tell me the location of the Navy ship, USS SUMMIT. We are trying to report to her. We were under the impression that she was going to be here today. We would like to find out if she's still coming here anytime soon. Could you find out where she is now."

He asked nothing else and responded with, "Wait one."

He walked over to an officer and tapped him on his shoulder. This officer raised up one hand indicating that he wanted to finish with the message that he was now receiving through his headset. About a minute went by before he took them off and placed them on the table in front of him. To my surprise, I could hear a baseball game broadcast coming out of his headset.

He told us, "The Mets might win one today. On the other hand, maybe it's yesterday or tomorrow that they are playing. I can't remember what day it is back home."

"These guys want to know the location of that SUMMIT ship."

He thought for a minute while looking at us and said, "My-Tho, she's anchored at My-Tho and has been for a few days now."

I told him, "Thanks a lot sir," believing that I covered all the bases.

He asked, "Anything else?"

Dan added in a question, "Any idea how long she'll be there, sir?"

Damn, I should have remembered to ask that question.

"No idea, she's been there a few days now and that's a few days too many."

Dan concluded with, "Thank you sir. That should be all for now except for one more item."

"You guys need your orders stamped?" The officer questioned.

"Yes sir, and thanks."

We both gave him a copy of our orders to keep, and he stamped the originals. With that completed, Dan and I made our way out, so this officer could get back to his ball game.

I looked over and said to Dan, "A baseball game, go figure."

"Yeah, I know what you mean."

"Now what are we going to do? I don't even know where this My-Tho place is?"

"No sweat. I believe My-Tho isn't that far away."

"And?"

"And maybe we'll try to hitch a ride. Let's take a walk and see if we can find the motor pool. Sometimes they'll have someone heading that way and bumming a ride for us will be a, no sweat situation." Dan said this with some disappointment in his voice, and I wondered if this was a bad decision or something. I was at least hoping that this idea of his was better for us than checking for a possible flight out to this My-Tho place. So far, I had gotten shot at while flying in a chopper and cruising on a boat and I had no idea what to expect with this ride down some highway.

I questioned, "What kind of ride do you expect to get?"

"It just depends. I've been the only passenger when a jeep was carrying a few spare parts. Another time, I was with a whole convoy of trucks, personnel carriers, and even a tank or two. Don't worry my confused friend. We just don't step outside the main gate and put out our thumbs."

"And if nothing is available for today, what then?"

"We'll just kill time all day and try to maintain a 'low profile' without being noticed by anyone needing volunteers for a working party. We can always take a walk into town and check out the local sites."

"Does this mean that we'll try to avoid anyone with a clip board," I asked, trying to be funny.

"Not bad my, anti-working party friend. You're getting the right idea," responded Dan.

"Dan, I have a question," I asked in a serious tone.

"Yes?"

"The Navy went to a great deal of trouble to provide me with a schedule of times and methods of transportation. You know, all the way from boot camp in Chicago to my home in Baltimore. From Baltimore all the way to Saigon, and that's quite a few thousand miles, and a number of flights. Yet, for the last 100 miles of my journey I must beg, borrow, and bum for a ride?"

"I realize that it makes no sense, but there are two things to remember. One, it's the military's way and it's not suppose to make any sense. Two, we are assigned to a mobile unit, and it's very mobile. The only people who really know where our unit is at any one time, are the ones who tell the fire support base commanders, and pilots, where not to drop their bombs. Otherwise, it's just a good guess."

"Yeah, but aren't we being missed? How long before we are considered a no-show, before someone starts looking for us?"

"You are not considered a, 'no show,' right now, you're just a nothing."

"But what about my orders?" I asked.

"No sweat. If you noticed, your orders said to report, on or about, a certain date, right?"

"Yes, but even that must have a limit."

"Look at your orders. I bet there's a three day difference between your arrival date at Saigon, and your, 'on or about' report date onboard our ship. Check-it-out, am I right?"

I took my orders out of my pocket and gave them a quick check. I found him to be correct. "Yeah, your right." I said.

"Take notice that you're given the same amount of time to get from Baltimore to Saigon as you were to travel the last 100 miles?"

"Yes, you're right again. Sorry I asked."

"No sweat, ask anything anytime."

Dan could tell that I was not completely satisfied with his answer. He turned to me and said, "Look, this is typical for anyone reporting to a mobile unit. There's a certain amount of hit and miss in trying to locate your unit. To cover our asses, each time we report to a Comm-Center, sleeping quarters or something like that, we just have them stamp our orders."

"Why?"

"This will show that we're attempting to find them and we can account for our time. Besides, we don't want them to count this as our leave time."

"No shit. You mean this might be counted as my vacation. I mean leave."

"No, no, no. I got it covered. Don't sweat it."

I was thinking, "Great. I could get shot at and have this count as my military leave and to make it worse, I didn't have any leave time built up yet." I wondered if I got any sick time.

Along with this issue, I also wondered if that my count of 365 days in-country started the day I arrived in Saigon. On the other hand, did it start after I arrived at my unit? Naturally, I hoped that it started when I arrived in-country. I was about to ask Dan this question when he stopped this Marine private walking by and asked for directions to the motor pool.

"Shit man. Id's don't knows no nothin' about no motor pool. Besides, Id's never got no reason to go visit no motor pool."

This guy sounded as if he came from the back hills where the Hatfields the McCoys fought each other and then married each other's cousins.

"Id's only knows" he continued, in his slow southern draw, "where I'd sleep, eat, work and the shortest way be to the bunkers. Id's ain't not never been no other place and that's all Id's knows."

With a sarcastic tone, Dan asked, "So that's all you be knows?"

"No man, Id's knows three more things," he quickly responded as if he had a canned answer. "Id's knows that the VC are outside the fence and us Marines are inside the fence."

Dan asked, trying all the while trying not to laugh at him or even crack a smile, "And the third thing that ya knows?"

"Ugh, the most important thing that Id's knows is that I'd only got six more days left before Ids gets to go home," he said proudly. He then smiled at the two of us and continued on his way. Wow, he told us I surmised.

"He may not be the smartest man around, but he's going home in six days and we're not. Serving and completing a year here is more important at times than having brains," Dan said as we continued on down the road looking for the motor pool.

After about thirty minutes of walking around and having asked two other Marines for directions, we found the motor pool. There was no sign that said, 'Motor Pool.' Just a place that looked like a parking lot where many vehicles were parked, and were naturally painted green, and brown. As I expected, there was someone walking around with a clipboard in his hand.

Dan walked up to what appeared to be a sergeant, the one holding the clipboard, and started talking to him as if they had been friends for a long time. Dan had a way with people, and I guessed he was aware of this and took advantage of it to the max.

A jeep pulled in and the guy with the clipboard pointed toward the front bumper and shouted to the driver, "So where did you bag the rat?"

After the driver stopped the jeep, he got out, walked toward him, and said, "I knew I hit him about ten miles ago."

He kicked the rat to make sure it was dead and said, "I was wondering what happened to him. I had him in my sights and I knew I hit him, but when I looked back, I didn't see him. I assumed that I squashed him so bad and that I flattened him flatter than a pan cake."

"Did you bring him back to eat, or to sell it to one of the locals?" The sergeant asked him.

Dan and I stood by while these two guys were trying to decide what to do with this very large and very dead rat.

"I'm glad that the cooks aren't around," Dan said.

"No way would they cook it for us. Right?" I asked.

"Of course not. Don't be silly. It'll be for the officers," Dan informed me as if he was telling the truth.

We could hear the driver of the jeep suggesting to the sergeant that they put the rat into this thing called the 'wash bucket,' whatever that was. Both men appeared to have struck gold with this idea of theirs and they were now going over the details. I could not hear all that much, but I would like to see what was going to take place here.

"What'll you think they're going to do?" I asked hoping to be included with whatever they decided to do.

"Don't know. Do you want to hang around and see? You know, we don't have a ride yet or anything," Dan asked giving the impression that he too wanted to see how this turned out.

"Yeah, why not," I answered in agreement.

The sergeant stepped to another jeep that was parked a few feet away. The driver looked down at the rat that he bagged and kicked it again to make sure that it was dead. He reached down, pulled it away, and dropped it in front of the jeep.

The sergeant returned with a bucket full of soapy water and cleaning rags. He looked over at Dan and I and said, "This is going to be cool."

"Let us in on this," Dan asked with a little boyish smile on his face.

"You see, when this guy comes back to finish washing that jeep, he'll find a dead rat in his wash water."

The four of us just chuckled and I think we all agreed that this was going to be a great trick. I only hoped that we didn't have to hang around too long to see the results.

With the rat mixed in with the rags, the sergeant returned the bucket next to the jeep where he found it. He hurried back to us as if he was a little kid playing a trick on a parent. The four of us got into some small talk to kill time.

A few minutes later, this guy was heading our way and the jeep driver said; "Here he comes. Don't stare at him or it might give us away."

Dan said, "How we gonna give it away? It was under two layers of rags and we can always say that we have no idea how the rat got there."

This guy was just a little kid that must have just turned 17 yesterday. Whatever, he was in for a surprise, and as mean as it sounded, I was glad that it was happening to him instead of me.

He just smiled and said, "Hello"' as he passed one very dead rat, and us, on his way towards this dirty jeep and wash water.

We all tried to appear normal and kept on talking, trying not to draw attention to ourselves. It did seem odd for us to be talking to each other while standing in a straight line and staring at him.

He reached down, picked up his wash bucket, walked to the other side of the jeep, and with bucket in hand, started to whistle to himself. I didn't recognize the tune, but he should have been whistling, 'Pop, goes the weasel.'

We were all quiet now waiting for him to put his hand in the bucket. He looked up at us because we had all stopped talking at the same time. With this, we just turned to each other and acted as if we were continuing with our conversation.

When he turned his head back toward the bucket, we all stopped talking again and went back to staring at him, waiting for the fun to start.

As expected, he reached down, grabbed a hand full of washrags, and slammed them down on the hood. The rat was under one rag, and I believed that I could see his tail swishing around from here. We were all smiling about this and had a hard time keeping a straight face.

He placed the top rag back into the bucket and for a moment started to wash the hood with the rat. We could see that the rat's tail and legs were doing fishy tails things in this guy's hand as he washed the hood.

Just then, he saw that it was a rat. He froze for a moment, then screamed and threw the rat straight up a hundred feet or more. I kept my eye on the, "rocket rat," and all I could hear was this poor guy running off away at ninety miles an hour, yelling something about mother.

We were so busy enjoying this trick that we failed to notice that the rat was going to fall somewhere and that it might possibility land very close to us. I then realized, that this was about a ten-pound rat, with five pounds of water, that was headed toward us, from a height of a hundred plus feet.

All I could say was, "Shit," and no matter which direction I tried to escape, I seemed to bump into someone. Even with that delay, we all made it far enough away that the rat did not hit any of us. Not even a splash of rat wash water got on our clothes.

I never saw anything as hilarious as this in my life. The jeep washing kid was out of sight, and all that remained of him was a trail of dust. All of us were doubled over with laughter. The only thing left to do now was to figure out what to do with this one dead, wet rat.

The sergeant said to Dan and me, "I know what to do about the rat, but what am I to do with you two?"

Dan answered, after catching his breath; "We need a ride to My-Tho. Do you have anything going that way today?"

The driver stepped in and said to the sergeant, "I'll just put the rat back into the wash bucket until we decide what to do with him."

"That'll be fine and we'll get to it later. I'm gonna check on a ride for these two, and I'll be back in a minute."

Dan told me to, "Hang loose, be right back," as the two of them headed toward what appeared to be an office or shack of some kind.

So here I stood, catching my breath from all my laughing and waiting for Dan to return. I watched as the driver retrieved the dead rat and put him back into the wash bucket.

After a few minutes, Dan rushed over to me and said, "We must get our bags as quick as possible and make it back here like, ASAP."

"We have a ride?" I asked.

"No, this is a drill, of course, we have a ride," Dan explained.

"Great," I answered

Dan continued, "Our ride is on a convoy and it left about ten minutes ago."

I questioned, "We have a ride and it had already left?"

Dan started toward the barracks and said, "The sergeant has a jeep that missed the convoy, and it will be leaving here in a few minutes to catch up. The convoy is going to My-Tho, and it's just what we want."

We ran quickly to get our things and made it back in time. Leaving our bags packed the way we had, finally paid-off. As he had said before, just in case we were to make a quick get-a-way. We were off again.

Chapter 8

We made it back in time for our jeep ride to My-Tho. To my confusion, I saw one jeep with four people standing by holding three sea bags. I asked Dan if we were all going to fit in one jeep, and he said, "No sweat my man, plenty of room."

The driver yelled, "Let's go. I got some time to make up, and I don't want to be out on this road alone when it's dark."

He made it sound as if we were boarding a train, or that we were on a wagon train that was heading west. I was expecting to hear him say, "All aboard," or "forward ho." This seemed to me to be an exciting way to start the day with a ride to the countryside.

Our five sea bags were placed in the space behind the front seats, and it was just enough room for them and nothing else. The driver got in the jeep along with another person up front, and two guys jumped on the hood. The two guys on the hood made it appear as if this were the normal way to ride in a jeep. I wasn't sure, but I didn't think that was right. Anyway, where were we going to fit?

I looked over at Dan and questioned, "No more room at the inn. What now?" Apparently, our bags had a ride to My-Tho, but we did not.

"We have the best seats in the house," he answered, as he headed around to the back of the jeep. Without much thought, he stepped up and stood on the little fender to the left of the spare tire.

He grabbed onto the roof of the jeep, looked around at his view of the area, and said with some enthusiasm, "Look, it's the best I could do with such short notice. Come on. It'll be a fun ride."

"Not 'exciting?' Just 'fun?'" I asked, walking around to join him. "This would make a great book," I said softly to myself.

"If one of our bags falls out, it'll be fun. If one of us falls off, then it will be exciting. So for now, what do you say if we just try to make it a fun ride? We can work on creating some exciting stuff another time."

"Damn . . . damn . . . damn. Why me, why me? How could this possibly be fun?" I said to myself under my breath. Again, I was thinking about the number of ways I could get killed over here, and now there was the added possibility of falling off this jeep. Oh well, such is life over here, in 'The-Nam.' Anyway, I have plenty of ideas for a book that I should write someday.

Dan must have been anticipating my thoughts because he told me, "If you ever do write a book about your time over here, don't forget to include this jeep ride."

I didn't respond to that because I was wondering how much time the driver needed to make up, in order to catch the convoy. I looked over at Dan and said, "Just like taking a crap off the boat, all I have to do is hang on, right? A 'no sweat' situation?"

Jokingly, Dan responded with, "If you have to, 'go' on this ride, I guarantee you that we'll have no tail-gaters."

"Yeah, and if we do, we can call them, brown nosers," came my comeback, that I thought was rather good.

"That's right," he responded. "And we have a bright side to all this."

I answered, "How can any of this have a bright side to it?" Yet, I still wanted to hear about the bright side. "This ride is not a good idea," I added.

"You'll get to see a great deal of this beautiful countryside. Some guys never get off their base or their ship while in-country. Just think of all the interesting things you'll be able to tell your family and friends that you saw over here," Dan explained.

"How can I think about going home, when all I can think about now, is how to keep from falling off the back of the jeep?" I questioned, as I grabbed the top of the jeep and quickly stepped on the fender on the other side of the spare tire from Dan. Before I was able to get a good hold, the driver, without asking if we were ready, started to pull away.

We were off now and you would think to see two guys standing on the back of a jeep, with two more on the hood flying across the base would cause some attention. Well, I was wrong again. I had never been anywhere in my life where the unusual seemed to be the usual.

We were flying down the base road, and at times, the road was paved and then it turned to just dirt. Just as fast as it changed from paved to dirt, it changed to gravel. Dirt, dust, and stone were blowing up all around us. I assumed that the driver had forgotten that he had two guys hanging on the back by the way he was taking the turns, and I was surprised that we had not fallen off yet. I was worried that this might be a long ride. No way would I be able to hold on like this for long.

"Dan, do you think that the driver has forgotten that we're hanging on the back? Don't you think he should slow down just a little?" I asked.

"This is a great ride, and we're gonna make good time. Anyway, how can he miss the two guys sitting on the hood? No sweat. He knows we are back here," Dan assured me, as if this was the norm.

After spitting out a few bugs from his mouth that blew in, he continued with, "Why are you suggesting for him to slow down? He is driving slow, because we are here on the base. Just wait until he hits the open road."

"You've got to be kidding?" I asked with some fear in my voice. Correction, not some fear, lots of fear.

"Relax and enjoy the ride. Don't sweat it, and hang on the best you can," was Dan's response, as if I should just get with the program and enjoy the ride.

I asked, "How does a guy keep his driver's license driving this way? Besides, if I drove like this back home, they would lock me up and take away my license."

"First off, it's easy to get your drivers license over here. All you have to do is to volunteer and complete a written test. To keep your license, all you must do is to stay alive."

I asked, "Why is, 'staying alive,' part of the deal?"

"Think about it," Dan responded. "If you were to shoot at a moving jeep, truck or tank, wouldn't it be to your advantage to shoot the driver first?"

"Yeah. That makes sense. I've never been in a situation before where I had to consider that I might be shooting at someone, or being shot at by someone, driving or not."

"Yeah, sure. Look, just consider yourself lucky to have such good seats."

After a little thought, I believed I had a great come back to his theory and that we didn't have the best seats.

"Say Dan," I said. "I do believe that the guy riding shotgun has the best seat in the house; I think that the two guys hanging on the back of a jeep make an easier target."

"Oh my, my, 'thinking too' hard friend. Let me fill you in on the finer facts and details of jeep riding," Dan started to explain as he yelled to be heard.

I was about to get another lesson about being in 'The-Nam.' Yet, there was still the possibility of my not thinking things out the military way; so I listened. Besides, no reason not to listen, and I had nothing else to do right now anyway, other than keeping my balance and hanging on.

"If the bad guy was to shoot from the passenger side of the vehicle, then he must shoot through the guy riding shotgun. In addition, the bad guy could be shooting from the driver's side. As an example, the bullet could miss the driver and then hit the guy riding shotgun, or the bullet could pass through the driver and hit him anyway."

"Okay, okay. Say you are right; aren't two guys standing on the back still an easier target to hit?"

"Yes, that's true, but of little value."

I responded with, "Well thank you. You mean that I almost got it right?" Some of my questions were not always out of line.

"In a way you are right. However, because we are the easiest targets, the VC might think that we aren't important enough to waste a shot. Besides, if he hits the driver, and we crash, then we'll be next on his hit list."

"Sorry I asked." I now knew how lucky I was with the ride to My-Tho; I was not the one driving, nor riding shotgun, nor one of the two guys riding on the hood. I also realized how safe I was to be hanging on the back of this jeep, because if we crashed, I would land on top of the jeep, and the jeep would not land on top of me. How lucky I was amazed me, once I figured out all the angles. I was amazed at all the things that I had become aware of, now that I was trying to enjoy the ride, and not doing any of the driving.

I noticed that every time we passed officer's quarters or an officer's club, that the roadways were paved; otherwise, it was gravel or dirt, I found that interesting. In all honesty, we probably were only going around twenty-five to thirty miles an hour. It just seemed faster with your face in the wind and the fear of falling off and rolling a mile or two before coming to a complete stop.

The driver slowed down as we approached the main gate. The guard looked at us and held his hand up for the driver to stop. The guard smiled as he looked at everyone. He took out a pad of paper, or a ticket book from his hip pocket and opened it.

"What's up?" I asked Dan.

"Don't know."

I was a little surprised that he did not have an answer. I asked a second question, "Is he going to give the driver a ticket?"

"I'm not sure what's going to happen, but I doubt that the driver will get a ticket."

The guard spoke to the driver and said, "Five bucks says that you don't catch up with the convoy this time."

"You're on. Five bucks says it's a done deal, and this time I will collect," announced the driver proudly.

The guard came back with, "What makes you so sure this time?"

"What else. My expert driving skills."

"You're carrying too much extra weight this time," the guard responded as he pointed towards Dan and me.

Damn, damn, damn. "Am I the extra weight," I thought to myself. "Dan, I have a great idea. Let's get off this joy ride right here and now and allow the driver to win his bet."

"Why?"

"Look, I don't want to fall off this thing at 100 miles an hour. I don't think that the driver will stop and wait for me to catch up. It might cost him too much time and he might lose his bet."

Trying to be persuasive, I continued, "You heard that the guard thinks that he's carrying too much weight. The driver will be more concerned about the five dollars than with us. You know what I mean man; we are this extra weight."

"No sweat, my scared, sissy friend. This bet could be to our advantage," Dan explained, as if he knew this to be true.

"How in the world could this ever be to our advantage?" I questioned as Dan looked at me as if I were crazy.

"Let me guess," I responded. "A fast moving target is a hard target to hit."

"Yes."

"The driver would rather win the five bucks than lose it; and of course, anyone getting shot would take up time."

"Yes."

"Sorry I asked," I said, still not convinced that this was a good idea.

"No sweat. You're starting to understand how things are done over here in 'The-Nam.' You must always remember that you are not home, and nothing here is the norm," Dan repeated the same theme to me about being over here.

After they consummated the deal, the driver and guard, knocked-knuckles and grabbed a few fingers. Something that I thought I saw on an old, 'Spanky and our Gang' movie.

"What is that hand shaking thing that the coloreds do? I've never seen that before," I asked.

"They just be a Dappin. I don't know what DAP stands for but they all seem to be doing it. Kind of cool, don't you think?"

I shook my head indicating that it didn't really matter to me. Before I could ask any more about it, the guard motioned to the driver to proceed, and with that, we pulled away. To my surprise, the driver pulled off slowly and came to a complete stop as we moved toward the main road. He looked up and down the road, as if trying to decide which way to go. No way can we be lost already.

I asked, "What is he doing? Is he looking to see if people have guns or not so he can decide which way to go?"

"Maybe so."

"For real?" Having said that, I realized what a dumb statement I made. At least back here, no one could hear me asking dumb questions.

"No man, I think he's just giving us a moment to settle in before he puts the pedal to the metal," Dan answered, as he started to look up and down the road. Dan continued with, "Or maybe we have to wait until those guys pass us."

I looked left and saw a convoy rolling by.

"They have the right of way," Dan added.

I asked, "Are we going to get in and follow those guys?"

"No such luck because it looks like we are heading left."

Following close behind the convoy was a couple of personnel carriers, and they seemed ready to fight. Maybe it was just as well that we were going the other way.

The driver and the guy riding shotgun were talking; but all I could understand was something about a bet. The driver gunned it, and around the corner we flew. The two guys up front yelled as they leaned back and held on. It looked to me, as if they were having fun. Still, I could see both of them trying their best just to hang on and to my surprise. They did not fall off and end up under the jeep. Even Dan and I had to hang on to avoid becoming road kill. The driver and the guy riding shotgun laughed very loud, as if someone were enjoying the ride.

I heard the driver shout, "Okay, they were able to hold on so far, but we're not there yet!"

"Dan," I announced with concern, "Did you hear that? Are they betting that we won't last the entire trip?"

"Relax, there might be a bright side for us on this bet," Dan answered, in a relaxed tone that didn't really calm me down.

Trying to hang on and not lose my balance, I responded with, "What can possibly be a bright side for us on this bet? I mean, here we are hanging on the back of a jeep for dear life flying down the road."

With another one of his damn smiles, Dan responded, "I believe that the driver is betting that no one falls off on this trip."

"I don't think so."

"Look, if anyone fell off, he'd most likely stop and pick them up."

"Most likely, yeah, right."

At that moment we hit a major bump in the road and I looked back to see if one or both of those guys on the hood were run over by the jeep. To my surprise, it was just a bump in the road, or maybe a large rat. The one guy sitting on the driver's side looked back at us, as if he thought it was one of us that fell off the back.

Dan looked over at me, and with his eyes almost closed because of the wind, he said, "I bet you thought we lost someone."

"Yes I did. Did you notice that the driver didn't even look back to see if we did lose anyone," I answered, with concern.

"No he didn't, and I guess he was hoping that you would take charge of that task. So, the next time we hit a bump, just check-it-out who fell off and let the rest of us in on it," Dan responded, giving me instructions.

I questioned, "Is everything always this easy for you? I mean, don't you think that it would be a serious problem if someone had fallen off? What if it happened to be me? Who will look out for me if I'm the one that falls?"

With another one of his pissed off looks, he responded, as if I was some kind of problem child. "Look, by the time we run over someone, the damage is already done. The only thing we can do is to stop and pick up the pieces. Feeling good or bad about it will not change anything, so just hang on, and enjoy the ride."

I wanted to maintain things on an even keel between Dan and myself, especially with this ride being a bet. So I spoke up trying to blend in, "How about betting on which guy we lose when we hit the next bump? No looking back until after the bet is made."

Dan's laughter was easily heard over the sounds of the jeep and wind. "You have a bet," Dan responded. "We can even bet on how many bones are broken."

"Okay," I answered. With the difficulty of talking back here, I turned my attention back to the ride, and enjoyed myself because it was an interesting view of the countryside, even with the wind and bugs in my face. After a few miles of checking out the countryside, I realized that I had let my guard down. I had to remember that someone out there might want to take a shot as us. Hell, they might even take a shot at me. Now I was looking out for the bad guy instead of checking out the sights and everyone I saw now looked like the VC to me.

We slowed and made a left turn onto a smaller road. It was not a dirt road, but a side road, and we were not making as good of time as before. I looked over at Dan and yelled, "This has to be a short cut because I can't believe that a convoy with heavy trucks would be able to drive on this road."

"You're probably right. No sweat, he knows where he's going," Dan responded, but I was not so sure of his answer.

I then thought, here we go again with his, all-knowing crap. So I asked him, "Why do you think that?"

"Simple, my need an answer for everything I say friend. Did you notice that our driver didn't stop at the corner and look both ways as if deciding which way to go?" Dan paused for effect and added, "When he got to the intersection, he just executed a smart left hand turn as if he had been here before," Dan explained, as a matter-of-fact.

I was about to respond to what he just said when the jeep pulled to a stop right in front of this little bridge. This bridge was even narrower than the road that we were on and was definitely a, 'one-vehicle at a time' bridge.

The guy riding shotgun got out and ran across the bridge. On the other side, he stood in the middle of the road. He stopped all the traffic from crossing over from that side of the bridge. He stopped little motor scooters, taxies, and even the people that were walking from crossing over.

The driver then yelled for the two guys on the hood to get off. They got down looking somewhat lost, as if thinking, what do we do now. Just then, Dan stepped down and said to me, "I guess this is a bridge that we're gonna have to cross on foot."

"Okay," I responded, as I got off and exercised my fingers. They had taken on a shape that was not natural and I hoped that they didn't stay that way.

Dan said to me. "What, you don't have any questions for me on why we're getting off here and having to cross on foot?"

I believed that he was just being smart with me, and I answered, "This one I can figure out for myself. I'm thinking that the driver knows that we might be too heavy for this little bridge, and he's taking our safety into consideration."

"Or," Dan said.

"Or?" I knew that he would have something to add no matter whatever I said.

"Yes, consideration for our safety. Maybe it's our weight and maybe not," Dan told me, apparently hoping that I would be able to figure this out from another angle.

"And why not."

Dan proceeded to explain to me slowly so that I would hear everything he said. "He'll be going slow across the bridge. We'll be an easier target for snipers, and if he does hit a mine, it won't kill all of us."

Now that statement renewed the fear in me as to where I was and why I was here. I asked Dan, "Shouldn't we get our bags off first in case something like that happens? That way we won't lose the jeep and all of our things."

I was only thinking about that part because of what happened last night during the mortar attack. I did not want to lose all of my stuff at one time.

Dan replied with, "My friend, if the jeep blows up, the last thing you will be wanting to save, is any of your personal things. You will be too busy focusing on saving your own ass."

Before I could debate that comment, the jeep took off and flew across the bridge coming to a screeching halt on the other side. The driver and the guy already on the other side of the bridge gave each other that handshake thing that seemed so prevalent over here. They seemed really pleased that the jeep didn't blow up.

Dan said, "Time to go," as he double-timed it across the bridge. Not wanting to be left out and on the wrong side of the river, I made it quickly across and ahead of the two guys that were on the hood. Those two were taking their time crossing the bridge and the driver noticed what they were doing. Now this apparently pissed him off, and he yelled, "I'm pulling out now, with or without you guys. You two can get onboard like ASAP, or you can get there on your own. Don't mean nothin to me."

They must have realized the seriousness of what was said, because they made it across and jumped on the hood in quick fashion. Without delay, we were off and flying down the road. After a few miles, the jeep started to spit and sputter a little and then picked up speed. A mile or two later it happened again; only this time, the spit and sputter part lasted a few seconds longer.

Dan and I glanced at each other and I believed that we were running out of gas. I said to Dan, "Think we're out of motion-lotion?"

"So much for the driver's bet if we are," Dan told me, looking as if he was ticked-off.

I was a little worried about running out of gas in the middle of nowhere and was concerned about the driver's bet. I would have been glad to give the driver the winnings if he would slow down a little. Well not, it was going to be hell for us to hang on, if we must stop for gas and make-up the time.

I asked Dan, as I hoped for a positive answer, "If we are carrying an extra gas can, does that mean that the driver will make an unscheduled pit stop and then drive even faster to make up for the lost time?"

"A good driver with a good pit-crew will probably try to add the gas without stopping."

Dan could not be serious about that. In 'The-Nam,' or not. No one really attempted stupid stuff like that. I started to ask Dan if he was serious when I noticed that he was looking all around the jeep as if checking for a gas can.

The spit and sputter started up again and this time it did not stop. With all the weight onboard and the airflow hampered by people on the hood and back fender, it did not take long for us to slow to a stop. The driver got out and he seemed pissed, mad, disappointed, and embarrassed, not to mention the problem that he was going to lose his bet.

"What's up?" I asked Dan as we both watched to see what the driver was going to do next.

With a look to the rear of us and then a look forward, as if trying to see over the horizon, he said, "I don't see the Texaco Star and that tells me that we might need to sweat a little."

"Surely, this guy must have a radio or something," I questioned.

"My name is not Shirley," Dan joked.

"I know that, you know what I mean."

"If my guess is right," Dan said as if taking up for the driver and our misfortune, "I bet that he left in such a hurry that he forgot things like gasoline and a radio."

"In so many words, what does that mean for us now?" Not wanting to know the answer, I got down from the jeep and allowed my fingers to return to their natural shape.

Dan stepped down and wiggled his fingers to take out the kinks in his hand. He then told me, “It appears that most military traffic on this road travels in convoys, and with the convoy ahead of us, it’s my opinion that we are all alone. I guess that there won’t be another one by here until tomorrow.”

“Dan,” I said, “I just thought of something.”

“And.”

“Didn’t we just turn off the main road? Maybe convoys don’t come this way at all?”

“Good question,” he responded.

“So, you think we’ll be okay? Do you think that we’re in any kind of danger?”

“As long as the local traffic keeps going by, we should be all right.”

“And when it stops?” I asked.

“Then there’s trouble in the air, and that’s when the locals know not to be anywhere near us,” Dan told me, as he looked around.

“Like in Saigon, when everyone cleared out from the other side of the street,” I said, remembering what happened the other day.

“Yeah, that’s right.”

“You mean this is something we should worry about?”

“Yes, this is a sweatable situation.”

One of those little buses pulled up, and everyone onboard smiled at us. They must have known that we were out of gas and thought it was funny. I would have found this funny also, but I would have helped out and they did not. That kind of pissed me off, and before I could mention this to Dan, our driver pointed to a small roadside stand a little ways up the road. He said with some excitement, “We have a solution, we have a solution.”

Dan and I both looked at this roadside stand about a quarter of a mile ahead of us, and Dan said, “No longer a sweatable issue; like the man said, ‘we have a solution.’”

I looked again and saw that it was just a very small roadside stand, and whatever it sold, it could not be much. It did not have a sign on it saying anything about what kind of stand it was. The only thing that was stopped in front of it was one of those small cabs. On the other hand, maybe it was a bus, because it carried as many people as a bus.

Now that I felt a little better, I joked, "So what are we going to buy, apples or oranges?"

"Gas, my confused friend. What we have there is a gas station for the local cabs and busses that use this road. I just hope they are willing to sell us some."

I could not believe that they would not be willing to sell us gas. I just had to ask, "And why wouldn't they sell us any. Is it not us Americans, that are here helping them out?"

"We are helping the South, beat the North, and if she's from the South, then she'll sell us some gas. If not, she won't sell us any, if she's voting for the North to win."

That thought would have never crossed my mind.

Dan said to me quietly, "If she doesn't sell us any gas, then we will assume that she's a North sympathizer and we'll just shoot her and take all her gas."

"This is a joke, right? You know, like the girl giving us the finger yesterday."

"Giving *you* the finger back then didn't leave us in harms way. Not selling us gas will."

Ah shit, I did not know whether to believe him or not. It did make sense but I did not believe we would shoot her.

I questioned Dan, "Why can't we just take the gas and not hurt her?"

With a look of disgust, Dan replied with, "Ass-hole, we aren't going to shoot anyone."

Again, I felt as if I belonged in Special Ed. This guy could be so convincing, that it was scary. The driver spoke out, and told everyone to push the jeep up to the little gas station. This was done easily and quickly with all of us pushing the little jeep.

The driver ran ahead as we got near the gas station. I guessed he still was focused on winning his bet. We pulled up along side, and could hear him bargaining for gas, with the young girl at the station. They were talking a lot, and it appeared that she saw his situation and was trying to commit highway robbery. I believed that he was only trying to get a good deal and not pay a fortune as quickly as he could. This went on for a few minutes and I could tell that our driver was starting to get angry. Their talk came to a halt as a cab, taxi, bus, or whatever these little things were, pulled up for gas.

After she filled the gas tank for the little bus, she and our driver talked a little more, and after some additional bargaining, our driver reached in his wallet, and paid the girl for a gallon jar of gas. It appeared to me that the gas was a little watered down, because it was rather clear, not the golden color that gasoline normally was.

As the driver approached us, he said in a loud voice, "I will not ask anyone to pitch in for the gas, that is, if everyone will promise not to tell anybody that I ran out."

Naturally, everyone just nodded yes, because we were just happy to be almost on our way. The driver emptied the gas into the tank, and then to my surprise, he took out his pistol that was strapped to his side. Damn, he just might shoot her. I looked over and the gasoline girl was talking with another driver that just pulled up for gas or directions.

The driver then handed the jar to the guy that was riding shotgun and said, "How high and far can you throw this thing?"

"Far enough to not shatter any broken glass on us," he replied most assuredly.

The driver saw the confused look on my face and explained directly to me, "With the price she charged me for a gallon of gas, I believe that this jar is a, 'no deposit, no return jar.'"

"Do you think it'll burn?" The guy holding the jar asked.

The driver smiled and said, "Don't know and don't care."

The driver got into a stance and held out his pistol with two hands pointing toward an open field. The guy holding the jar took a few steps to his side and said, "Ready?"

The driver responded with, "Pull."

The jar was thrown up and out toward an open field. The driver took aim, shots three or four times, and hit the target. As dumb as this may seem, it was somewhat cool. Besides, with the breaking of glass into a million small pieces, it generated a million small sparks. This only lasted for a split second, and it appeared that each spark blew out as quickly as it started.

Even with all that going on, the traffic kept passing us by, as if this was the norm. If this had taken place back home, this would have caused a traffic jam with everyone rubber-necking to check out all the excitement.

With nothing more to shoot, the driver placed the barrel close to his mouth and blew away the smoke to signify that he knew that he was a good shot. With a cocky attitude, our driver sat himself down in his seat, as if this was his throne and that he was king.

Everyone followed the driver's lead, and we got back onboard the jeep. It only took a turn or two for it to kick over, and we were ready to drive crazy again.

Just as we are about ready to pull off, the guy riding shotgun looked back and said in a calm voice, "Fire, you caused a fire."

We all turned to see that a small fire had started where the debris landed. The driver replied with, "Shit. Oh well, I got a bet to collect. Besides, what did anyone expect?"

Every one of us, except the guy riding shotgun, gave the driver a confused look. As if he was talking to a group of retards, he responded to that look by saying, "You know, gasoline, fumes, sparks, and a gun, it's kind of like giving birth to a fire."

With this, we just drove off as if that was no big deal. Especially with no one wanting to be left behind. And for now, the fire would burn unchecked. Looking back, I could see that the fire was spreading rather slowly. Not a big deal, but big enough that we should have tried to put it out before it got out of control, and became a big deal. Yet, no one said anything about this to the driver, and he was not paying any attention to any of us anyway. I would like to see how this fire turned out but I was not aware of any news source that would be covering this fire.

As we passed by our little gas station, I noticed that she had about two dozen, one-gallon jars of gasoline on the shelves. I saw that not all of them were the same color. I guessed that she had high test and regular, or maybe not watered down and not so watered down gasoline.

I looked back at the fire that had now developed flames about two feet high and was smoking a great deal. Dan looked at me and asked; "Do you see a problem?"

Now what was I going to say to this? Everyone knew that we started a fire and I was the only one even taking the time to check on it. "No, no problem to report. I guess fires often break out when people run out of gas."

"It just might be the driver's way of giving the gas station girl a pay-back for the price she charged him for gas," Dan said with a snicker.

"What if it spreads towards her station?"

"Then it'll be some sight as she tries to save herself and the gasoline," Dan told me this, as if he really didn't care what happened to this girl, or her gas station.

This seemed somewhat mean, and I wondered if this kind of thing happened all the time.

Dan continued, "I can see it now. She's taking the gasoline from her station and moving it out of danger and hoping that no one steals any of it in the process."

With that comment, I dropped it. It appeared to me that no one was concerned for the girl's safety. I had to place my thoughts on things that were more important, like how to keep holding on. No need to fall off this thing at sixty miles an hour and land in a forest fire.

We drove for about ten or fifteen minutes, and turned back onto a main road. We started to make good time, when the driver pulled over to the side of the road.

I asked Dan, "Let me guess. We didn't get enough gas and we're out again."

"Don't think so this time. Look what's coming our way," Dan said and pointed up the road a ways.

What I saw was many trucks coming towards us. Another one of those jeeps with a machine-gun mounted on the back was leading the way. There were only around a dozen or so trucks in the convoy. Every driver in the convoy gave us a major look-see. I knew that we were something to see, with guys sitting on the hood and us two hanging on the back. A few drivers even slowed down to take our picture.

I noticed that each truck only had one driver and I said to Dan, "At least they have a safe and comfortable ride."

"Not everyone," he responded.

"I could see where the guys in the first jeep were a bigger target."

"True, but the guy driving that truck was certainly a nice target. He'd make a big bang, if he ever got hit.

Not knowing what he was talking about, I gave that particular truck a look. He was right because it was carrying a load of bombs or rockets. After checking that out, I didn't have any reasons to complain about my present accommodations.

The convoy arrived quickly, passed us, and was promptly out of sight. After the convoy had past, and with little delay, our driver took off extremely fast. I assumed that he was going to try to make up this additional time lost.

We drove on for a few minutes without incident; and then up ahead of us, I could see a roadblock that appeared to be manned by the local Army. At least I hoped they were the local guys. Our driver started to slow down, and came to a complete stop about 100 yards from the roadblock, while another vehicle was being inspected.

"Dan," I asked, "why are we stopping so far back? Is he planning to run this road block or something like that?"

"I don't think so. He's just gonna check them out from here."

The driver stepped out of the jeep, and with a pair of binoculars, started viewing the guards at the roadblock and the surrounding area.

I questioned Dan, "Is he looking for the VC?"

"Maybe and maybe not," Dan responded. "He might be seeing if he owed any of them money from a previous bet."

I started to think how much sense this made. Yet, in the back of my mind, this could be a trap or something. "Would the VC set up a simple road block like this?"

As if thinking of an answer, Dan replied with, "I don't know, but that's a good idea, to get a vehicle stopped with everyone's guard down, don't you think?"

Just then, the vehicle in front of us moved and now it was our turn. The driver returned to his seat and slowly drove toward the guards. As we approached, I noticed that two of the guards had their weapons slung over their shoulders, but still aimed at us. The one guard held up his hand, and as we stopped, he gave the jeep and us the once-over. It put a smile on his face to see so many people in one jeep. He said something to the other guards and all of them started laughing. I did not know what they said, but I smiled back at them, just to be polite.

"Do you think he'll give us a ticket or something?" I asked. "You know because we have too many onboard."

"Nah, he'll just shoot one of us if that's the case. It'll be less paper work than writing a ticket," Dan explained.

I hoped that I was right about this being a joke. Somehow, I was not 100% sure.

Dan looked at me and said, "I hope you're not thinking I was serious about that comment?"

I looked back at him, and before I could respond to that, he told me, "You're a gullible, ass-hole kind of guy. You should have figured out for yourself that it would involve more paper work if they shot someone instead of giving out a ticket or two to the driver."

"I knew that." I hoped he would just shut up for now and drop the subject. I wanted to spend the time thinking about how to get my fingers working again. I didn't want to focus on the joke; or, which one of us the guards would shoot first. The only good thing about these stops was that my fingers could start to return to their usual figure.

The guard that stopped us, asked the driver to step out of the jeep. He did, and was asked a question or two that we could not hear. The one guard made a comment back to the other guards, and they laughed again, at what he said.

Dan said to me in a whisper, "At least whatever is going down seems funny to the guards."

I asked, "Funny in their favor or ours?"

"Don't know, but that's a good question."

"And here I thought you had all the answers."

In a whisper, Dan replied with, "It's a hard call to make. What we have here, is that the same ones laughing at us, are also holding loaded rifles." He continued after a short pause, "That are aimed at us."

This was definitely an, unsure, sweatable situation that we were in right now. I hoped that those guards were on our side. Even with what was going down, I figured that Dan did not care, and the driver was more concerned about losing his bet, if we were here too long. Just as I was about to ask Dan another question, we heard an explosion from behind us. I looked back and it appeared as if it was the gas station. I could see a fireball rising in the air, as if a couple of gallons of gasoline exploded. Next to the explosion was a lot of white smoke that must have been from the field that was on fire when we left.

Out of nowhere, Dan pointed toward the fire and yelled, "VC, VC!"

I realized that I was the new guy here and all that, but I did not think that the VC had anything to do with the fire and explosion. Our driver pointed toward the explosion and yelled the same thing, "VC, VC!"

The next thing I heard was a lot of excited, gook talk from the guards. I didn't know what they were saying but I could see that they were in a hurry to get into their jeeps, that were parked along side the road. All that they were going to find was a small brush fire with a couple of gallons of exploded gasoline and no VC.

What happened next was a surprise to me. In 'The-Nam,' or not, it was still a surprise. The Vietnamese Army guys piled into their jeeps and took off, away from the explosion. These assholes were headed the wrong way! No wonder they needed us over here; someone has to fight the VC.

Right now, I was full of questions about the explosion, the status of the girl at the gas station, why Dan yelled about the VC, and where in the world were those guys going. Before I could get out a single question, the driver told Dan, "Thanks, great idea."

I thought, what the hell was he talking about, as Dan told him, "No sweat, now we can di-di-mau out of here while we can."

The driver got back into his seat, and we quickly pulled away. Dan and I had just enough time to jump onboard to avoid being left behind. I believed that with the way things had transpired so far on this trip, we would have been left behind for sure.

Our driver was driving so fast that we started to catch up with the cowardly guards.

I yelled over at Dan and asked, "What was our driver trying to do?"

"He's just trying to catch up with those guys."

"Now why in the world would he want to do that?"

"Because passing them would be too dangerous on this road."

"No, I mean why he would want to catch up with them."

"Because they had their sirens on for people to move over, and we'd make better time by staying close to them."

Damn, these cowards were in such a hurry that they even had their sirens blaring. "Aren't those Army guys going the wrong way, siren or no siren?"

"Yeah, maybe. They might not have even been regular Army guys. They could have been highway robbers or even the VC themselves."

"You don't think that they were Vietnamese Army guys."

Dan thought for a minute and replied, "Could have been regular Army, and if so, this would give credibility to the color of their country flag."

I knew that it was hard to hear with the wind rushing by, but I had to ask him what he was talking about this time. "Country flag, what do you mean?" I asked.

"It's had a yellow background to show how most of them were cowards. Then there are three red lines going across long ways. One red line represented the French that shed their blood trying to save them from the communist. The second red line represented the blood from Americans that were trying to save them from the communist."

He paused for a moment to get another handhold and then he continued, "And I guess the third red line is for whoever comes in after us to save them from the communist."

I started to see that the people here, just might not be up for this war that they started. I said to Dan, "You're right, I do remember that the French lost."

Dan's comeback for that was, "That might not be as bad as it sounds."

"What do you mean? Isn't it bad to lose a war?"

"True, but the French are always losing their wars."

As if he was on a roll, he continued, "Do you know why most of the main roads in Paris are tree lined?"

"No, but you can tell me why."

"It's to allow the invading armies to march in the shade," Dan answered laughing to himself.

As if he was, on a roll, Dan added, "Mayday. Even the word Mayday is French. It simply means, 'Help me.' The French always need help."

Being inquisitive, I asked, "Is S.O.S. a French word?"

Dan pondered for a second and said, "Well my inquisitive friend, if S.O.S. meant Save Our Ship or Save Our Souls. Then yes, it would have come from a French word and with an embarrassing French history story to go with it. Hell, even if it meant Shit on a Shingle, it would have been French. However, S.O.S. is just very easy to send and understand in Morse code."

I gave Dan another confused look, he added, "Three short, three long, three short, and that makes up S.O.S."

This guy was so full of shit today and yet, he could be telling me the truth. I could keep him from telling me dumb stuff by not asking too many questions. At any rate, we were presently making excellent time by following behind those two jeeps; however, and as expected, it did not last long. They slowed down and had their sirens turned off. So we passed them. I didn't know why, but I did not look back. I suppose I just didn't want to make eye contact with these cowards. I did not think that these guys could have been the VC. If they were, I would have thought that they would have shot us by now.

I did want to look back and see if the fire was spreading, and if there had been any additional explosions. However, we were in an area where there were some low hanging tree branches and stuff. The last thing I needed was to be knocked off the back of the jeep. In some ways, I felt a little safer on the patrol boat, even though we were involved in a firefight.

Because of the slow traffic in front of us, we came to a stop. We were held up behind a cart that was being pulled by an old man. It was not only slow going, but also hard to pass, because he didn't want to move over. Off to the side were a couple of kids that were laughing and pointing at us. All I could do was to smile back at them and wave. They laughed some more, and started calling other kids to come over to, check us out. This was a little embarrassing, but I would get over it, as long as the crowd didn't get too big. Lucky for me, we were soon off again and flying down the road.

Dan yelled over at me and asked, "So my man, which mode of transportation have you enjoyed the most so far?"

"Let me think about that for a minute." I came back with, "The patrol boat."

"But you were shot at and had to fire a weapon. Then you were made to take a crap over the side, and you had beer clean-up detail."

"I remembered the part about being shot at, but I did forget about all the other stuff."

Dan inquired, "Same answer?"

"Yes," I said. "The chopper was exciting, but I didn't have that great a seat or view, and the flight was too short."

"Are you saying that this was the worst of the three? I don't know why. You weren't shot at or anything."

"Not yet anyway, but I might get an injury out of this."

Dan thought for a minute and asked, "Are you expecting to fall off, get shot, or something like that?"

"No, definitely nothing like that. It's my fingers that concern me. I don't know how much longer I can hang on, and still have my fingers return to their normal shape and size."

"It won't be much longer," Dan yelled over at me.

"How much longer?"

"I'm not sure, but we have to be close."

Now how in the world could he figure that out? If you do not know where you are, and where you were going, how could you figure out how far we had to go?

"Say Dan, how did you figure out that we're almost there?"

"Simple, I heard that it was an hour or so jeep ride and almost an hour has gone by since we left."

"But we did make two unscheduled stops, and that should have added time to our trip," I added.

"True my friend, but we have been making better than average speed, and the driver wants to win his bet. And lets not forget the short-cut we took."

No sooner did he say that, when we started to slow down. Before I had a chance to figure out where we were, we pulled up to the guard shack. I assumed that this was the main gate to the base near or at My-Tho. It could have been a side or back gate of another base in another city. What did I know?

Dan said, "Told you."

The guard came up and started to count aloud everyone that was on the jeep. I was thinking that this guard would issue our driver a ticket this time for sure. However, not that I should have been too surprised at this, he gave the driver a hand shake and said, "You did it."

While getting out of the jeep, the driver responded with, "Not yet, you have to call this in first."

"No sweat," the guard said and returned to his shack to make the phone call.

Another jeep pulled in behind us and blew the horn. The guard waved his hands indicating to the jeep driver behind us to hang on a minute.

The driver of the other jeep got out and approached the guard shack. After the guard hung up the phone, those two talked for a second. Then the guard made another call.

"What's up?"

Dan said, "My first guess is that he's another driver that also has a bet going."

"And what does that mean?"

"It means that the guard is placing a call to the guard shack where the drivers started. When it comes to collecting or losing a bet, no one takes anyone's word on anything. At least this way, it can be verified."

"I see that there was at least one thing that the military has organized," I added.

"Just remember one thing, if you lose a bet, it's to your advantage to pay in full and pay on time," Dan told me suggesting that I remember this.

Our driver gave the guard another handshake, jumped in the jeep, and off we went. "What do we do now?" I asked Dan, hoping that our trip to find the SUMMIT was concluding.

"We'll get off, grab our bags, and, of course, we'll do this after he comes to a complete stop."

"I figured that part out already. After we do all that," I inquired.

Dan looked at me as if I was asking too many questions. So, before he could respond, I continued with, "Let me guess, we'll take a walk down to the river and do a look-see for our ship. If we get a no-hit with our look-see, then the next step is for us to find a Comm-Center and ask about her location. Not forgetting to get our orders stamped."

Dan now looked surprised. I didn't know if it was because I said the correct things in the correct order or that I was so far off base with this that he was just holding back his laughter.

Dan replied with, "Okay, we'll do it your way."

I need clarification on this because of the way he answered me. It was as if he wanted me to mess up, assuming that my agenda was workable somehow. "Is this the way you would do it, or not?" I asked.

Just then, the jeep stopped and the driver yelled out, "Last stop, everyone get out of my jeep and take all your things. I do not, and I repeat, I do not run a lost and found. If you lose it, and I finds it. It's mine."

One of the two guys on the hood told the driver as he got down, "That ride was more dangerous than being out-numbered and alone in a firefight."

He responded with, "No sweat, glad I could help. And by the way, you might want to clean off the dead bugs that are splattered all over your shirt and pant legs."

As the other guy that was riding the hood got off, he said as he was picking at his teeth, "Yeah, and let's not forget the ones I didn't swallow that were stuck in my teeth." He looked around and continued with, "Anyone have any dental floss?"

Another time and another place, that might have been very funny. Except for the fact that my shirt reminded me of the front grill of my dad's car, after getting home late on a hot summer night.

Before I was even down off the jeep, the driver had all the sea bags off-loaded, and was back in his seat ready to pull away.

While I was rubbing my hands and fingers together and working out the kinks in my legs from the ride, Dan was over talking to the driver. I could hear him saying, "Thanks for the ride. Just remember when you get back home, it might be hard to keep your drivers license and drive the way you do."

"What license?"

"That's cool," Dan replied with laugher.

"You see my man, they can't take away something that I don't have," and with that, he drove off spinning his wheels on the dirt road, spitting out dust and small stones all over us.

It only took everyone a second or two to pick out their sea bags. The guy riding shotgun stayed in the jeep, and everyone else looked around trying to get their bearings.

I figured that I would speak up and get things started with Dan and me. "Okay, why don't we head on down to the river for a look-see."

"Now why would you want to do that first?"

Wanting to show him that I was no idiot or a retard, I responded with, "Because there is no reason to search out a Comm-Center, if we can see that our ship is already here."

"That's true."

The only thing I could respond with was, "But?"

"Now this is just a suggestion, and we can still do it your way."

"Okay, I'm listening, what's up?" I questioned.

He pointed to the building behind us, and said, "We are presently standing in front of a Comm-Center, and we can ask about our unit while we are here. If the ship is here, they will tell us that, and we can still head on down to the river. If she's not here, they will tell us that also, and that information will save us a walk down to the river and back."

"That sounds like an acceptable modification." And why not? It did make sense, and I had no desire to carry my bag around with my fingers crippled up they way they were.

With little delay, we made our way to the Comm-Center. Just like the other Comm-Centers, it was just a room filled with radios, maps, and lots of radio static. We asked about our ship and not that I was surprised, but disappointed just the same, our ship was not here. Dan asked about its location, and then with our orders stamped, we were off to a place called Cam-Ranh-Bay. Once outside, I asked how far away this place was.

He answered, "I've been there a number of times before, and I know where Cam-Ranh-Bay is, but I'm not sure how far away it is from here."

"I'm just a little curious. If you know where we are, and you know where we need to go, how come you don't know how far away it is?"

"Simple, my inquisitive friend. If we travel by jeep, it will take more than a day. If we luck out with a direct flight, without a working party that is, maybe an hour or two."

"Whatever. May I suggest that we look for a flight out, instead of booking another jeep ride," I suggested.

"Didn't enjoy your last jeep ride?"

"I had a good time, and that was very educational; however; it's my fingers that may never work properly again," I answered him showing him my deformed fingers.

"I agree. What do you say we try and find us a flight out of here?"

"Great idea, and I don't care if it's low and slow or high and fast," I informed him.

"Sounds like a good plan for now. Let's get ourselves a flight out, and if we have some free time before we leave, we can do lunch here."

Wanting to be part of the planning, I added, "And if we're lucky enough to get out of here right away, then I'll get us lunch at this Cam-Ranh-Bay place."

Dan smiled and said, "I see that we have an action plan."

I thought that this was not all that great of a plan. Besides, here we were again, at the wrong place at the wrong time, with no real assurance that our ship was going to be where it was supposed to be. Whatever, after getting directions from a guy sitting nearby in a parked jeep, we made it to the runway and found a number of choppers and small cargo type planes lined up in neat military order.

Dan said to me, "I hope we can find a flight out of here soon."

"I thought you weren't in a hurry to report to our unit?"

"I'm not, I just don't like this place."

"Any particular reason?" I questioned.

"None really, it's just that Cam-Ranh-Bay is the place to be."

"And why is that?"

"It's a party town, and it has a great beach. If you can't make it to an R&R place for your R&R, Cam-Ranh-Bay is the next best place to be," Dan informed me.

Before I could ask him more about this, he told me, "Hang loose, I'll be back in a minute." With that, he dropped his sea bag down next to me. He headed toward this old airplane, with its engines running, that looked like one of the planes used in WW II. Just as he stepped onboard, the door closed behind him and it started to taxi away.

"Oh shit," I shouted, because this was not part of the plan. I had no desire to be stuck here with two sea bags and fingers that hadn't fallen back to their original shape. I was gonna have enough trouble getting around just taking care of my one bag, and that was if I knew where I was going.

Luck must be with me today, because just as the plane turned around, and as I thought it was going to take off, it came to a complete stop. There wasn't a door on this side, and I could not see anything in the windows. I did not know if I should stand here and wait for Dan to signal me, or to make my way to the other side of the plane, dragging these two bags behind me. The easier of the two was for me just to stand here. No reason for me to drag two bags over to the plane, just to drag them back. Besides, I had his bag, and I did not think that he would leave it behind. He might leave me behind, but not his bag. My fingers were starting to hurt in anticipation that I might be dragging these two bags around with me.

Right then, two legs appeared from under the plane where someone had jumped down to the tarmac from the other side of the aircraft. Because everyone over here wore the same boots and pants, it was impossible for me to make out who it was. Well, good news for me, because it was Dan and he was looking at me from under the plane. He waved for me to come and to join him. Without hesitation, I dragged the two bags around the tail end of the aircraft, and he helped me throw them onboard the plane. As soon as I was onboard, the door closed behind me, and the plane started to taxi again. I had just enough time to sit in my seat and buckle in before the plane was airborne.

I hoped it was headed to that Bay place. What did it matter anyway? I was along for the ride with my tour guide, and I might as well sit back and enjoy it.

Chapter 9

What an interesting airplane we were on. There were no regular passenger seats onboard. Just cargo-net type seats that ran the length of the plane on both sides. And we faced each other instead of facing forward, not to mention the fact that the plane did not have a wheel under the nose, just a little wheel under the tail that made the plane sit low at the tail end. I didn't know if we were in a DC-3 or DC-5, but in some ways, it was rather cool to be in an airplane that was this old.

Dan asked, "So, what do you think about our ride this time?"

Getting my breath back, I answered slowly with, "It's okay. I especially like the fact that I do not have to sit on the wing or hang onto the tail. I thank you that we at, least, have an inside seat this time."

"That's good, because I didn't have time to review other options that might have been available," Dan informed me

"Where are we going? Are we still heading for this Bay place this time or someplace else?"

He answered with, "Cam-Ranh-Bay, yes, and no."

"Well that's good news. At least we're heading in the right direction to find our ship."

Dan answered that statement with, "Well, yes, maybe and maybe not."

Damn, damn, damn. What was he up to this time with that answer? So I asked him, "Okay, let's hear it. What yeses, maybes and maybe nots are you talking about this time?"

"Yes, we are heading to Cam-Ranh-Bay. Maybe it's the right direction, maybe it's not, and that depends if our ship is there or somewhere else. We'll find out when we get there, if we are in the right city at the right time."

Whatever. I was not going to worry about it right now. I was just going to relax and enjoy my flight. If she were there, great, if not, that would be okay too. I could wait until then to find out if jumping on this plane was a good move or not. I wanted to change the subject, because this hit and miss stuff, was starting to get old; so I asked him, "What are we flying in today?"

Dan gave me that look as if I was the village idiot. He answered, "A cargo plane. You see, there are no helicopter blades above us and no passenger seats onboard, which makes this a cargo plane. Can you say, 'cargo plane?'"

"No, not that, I know what a cargo plane is. I am only asking, what is it, that we are flying in this time. I am curious about the type of aircraft this is. Is this a DC-2, 3 or a DC-5?"

"You didn't ask if this was a DC4."

"I've never heard of a DC-4, and I don't know what they look like. Is this a DC-4?" I asked.

"I don't know, but you could always walk up and ask the pilot. I don't think he'll mind your visit."

"Nah, it's not that big a deal to me," I said that even though it was important to me, and I was curious. I did not want to set myself up for trouble. The mere fact that he suggested that I walk up and ask the pilot told me that it was not the right thing to do.

Two guys sitting across from us were having the same conversation about the type of aircraft that we were in. One guy told the other to walk on up to the cockpit, and ask away at what you want. And that's just what the guy did. He headed to the cockpit door and knocked. The door opened just a little and a small conversation started. After about thirty seconds or so, the door opened all the way, and he went on in.

I did not wish this guy any harm, but I hoped they chew his ass-off. You could not just walk up and enter the flight deck while a plane was in the air. Nevertheless, of course, this was 'The-Nam,' and I should not be surprised with what was acceptable, and what was not. Ten minutes went by before the guy returned to his seat. I could not exactly hear what he was saying, but it appeared that he had the time of his life in the cockpit. The way he was talking and acting gave me the impression that they let him fly this damn thing.

Oh well, I was not feeling too bad about that until Dan stepped in and made the comment, "I told you that you should have gone up there and asked your questions. That guy did, and they apparently did more for him than answer his questions."

"I see that now," I responded knowing that I screwed up by not going.

Dan questioned, "You just didn't trust me, did you?"

"Yes. No. Yeah, sometimes. No, I thought I would have gotten into some kind of trouble, and you would have made even more fun of me."

"Don't sweat it my friend, I have plenty to laugh at when you do your own stuff. Besides, there's no need for me to add anything additional to the dumb-shit stuff that you pull."

"I'll keep that in mind," I answered, feeling a little uneasy with the way he sees me.

Dan sat back and closed his eyes. I doubted he was mad or anything. Oh well, with nothing else to discuss, I too, settled back and closed my eyes.

After a few minutes of flying, I started to notice how hot and humid it was in here. I felt the sweat roll down my face and back. I assumed that there was a puddle growing under my seat, from all this sweat that was running off me, as if I forgot to dry off after taking a shower. Adding this to the heat, this was also an uncomfortable flight. It was extremely bumpy, there was a breeze of all things, and I could smell jet fuel. It was probably called propeller fuel for this plane. I could even taste oil in the air, and it would not surprise me if they had to mix the oil in with the gas. You know, the same way you would mix oil and gas for outboard motors.

I looked over at Dan and said, "This is a very uncomfortable ride, and I might be getting sick. Do you know how long our flight is going to be this time?"

"Let me guess. You were expecting air conditioning or something like that. Did you really expect that a plane this old would have air conditioning installed and in working order?"

"Yes and no," I said.

I could answer two questions at a time just like him. I continued with, "The pilot could at least avoid the bumps up here. And what's with the breeze?"

"This plane does not come equipped with an air conditioning system and is not pressurized. As far as the bumps go, well, we just can't fly all that high either. Just be grateful that a plane this old got off the ground and is consistently flying straight and level."

"You're right," I answered and just maybe I expected too much.

"Besides, Cam-Ranh-Bay is the place to be, and it'll be worth the trip," Dan said to cheer me up a little.

"No sweat," I answered, as I noticed that the only thing that this plane was carrying, was two other guys and us. With no cargo onboard, that gave me another question for him. "Dan," I asked trying to ignore the smell, heat, and this bumpy ride, "I noticed that our plane was not carrying any cargo, just us four guys. Does that mean that it was returning from a delivery, or was it that it had to pick up cargo? If so, are we the loaders?"

"Don't know about that; however, when we land and the doors open, we'll grab our bags, jump up and get out quickly. Now when I say quickly, I don't mean step off and look around. I mean as soon as your feet hit the tarmac, start walking away as if you know where you are and where you are going. No matter what you hear, don't look back. And most important, don't bring attention to yourself. Again I say, do not bring attention to yourself."

"And what do we do if someone is yelling at us?"

"What?"

"What do we do if someone is yelling at us?"

"What?"

Finally, I got it. "Okay, you are saying that we just pretend that we don't hear anything, right."

He answered again with, "What?"

After a few seconds, Dan added, "We can't disobey an order if we never heard it."

"What," I answered because I had a sense of humor, too.

He smiled at my comment and closed his eyes because he was apparently going to try to finish his nap. Nothing more was said between us for the remainder of our flight. I wanted to look out the window but it was too much trouble to turn completely around for a look-see. So with that, I closed my eyes to give them a rest from our jeep ride and this soon developed into a nap: a bumpy, smelly nap, but a nap just the same. I hoped that I would not throw up in my sleep. I had just gotten the buffalo crap cleaned off my pants.

I was jolted from my nap by a hard shake from Dan. Next was the opening of the cargo doors followed by the sun that beamed brightly on me from the doorway. For such a rough and uncomfortable ride, the landing was so smooth that it didn't wake me. I remembered what Dan said earlier about getting up and out quickly. I grabbed my bag and made my way towards the door. With just one step, down I went and out the door I fell after rolling down the aisle. I would have fallen flat on my face, but instead I fell on top of my sea bag, and then bounced off and rolled onto the tarmac.

Dan stepped off the plane, stood beside me and said, "You are one funny guy. Most people can make a grand entrance, but you know how to make a grand exit. So much for you trying, not to bring attention, to yourself."

"How did I do all that? All I was trying to do was to get myself quickly off the plane. You know, as you suggested earlier. Besides, I had done this quick exit thing once before," I explained dusting the tarmac dirt off my shirt and pants.

After laughing at me, Dan placed his bag on his shoulder and said, as he started to walk away, "You had a couple of things going against you my comedy caper friend."

I caught up with him, and in some ways, I did not want to hear how he was going to explain any of this to me. Yet somehow, I did not want this kind of excitement to happen to me again. I asked, "Okay, I give, what things are against me? You don't have to add in the parts about being in the Navy, or me being over here In-country, in 'The-Nam,' or that I was from California."

It appeared to me that he was going to answer this, as if he had the answers to every question ever asked by mankind. "You woke up quickly with sleep in your eyes, and that affected your vision. The sun in your eyes, on your way out the door, didn't help either. Your fingers were probably still hurting from our jeep ride, and you didn't get a good grip on your bag, which caused you to drop it, which made you fall over it. Dehydration had probably set in, because of how hot it was on the aircraft, and you hadn't had a drink for some time. Your beers earlier influenced your thinking, and you were probably trying not to throw up from the smell and taste of gasoline and oil in the air. The last thing you remembered, before your nap, was our conversation on how quickly we needed to exit the aircraft. This caused you to jump up and head out quickly without thinking about anything else."

"Okay, I can see all that. Thanks," I answered indicating that I had heard enough already.

"I'm not finished yet."

"Sorry, please continue to put me down," I said with some embarrassment. At least no one was around to listen in.

"I'm not putting you down because you can do that all by yourself. I'm just answering your question. So, should I continue on, Mr. Excitement?"

"Yeah, sorry."

"I know you're a sorry kind of guy, but I'll continue anyway."

So far, he was right, I was sleepy, and I needed something to drink. Not a beer kind of drink, but a cold soda right now would be just fine with me.

He continued with, "Plus, the plane has a floor that was slanted down towards the cargo door and I bet you forgot that part, and you assumed you were on level ground."

"Thanks for the information and, for the most part, you are correct. Why didn't you say something to me when I first got up? That way we could have been saved from being embarrassed?"

"What's this, *us* stuff? You didn't humiliate me."

"Right, I forgot. I could have saved myself from embarrassment."

"I tried," Dan said, "but you must have remembered the other thing I told you before your nap or you didn't hear me."

I asked, "You told me to quickly jump up and out the door."

"Yes, and I also said the part about ignoring anything that you hear as you are exiting the aircraft."

"Yeah."

"I was trying to tell you to watch your step, as you were doing your Buster Keaton imitation. You ignored me and down you went, face first. Lucky for you, your sea bag went first to break your fall and save you from additional scars."

"Additional scars," what was he talking about this time?

"You must be getting mental scars from all the dumb crap that you pulled, and falling on your face could have given you some physical scars."

"I'm glad that you find me to be an amusing kind of guy," I answered thinking that back home, I was a normal kind of guy. Over here, things sure were different.

"No sweat, because you make things interesting for me and that helps pass the time. I spend part of my time watching out for the VC and the rest of my time watching you pull dumb stunts like that." He laughed for a moment and added, "I'm just surprised that you didn't fall face first into some buffalo shit."

"There are no buffalo around here, on base, or on the runway," I said, wanting him to realize that I was not that dumb and that there would not be any water buffalo near the plane.

"True, but if there were any anywhere near by, you would have found their droppings."

"At least I followed your instructions," I said, hoping to put a positive end to this.

"Yes, you did, and so did Custer's men at Little Big Horn."

Damn, this guy was still putting me down, so I asked him, "And what does that mean?"

"Well my Special Ed friend, I was yelling for you to stop because I knew you would forget the slanted floor and fall out the plane."

"At least I'm following your suggestions from earlier."

"I didn't tell you to fall flat on your face."

"Give me a break."

"No sweat man, I was just making a conversation with you. You know, small talk. Now do you feel any better?"

I thought for a minute and said, "Yeah, that was rather funny, and at least I didn't fall into any buffalo shit."

Wanting to change the subject, I asked, "So what's up for now?"

"What do you think?"

"I think we go and do just as we do each time we arrive some place new. We'll try to find our ship, and when we realize that she's not here, we will check in with a Comm-Center. We get our orders stamped, find out where the ship is and either make reservations to stay for the night, or find another ride out. Did I get it right this time?"

"Almost."

"Now wait, how can this stop-over be any different from our previous stopovers?"

"This is Cam-Ranh-Bay."

Starting to tire with all this, I said, "Here we are and it is the wrong place again. Cam-Ranh-Bay or no Cam-Ranh-Bay. We got to check in sometime. Right?"

"No sweat my man, relax. We'll find her soon enough and you'll be very grateful that you had this little bit of free time before you start to earn your pay and make your contribution to the war."

I guessed that I might as well develop his attitude towards our attempts to find our ship. He was right. As long as we got our orders stamped and kept making an honest attempt, we should not get into any trouble. I came back with, "You're right. What we have here is a 'no sweat' situation."

"Great. Look over there," he said to me, pointing towards the only building anywhere near us.

I responded with, "That must be the Comm-Center and control tower all rolled into one."

"Yeah, I bet that anything we need to know can be found out there."

"You don't know? I thought you've been here before."

He responded with, "I've been here before but not over there."

With that, we headed over and when we got inside, we asked about our ship. No one knew anything about any ship called the SUMMIT.

Dan looked at me and said, "This is not good."

"You can say that again."

"This is not good for a number of reasons."

"Damn, damn, damn. You mean this is worse than just not finding her here?"

"Yeah, because not only is she not here, they have never even heard of her. And they don't have a suggestion on how to find her."

I asked, "Is there anyone that you can call? You know, like the Navy Department or something."

"Now that's a great idea," Dan said to me as he asked to use the phone.

I thought that he was going to call the Navy Department in Washington, because they just had to know everything, but to my surprise, he asked for a phone directory. He was given a sheet of paper with numbers on it and he selected a number and called it. Apparently, there was no answer because; he hung up and called the next number. Someone finally answered at the other end and to my surprise, Dan did not pretend he was someone else. I had him pegged to imitate some officer to get answers about our ship's location.

As Dan started to explain our situation, he was apparently told to hold-on. He looked at me and said, "We'll be getting an answer soon. I was told to, 'wait one.'"

"Who are you talking too?" I asked.

"Don't know, just some gook."

"Now how do you know that?"

"Simple, my friend. He just answered, 'can I help you Joe?'"

That was funny, but I could not believe that it was true.

Right then Dan started back on his conversation with the gook. He ended the conversation by saying, "Thanks for the info, Joe."

"Well?"

"Well my friend, you were right about her location the first day you were in-country."

"What, that she's located in the Saigon harbor or out on Yankee Station?"

"No and Yes."

"No, that she's not in Saigon and yes, that she's on Yankee Station."

"Yes and yes," he responded to me as if I was some kind of little kid.

"It doesn't matter, just as long as we finally get there, wherever, 'there' is. So how do we get out there?" I asked.

He thought for a minute and said, "Yankee Station is a very big place. I have no desire to spend any time out there on a small ship trying to find her. Our best bet is to find a flight out to her. We can do that tomorrow."

I was tired of traveling today anyway and I answered with, "Not a problem with me. I could use a break in the action."

"Fine then, we'll find ourselves a place to stay and check out the night life."

I happened to be hungry, so I asked him, "What about lunch or brunch?"

"No problem, we might have time for 'lunnier' after we find a room and get settled."

What was he talking about this time? I asked, "What is a lunnier?"

"Brunch is between breakfast and lunch. Lunnier is between lunch and dinner. So I call it lunnier."

I should have known it would have been something stupid like that. "Whatever, I'm game for lunch or lunnier, as long as we can check into someplace so that I can put my bag down for a few hours."

"Cool, let's get to the main gate and get ourselves a cab into town," Dan instructed.

We only had to walk a very short distance to the main gate. Cabs were already lined up and waiting for anyone going anywhere. Dan gave the driver the name of an intersection and off we went. Our ride only lasted about ten minutes before our cab stopped, and we got out.

Dan pointed to a building across the street from where we were and said, "We'll go and check out that place. I was there before, and it was most acceptable."

I noticed that the building did not have the screen netting around it like the BEQ we stayed in while we were in Saigon. We crossed over and just as we entered the hotel lobby, two Americans, Navy guys in jungle utilities came out and we almost collided with them.

To my surprise, Dan told the one guy to, "Grow up and watch your step boy."

This poor guy turned around, and there was anger written all over his face, as he stared-down Dan for making that, un-called-for comment. He immediately settled down. I believe he saw how tall Dan was and apparently did not want his ass kicked.

As usual, and to my surprise, the two guys smiled at each other and then gave each other a regular handshake, not that jive handshaking, knuckle-knocking, and finger-grabbing thing that the coloreds did. It figured, these guys were friends, and for the next five minutes or so, both men spent time catching up on what had happen to each other since the last time they were together. The other guy with him and I struck up a conversation on our own, because Dan and his friend totally ignored the two of us.

Finally, Dan looked over at us and made the introductions. Their names were Bill and Bob, or was it Bob and Bill, whatever. Dan continued by telling me that there was a birthday party going on that we could go to. These two guys appeared to have already been to a party because they were both already drunk.

The guy I was talking to said, "You ought to come. It's Bertha, and with Bertha, everything she does and is, is big."

All three of them laughed at that comment, and I didn't know why. I said, "No sweat, I'm there man."

Dan looked at Bill and Bob and asked, "Any women going to be there?"

One of them answered, "Always man. Bertha knows a lot of girls."

The other one answered, "Some of these ladies are Marines. Mixed in with them are some Navy waves like Bertha. So yeah, there will be some women there. Horny, away from home for the first time horny women."

Dan told the guy that he was talking to that we would check-in first and that we would be down in a few minutes. This guy said that he would wait for us, but he would only wait for ten minutes and no more. With that, we checked in, got our alarm clock, keys, and towels. After locking up our bags in the bathroom, we made it down in less than five minutes.

These two guys were sitting in the lobby waiting for us because it was cool inside and it had just finished raining. Once they saw us, they got up and headed towards the door. They did not wait for us to catch up with them, but they did say, "Lets go. This party won't last forever."

"We'll catch a cab out front and you guys can follow us," said Bill, or maybe it was Bob. Whomever that might have been, Bill or Bob, I did not remember.

"No sweat," Dan told them and we were on our way to a birthday party. Somehow, this seemed to be an odd thing to be doing, but I was just going to go along with the flow. Cabs were everywhere. There definitely was not a shortage of cabs in this city.

Dan said to me, "For a country that's at war, this place has more cabs than tanks and jeeps put together. You know, that should tell you something about their priorities over here."

There were a few cabs with the little taxi light on top, just like what we had back home. A few others were motorcycles that had passenger seats in the front, and some with seating behind the driver. All the motors were loud and were burning oil that you could see, taste, and smell.

Before we could select our ride, the two guys that we were going to follow had already jumped into a rickshaw cab and pulled away. I was wondering that if these guys were in such a hurry, then why they would pick the slowest ride available.

Dan jumped into a rickshaw that was behind the one that just left. I followed him and here we were in this rickshaw thing peddled by some kid that probably weighed less than a hundred pounds. The rickshaw had just enough room for the two of us and it was a good thing that we didn't have our sea bags with us.

Dan told the driver to, "Follow that Cyclo."

Our poor driver was running his ass off trying to catch up with the other, rickshaw, cab, or Cyclo, assuming that a cyclo and rickshaw was the same thing. Anyway, luck was with us because we caught up with them as soon as we hit some slow traffic. At the next light, we are able to pull up beside them.

They noticed that we had caught up with them. I heard one of them tell the driver to, "Lose them." The other guy added, "We'll give you a nice tip."

Apparently, Dan overheard that and told our driver, "Don't lose them, and I'll give you a numba-one tip."

Overhearing what Dan had said, Bill, I mean Bob, told his driver, "I'll double your tip if you let them eat our dust."

I figured I might as well get into this betting frenzy so I told my driver, "Beat them there, and I'll double your tip." What a deal that was. We took off first and got ahead of them. I looked back and felt great that we were winning.

At the stop sign, we were side by side and Bob; or, Bill yelled out to my driver, "Yeah, if you get there first, we'll double your tip too."

Our driver looked at them and then at Dan and I. When the traffic allowed, off we went cutting and weaving through traffic. Only at four or fives miles an hour, but it was still fun. Our driver took off in hot pursuit but he was not making much effort to speed past them, although there were a number of lane openings he could have taken.

I said to Dan, "I don't understand, this guy can make big bucks by just getting there first. Why doesn't he just pass them when he has the chance?"

"You ass-hole."

"What? What are you talking about?"

"Okay fine, let's say that we have the fastest rickshaw in all of South Vietnam. Let's assume that he really wants to win all that money that both sides are offering. He has motivation and ability for him to win this bet, correct?"

I didn't know where he was going with this, but I answered with, "Correct."

"Okay, now where are we going?"

"To a birthday party for some girl," I answered knowing that I knew where we were going.

"Your right so far. Now, where is this party?"

"Oh yeah, I didn't know," I responded feeling like the ass-hole he had just called me.

"Good, now just sit back, enjoy the chase, and don't place any more bets with our driver."

Therefore, I did just that. I just sat back, hung on, and enjoyed the ride.

Now, riding beside us were two cute girls. The one driving ignored me completely but the one in the back was smiling at me. At least I thought she was smiling at me and not Dan. I didn't know if it was a pick up smile, or just a smile because we were funny looking to her.

I said to Dan, "Check'em out. Maybe they will want to join us for the party?"

"I don't think so," Dan said, as Bob and Bill made a quick right hand turn that almost tipped them over.

Our laughing at them ended quickly as we made the same hard, right hand turn, and then did tip over. Now it was just a small crash, and everyone got up laughing. However, we did cause a slight traffic jam, and I got another smile from two different girls behind us. Dan was correct about this place, things out of the ordinary sure happened all the time over here.

At any rate, the first two girls kept going straight and so much for that.

Before we could talk about what had just happened to us, I caught a glimpse of an empty beer can being tossed at us from the guys we were following. It did not come close to us or anything; I just was not expecting that to happen at all. Besides, where did they get the beer?

Dan yelled at them, "Do you have any more beers?"

"Yes, if you want one, come and get it," was the response we got.

Surprisingly, Dan jumped out, and ran, and caught up to them. As he ran alongside them, they handed him two beers. At the next corner, when they had to stop to make another turn, Dan jumped back in and handed me a beer. I quickly opened it, only to have half of it spew all over me and our driver.

I said, "Damn, I wasted half of it."

"What did you expect would happen?"

"What?"

"You don't drink much do you?"

"Some, I drink some," I said looking at him from beer filled eyes.

"Right, and you always open your beers when they are warm and shaken-up."

"No sweat, not a big deal. I was just caught up in all the excitement," I responded thinking how this whole thing was funny, very, very funny.

Lucky for me, we stopped in front of some building before Dan could continue to put me down over a little spilt beer. After all this racing we did, we arrived at almost the same time and I would call it a tie. I assumed Bob and Bill felt the same way, because they were telling their driver that he did not deserve a numba-one tip.

Dan told me to give our driver a dollar and I did. Dan also gave our driver a dollar and told him that he did a numba-one job in catching up with them. With everyone's driver paid, we all headed into the lobby and ran up the stairs.

After a few flights, I noticed that Dan had started to spill some of his beer, so I said to him, "Can't hang onto your beer? You got to spill it all over the stairway?"

He came back with, "No sweat, I bet there is plenty of fresh, cold, unshaken beers for us to feast on to replace what we've lost."

After running up about four or five flights, I followed Dan, Bill, and Bob inside and found that we were in a rather large hotel room. I had only seen hotel rooms this size when watching old black and white movies. Movies that starred actors such as Fred Aster, the Marx Brothers, and W.C. Fields. After looking around at the room, I figured there were thirty or forty people in the four or five rooms.

Many things about this party seemed like a normal party back home; like the noise from everyone talking, the smell of beer, plenty of bags half-filled with chips and pretzels, along with the heavy haze of cigarette smoke filled every room. With a little imagination, you could think that the uniforms we were wearing indicated that everyone here attended a local catholic high school. Everyone that was not in some type of military uniform, was wearing shorts and brightly colored Hawaiian shirts. The Joe College look and the Jack Purcell tennis shoes were not here today. I take that back, one guy had on a pair of fake JP's. The only thing that really stood out was that some of the guys had side arms. There were even a few M-16's stacked in the corner.

In another corner were two huge speakers with an 8-track player on a table near by. There was only one 8-track to select from and that kept playing repeatedly. It was a tape by Iron Butterfly and it was very loud.

Two girls came walking by and they both caught my attention. Not only because they were both attractive, which they were, but mostly because they dressed alike. The taller of the two, turned and looked at Dan. She smiled, walked right up, stood between Dan and I, and said to Dan, "So where have you been lately. I'm surprised that you haven't called me like you promised." I did not know what that was all about, but it sounded like something you would hear back home.

Dan responded, "Well hi Jackie. Forgive me for not calling you. I have been very busy lately, you know, with the war going on and everything."

With a pissed-off look, she responded to him by saying, "Jerk, my name isn't Jackie."

I was thinking, 'Nice going. Way to go Dan. You get an attractive looking girl that wanted you to call her and here you go and call her by the wrong name.' What was I thinking? No one calls anyone over here. I could not even make a simple phone call home, and everyone wanted to call home.

Dan responded to her nasty tone by answering, "I know your name isn't Jackie, I was just checking to see if you remembered your name."

"Of course I remember my own name. You're the one that always gets it wrong."

"Okay, then what is it?"

I was wondering where this conversation was going. It seemed somewhat dumb to me.

"Gail."

"That's right," Dan said and gave her a hug and a kiss on the lips.

I did not know if I was reading this correctly or not, but I believed this was one stupid, but good-looking girl.

After their short kiss, Dan asked her, "You know, what about this new, women's movement thing that's going on now? I thought you guys wanted to be treated equal and all that. So with that in mind missy, why haven't you given me a call?"

I did not know where he was taking this, but this had to be good. She thought for a moment and I believed she was really stuck on that question.

Finally a response, "You never gave me your number, remember?"

This girl was not very quick, and, if you were to talking to her on the phone, you would bet that she was a blond.

Dan then old her, as if he thought he was God's gift to women everywhere, "The last time we were together, I thought you only wanted me for my body, and that you would have never given me a call anyway, after you took advantage of me."

This role reversal was great, and Dan was getting away with it. She was totally confused and she was searching for what to say next. Still looking stupid, dumb, and cute, she gave Dan another kiss and hug, and attempted to apologize to him. Looking over her shoulder at me, Dan gave me a smile and wink. With their second hug and kiss out of the way, she asked, "So, do you want to give me your phone number now?"

"I don't have one where I'm staying, but I'll give you my number back in the states and you can call me there, when you make it back home," Dan told her.

Looking totally excited, like a kid opening packages on Christmas morning, she whipped out pen and paper and asked, "And what is your name?"

Dan, apparently without thinking, replied with, "Dan."

She came back with, "That's correct, now do you remember your phone number?"

With a big smile, he gave her a phone number. She wrote the number down and after putting away her pen and paper, she asked, "So, who is your good looking friend here?"

She was pointing to me and she thought I was good looking. Maybe she was not as dumb as she acted. Wanting to respond before Dan cut me down, I said, "My name is Charles. I would have never forgotten your name." I could not believe I said that and it did sound rather smooth. Damn, that was a good pick up line I thought praising myself.

"You must be a friend of Dan's because he used the same line on me when we first met."

I had to have a come back on that one because, no way did I want this dumb girl putting me down, good looking or not.

"I have only known him for a few days and I mean what I say," I told her hoping that she would just be polite to me and not put me down again.

She responded to me before turning back to Dan, "Nice try."

Oh well, that's the way it goes. I never expected to meet any girls over here and this one meant nothing to me anyhow. With that, I turned around to the table and grabbed a few chips.

After a few minutes of eating chips and finishing off a beer, Dan questioned, "Having a good time?"

"Yes I am. What happened to Jackie? I thought that the two of you were going to take off together and get it on or something."

"You mean Gail."

"Yeah Gail, right, she does look like a Jackie to me."

"I have no idea what or whom she was into right now. I can only guess that she's looking for someone else to take her on for tonight."

"What? I thought you two knew each other."

"I never met her before in my life. I think she and her friend are in the Air Force or maybe they are both in the Army. Not smart enough to be in the Navy or the Marines," Dan explained.

I asked again, "You don't know them at all?"

After giving this some more thought, Dan answered, "I had no idea who they were, and I did not want to find out anything more about her."

"What part of this story am I missing here? I believe that we could agree that she was good looking, and apparently she wanted you and your phone number," I asked because I had to get an answer to this one.

"She and her friend had been trying to pick up guys from the minute they walked into the room and most likely from the minute they arrived in-country."

I asked in confusion, "She had a friend? Where is she?"

"She's over there and they are both wearing same-same."

Her friend was good looking too. I told Dan, "Hey, she's very attractive, same outfit or not. Hell, we have on the same outfit, along with almost everyone else here."

"Good point, but you do not want either one of them."

"Why not? What's wrong with them? Who wouldn't want a cute, stupid, round-eyed girl, ten thousand miles from home trying to pick me up at a party?"

"It's because of what she said to her friend when they first came into the room."

I had to hear this one. What kind of statement could a girl as cute as that make that would turn him off from wanting to go out with her? "So what was this horrible thing that she said?"

"She told her friend, after looking into the room, that there must be at least ten feet of peter in here," he answered, looking at me intently to check my response.

"You're right, that would have turned me off. So what did her friend say in response to that?"

"Her response was, 'that's good, that means we'll have about five feet of peter each.'"

How about that, girls that talk as crude as guys. "So why did you give her your phone number?"

With a smile, he replied, "I didn't give her my number, I gave her your home phone number."

I was a little surprised and pissed at his answer. I asked, "Why did you do that?"

"Relax dummy. I don't even know your phone number. Remember? You never told me and I never asked."

"Oh yeah, right. Sorry about that. I just had sickening thoughts about her calling and talking with my mother, and that would not be acceptable."

At this point, we just dropped the subject and walked over to get another beer. With a cold beer in hand, we stepped over to check out another table covered with a spread of lunchmeat, bread, chips, and dip. All of a sudden, the room got dark. The same kind of darkness that occurred during a lunar eclipse, except that we were inside.

I heard this feminine, man's voice, say to me, "Who are you guys?"

I turned around, and standing between the window and me, was this huge woman. On the other hand, it could have been a five hundred-pound polar bear in a woman's dress. And she said, "My name is Bertha. It's my birthday today."

I was so stunned with the size of this woman that I could not respond to what she just said. Lucky for me, Dan spoke up and said, "I'm Dan, and this is Charles. Happy Birthday."

I was able to muster up and say, "Happy Birthday," but with some difficulty. I still could not believe that she was that big. She was just as wide as she was tall. I bet that if she had a window seat on an airplane, the pilot would have a hard time flying straight and level. Damn, she would have taken up window seats that were on both sides of the plane at the same time.

"Well thank you Dan and Charles. Welcome to my party. You can stay as long as you want; but don't eat all the food."

What she said caught me off guard, because I thought she meant that because she was hungry and was planning on eating it all herself. I had this horrible feeling that Dan was about to make a cruel joke about what she had just said, but he did not. She continued with, "I want to dance with you guys when the 8-track by Chubby Checkers gets here."

"No sweat, we'll be here," Dan informed her with a smile from ear to ear. "Charles here is a dancing fool and he does a mean twist. He loves Chubby Checkers."

"Oh really," she responded, as she looked at me as if I were a hamburger, large fry and chocolate shake.

Before I could say anything, Dan added in a little more crap about me, "Charles here was saying to me as we walked in that he wished that someone had a twisting 8-track to play."

She smiled at me and said, "When it gets here, I'll be sure to look for you, and we'll see just how good you are."

Still, I could not say a thing, and I was hoping that there was enough beer here for me to get drunk, so that I would not have any memories about what might happen to me, if I had to dance with her.

Then she said, "Got to go, I have more guests arriving."

As she walked away, the sunlight from the window returned that she had totally had blocked out. She even looked bigger walking away. The flowers on her dress looked like a huge field somewhere in the country where there were lots and lots of room. With a little imagination, I could see a wheat harvester going across her butt.

"Thanks a lot," I said to Dan.

"No problem my man. I thought you might want a girl friend while you're over here."

"No thank you. I don't want her as a girl friend, friend, dance partner or anything else you could try to set me up with." Finally, seeing the humor in this, I said to Dan, "Now, the second I hear Chubby Checkers say, 'Come on everybody,' I'm out of here and on my way back to our hotel room, with or without you."

"No sweat," Dan answered.

With that, we started to mingle around the party. Just like any party back home, there was plenty of people, beer, chips, and loud music. Not too many girls, but the ones that were there were okay. Well, except for Gail, her friend, and the Big-ass Butt birthday girl.

A little later Dan said to me, "If you got to make a head call, now would be a good time my friend."

"Yeah, I do, but why is now a good time?" I had better pay attention to this because he might have me doing it out the window or somewhere that will get me into some kind of trouble.

"Not a big deal or anything. I went a minute ago, and there was a line. There's no line now, and I was just trying to be helpful. No sweat. Go when you want."

I told him, "Thanks, good idea, and I'll be back in a minute."

I figured that I might as well go, because I did notice a long line earlier. However, before I closed and locked the door behind me, I did make one quick check to see if Dan was doing anything suspicious that might cause me to be on my guard. He was looking the other way and talking to some girl. I did not know why I was acting so paranoid; I mean, I only wanted to pee, and this was a bathroom. An inside bathroom, and in 'The-Nam,' or not, a bathroom was just a bathroom.

So here I was with my zipper down, relieving myself, when all of a sudden, the shower curtain flew open, and there was the birthday girl with a camera in her hand, flashing away at me.

My mind tried to react quickly, as if I had four hands. I thought that I had one hand available to hold myself, one to close the curtain, one to put in front of the camera and one to pull up my zipper. Naturally, I only had two hands and the only thing I could accomplish was to pee all over the toilet, floor, and myself. It was not as bad as having an uncontrollable fire hose, but still, I was not in control for a second or two. I was using both hands trying to close the curtain, and grab the camera from her.

She backed up and kept on taking pictures, all the while excitingly yelling, "More. Show me more."

I could hear Dan banging on the bathroom door, and he was yelling, "Everything okay in there? Does she have everything in hand?"

Of course, everyone out there was laughing at me. I could not decide whether it was best to go out there or to stay inside here with Big-Ass Bertha. I quickly decided that I would rather be in with a crowd of people with pee spots on my pants, than to be alone in here with her. Damn, she was even uglier up close and in person.

Still having to relieve myself, especially because I had only half finished, I decide to tuck-in, zip-up, and leave Bertha in the shower, along with her camera and smile. I just had to continue with it later, pain or no pain. After unlocking the door and stepping out, everyone looked at me and laughed.

Dan said, "So did she give you a hand?"

More laughter from everyone as he continued with, "What part did you like best?"

"The part I liked best?" I might as well join in on the joke.

"Yeah, what was the best part?" Someone else yelled at me from the back of the room.

"The best part was that she still had her clothes on." At least now, everyone appeared to be laughing with me instead of at me.

Bertha came out of the bathroom holding up the camera and said, "Anyone want copies?"

A girl in the back yelled out, "I do. What do you have?"

It figured she was the one that Dan and I were talking to earlier. She started to sound increasingly more like a slut and apparently; she did not care what she said.

Bertha-Butt answered her back, "With this guy, I only have the little wallet sizes, nothing bigger than a 2x3." That brought a new round of laughter from everyone. That was rather funny and now the joke was back on me. I knew I would recover from this.

"Yeah, but that was a head on shot. Let's go back inside, I'll stand sideways for you, and this time you'll need your wide angle lens."

Right now, everyone was back to laughing with me and this was not so bad after all, although I still had piss-spots on my pants. Still having to go, I quickly sneaked passed Bertha and closed, and locked the door behind me. I finished-up, washed-up, dried-up, cleaned-up, hurried-up, and returned to the party.

Once I got outside of the bathroom, no one paid any attention to me. I assumed that the joke was over with and all forgotten about by now, especially with other things happening. I meant, this was a party, there must be more important or funnier things going on, and that was okay with me.

I found Dan and asked, "Did you know that she was in there hiding?"

"I knew she was in there, but I didn't think she would be able to hide from you. Where was she and how could you not see someone that huge in that little bathroom?"

"She was in the shower hiding behind the curtain."

"Didn't the shower curtain bulge out?"

"I wasn't taking notice of the shower curtain. Man, I just had to pee and the only thing I was looking for was a target."

"Want another beer?" Dan asked, trying to get back on my good side.

"Nah, you don't have to get me one right now."

"I wasn't going to get you a beer. I figured that if you wanted one that you would bring one back for me."

"Funny man, real funny."

"Relax," Dan said, "You're having a good time, right?"

"I am, but of course that would have been funnier if it were played on someone else."

With that, we smiled, laughed, and made our way over to get ourselves a beer. What a great way to spend part of my tour, I thought to myself.

Two guys came over beside us and helped themselves to a beer, and I overheard the one telling the other that he had just gotten there and has brought his twisting 8-track tape with him.

I clearly asked Dan, "About ready to head out of here?"

"Yeah, now would be a good time to exit the party," Dan responded, apparently having also heard about the arrival of the 8-track.

"Let's make it quick before they play that tape. Besides, we've been here long enough," I instructed, not suggested, but instructed. I wanted to leave soon.

Dan agreed and turned towards the door. We started to head out, but Dan came to a quick stop, turned to me, and said, "We can't leave that way. We have to find us another way out of here, or we be in deep-shit."

"Why? Is there a problem? Come on man, you know I must get out of here."

I could not imagine a problem in leaving by the one and only door. So, I looked over at the door, and I could see that nothing was blocking our way. There happened to be a small group of people by the door; however, there were small groups of people all over the place. This was a party, and that part was normal.

Dan walked past me and said. "We'll try a window."

He looked very serious about this. I caught up with him and asked, "Why do we need to leave by a window?"

He stopped and said, "Look over at the Big-Ass Bertha-Butt Birthday girl, and tell me what you see."

I glanced around the room and I could not find her.

Dan said, "Look by the door ass-hole, you know, our way out of here."

Initially I thought that because Bertha was very fat, that maybe she was stuck in the doorway, and no one could get past her. The only thing I noticed was that she was giving some guy a kiss. It looked like Bill, or maybe it was Bob as the, 'kiss-ee,' or the 'kiss-er.' Whatever, nothing else seemed out of place and the doorway was not blocked.

"Dan, I still don't see a problem."

"Look my friend. She's giving everyone some lip because she's expecting a birthday kiss from every guy that leaves."

"That's it? For that, we must find another way out. Even Bertha-Butt, with her massive physical ugliness, should at least get a quick peck on the cheek for her birthday. I mean this was her party and everything. If this were my party, I'd certainly want a little lip from all the attractive girls that were there for my birthday."

"Okay my friend. You can leave that way if you like; however, as for me, I'm using a window."

I still didn't see a problem with that and I believed that he was thinking too much about himself to avoid such a simple task. Besides, we were a couple of floors up. I asked him again, "What's the problem with a simple peck on the cheek? We did get lots of free beer and food while we were here, you know."

Dan placed his hand on my shoulder and pointed toward Bertha-Butt who started kissing another guy that was attempting to leave.

"Watch what happens as this guy attempts to give her an, as you say, a quick peck on the cheek. He's apparently trying to show her his respect and appreciation for being invited to this party; with its free beer and food."

"No problem, I can check-it-out for myself," I explained not knowing for sure what I was looking for.

As this guy tried to kiss her on the cheek, I saw, to my horror that she turned his face so that their lips met by grabbing onto both his ears. She clamped a lip lock on this poor guy, and we could hear over the music and all the people talking. Even from fifteen feet away, I could tell that she was all tongue and was not letting him loose to come up for air. His hands and arms were flapping about as if he were trying to fly. I could see fear and the whites of his eyes, as he was trying to catch his breath. Instead of sucking in air, he was sucking in tongue.

Dan added, "Check out how many guys are able to sneak out while she has that guy in a death-lip-lock."

He was right. I could see that two guys were ducking down low and were passing quickly through the doorway making their escape. To no surprise, they did not even look back. Once in the hallway and out of her range, they gave each other a high five. By this time, the guy in her captivity appeared to be starting to lose consciousness. I didn't know if she had cut off his air passage or killed him with her bear hug. She might have even scared him to death. Whatever the reason, I did not want the same fate for me.

After a few seconds of watching in amusement and horror, Dan said, "Like I said, as for me, my suicidal friend, I'm leaving by the window."

I looked over at Dan and nodded my head in agreement. I looked back at this poor guy and I could see that his hands and arms were no longer trying to take flight. Maybe he did pass out, and with her, that might be a blessing.

A few girls near Bertha's butt were laughing and edging her on to go for the gold. Some guys near them, without the sense to get out of her reach, had looks of fear and disbelief. These guys must be stupid if they didn't leave now, while they had the chance.

Dan said, "Look over there, those two have the right idea."

I looked over and saw in the one bedroom, that those two had the window opened, and one guy was already half way out on the ledge. I found myself so excited about a way out that I walked right past Dan.

"I see that you have changed your mind," Dan said as he got in behind me.

I responded with, "Yeah man, I can live with a few piss spots on my pants and a quick peck on the cheek, but I can do without her death hug and tongue dipping."

I did not take the time to check out the details of our escape route, because I wanted to get out before we were discovered. Dan was right behind me, and we found ourselves four stories up on a one-foot wide ledge. The first two guys ahead of us were going into a window about twenty or so feet away. I didn't care where it led; I just wanted to get away from Bertha and off the ledge.

Dan asked, "So, are you having a good time?"

"Yeah, only in 'The-Nam,' can anyone have this much excitement."

"Of course, if you fall and get hurt, you won't get a Purple Heart," Dan explained as if I might really fall.

Now that was a pleasant thought. I asked, "Dan, do you write home about this kind of stuff? Did you ever tell your parents or your sister or brothers any of this?"

"No way man, besides, if I did, no one would ever believe me about this one. Know what I mean?"

"I roger that. I do not believe this to be true and yet, here I was, way up on this window ledge, running away from a woman that only wanted a birthday kiss."

To our luck, the room that we slipped into was empty, and those escaping ahead of us had left the door to the hallway open.

I waited for Dan to make it inside the room before I started for the doorway. Once in the hallway, I turned left and saw right away that it came to a dead end. Without thinking, I made a U-turn, and before I took my first step, I stopped dead in my tracks.

Dan bumped into me and asked, "Why'd you stop? Did you want to go back and have your tonsils extracted?"

I could not speak a word as I pointed down the hallway. To my surprise and disappointment, Bertha-Butt was there, and she was taking up most of the hallway. She was now giving one of the guys, one that tried to escape ahead of us a bear hug. Just like her last victim, his arms were a flapping away in a futile attempt to escape.

Knowing that I would have to make my escape while she was interrogating his insides with her tongue, I thought about my next move. Dan and I must have had the same idea at the same time, because we both made a quick dash to get by her. Dan went for her port side, and I headed to starboard. I ended up scraping the wall for about eight or ten feet. However, I made it by her with just a few scrapes and bruises, and based on the alternatives, those injuries were most acceptable. I did not think I was the lucky one because of my minor injuries, until I turned around to see that Dan did not make it past her at all.

The only flaw in our plan, was that we should have followed one another past her on the same side. However, we were in such a hurry and in our panic, we tried to pass her on both sides at the same time. You see, Miss Bertha Big-Ass Butt was about the size of the hallway and there was just enough daylight on one side to allow an escape and only if we had passed in single file. We had both taken off thinking every man for himself. Apparently, we should have acted as a team.

"I got you, you little tease," shouted Bertha-Butt, as she grabbed Dan and recoiled him into her arms, as her last victim dropped lifeless to the floor.

I knew that I was unwilling to help him for a number of reasons. One reason was that she was bigger than the two of us put together. I did not want to increase the odds that she would get a hold of me. Moreover, and most importantly, I enjoyed watching Dan get it. It was cool to see him getting, 'licked' for a change, and I wanted to see him talk his way out of this one. To my surprise and disappointment, Dan put his arms straight up and slid right down between her two huge tits. With that trick, he was out of her grip, and she was unable to bend over far enough to retrieve him. On his knees, he quickly moved away from her and yelled, "Run! Run for your life! She'll suck the life right out of you!"

He and I made our way down hundreds of stairs and out of the building. Not once did we look back in fear that it might have slowed our escape. I realized that she could not run that fast, but I was not taking any chances.

"Thanks for your help," Dan said to me as we reached the bottom level.

"I figured that you had it under control, and I didn't want to interfere."

"Yeah, right. You had it figured wrong my friend. You probably didn't want to risk the chance of being snared yourself by Ms. Big-Butt."

With a smile on my face, I answered with, "That was one of my reasons."

Dan started to pull himself together. He straightened his cap, re-buttoned a few buttons, tucked in his shirt, and pulled his belt buckle back around straight. Even his eyebrows were messed up and crooked.

"So was it good for you?" I asked.

"She's really in heat. If she's that way for a birthday kiss, I'm afraid to imagine what she is like when she's horny."

We both laughed, and Dan continued with, "So, if I hadn't gotten away from her when I did, how long would you have waited, before you would have come to my rescue?"

"Good question, my friend. The first thing is, that I would have given you two a few minutes together. Naturally, I wanted to be sensitive to your needs and not step in too early."

"And after that?"

This time, I could make fun of him and I was going to do just that. "I would have first wanted to make sure that you were really in trouble. I would have needed a little time to review your situation, because I could not tell by your facial expression whether you were having a good time, ready to climax, or about ready to pass-out."

"You think I was having a good time with the She-Devil?" He asked, in a not so friendly manner.

"Not really; however, I would have waited until you were very close to death, before I would have stepped in to assist you."

"And I assume you had a plan for this?"

"Yes, I would have found a fire hose, turned it on, and hosed her down like an out of control fire. My plan was to get her body temperature down to 98 degrees. Then as the hallway filled with steam, I would have pulled you out to safety, fresh air, and saved your life."

Enjoying this moment, I continued with, "However, if you would have needed mouth to mouth resuscitation, I would have let her perform that work on you."

"I'll remember that the next time you need assistance."

"No sweat," being careful not to carry this too far.

"The next time she has a party, free beer or not, I'm not going," Dan said as he continued to pull himself together. It appeared that even his T-shirt was crooked under his shirt.

"I have an idea what we can do now," I only said that because I really wanted to keep this Bertha-Butt thing going on a little longer. I truly enjoyed seeing him getting it.

"And that is?" He responded as if he knew this was not in his favor.

"I know a great bar that I'll let you walk into first. There the girls will take little Danny and the twins for a little stroll and give'm some fresh air."

"Very funny and I'm pleased to find that you're looking out for me, now that my ordeal is history. The truth is, after my escape from Bertha-Butt, I may never want to be near another fat woman again."

"Was it really all that bad?"

"Yes it was. When I slipped between her tits, it felt, and smelled, as if I fell into a clothes hamper. If it weren't for her body sweat, I never would have slipped out as easily as I did. I'll bet that one of her tits weighs more than I do."

"I like that and that's one to remember."

"I had many strange thoughts while I struggled to get out from her grip. I couldn't tell up from down. I didn't know my right from my left, and I thought all the lights went out. I got the sensation of being squeezed by a three hundred pound python, and breathing was starting to be difficult for me, for real."

"That's funny man, this is good stuff, and you sure have a great imagination."

With a sad look on his face, he responded with, "I didn't say it to be funny, it was bad. It'll probably give me nightmares for the rest of my tour and maybe for the rest of my life."

I wanted to chuckle with that comment but it appeared that he was serious.

"When she had me in that head lock, I was thinking that our two inch regulation hair should also pertain to the hair under her arms. Either she had long hair under her arms, or she was hiding a cocker spaniel puppy in each arm pit."

I questioned and laughed at the same time with, "You've got to be kidding?"

"The smell, I'll never forget that smell," Dan explained, as he spitted three or four times on the ground.

"Like what?" I just had to ask.

"Tiger Balm, good old Vietnamese Tiger Balm. It's a foul-smelling oil kind of crap to scare away evil spirits." After a pause, he added, "I bet it works. I'll never go near that monster again. In fact, there needs to be a Three-Mile limit placed around her body."

As he was shaking his head back and forth in apparent discuss with himself, I watched him pull a long black hair from his shoulder that apparently came from her. With that, Dan said, "This strand of hair is probably as strong as a 50 pound test fish-line."

Now that was some nasty looking armpit hair. "Yeah, it also looks long and strong enough to be used on an archer's bow."

We both stared at this hair as it fell straight down to the ground like a rock. I bet that if it wasn't for the sound of traffic, we could have heard it hit the ground with a thud.

We both had a good laugh about his experience and we continued on down the street.

Chapter 10

At the next corner, we stopped for a light and I noticed what appeared to be a hooker on the other corner across from us. She was extremely obvious with her appearance and mannerism. She had on a short skirt, go-go boots, fish net stockings; a cigarette in her mouth, her purse thrown over her shoulder, and let's not forget that she was leaning up against a pole. As with most oriental women, she had long, straight, black hair. She wasn't bad looking for a woman about thirty years old.

I commented to Dan, "I guess that's a hooker."

"You can not tell?" He questioned.

"No man, that wasn't a question. I was just saying that there's a hooker on the corner, and that I've never really seen one in person before."

"What about all those girls in the bars trying to get you and your money? What do you call them?" Dan inquired.

"Okay, they were hookers too. But they seemed different, and most of them were a lot younger than this one."

"I guess she doesn't have a bar to work from. She might be an independent, enterprising young lady," Dan explained cracking a joke.

We watched her for a few minutes before crossing the street. She was walking up to any man that walked by himself, and said something into his ear. Each man in turn would either ignore her completely or apparently had told her no. Again, she did this to every man that was walking alone.

I said to Dan, "I wonder what she is saying to these men?"

"She's just doing her job and trying to score a hit," Dan answered, as if I should have known better.

I had zero interest in her, but I was a little curious about what she was saying. "Honestly, what do you think she's saying?" I questioned again.

"Don't know for sure. Why don't you go and check-it-out for yourself."

I answered quickly, "I don't want to do anything with her. I'm just interested in what she was telling or asking all these men."

"Well then, walk on by her and see for yourself. You can do that much without putting anything out, as in your little Charlie or your money."

"You know, I'll do that. Wait here. I'll just be a minute. I really want to hear what she's saying," I told him as I made my way towards her. At least in public I doubt she would grab me or anything.

He responded, "No sweat, and good luck. Oh, by the way, get a price on that thing."

Now why would I need any luck for this, question and answer time? How hard could it be, I thought to myself as I crossed the street.

I walked past her and timed it so that I would be the only man approaching her in either direction. To my surprise, she ignored me completely, and I was hurt and embarrassed to say the least. Dan on the other hand was laughing so loud that I could hear him all the way on this side of the street. At least he was enjoying my little adventure.

Assuming she just did not see me, I walked by her again; and this time, I walked a little slower. Before I even got all the way past her, I could hear Dan laughing even louder than before. Oh well. I crossed the street and as I approached him, I asked, "What?"

Trying to talk and not laugh at the same time was proving to be more difficult for him than I thought it should be. Catching his breath, he answered, "I've never seen anyone, anywhere, that got ignored by a hooker during working hours."

This was truly embarrassing, because it was not as if I was retarded or anything. It must be that she just did not see me. She could not be all that selective because she approached every man that was alone, whether he was old, young, colored, white, military, and civilian alike. Wanting to remain cool and not give him any more reasons to kid me about this later, I said to him, "She just didn't see me."

"Twice she didn't see you. I don't think so, my friend, because she just down right ignored you."

"Watch and learn," I told him.

"Yeah, I can learn what not to do," Dan responded.

Thinking to myself on how I hoped this would work, I crossed back over, walked right up to her, and said, "Hi."

Now what happened to me next, must have never happened to anyone since the beginning of time. She looked past me as if I was not even there. I told her, "Hi," a second time, and with that, she told me to, "Go away little boy."

Go away. How could she say, go away? This lady was working, and I was a customer. How could she tell me to, go away? This just was not right, little boy or no little boy. With my head held low and my tail between my legs, I quickly retreated to Dan to an even more embarrassing situation. Being here in, 'The-Nam,' was just too much for me at my young age of eighteen, well, almost nineteen in a few days.

I had to think of something to tell Dan before he had a cow over what just happened to me. However, before I had a chance to respond, Dan excitingly repeated, "Go away. Go away little boy."

I gave him that, 'deer into headlights' look.

He repeated, "Go away? A hooker on the prowl telling someone to, go away. How is that possible, my man? Or should I say, my woman?"

"She's very particular, that's why. I believe she thinks I'm not old enough, and she probably knew that I did not have the money to pay for her."

Unable to hold in his laughter, he continued, "Oh yeah, I get it. You were told to go away because she's selective and you're too young. Yeah, right."

"She has the right to be picky," I responded not knowing what else to say.

"Let me see if I can help you figure this out. She doesn't like men with all their teeth. Maybe leprosy is a favorable feature; or, she noticed that you didn't spend any time scratching yourself between your legs. I get it now. Maybe it's because you didn't pick your nose or cough up blood."

"If you're done having a good time at my expense," I interjected. "We can move on to something or somewhere else. As I said, I assume that she thought I was too young to be spoiled by her. She's doing me a favor and allowing me to save myself for someone else."

Still laughing at me, Dan responded with, "Yeah, that's the reason."

I came back with, "You know. I had another possibility to explain, and I wanted him to hear this. "She could be a cop on a stake out and was giving me a break."

"Sure, we're in a country that doesn't have health inspectors, but they do have sting operations to catch people with hookers."

"Give me a break," I said as I started down the street. He caught up with me and continued with his insults. "I only hope that the VC avoid you as much as she did. Your presence might come in handy when we get into another firefight."

Wanting to conclude this with my having the last word, I said, "I believe there are two reasons for this, 'lady of the evening,' denying me a working relationship with her."

"Oh, this has to be good. Let me hear it so I can use these excuses the next time I am turned down by a working hooker."

"Okay, listen up, my man. One, she knew before hand that I only wanted to talk to her, and this would have taken up valuable time from her solicitation."

"Okay, that's a good one. Not really, but I'll give it to you. Now, how about reason number two," Dan asked, apparently in anticipation of new ammunition for cutting me down. However, for some reason, I believed that he was being sincere. I kept my guard up just the same.

"Two, she saw me as a young kid and was being kind, by not having me spoiled by her."

There, I made up two good excuses, and I believed them myself. Besides, I was not going to do anything with her anyway. In addition, I did look younger than I really was. I only started shaving a few months ago.

"No sweat, I'll give this one to you," Dan said.

Surprisingly, he dropped it and did not bother to bring it up again. I still wanted to have the last word on this subject, so I said, "I don't know which is worse?"

"What?"

"Which of these two examples are worse? Being rejected by a hooker or spending a close, but brief encounter with Bertha-Butt."

Dan thought for a moment and responded, "You have a good point, my getting even friend. What do you say we both forget that these two incidents ever happened, and never bring them up again?"

"That's a deal I can live with," I said with much relief.

After a few minutes of walking around, Dan asked, "You hungry?"

"Hungry? No, not me, but if you want to eat something, I will join you."

"I'm okay, I was just checking on you. What do you say we catch a cab ride back to our hotel?"

I guess he was tired of all this walking around, and I asked, "Are you tired?"

"A little, but for the most part, I'm lost and I don't feel like walking in circles trying to find our way back."

"No sweat, a cab ride back would be fine with me."

At that moment, almost every cab driver in South Vietnam must have known we wanted a cab, because about a dozen of them showed up next to us in a manner of a few seconds.

Dan said to me, "Pick a ride, any ride. For the most part, the price will be same-same."

Given the choice, I wanted to try something different this time. There was the rickshaw from earlier, and it appeared as if he was still out of breath from our race. Besides that, it was too slow; nice and entertaining, but slow just the same. The guys pushing the carts on the boardwalk in Atlantic City New Jersey made better time than this guy did. This time, I selected one that was motorized. It was a small scooter bike, with a large seat for us that also doubled as a front fender, and the driver sat behind us.

We sat down, gave the name of our hotel, and off we went on an adventure like no other. Our driver flew down the road and tailgated everything and everyone. He went in behind a bus, and the exhaust blew right in my face. If we stay behind this bus any longer, I might be forced to puke up all my beer and chips. Our ride was more frightening than a roller coaster. On a roller coaster, you had a good idea which way you were going, because you could see the track that was in front of you. Here, we had no way of knowing which way our driver was going, or if he would even slow down or stop. Except for the exhaust from the vehicles in front of us, this was an exciting ride, and we were making excellent time. Our driver made lane changes more often than he drove straight in a single lane. After a few quick lane changes, Dan and I caught on to the fact that we must lean into the turns so we did not tip over. Once the driver realized that we were helping and improving his turning with our shifting weight, he started to go faster and he made even tighter turns. I didn't know if we were screaming because of the fun we were having or that we really were scared to death.

Dan said to me, "Good selection for a cab ride, but next time, let's try this sober and see how we like it."

"No problem, but we must survive this ride first," I answered holding on for dear life.

We now approached a major intersection that was not controlled by a signal of any kind. A normal person would have slowed down; however, our driver sped up, and because of that, we had a number of extremely narrow escapes. Now I was a little more frightened than before. At one point, I placed my hand out to help miss another cab.

After we made it across the intersection unscathed, Dan said, "That was cool."

"I'm surprised that we didn't have a fender-bender or something. I bet the body shops around here keep pretty busy."

"What kind of body shops are you talking about my man?"

Now that sounded like a somewhat dumb question that I would have asked. I answered him with, "You know, auto body shop."

"You need to review your present situation my friend, because I was not talking about an auto body shop."

"What are you talking about?" Talking to him sometimes was like talking to the Riddler on the TV show, Batman and Robin.

Dan answered, "Your feet are the front bumper; your lower legs are the front grill; your upper legs are the hood; and what's between your legs could be the hood ornament." As he continued, I started to sit with my legs together, and keeping my arms inside. "Your chest and face are the wind shield, and the top of your head could be the roof. They are the body parts that I'm talking about my friend."

"I never would have thought about that when I selected our ride," I said, as I realized that maybe I made a bad choice. Next time, give me something with a back seat and doors.

"No problem, at least we only have a little ways to go," he said as he pointed up ahead and added, "Look, there's our hotel."

I was never so happy to exit a cab in my life and I said, "At least we kept all our fingers and toes."

Dan responded with, "And most importantly, we kept our hood ornament attached."

We made our way to our room and, once inside, I tried to find the pull-string to open the curtains as Dan made a head call. I was having a hard time finding a way to raise or move the curtains until I realized that there was no pull-string. The curtains were nailed above the window onto the window frame. Again, another simple task was made impossible over here. Dan came out of the bathroom, and I told him, "So much for letting some light into our room."

"What light? It's dark outside."

"I know, I just said that. Did you know about the curtains being nailed to the window frame? Is there a way to open these guys?"

Dan walked over and took one end using the hole that was already in the curtain and hooked it to another nail hook that was already on the wall. "There," he said, "Anything else I can do for you before I pass out for tonight?"

I did not respond to his comment, I only wanted to look out the window and check out our view. As I looked out, I noticed two guys across the way walking out on a ledge a few floors from the sidewalk below. I said to Dan, "Check out those two guys. They look like Army guys on some kind of army maneuvers or something.

Dan looked over and after a double take, he started to laugh and fell back on the bed.

I looked out again and saw nothing all that funny about those two guys. It appeared that they were Americans and not Vietnamese because one of them was blond and tall. I also saw that they were not carrying rifles or anything like that.

"What's so funny," I asked.

"Doesn't that bring back any memories?"

I looked back again and saw nothing familiar about anything. "No," I responded. "What are you talking about?"

Making himself stop laughing, he told me, "That, my short memory friend, is the exiting of military personnel from a very big party."

"Party. Big?"

"Yeah," he answered.

"Yeah. What?"

"Remember?"

"Remember what," I questioned him a little tired of having to ask a lot of questions.

"Look at those guys. You can see that those guys are escaping the same way we did."

I could not believe it, because that was where we were, and it was only a block away from where we were now. I joined right in with Dan and laughed my head off. Truly enjoying the moment. Both our cab drivers took advantage of us, and took us for a ride, by going the long way to the party and back.

"Damn it my man," I said to him. "It would have been quicker just to walk the two minutes around the block instead of our fifteen minute cab ride."

"Those guys really took us for a ride and on top of that, we paid them," Dan explained.

I hate being cheated out of anything, especially my money. With that, I said, "Is there anything we can do about that?"

"Let me guess," Dan questioned. "First you expected health inspectors to check-out our food, and now you want someone to follow the cab drivers and enforce their non-written laws on cab fares."

"When you put it that way, of course not," I responded feeling cheated.

I looked back towards Bertha's place and noticed that the lights were out now. I told Dan, "I guess the party is over."

He looked over and we could see some movement in the darken room. Dan said, "I guess that Big-Ass-Bertha is trolling the room for guys that have passed out and not escaped."

Remembering what I saw her do to a few guys earlier, I asked, "So what do you think she'll do to anyone that's unlucky enough to stay behind."

He thought for a moment and said, "For those guys, their lives are over."

"I guess these guys were very unlucky to pass out when they did," I said trying to be funny.

Dan replied with, "Not really."

I had to ask, "What do you mean, not really."

"They were lucky enough to pass out when they did. Imagine how unlucky they will feel when they wake up next to, under, on top, or around Bertha."

"I agree. Now that's a horrible thought to wake up next to her."

He came back with, "If that would have happened to me, I would be volunteering for point-man on every mission I could get. After spending time with her, anything else life can throw at me would be a piece of cake."

I added, "I agree, I'm tired, and I'm going to bed."

Just before I fell asleep, I asked Dan, "What time we getting up in the morning?"

"Don't know, don't care. Wake me when you're up," came his last words, before he turned over and placed his covers over his head. Oh well, "Good night," I told him.

Chapter 11

To my surprise, we slept until noon. The only reason we did not sleep any longer was that someone was banging on our door, because we apparently had slept past checkout time.

After answering the door and sending the guy away, Dan told me that he was going to go down and ask if we could stay another day. I didn't want to stay any longer, but I was just going along with him, because Dan must have known what we were going to do today. It wasn't as if we had anything scheduled anyway. Well, maybe I did. I really did want to find my unit, and get checked in.

Dan returned a few minutes later and said that everything was taken care of. I got dressed, we locked up our bags, and had breakfast at a little place next door to our hotel. We just had eggs and toast for breakfast this time. They had lots of chickens over here, and eggs were plentiful and cheap.

Outside the restaurant, I asked, "So how are we going to spend the rest of our day?"

"We'll just walk around for a while, check out the sights, and if we should see anything of interest, then we'll check-it-out and kill some time."

"Sounds okay with me," I answered, agreeing with him, as if I had a better idea.

After a few blocks, Dan suggested, "Let's take a break and check out that Farmers' Market over there. Sometimes you can get good deals on stuff to send back home. Also, while we're here, you can give it one of your health inspections, and be sure to let me know if it meets your standards of public health."

I had a headache, and I didn't have any need for any of his crap this morning. "No sweat," I said. I only hoped that I didn't find myself being taken advantage of in front of Dan if I bought anything. It would just give him additional ammunition to tease me with. What was I saying, I had no desire to be taken advantage of at all, in front of Dan, or not. I was just going to keep my guard up. No more Christmas Cards for me.

Looking around, I could see that it was just like the farmers' market back home. There were plenty of booths, selling all kinds of stuff. He was correct about this place selling anything and everything. A few stalls had the typical items like vegetables, clothes, and animals. Some sold TV's, radios, 8-track players, and 8-track tapes, along with a few items that I had no idea, what they were.

"Anything here that you can't eat is probably black market stuff. Remember to always work out a deal with them on anything you want to buy," Dan reminded me, as if I had forgotten what he told me before, about buying stuff over here.

"Okay," I answered.

"What ever you do, don't make a shopkeeper angry."

"Why?"

"They'll shoot you, cut you up, and sell the parts. Well, maybe not your uniform," he responded, giving me a look as if I was a homeless person, because of the way my clothes fit.

"Very amusing. I'll try to keep that in mind," hoping that he was joking about the, 'getting shot' part.

We made our way in around the aisles, and there were lots to see, especially the people. There was a mixture of the old-culture clothing, new hippie style clothes on some of the kids, and many people wearing bits and pieces of military uniforms. Green and brown were the prominent colors that everyone seemed to be wearing. Somehow, it still seemed a little odd that so many people were carrying rifles, wearing side arms, and flip-flops instead of shoes. I guessed this was something I had to get used to. I guessed the fashion statement here was not the style of clothing that you had on, but was based on the caliber of your weapon. The bigger the gun you carried around, the bigger the man you appeared to be.

Walking around, I noticed how the smells would change from stall to stall. I could not tell if it was as bad as before; or, if I started to become used to it. There were many kids running around with older people selling stuff. I guessed it was because everyone else in the middle age group was in the military somewhere, and not here.

Dan pointed at a small crowd and said, "Let's go and check out the auction."

I did not have a chance to answer him because he was already on his way. The parking lot was unusual because it was paved and the lines for the parking spots were freshly painted. This must be the only lot in town that was paved. It appeared to be new, and possibly not opened to the public yet. In some ways, compared to the rest of the country, the lot looked somewhat orderly, even without any cars on it. Now, instead of cars in the spots, each spot was being used like a table at a flea market. Each space was numbered, and it appeared that each person had a designated space to display his or her stuff. No one had anything even touching the painted line. It was as if taking up more space than was allotted was not permitted.

We heard an auctioneer doing his thing, and made our way over to where he was. There we found a small crowd that trailed the auctioneer as he walked from space to space, using a long stick to tap an item that was up for auction. To hear his voice in his native tongue added to the auctioning part. Well, that alone was worth the trip to 'The-Nam.' This went on rather quickly because the auctioneer was not tapping on every item. He apparently skipped some of the junk stuff, just like they do back home.

Dan said to me, as he pointed to our left at some kids, "Check out those two over there."

In some ways, I was not interested in turning around to check out any kids. I found it interesting with what I was already watching. Besides, I didn't want anything that these kids might be trying to sell me.

Dan started talking as if he thought I was listening to him, "Real smart little gooks. That's a very bright idea that they have going for themselves if it works. Don't you think?"

I might as well look, what could I lose besides my money and self-esteem. After checking out these two kids for a few minutes, I didn't see the attraction. It appeared to me that as the auctioneer moved on to the next pile of items, leaving the owners with what did not sell, these two kids were taking everything that was left behind by the original owner. Nothing like collecting junk, that no one wanted.

"You call that, smart?" I said to Dan. "All they were doing was taking junk that no one wanted to buy. The original owners didn't even want it back."

"Yeah, but check out what they're doing with it," he suggested pointing at them.

I kept an eye on the older of the two kids. He grabbed up the junk items and ran them to the end space, in the direction that the auctioneer and the small crowd were heading. He would then place them down, being careful to stay within the lines, even taking the time to make it neat by placing the tall items in the back with short, or flat items, in the front. Only the auctioneer, Dan, and I noticed what they were doing.

Then I got it. These two kids were going to try to sell this stuff. They were even clever enough to run behind the people doing the buying so as not, to be noticed. "I like it," I told Dan.

"I bet that whatever they can't sell, they just walk away and leave it. No need to keep junk inventory with items that got ignored twice in one day," Dan said.

We decided to follow along and see how well the kids did. They kept running back and forth with additional items until the crowd and auctioneer got near their space. They appeared to have enough sense to know when to stop, so not to be noticed by anyone. Besides our original crowd of buyers, every now and then someone new joined in the group and viewed the stuff for sale. I figured that there were between twelve and fifteen buyers.

Sure enough, once the group reached their space, both of them stood behind their items, as if they were the proud parents showing off their new baby. The auctioneer did his thing, and a number of items were sold.

Dan asked me, “You want anything?”

“No way, not me,” I answered, still impressed by these two little kids.

As the crowd dispersed and headed away, I watched as the two kids divided-up their money. The older kid made his way to the auctioneer and gave him a little money. The two kids then walked away with smiles on their faces leaving behind the second-hand, twice rejected, pile of junk-junk.

I said to Dan, “Those two kids should teach economics or some money management class. They both have real sales savvy in their blood.”

“Real cool. Not bad for little gooks,” Dan added. “They will make good used car salesmen someday.”

I saw something interesting and said to Dan, “Look, that old man must be one of their former students.”

Dan looked over and we could see some old man with a cart picking up everything else that was not sold today and left behind. He did know enough to leave behind the kid’s junk-junk. I guessed he now had his inventory for tomorrow.

I asked Dan, “So, where can we go for a cool drink? I’m dying from this heat, and a cold drink would hit the spot just fine right about now.”

“I’ll find us a place,” Dan assured me with confidence.

Not wanting to experience something that might get me killed, or even worse, having my little Charlie dragged all around a bar, I said, "Now, I'm only looking for a cold drink, not an experience that will harm me for a lifetime."

"Do you want some ice cream with a waitress coming out to us on roller skates and wearing a little skirt? We could always try to find a Diary Queen if that's more to your liking."

"They have something like that over here?"

"Sure, and maybe we can order a Gino Giant with fries."

I just fell for that one, so I responded quickly and acted as if I was joking. "Yeah, and we can pull in to Ameche's; or, to the Thunderbird on Eastern Avenue for a shake and onion rings."

Dan continued with, "Yeah, we can pick up some chicks and head up to Lock Raven, and watch the submarine races."

"You did that too?"

"Yeah, hasn't everybody been to Loch Raven?"

Thinking of better times and a better place, Dan said. "Up at Loch Raven, what I did was to tune my radio to a station out west, and sometime I would pick up a Chicago station."

"Why would you do that?"

"They would always announce the time on the radio."

"Yeah, they all do that," I questioned.

"True, but it's an hour earlier in Chicago, and that meant that I could stay out an hour longer and have a good excuse. However, I was only able to get away with that trick once per girl."

After a few seconds of reminiscing, he added, "I knew a girl or two that I could pull that trick on a few times."

I was thinking that this guy had an angle for everything. If I paid attention, I might pick up a few for myself because I really liked his Loch Raven trick. What was I thinking? I was going to be here for the next year, and I had no idea where the Navy would send me for the next three years. In reality, it might be four years or more before I could make it to Loch Raven. Maybe I should just focus on getting checked in and staying alive for now.

At this point, we just kept on walking. I assumed that he was thinking about home as I was. I had only been gone a few days, and it was rather hard to imagine that I was not going back for at least a year, and even then, it might only be for a visit.

Dan said to me, "You feel like taking a break with some music and girls? It'll kind of be like home, in a way."

"Yeah, I guess," I answered not knowing what he was talking about . . . again.

I started to hear a band playing as Dan pointed and said, "It's just around this corner, and there's plenty of dancing for everyone. Some of these dance places never close."

"Is it hard to pick up girls here?" I didn't know why I even asked that question. What was I going to do if I did pick up a girl? I didn't have a car, and if I did, I didn't have a place to take her.

"My man. Not even a problem. Don't sweat it. Look, it's the same over here for the guys as it is for the girls back home."

"And what does that mean?"

We turned the corner and Dan continued, "Back home, the girls at the clubs just stand around, and the guys must always ask if she wants to dance. Even if she is standing there, next to the dance floor and moving her hips with the music, she still controls the situation. She'll give you the once over and decide yea or nay, because you're at her mercy. They like it that way. They like it that way a lot and they'll keep it that way."

"True, but why is it like that for us over here?"

"The girls here want to dance with you. They'll tell you how good looking you are, how well you dance, and maybe you can be her numba-one guy and she'll be your numba-one girl."

"Let me guess. Then you would take her back to your table and start buying her drinks," I said because I thought I was now starting to pick up on this.

"That's right my friend. You may not get to dance with her again for the rest of the night because she would be ordering drinks until you were out of money. Then she would dance with someone else, anyone else, hell, whomever else, and drink up his money until he was broke."

"So how do you deal with it?" I asked, because I didn't want to find myself in a scam like the Christmas Cards the other day. Crap, if a little kid could rip me off there was no telling how much damage a pretty girl could do to me.

"If you want to dance, then dance. When the music stops, just say thank you, and walk away. Remember how it was back home?"

"Kind of," I answered that way because I didn't want him to know that I had never been dancing before.

"You know what I mean. There are the girls who only want to dance because of the song and not because of you."

"Yeah? I remember."

"She would just say, no thanks, and walk away. Do the same-same over here, and it will make you feel cool. The girls back home love doing that to guys. I bet that some of them even keep count of how many guys they tell to kiss off every night. I'll bet that they have contests, between themselves on who can tell a guy, 'no' to, the most times."

"Yeah, okay, I know what you're talking about now. I remember how a girl could at least get a dance and a free drink out of you before you were dismissed."

"Back home, yeah, over here, no. You must dismiss them," he added for my benefit.

"Okay," I answered, thinking that this might be cool. I might just enjoy this after all.

"As for me, I like to dance, and I like to keep score. I'll be able to get a couple of dances in with a few girls before they figure out what I'm doing," Dan explained, convincing me how sure he was of himself.

"Figure you out? What do you mean?" I hoped this was something that I needed to learn and not something that he had made up as he went along.

"Yeah, after a while they notice that I'm dancing and not buying. They also keep track of what's going on, and then they soon start to tell me, 'no.' And that, my dancing fool friend, is not a problem for me. I'll get in a half-dozen dances with a half-dozen girls, and then I can call it a good day."

"Is this anything like the bar you took me to my first day here? I do not want to dance with a girl that is holding something of mine besides my hand. You know, I do not want to be doing the Jerk, or Hand Jive, or being used as a Limbo stick."

Dan responded with laughter, "Nah, this is a dance place. Pool tables in the back if you don't want to dance, and they even have a small menu."

"I like to dance. I'll just try your method and see how many girls I can tell, 'no.' Naturally, I wouldn't be telling them all 'no,' because I do want to dance some myself," I cautiously explained, because after all this, it could still be a trick of some kind.

We both had a laugh with that and went inside. Naturally, I kept my privates guarded just in case they wanted to stamp something besides my hand, to show that I paid to get in.

There wasn't a problem on our entry, and we had good seats right next to the dance floor. For us to get up and dance, we had to walk around this chain and pole set up. The kind you find at banks and movie theaters with poles about four feet high, that were about five or six feet apart from each other. I guess it was to keep everyone on the dance floor from dancing in our laps.

We ordered a couple of beers, and settled down to relax and take in the sights. The band was rather good, and not as loud as the ones back home. The music was a decent copy, but the voices were very oriental. It was hard to appreciate a good country-western song from little gook guys that sort of sounded like Alvin and the Chipmunks after they had had a few beers.

The band, with their brightly colored outfits, looked like a group of little clowns. The only thing missing was a red nose and orange hair. I didn't know why I was complaining. I mean, I got in free and no one grabbed my little Charlie.

Our beers came, and two girls wanted us to dance. We both told them, "No, not now, maybe later." I just wanted to sit back and listen to the band. When I felt like it, I would dance with someone of my choosing. With a good band, air conditioning, cold beer, and girls that keep asking ME to dance, how much better could things get.

Dan and I, with raised beers, tapped them together and said at the same time, "Cheers." So, for now, here we sat watching everyone dance instead of watching guys on a working party, loading up a C-130.

Right in front of us, one guy had his hands all over a girl with whom he was dancing. His hands were going up, down, and all around her ass and she didn't seem to mind a bit. Her dress was almost up to her neck now with her red panties swaying to the music.

I said to Dan, "You don't see that very often back home."

He laughed and answered, "I have, and it's always at a wedding reception. It's usually the girl without a date with her ass hanging out for everyone to see, like a mating ritual."

He was right about that. I added, "Yeah, and she's the one that would kill to get the bouquet. She would use any excuse to have some guy lift up her dress to put the garter on.

Dan added, "Then she would always put the move on the guy who caught the garter."

We laughed and tapped our drinks together. Dan then toasted to the following, "To horny women at wedding receptions that don't have dates. May they always remember to wear clean panties for all to see."

"And if they can't keep them clean, at least try to remember that yellow goes in the front and brown goes in the rear."

Dan looked at me and said; "Now that's nasty, but I like it."

Another tipping of our drinks and we quickly finished off our beers. Dan motioned our waitress to bring us another round. We sat there and continued to watch everyone dancing and turned girls down that wanted to dance with us.

Back home, usually everyone danced the same-same. Over here, because everyone was from everywhere, no two people seemed to dance the same. It was amusing to see because the colored guys were dancing with arms and legs going in every direction. The white guys kept their hands and arms down to their sides. The Vietnamese guys and girls copied a little bit from each. It was entertaining for me to see little oriental guys trying to dance as if they were colored.

There was this big guy that looked like a farmer, he was dancing, and it looked as if all he really wanted to do, was crash into everybody. I didn't know if he was too dumb, or too drunk, to know what he was doing. With size in his favor, almost everyone that was bumped gave him a dirty look when he faced the opposite direction. Hell, if he bumped into me, I wouldn't say anything to him either. Some people were just too big to mess with, even when they acted the way he did. This guy was also a very ugly man, and he was so big, I was surprised that his knuckles didn't drag on the floor.

I said to Dan, "Check out Paul Bunion out there. This asshole is trying to clear the dance floor for himself by process of elimination."

"I see him."

"I'm surprised that no one has said anything to him. Don't you think that the girls who work here would at least say something about him to someone?" I questioned.

"Nah, if they did that, and he becomes pissed, there might be a fight; then people would leave, and the bar would lose business."

"Yeah, but wouldn't people leave if he kept doing that anyway?" I asked.

"I suppose that some would, but most would just dance and give him some room. Still, others won't dance and that means they'll be buying more beers for the girls."

I didn't know about anyone else, but it looked as if he was trying hard to purposefully, knock into people. He didn't care if it was a man or woman that he banged into. He really was an asshole. He reminded me of bowling. He was the bowling ball with everyone on the floor the pins. He tried to get a strike before the song ended. If he missed anyone, he treated them as if he was willing to settle for a spare. I decided that I would dance later, when he was off the dance floor.

A girl stopped over and asked Dan to dance. He smiled at her, and told me that he would be back in a little bit. They headed up to the dance floor, and started dancing far away from Paul Bunion. I finished my beer and asked for another.

This very cute girl asked me, "You want dance?"

"No thank you, not now. I dance later."

"You no can dance? I teach you Joe," she suggested to me very convincingly.

Still, I responded with, "No."

I could not believe that I just told another very cute girl that I did not want to dance. If we were back home, guys would be in line to dance with her. However, I was over here, and she and others just as cute would be back. It was strange to have all these girls wanting to dance with me. I must keep in mind, that this was their job, and that I was not all that special. I might as well enjoy it while it lasts, though. I could see now why the girls back home did this, 'no, not now, maybe later, thing.' It was rather cool, and I liked doing it.

I paid for my beer, opened it, took a good swig, and glanced back out at the dance floor. To my surprise, Dan, his girl, and the big guy were now only a few feet apart. I knew that Dan did not like little guys with no balls. I wonder how he felt about big guys with no brains.

Sure enough, Big Foot hit Dan and his dance partner at the same time. Both of them ended up bumping into another couple. The four of them just gave the big guy a dirty look. The one couple walked off the dance floor, but Dan and his partner kept dancing. Just then, the band stopped, and a few people left the floor. Others were standing around waiting for the next number before deciding whether they wanted to dance or sit.

Dan looked over at me and yelled for me to, "Watch this." He was standing behind the big guy and I could not see what he was about to do. I could only smile back and wondered if he was aware that he might get his ass kicked for whatever it was that he was thinking about doing. I really hoped he didn't expect me to jump in and help if monster man got pissed. This guy was so big that it could take everyone here just to take him down. Even with that, we would have to call in reinforcements to hold him down.

I could see the people sitting behind Dan, as they started pointing and laughing at him. He had taken the chain off the pole, the chain, and poles that separated the dance floor from the tables, and hooked it to this guys rear belt loop, and the big guy never knew it. It was done in one swift, smooth move, and then Dan headed toward me with a big smile on his face. His dance partner, who saw what he just did, yelled to some of her friends apparently letting them in on the joke.

The big guy was standing still and just talking to his girl. I could see that one member of the band was pointing and telling other band members, about what would soon happen. Dan returned to his seat without his girl. I assumed that she went back to her friends. Dan must have used her for those few dances only.

"This should be fun," Dan said with a childlike expression.

"Where do you dream up these ideas?"

"I've done this a number of times before. I was gonna do that to you; however, this guy needed to be taught a lesson."

"So you're telling me that this ass-hole is saving me from being made an ass-hole?"

With a smile, Dan replied with, "Yeah, I guess you could say that."

Dan took a swig from his drink and for a moment, we almost forgot about the guy chained to the pole until we heard the clanging sound of one of the poles hitting the dance floor. Sure enough, he had made one step too many and now the chain and a single pole trailed behind him. He turned around to see about the confusion and this only pulled more on the chain. Another pole clanged down and those who were not initially aware of this trick, were now watching, and enjoying it. This was very loud because these were metal poles and chains hitting on a wooden floor.

He turned again the other way to see what was behind him and then a third pole crashed down making even more noise. He now had about twenty feet of chain and three poles for a tail. The drummer in the band was now adding sound effects with his drums and cymbals to blend in with the action. It was more entertaining than watching the Ed Sullivan show.

This jerk, with a tail, was now alone on the dance floor, which was now his stage. He was a one-ring circus. He was either too drunk or too dumb to figure out what his problem was. He started to turn in a circle and that only made it more difficult for him. He was acting a lot dumber than he looked, and the crowd loved it. Everyone, and I mean everyone, was laughing at this main attraction. I had tears in my eyes because this was the funniest thing I had ever seen. However, this was no laughing matter to him. He looked angry and it appeared as if he wanted to kill someone, anyone. To add to the excitement, he started to growl like an animal. I had never heard a person growl like that before.

He was so big that he was unable to reach behind himself to unhook the chain. Now, there were four poles clanging on the floor with about twenty-five feet of chain around and behind him. The way the crowd responded with their laughter and cheers, it started to sound like a major sporting event. The crowd was going wild, and you would have thought that Johnny Unitas just threw another winning touchdown in the last few seconds of a game.

To my surprise, Dan stood up and motioned Mountain Man to turn around and back up towards him. It appeared that Dan was going to help this guy. Some people in the crowd were booing him for cutting short all the excitement. I could only guess that Dan figured that if he was to help him, that maybe he would not be considered as the one that did this.

He backed up to Dan, still growling, acting as if he was some big ape. He was humped over from exhaustion and too many drinks. He seemed frustrated, angry, and out of breath.

The dance floor was empty except for him, the poles, and the chains. Others in the room were standing on their chairs and some of the girls were standing on tables to get a better view of the action. Everyone continued to laugh at him and the crowd started to "Boo" Dan.

After the big guy backed up to Dan, Dan asked me, "Are you ready to leave?"

I was about to say "No," because I was enjoying all this, when I caught a glance of what he was about to do. Before he unhooked the one chain, he hooked the chain from this side of the dance floor to big foot's belt loop. Now I could see the reason for him wanting to leave.

Dan handed him the first chain and big foot held it up above his head as if it was a trophy or something. I heard him roar like an animal in heat. He didn't bother to thank Dan and he started to walk to the other side. As expected, down came the additional poles trailing behind him on the chain. The laughter was greater now than before. His anger doubled and it was now all directed at Dan. I doubt it was my imagination, but I could swear that I heard the big guy roar like a bear.

Dan said, "Ready? Now is a good time my friend."

I did not have time to answer him because he was already halfway out the door. I looked back and saw that Big Foot was tangled up, and had fallen down. The dance floor was filled with chains, poles, laughter, and one big ass-hole. I guess we could never come back here again.

The crowd had opened up a lane for Dan's escape, and he was getting high-fives from almost everyone, as he left in a very quick fashion. I caught up with him outside, and he said to me, "You hungry? Want to find someplace quiet where we can get a bite to eat?"

"Sounds good to me," I answered being almost out of breath. With all this excitement, I forgot that we just ate a little while ago. I could not believe that Dan wasn't continuing to run away in order to put great distance between us, and the big guy; he was just doing normal walk.

I asked, "Don't you think we should put some distance between us and Big Foot? You know, in case he gets loose, and wants to kill you."

"I believe we will hear him coming. The sounds of the clanging poles and chains should carry a good ways," Dan explained most assuredly.

I agreed with that, but I would also keep looking over my shoulder for a few blocks just in case. At the corner, we stopped and waited for the light to change. A jeep pulled up and inside were four colored Army guys. This in itself was no big deal except for what Dan said to them.

"Damn, I've seen four niggers together before but, never, and I mean never, have I ever seen four very ugly niggers together at the same time."

This guy was crazy. Wasn't it enough that he wanted a giant to kill us? Now he wanted these four colored guys to do us in. To top it all off, he had given all of them a good reason to kill us, and I agreed with them. I should kick his ass for what he just said to these guys. I guessed that I must watch out for the VC and the crap he pulls. Either way I, I mean he, he would get me killed. At the exact moment these four guys turned and faced us with a desire to kill, we heard, off in the distance, the clanging of poles and someone yelling, "I'm going to kill you. Don't try to get away from me."

What timing this was. Here comes the, big, ugly guy; and naturally, he was pissed and set in motion to kill us. And now, four colored guys had the same idea. I had visions of my immediate future with Dan. The five of them would team up, shove the poles up our ass, tie the chains to our balls, and string us up to a tree. The four colored guys would then give each other that hand shake thing that they do, and Big Foot would just stand there saying, "Cool man." This was not a good situation to be in, and I did not start any of this. This time, however, I was going to be killed just the same.

These four guys then turned to look at the noise that Big Foot was making and saw him coming our way, like a runaway train.

This slight diversion might be a good time for me to run away and hide from these colored guys for the rest of my tour.

Of all things to say, Dan said to the four guys, “How about a ride out of this neighborhood? And if you don’t mind, no need to wait for the light to turn green.”

Dan was crazy. I mean very crazy-crazy. You don’t go and call four colored guys niggers, and then ask them for a ride. It was like saying, “Take me to a place of your choosing, and kill us.”

“No sweat Dan, you and your friend get on the back and hang on tight.”

Dan jumped onto the rear fender, looked at me, and said, “What are you waiting for, a private invitation? You did this back-fender thing before.”

With Big foot almost on us, and because one guy knew Dan’s name, I supposed that my only choice was to take these guys up on the ride. At least I could cut my two issues in half. Now I could focus on how not to be killed by these four colored guys.

With my one hand and foot on the jeep, it pulled right through the red light, just as Big Foot arrived on station. Just missing me by inches was one of the poles thrown by Big Foot, at least he missed, and we were soon out of the area.

One guy in the back of the jeep turned to Dan and said, “I have two questions for ya.”

“Yeah, what’s ya got? I’m the answer man,” Dan responded yelling over the noise.

He probably wanted to know which one of us wanted to be killed first, I thought.

“One, did you hook that guy up to the chain? I saw you pull that one before on one of the brothers. And two, which one of us bronze beauties did you say was ugly?”

“Yes, that was my work of art, and he deserved it big time. And I didn’t say that one of you’s were ugly, I said that all four of you’s were ugly.”

He was still trying to get his ass kicked and yet, somehow with that comment, he got them laughing. I didn’t know for sure what kind of laughter this was. Did they think what he said was funny and it was okay for him to say? On the other hand, did they think that it was not funny and they were going to kill us?

The driver came back with, "Okay, but which one of us niggers is the ugliest of them all."

By now, I figured that these guys had to be friends to be talking this way to each other.

Dan responded with, "I don't know, it's too close to call. You all do look alike, don't you know."

One guy in the back tapped the shoulder of the guy-ridding shotgun and said, "It must be you."

"Why me nigger?" He responded angrily.

"I heard that when you were a little kid, that you mother told you that you were white so no one would call you an ugly nigger."

"Bull shit man. I heard something about you once from your one and only girlfriend. She told me that when she made love with you, that one and only time, that she kept a bag over her head in case the bag over your head came off."

Dan added in, "You mean like a double bagger?"

"No man, that nigger girl that he dated, well, she couldn't count that high. She got as high as 1 then 2, and she couldn't go any higher."

The guy that was being cut-up responded with, "Yeah, I heard that when you were a baby, your mother was stopped for shoplifting when she carried you out of a pet store."

"Is that right, nigger? You were so ugly that your mother had to tie a bone around your neck so the neighborhood dogs would play with you. And I heard that you were buried twice," responded the guy driving.

"Shit man, I heard that when you were born, the doctors didn't smack you, they smacked your father and mother."

"Shit nigger, I was told that once you and your girl had trouble leaving the zoo."

"What you be talking about man?"

"Yeah, she was so ugly that she had to show them some ID, before they let you take her out of the park."

"Oh yeah, I heard that when you were a kid, that you liked to wear cowboy hats and everyone started to call you, 'Leroy Rogers.'"

"That ain't nothin, man. I heard that your girlfriend always turned in circles like a dog before she lay in bed."

It was hard to keep up with everyone talking back and forth they way they were. At least everyone was laughing as the driver said, "Yeah, and every time you rubbed her chest, her leg kept kicking you, and the only way you could calm her down was to rub behind her ears and say to her, 'good girl, good girl.'"

The guy ridding shotgun joined in and added more insults, "And your mother told you that as long as your nose was cold, that you weren't sick and had to go to school."

Everyone was starting to take these cuts at each other. I could not help but notice that everyone was calling everyone a nigger. Even Dan was joining in with the nigger calling stuff.

"You know these guys?" I asked. Now that was an understatement. I just felt like saying something.

"Yeah," Dan replied loud enough for everyone onboard to hear over the noise of the motor and wind. "The driver and I went to high school together."

The driver made a quick look back at me and said, "Greetings and salutations from South Vietnam. My name be Marvin."

That was easy enough to remember. "Hi Marvin," I shouted. "I'm Charles from Baltimore, Baltimore Maryland. Glad to meet you."

Dan continued with, "Riding shotgun is my man, John. Now I didn't say he was a John, just that his name was John."

Now John looked like he was ready for war. He had on his flack-jacket and helmet. He did seem out of place dressed the way he was, but what did I know. I would have thought that everyone would be wearing a helmet and flack-jacket, or that no one would be wearing them. Again, what did I know? "Hi John," I shouted to him.

He quickly came back with, “What? You not be glad to meet me?”

I glanced over at Dan and questioned, “What?”

“Man ole man. You need to show consistency. You said that you were glad to meet Marvin, but you didn’t say that to John here,” Dan explained.

Oh yeah. Okay. “About that, sorry John. I am glad to meet you, too.”

Dan then proceeded to explain, “You see, John here thinks that everyone hates him, and that he doesn’t have any friends.”

Dan leaned close to me and continued to explain, “He’s always wearing his steel pot, that’s a helmet, and flack-jacket, even to bed and in the shower. He believes that there is always someone out there that wants to shoot him.”

“Is that true?” I questioned, almost believing what Dan had said. I mean, this guy was wearing all that stuff and this was just a joy ride.

Dan ignored the question as he introduced the next person. He pointed to the guy right in front of me that had a dent in his head. Now this dent could pass for a birdbath if it was filled with water. Even with us flying down the street and hanging on for dear life, this dent in his head had my total attention. Except for the color, the dent also reminded me of a bad dent in the middle of a baby moon hubcap on a 57 Chevy. Anyway, Dan introduced him as Anthony. I never knew a colored person named Anthony before.

“Hi Anthony. Glad to meet you,” I said, remembering to add the, ‘glad to meet you part.’

“You can call me Crash. Everyone calls me Crash,” he explained, as he turned around to shake my hand the regular way.

Still trying to fit in, I asked, “Why do they call you Crash?”

Everyone laughed at my request as if they had all heard the story before. For my benefit, he began to fill me in. “When I was a little boy,” he started.

Dan broke in and said, “When you were a boy. Damn man, you’re still a boy.”

Now that was funny, but not a very nice thing to say. I made a point of ignoring what Dan just said.

Crash quickly responded to Dan's comment angrily with, "Shut up white trash. I've got a story to tell your white friend here."

Dan submitted to his request as Crash continued, "When I was a young man, a very young and good looking young man, I crashed on my bicycle and went head first into a fire hydrant."

"Wow. I'm sorry to hear about that," I told him, being very sincere.

"Mans, don't be sorry about that, that was a good thing for me to run into," he told me as he turned to look at me, while he rubbed the dent in his head. "The hydrant, you see, stopped me from crashing into a busy street filled with traffic."

Not knowing what to say or ask next, I stumbled with, "So, what happened to your bike?"

He turned back around and thought for a moment. "No one has ever asked me about that before. I do remember that the last time I saw it. It was wrapped around the back set of wheels to a tractor-trailer. That tractor-trailer never did stop, now that I think about it. I doubt that the driver knew anything about it."

Dan shouted and changed the subject with, "Well, now that you made everyone here sad, let me complete the introductions here with Mr. President."

The guy in front of Dan turned to me and said, "Hi. My name is Monroe. Some of my friends call me Mr. President and some call me Monroe. You can just call me, Prez, that's short for President, don't you know."

I answered him with, "Hi Prez. I'm Charles from Baltimore, Baltimore, Maryland."

He turned around as if not impressed with me and said, "Yeah. Yeah. Yeah."

Dan started to explain, "Mr. President Monroe here wants us to believe that he's the great, great grandson of President Monroe. And, of course, everyone believes him." Dan said, as he finished it off with a wink, indicating that this was fictional story.

Prez turned around and told me rather loudly, "I am the former President's great, great grandson. Everyone here is just jealous, and I can live with that." He turned back around with his arms crossed and sat up straight indicating that he was on some kind of high horse.

Dan added in a low voice so as not to be heard by Monroe, "One day, this guy will be king somewhere on a tropical island. And when he is, he will start a war with the United States.

"For what purpose?" I asked, and this time it was easy to keep my voice down because of all the noises already around me. "He'll lose the war, right?"

"Most certainly he will lose the war. Then the US will send him some foreign aid, and his country will thrive and he'll be rich," Dan told me and I found this very believable.

John yelled back at me, "So Charles, what do you think about Dan?"

I had to be careful here and not to offend anyone, especially Dan. "He's okay. I've only known him for a few days now. We're checking into the same unit."

"Yeah. We think he's okay too," John responded. "Not bad for a white guy that thinks we all look alike."

The other three guys laughed and John directed his next question to Dan. "Now what do you think would have happened if you had make a mistake and we were someone else?"

"You mean like four other ugly niggers?"

"Yeah, that's right."

Now that was a horrible thought. I didn't even want to think about what might have happened to us.

"No way man, no mistake. I can spot you ugly, four of a kind uglies, from far away," Dan boasted.

At least they were continuing to laugh.

John stopped at a light, and Dan looked behind us. I guessed it was to see if that big guy was still following us. He turned to me and said, "Well, we just got away from a possible bad situation."

As the jeep pulled away from the light, I said, "Yeah, but I thought you were trying to make it worse for us by calling these niggers, 'niggers.'"

I got a surprised look from Dan and mean looks from everyone else. It was obvious to me that I had messed up somehow. I was back to the place where I felt that they wanted to kill us, well, me anyway. The jeep quickly pulled over to the side of the road, and everyone looked at me as if I had two heads. I had no idea what it was that I said, but I was sure that someone was going to be telling me very soon.

Dan gave me a look of disgust as if I was some kind of idiot. He said to me, "Look, a nigger can call a nigger a nigger, but never can anyone else call a nigger a nigger. And it especially can't be coming from a white guy."

I looked around at everyone and answered to the group, "But, but Dan called you guys niggers. I just thought that it was all right. Am I wrong?"

The driver said, "Yeah, dead wrong, you white trash, motherfucker."

Dan said, "Just tell them how you are from California, and in California, everyone calls niggers, 'niggers.'"

Here we go with the California bit. If it would save my life, I would say that I was from the moon.

John added in his anger by saying, "California, you say? What do you say I put my M-16 behind your ear instead of a damn flower?"

The Prez added, "Yeah man, that way he can sing how he left his heart in San Francisco and his brains in Saigon."

Everyone laughed at that one, but I didn't think it was enough to get me off the hook just yet.

Crash spoke up and said, "I say we cut off his balls so he can be one of those California hippies that talks funny."

"Hell man," I guessed this was a good time for me to say something. "I can start talking very funny right now, and save you the trouble of having to cut off anything. Know what I mean?"

I was trying to create a joke that might calm things down for me. Everyone was laughing now, which was a good thing.

John pulled away from the curb, and down the road, we went.

I felt relieved that my life had been spared, and maybe everyone would ignore me from now on. I must watch my P's, Q's, and niggers.

I glanced over at Dan and he was just smiling at me. I asked him, "What?"

"I'm liable to get a medal for all the times I have saved your butt from getting killed. I can't wait to see how well you do in a combat situation. I know you are part, 'AH.' Is the other part of you, 'VC?'"

"I'm no VC, but what's an 'AH?'"

"Ass-hole."

At least with that comment, everyone was still laughing. John yelled back, "Yeah man, you are one dumb-ass white boy."

I looked over at Dan and said, "Don't sweat it man. I owe you one."

Dan said, "Look. You are probably wondering, why is it, that I can call them niggers, right?"

"Yeah, I would like to know. Not that I would ever think of calling them anything like that again."

"You see in high school, most of the time I was the only white guy in class. After a while, you kind of know what, when, and how you can say things. For the most part, I can say almost anything about almost anyone and usually I get away with it."

Then John, overhearing us, said, "In high school, Dan taught us niggers something that we once believed to be an old wife's tale."

I looked at him and said "Like what?"

"We always believed that you white guys always looked alike. But, because Dan is so ugly, we found ourselves being grateful that all white guys didn't look like him."

Everyone broke up and started to laugh again. I didn't know whether to laugh with them to get on their good side or not. On the other hand, if I did, then I might not be on Dan's good side. I best just smile and let it go at that.

"So where are we heading?" Dan asked.

John spoke up, and said, "We aren't heading anywhere that we can take white, red-neck trash to. Let me know when we can drop you guys off, and I might slow down a little."

"Oh, I get it. Going to one of your all colored party things?" Dan questioned.

We got a dirty look in return and Dan immediately responded with, "The next corner will be just fine, and I do appreciate the ride and rescue. I owe you one."

I think Dan just made one comment too many that time. If there was ever a line for Dan to cross with these guys, I believed he had just crossed it. At least he knew when to bow-out.

"With the size of that guy that was after you, I would say that you owe us all two, not one; not to mention the fact that we didn't kill your California, ass-hole, friend here."

"All right already, two. I owe you guys two. Now if you will just slow down to make the departing of two helpless, white trash guys easy, it will be greatly appreciated."

Dan looked at me and said, "I do believe that we have out-stayed our welcome."

"Dan. You didn't outstay your welcome, because you were never welcomed in the first place," said the driver.

"No sweat, nigger. With that comment, I'll take away one that I owe you," Dan replied, and I thought he should have just kept quiet. At least he was able to keep them all laughing as we prepared to jump off.

The jeep did slow down a little, but it never did come to a complete stop. Regardless of that little detail, I got off, and after a short run to keep from falling; I glanced over at Dan as if he had two heads. To analyze what happened to me in the last thirty minutes would take me the rest of my tour to figure out. I was not going to ask him any more questions about this. I had to let this go.

With a childish smile on his face, Dan asked, "Still hungry?"

Chapter 12

"Hungry?! Hungry?! I'm just grateful to be alive. We could have been strung up or sitting at the bottom of a river because of you. Hell man, we were almost killed twice in the last half-hour and they aren't even the VC. Between the crap I pull, and the crap you just pulled, no way will I make it twelve months," I yelled.

As if I hadn't said a thing, he came back with, "Simple question, are you hungry or not?"

"Yeah, I'm hungry," I replied. "Besides, with all that has happened today, there's no reason to skip a meal. We might as well do something normal for a change."

After a short pause, I continued with, "Normal. Okay. I would like a normal meal."

"No sweat my man, in fact, you choose," Dan suggested, apparently trying to calm me down a little. It worked.

Looking across the street, I could see a row of restaurants that were opened, and I suggested, "Let's check out that side of the street."

"Okay. I'm with you."

We made our way across the street without incident. We entered the first restaurant and took a seat, away from the window. Immediately, a middle-aged lady was there to give us a menu to read. To my surprise, the only thing I understood was the Coca-Cola logo at the bottom of the menu.

"So, how do we order? Can you read this?" I asked, thinking that I made a bad decision on where to eat. Ordering the wrong thing here was something that I would like to avoid today.

"Nah, just order like a child," he said as he scanned his menu.

"What are you getting?" I asked trying not to sound like a child.

He responded while running his finger down the menu, "Third item down, and second one over to the right, and a Coke."

I get it now. This was sort of like going to Howard Johnson and checking out the pictures of the meals. His third one down, and the second one over, looked like a hamburger with fries. Now that looked okay to me. "I'll get the same," I said, sounding rather proud of myself.

A moment later, the waitress returned, and Dan pointed to his order. First to the sandwich with fries and then he pointed to the coke. He didn't say a word and he made it seem quite simple, child like.

She made a few quick notes and looked at me. I said to her, "I'll have the same."

She says, "No got same. What you want Joe? No same on menu."

"The same as him, you know, burger, fries and a coke."

"What want," see asked me again.

Laughing at me, Dan said, "She doesn't understand same. Just point to your selection, and she'll be on her way."

Damn, damn, damn. What was the big deal here? Anyway, I did as suggested. I pointed to my order and held up two fingers indicating that I wanted same-same. With that, she made a few notes on her pad and off she went.

"I didn't know you liked water buffalo," Dan inquired.

"I've never had it before, can you get it here?"

"Oh yeah, you can and you just ordered it."

"I just ordered a water buffalo burger?"

"Yes, with fries and a coke. Good choice, so don't sweat it. It's almost as good as a regular hamburger."

"What do you mean, almost?" I asked thinking that I should have let that one go.

"It's a little tough, but almost as good. They eat it over here all the time," Dan explained, suggesting that this was the norm, and I should just get with the program.

"Tough?"

"You see, back home a cow is slaughtered when it's just big enough to eat."

"Okay," I answered cautiously.

"No reason to feed it for any longer than needed. Cuts back on the profit and all that, you understand. A young cow is kind of tender and easier to eat."

"And over here?" I asked thinking that they would have the same profit motivation over here.

"Over here, they work the cows and buffalo to death until they die. Then they drag it, push it, or pull it to the nearest slaughterhouse to cash it in. After a few cuts with a dull blade, it's made into a buffalo burger."

"You sure? Is it any good?"

"Yeah, I'm sure. I ordered it, didn't I?"

"Yes," I answered believing that I might have made a bad decision.

"But, just don't eat it too often," Dan said. He just had to add in that part.

"Why not?" Not that I wanted to order this a second time after what he just explained. With a serious look, he explained, "If you eat too much, you'll have a strong desire to walk in some rice paddies in your bare feet pulling a plow."

"Is it really okay to eat?" I questioned a second time.

"What's your problem? Do you think I would have ordered it if it wasn't okay to eat?"

"I'm not totally sure," I answered just trying to get the facts.

"Look, the locals here eat it all the time," he assured me.

With a little thought, I answered, "Maybe so, but look at them. Almost everyone I see here is less than five feet, and some of them, could be the poster child for the starving people of Ethiopia."

"Good point," Dan agreed. "Then we must off-set this meal with a large order of fries."

Damn, this initially started out just having a burger and fries kind of lunch. Now it was giving me visions of pulling a plow in the rice paddies and being a foot shorter. I bet I would have nightmares because of this. Anyway, on the positive side, this was just one meal. I wanted to keep this menu as a souvenir to take home. My mom would enjoy hearing about my eating buffalo burgers.

Our burgers arrived, and to my disappointment, my coke was warm, and my fries were cold. However, after a few bites, I could say that my burger was very delicious. It was not a bad meal at all and I would order this again. In fact, my burger was so good that I didn't give my warm coke and cold fries a second thought. I had already forgotten that it wasn't regular hamburger, because it was so good.

Now my meal was going just fine until Dan asked, "How's your buffalo?"

Then it hit me like a pound of rice. I almost forgot about what I was eating. This was buffalo, a buffalo burger. Not the good old American, Grade-A, ground beef that my mom would get at the A&P. The only real difference was that I had to chew it a little more than normal. I needed to ignore Dan. "Good," I replied. "I might want to order a second one."

"Not me," said Dan. "One buffalo a day is enough for me."

I didn't care. I was going to enjoy my burger, cold fries, and warm drink anyway. After completing my meal, I quietly placed my menu in my pocket without anyone seeing me.

Our waitress came over and left Dan our check. I asked him, "What's my part?"

He gave our check the once-over and said, "Give me a dollar, and that'll include the tip."

I thought that we got a good deal for only a dollar. We got up and headed out the door. Just outside, I felt this tug on the back of my shirt. I quickly turned around to find our little waitress yelling at me and waving her hands all around my face. I could not make out anything she was saying, other than the fact that she was pissed at me, for some unknown reason. Maybe Dan didn't leave her a tip or something. Hell, I didn't know.

"Her menu. Give her back her menu," Dan told me. How did he know? I thought he didn't see me put it away. Just wanting to get away from her as quickly as possible, I took the menu out of my pocket and handed it to her. She said something to me that sounded ugly, and returned to the restaurant.

"What was she yelling at me? Did you understand what she was saying?" I asked as I turned to walk away as fast as I could.

"I didn't know what she was yelling at you, but at the end, I doubt that her last words were, 'thank you,' or 'please come back again.'"

"Now that wasn't all that bad. I almost got away with it," I said trying to make light of the situation, especially now that we were away from her.

"Not bad? Damn man, you were lucky this time," Dan explained.

I didn't know if I would call that confrontation, 'lucky.' I asked Dan, "Why do you think I was lucky this time?"

"If she would have been from the North, you might have gotten shot."

I never gave that any thought. What a horrible little country this was. "Next time, can you warn me," I asked with a most sincere look on my face.

"Warn you. Nah. I'm enjoying the entertainment you are providing, and that last skit of yours was most enjoyable."

"All right, that was wrong. Won't happen again," I answered knowing that he was right.

"Thanks. Besides, there was no real good reason I could think of that would have warranted anyone getting shot over cold fries and a warm soda."

I added in, "And buffalo burger. Let's not forget about the buffalo burger."

"So, you liked your buffalo meal. You can always order that one again, but I would suggest that you try another place," Dan advised seriously, with some laughter mixed in.

After a short walk, we stopped at the corner and waited for the light to change. I was surprised that the same four colored guys from earlier were in their jeep at the red light. No way was I going to say anything about, 'ugly this,' or 'ugly that.' Of course, no way was I going to say 'nigger' about anything or anybody, either. Damn, I wasn't even going to think the word.

Dan saw them and yelled, "So, are you guys still lost? Still can't find the place? It appears that you guys are ugly, dumb, and lost."

"No man, we'd not be lost. We'd just heading to the air base to meet his cousin that he's never met before," John, the driver said as he pointed to Monroe in the back.

"Never met him before?" Dan asked.

"Isn't that what I just said?"

"Just verifying the facts my man, just verifying the facts. If you want, I have a great trick to play on your cousin," Dan said with a gleam in his eye.

Somehow, this would be either extremely funny or very bad news for us. Monroe, whose cousins we were talking about asked, "This great trick of yours, what is it? You wanna hook up a few feet of chain with some poles hooked to his ass?"

"Take us with you and let me meet your cousin. I'll pretend I'm you. Naturally not as ugly and dumb as you, but you just the same," Dan explained to the group who were apparently listening to his suggestion.

"And what would that prove?" John asked. I didn't know why, but John seemed to be in charge, here with these guys.

"Now, how do you think he would respond to seeing me? You know, a red-neck, white-trash kind of guy and all that," Dan explained trying to convince everyone about his idea.

"Yeah man," they all seemed to say at the same time, as they started to talk between themselves.

Dan continued, "You guys can stand nearby to check his response. I can share with him that there's some white blood on my side of the family."

John said, "That will be funny. I'd love to see his face. Let's do it."

"It's my cousin, I'll decide," Monroe said.

Everyone gave him a stare, as if suggesting, 'what's your problem?' This sort of thing would be something we could tell our grand children about when we got older. With Monroe smiling and shaking his head yes, as if showing approval, Dan and I stepped onto the back of the jeep, and down the road, we went on an adventure. Moments later, we arrived at the air base and easily found our way to the terminal.

Monroe explained, "I told him in a letter to meet me right outside the terminal after he gets his luggage."

I asked, "How will you know each other?"

He showed me a picture of him. He was standing with some friends in front of a Pontiac GTO. He said, "He's the one on the end; he's kind of tall and dark skinned. I told him to come out the main door and stand near the buses, but not to get on."

Dan asked, "What's his name? And what's his mother's name?"

"His is William, and everyone calls him Willie. What do you want with his mother's name?" He asked as if suspecting a scam or something.

"That way I can say, Hi Willie, how is Aunt what's her name?"

"It's Vivian. She would be your Aunt Vivian," was the answer.

"Okay, good, I got it, Aunt Vivian. Now, does your family hug when they meet or do you guys do the hand jive, handshaking, knuckle-knocking, and finger-grabbing thing?"

"Man, we do the hug thing back home. Our brother to brother, power hand shake greeting is only done over here, for now."

"Got it," Dan replied as we made our way out front, to where the buses were parked waiting for the next incoming flight.

Once outside, we only had to wait a short time before some military personnel started filing out of the main doors. Apparently, a flight just had arrived. I could easily tell who just arrived in-country by the way they were dressed. The ones in jungle utilities, for the most part, came out first, and walked smartly to their buses, because they knew where to go. The ones fresh out of boot camp, in their dress uniforms; or, the ones here for the first time, came out and looked all around trying to decide which way to go. There was one guy out here with a clipboard, just like the one in Saigon. He was also yelling and giving directions for everyone to board their buses.

Dan butted into my day dreaming and said, "I wonder how many of those guys will check into their units before you do."

"Not funny. Not funny at all," I answered.

"Didn't say it to be funny," he responded.

Before I could answer to this cut of his, I asked Monroe, "Do you think his flight arrived early?"

He answered, "Don't know, let's just wait over here, and see."

As if on command, the six of us walked over and stood in the shade with a good view of the bus loading area.

Dan began to talk to the group, "Let me see if I have it straight. His name is Willie, and his mother is my Aunt Vivian, right?"

"Yeah, you got it. So when do you want us to step in?" Marvin questioned.

Dan thought for a moment and said, "Let us talk for a minute, and then you guys can mosey on over, and I'll introduce you as my friends. Then we'll improvise from there."

"Is that him?" Crash questioned.

Dan said, "Give me the photo."

Dan got the photo and took off yelling, "Willie, Willie, is that you?"

Although we were some fifty or sixty feet away, the look on the cousin's face was unmistakably shaken. Dan gave him a hug and started talking away, as if they had been close cousins for years. Dan picked up his sea bag and started walking slowly in our direction, and he talked all the way back to us.

Willie still had not said a word. Even with his mouth wide-opened, still, nothing came out. Now we could pick up on what Dan was saying, while this 'blank look' stayed on Willie's face. The four guys with me were all trying their hardest not to bust out laughing.

I could hear Dan telling Willie, "I didn't know that you were that dark skinned. Hell, on my side of the family, most of us look white. We even have a few, 'high-yellow' cousins mixed in, and some times we get called, 'white trash' and 'nigger' all in the same sentence."

Everyone was still able to hold back his laughter and only smiles were slowly slipping by.

Dan approached us and said, "These are my friends, brothers at arms. The white guy here is our driver. Don't mean nothin' about how our jeep be overloaded. The white guy just drives and does as we tell him."

Willie still had not said a word, as he shook hands with everyone while Dan did the introductions. It was obvious that Willie didn't know a thing about the jive handshaking, knuckle-knocking, and finger-grabbing business, because he did his handshake the regular way.

Dan handed his sea bag to me, and said, with much authority, "Stow this in the back of the jeep for my cousin, boy."

To continue with this joke, I responded trying to sound like Amos from the Amos and Andy Show with, "Yes boss, right away boss."

Willie looked to me as, if he wanted to get back on the plane, with everything a total surprise to him. He was meeting a family member that looked white for the first time. Whites taking orders from a colored; and to top it all off, a white guy was driving colored guys around, and taking care of the luggage. It was at this point that everyone lost it. Laughter from everyone was so overwhelming, that the cousin took a few steps back, so as not to catch whatever it was that we had. No way was he going to get into the jeep with us now.

His real cousin stepped up and said, "Willie, Willie. It's okay man. I'm your real cousin, not this white cracker here. This has all been a joke in your honor my brother."

A relieved look came over the cousin. He finally spoke up and said, "I was a little surprised about him being white and all that, but I wasn't going to say anything."

This was cool, and he took the trick well; at least he had a sense of humor. Everyone was now laughing and jive handshaking each other. The trick was a hit.

Willie added in, "Back home, no whites on my side of the family, just us Mahogany Marvels. As for me, I'm a Bronze beauty."

That statement got all kinds of comments from the guys, even though I didn't fully understand it. It must be a colored thing. No way was I going to ask any questions, about any of this.

Dan said to me, "Its time for us to mosey along because soon they will be a hugging and a kissing and all that. You know what I mean. Then there will be those lessons on how to greet each other with their jive-ass, handshaking, knuckle-knocking, and finger-grabbing, and butt-bumping thing they do. And you know that's not a very pretty sight."

Since everyone was apparently ignoring us anyway, I guessed that Dan was right about wanting to leave now. Dan butted in on these guys, and told Willie that it was nice to meet him. And how sorry he was that he had the one guy for a cousin and the rest as brothers.

He responded with, "No problem white boy, anyone is better than you."

This got a laugh from everyone. Dan and the cousin did a regular handshake, and we headed away.

"Hungry?" Dan asked.

"We just ate," I answered.

"That's right. I forgot."

"While we're here," I asked. "Do you think we should check on the location of our unit?"

"Yeah, we can do that."

Marvin yelled at us as we were walking away, "Dan! That trick be cool man. We even-up now, my friend, even-up."

Dan turned and gave him the peace sign. Wanting to fit in, I did the same. We walked back to the terminal and the first thing that I noticed, was that the same guy that sold me the booklet on Vietnamese Phrases, my first day in-country, was here. This guy really gets around.

Dan saw him and said to me, "So, do you need to buy the latest release?"

"Nah, one copy is enough for me."

This guy really made me mad because he was still taking advantage of the FNG's. Not that I was seasoned or anything, but this was my second time here. I should say something; maybe even ruin a few deals for him.

Dan read my mind and told me, "Drop it, and let it go. No matter what you say or do to this guy, he'll be back here or someplace else tomorrow, doing the same thing."

"You're right. That kind of thing pisses me off, you know; especially because it happened to me." However, I took his advice and as we walked on passed him. I didn't say a thing, even though he was making a sale at the time. After following Dan around for a few minutes, I asked him, "Do you know where you are going?"

"Kind of. Somewhere in here, there must be a flight operations office. We'll give them a try this time; they might have a better idea of the location of our unit."

I questioned, "You used them before?"

"No, I've always gone into town first, like we did the other day. I figured since we were here, I would give it a try."

As he was saying this, I saw a sign on the door down the hall that read, 'Flight Operations.' Quickly, I said, "That must be the place."

"Great, you are good for something."

He could have just said, 'thank you,' and left out the insult, but whatever.

Inside, we saw a very large map of South Vietnam on one wall. On another wall, was what appeared to be a schedule of flights in and out of here.

Dan and I walked up to the counter, and an Air Force colonel greeted us. I didn't know what kind of colonel he was, but he was a one star colonel. I had never spoken to anyone with a rank that high before, and I hoped Dan would do all the talking. Of course, this time, he said nothing. He just stood behind me, as if I was the one that was going to ask all the questions.

Damn, damn, damn, I hoped that I wasn't going to mess this up. Whatever, I took my time and asked, "Sir, we are trying to locate our unit, the USS SUMMIT. Could you help us out?"

"Why would you sailor boys think that I could help you? The only time we ever look for anything in the water is after a crash," he proceeded to tell me in an un-confrontational, and an un-authoritative way. It really seemed that if he could have helped us, he would have, or that he could have been teasing me a little.

"Yes sir. I realize that and I do not mean to waste your time. However, if you knew her location, then you might have been able to assist us in getting there."

I thought I said that rather well and was rather proud of myself until Dan added in, "Sir." Damn, I forgot to end my last two sentences with, 'sir.'

He returned a smile at me as if he was not going to jump in my face for my error, and for that, I was very grateful. He said to us, "Very well, wait one, and I'll check."

He turned and made a phone call. I saw that Dan was trying to remember the number that he was dialing. With no answer, he hung up and dialed another number. This time, someone answered. He asked a number of questions, but he spoke so low that I was unable to hear what he was asking.

He hung up, turned around, and said to me, "Just a minute."

The Colonel walked over to his desk and browsed through his clipboard. He was apparently making some mental notes to himself, before he returned and proceeded to tell me, "Here's what you want to do. I have a C-130 that's leaving in two hours. It's going to quick drop some cargo on the tarmac, not too far from here. The cargo is going to be picked up by a helo, then it will be heading out to an LST. From the LST, you can make your own way to your ship that should be close by."

Before I could ask either one of them what an LST was, Dan asked, "Sir, which C-130 should we board, sir?"

"I don't know the number yet because it hasn't been assigned. However, here's what you want to do. You want to follow the cargo. It's the cargo that going to your ship."

I asked, "Sir, where will we find this cargo, sir?"

He answered with, "Follow me."

We followed him as he turned and walked out of the office and down the hall. We came to a door that led to the outside and we stepped out with him. As he pointed to the cargo on the tarmac that was just a few feet away, he said, "Follow that pile of supplies; it will be leaving in about two hours."

Dan and I both thanked him at the same time followed by a salute. He returned our salute and walked away. I asked Dan, "Is this a, 'rush to get our things,' and 'rush back,' kind of time?"

"Sure thing. We'll catch a cab, have it wait for us, and ride it back."

With nothing else to say, we did just that. We made it back in a little more than an hour, and it was quite a relief to see that the pile of cargo was still sitting there. Standing next to this pile, I asked Dan, "What do you think is in these boxes?" I wanted to at least peak inside.

"No idea and before you get any ideas, leave them alone."

"I wasn't gonna do anything to them, I was just making conversation."

Before he could cut me down with one of his comments, a small pickup truck pulled up. The driver started to load up his truck with the cargo. Dan and I gave him a hand, and he looked at us, not sure what to think about our unsolicited help.

Dan broke the ice by saying to him, "We need to follow this cargo. I understand that it's going to be loaded onto a C-130. Is it okay if we ride with you?"

He responded, "Don't know and don't care. If you need a ride, and I'm going that way, no sweat man, get on the back."

We finished with the cargo loading, and rode to the other side of the base, in the back of his truck. We ended up at hangar six. Hangar 6 was where we started out my second day here, and sure enough, there was a C-130 there, just like before. The truck stopped, and we helped unload the cargo onto a pallet with wheels. It only took us a minute to complete this task before two other guys came over, placed a cargo net over everything, tied it down, and rolled it onboard the C-130.

Dan followed the cargo onboard and took himself a seat, as if he already had a ticket. I would have thought that he would have had to ask someone if we could get onboard, or at least find out where it was going.

Oh well, another adventure. With that, I sat down and buckled myself in, as the cargo doors closed, and we started to taxi. In no time at all, we were airborne and on or way to wherever.

Just after take off, one of the crewmen walked by and Dan asked him a few questions. They spoke for a few minutes before he walked away. I could not hear anything that was being said and Dan did not fill me in. The only thing Dan said to me before he closed his eyes to nap was, "It'll be a cool ride."

With that, I did the same, and assumed that he knew where we were going and that all was well.

Chapter 13

After about thirty minutes, the loadmaster came up to Dan and I, and said, "I want you guys to be ready to jump off, as soon as we make our turn. It'll be safer if you both wait until the cargo is off-loaded first. Remember what I told you earlier?"

Dan shook his head yes, closed his eyes, and continued with his nap.

Now, should I ask Dan about this 'jump off' thing, or assume that it was just an expression. Yet, he did say this would be a cool ride; and so far, nothing cool has happened. It could not mean to jump, as in parachuting. That might be cool, but I could not do that, because I didn't know how to parachute jump, and in no way did I want to learn today. I might as well ask, even if I had to wake him. Besides, the crewmember told him something, and I didn't know what it was.

"Excuse me, Dan. I don't mean to wake you, but I have a question."

"If you don't mean to wake me, then don't."

"I only have one question," I prodded.

"Let me guess, you heard the word, 'jump,' and you want in on some of the details."

I questioned, "Yeah, what is this, 'jump-off thing,' he was telling you about a minute ago?"

"It's not what you're thinking."

"What am I thinking?" I asked because I didn't know what I was asking.

"You're probably thinking that we're going to jump, as in parachuting, right?"

"Okay, right, yeah. Besides, how many ways can anyone jump out of an airplane?"

He sat up in his seat, wiped the sleep from of his eyes, and said, "Simple, my scared shitless friend. The plane will land first and it will only slow down a little."

"You mean like a, touch and go?"

"More like a touch, turn, drop, and go."

I tried to picture in my mind just what he tried to explain to me. Are we going to be dropped-off, if we don't jump?

Dan continued with, "After we land, and at the end of the run way, the plane will make a U-turn, at which time the ramp will be lowered. The cargo will roll out, as it starts to pickup speed for take-off. It's at this point, between when the cargo is off-loaded and take-off speed is obtained, that we will get off, or jump, as I said earlier."

"You mean that the plane will never actually come to a complete stop? You know, the plane might run over us. How dangerous is that?" I had a million other questions, but these few would do for now.

"Not a big deal at all. Hell man, wasn't it the other day that you jumped from a chopper onto a boat and both of them were moving? This won't be as cool, of course."

"Won't we get run over?"

"Impossible," Dan assured me. "Besides, the plane can't run over you if you are jumping off from the back."

"Of course," I responded, as if I already knew that.

"Just remember to throw your sea bag off first. It'll be too hard for you to catch up with the plane, if you forget and leave it onboard."

"So how fast will the plane be traveling when we jump off?"

"So slow that you might just step off with your bag on your shoulder."

"Oh good," I answered as if I was thrilled about this.

"Naturally my man, that's assuming that you have it timed just right."

"You had to say that, didn't you."

Dan responded with, "Just trying to keep you informed, my un-informed friend."

"I do feel a little better now. I had visions of you jumping out with a parachute, and me just waving bye to you."

"You mean you would not have jumped?"

"No way, I've never done anything like that before. Even if this is 'The-Nam,' and all that, I don't think I could have done it."

"Okay, my sissy man friend. If you don't have any additional questions for me, I'll get back to resting my eyes," Dan informed me and he did just that, closed his eyes, and ignored me.

"No sweat, I'll be doing the same as you; and I am not a sissy man," I fired back wanting to get in the last word. No response from him, but I just had to end our conversation with that.

Our flight continued for another fifteen or twenty minutes before I noticed we were starting to descend. To my surprise, and while we were still in the air, the ramp started to slowly open and we now had a spectacular view. The ramp continued to open so wide that you could have driven a truck inside. Again, I had a view that put to shame the little airplane windows on commercial flights. The motor and wind sounds were extremely loud, now that the ramp opened.

The two loadmasters were up and walking around, doing whatever it was that loadmasters do in flight. I stood up to get my things together, when the one guy told me, "You need to stay seated and buckle-up."

Now I figured that this guy only wanted to give out orders. With that, I came back with, "First off, I don't take orders from an enlisted person. Second, why is it that at 20,000 feet and moving at 200 miles an hour, we can walk all around the aircraft, and now that we are landing, I have to get back in my seat? And third, don't sweat the small stuff. Since I've been here in 'The-Nam,' I don't sweat the small stuff."

I looked over at Dan believing that he would be so proud of me for talking this way. However; he looked surprised, and I assumed that was because he didn't know I had it in me. Anyway, this was not an officer that I was talking to this time. I could say what I wanted to. With me being on a roll, I continued with, "And four, I know that a slow moving airplane filled to capacity with cargo makes a grand target for snipers. No way am I staying buckled up."

This guy gave me a look as if he wanted to throw me off the plane, right then and there, and save me the trouble of jumping off after we landed.

I proudly informed him, "I've done this jump thing before, and it's no big deal to me."

Dan grabbed my arm and said, "Sit down, be still, shut up, you ass-hole."

Now Dan told me to sit down and be still. What's up? Did I mess up?

The other crewmember came over; and now both were in my face, and with Dan taking their side; I had this feeling that I had screwed-up. I guessed that I would be filled in with the details later. So for now, I would just take my seat and stare at the floor. I was finally learning that being in the military was not a place to speak without thinking first. Yet, I thought that I had thought this thing through. I had done this before. What could have gone wrong?

The two crewmembers were still standing there looking at me as if I was crazy. I said to them, "No sweat, I'll stay seated until you tell me it be okay to get up, sorry."

With that said, the both of them returned to checking out the cargo and other stuff that they do.

Dan leaned over and said to me, "And what was that all about? Do you want these guys to help you jump out? What is your problem man?"

I didn't feel like talking about it, I just kept starring at the floor.

"Come on man. Help me out with this," he repeated.

I might as well answer him, so I said, "I thought this was like our flight into Saigon. You remember, get up, and get off, quick-like. Besides, he's a little short guy like the one guard at the Comm-Center. You do that kind of stuff, and talk that kind of way and it's all right. Yet, when I try it, it seems to be bad news for me."

"Did you happen to take notice, that these two guys happened to be wearing safety harnesses, you know, to keep them from being sucked out of the aircraft, and that maybe it was for your own safety to stay seated and buckled in until we were on the ground. I mean, look around man. The door is wide open, and there is enough room for the two of us, the two guys, and all the cargo to get sucked out. And all at the same time."

"I didn't notice that part, I was just trying to fit in," I explained, knowing full well that I screwed up.

"Next time you want to fit in, think about it first, and ask me about it second, before your 'fitting-in' gets you 'sucked-out.'"

"No sweat, I'll keep that in mind."

After a few minutes had gone by, I looked up to check things out. With Dan finished talking down to me, and the two crewmembers back doing their thing, at least now I could hold my head up and check out the view from the opened cargo door. Ignoring what happened to me, this was starting to be an interesting flight anyway. It was not often that you saw a view like this.

The lower we got, the rougher the ride started to be. I could only guess that having the cargo door open, while in flight, kind have messed up flying this thing. I didn't know if the pilots wanted to keep the plane trimmed or calibrated.

Moments later, we landed, and the engines got very loud. I assumed they were reversing, to slow us down before our U-turn. Almost as quickly as we landed, the plane slowed and started to make its turn. Cargo started to roll out, and Dan was walking right out behind it. Lucky for us, the plane was almost at a complete stop making our exit easy. However, just as I was about to step off, the plane started to race forward. Again, with luck in my favor, I made it off just in time, only to have the prop wash almost knock my sea bag and me down on the tarmac.

Dan looked at me as if I was some kind of retard by the way I tried to keep my balance. He said to me, "You are one amusing kind of guy."

"Thanks. At least I got off without breaking anything."

As expected, the C-130 started down the runway while she was raising her ramp. It only took a few seconds before she was airborne. Now this was another interesting view for me. I mean, here we were standing in the middle of the runway watching from this angle. This was rather neat and only in 'The-Nam,' could anyone expect to get this view of a plane taking off. I did turn around to make sure that nothing was coming in to land behind us. However, before could check-it-out, I got this beep from behind me. I should have figured that someone would be out here quickly to pick up the cargo, now that it was sitting here in the middle of the runway.

Dan said, "We're in luck. Here's our ride to the terminal area."

It was just one of those, front-end-loaders, and it soon picked up the cargo. I watched as Dan got up and began talking to the driver. I could not hear what was said, but after he got down and threw his bag on top of the cargo, I figured that I had better do the same.

By the time I turned to retrieve my sea bag, the front-end-loader raised the cargo a few feet higher above the tarmac. It was so high that the driver could see under the cargo and that made it easier for him to drive; however, it would not be easy for me to load my bag on, but I was glad the driver was happy. I made two attempts to throw my bag on top of the cargo and missed both times. Not only did I look like a wimp, I felt like a wimp. In addition, I had an audience that enjoyed my situation. Dan and the driver enjoyed it so much that now the driver raised the cargo even higher to the encouragement of Dan.

The driver apparently felt sorry for me or maybe he was tired of waiting. He finally lowered the cargo, and made it easier for me to throw my bag on top. I felt like a kid that was unable to shoot a basketball because the rim was too high.

Dan yelled at me, “Come on man, you only have twelve months to go, and you might run out of time.”

With my bag onboard, I jumped on and sat next to Dan. I hoped he had nothing more to say to me about that, but of course, he could not let that one go.

“What was the matter, was your bag too heavy?”

“Yeah. Remember I was carrying all my stuff and you were only carrying part of your stuff. I have in my bag, my dress blues and pea coat, and that’s extra stuff that I don’t need over here.”

“Relax man, just kiddin’ with you. Don’t sweat the small stuff,” Dan told me loud enough to be heard over the noise of the front-end-loader.

He was right; this was a ‘no sweat’ situation. It was just a short ride to the control tower, well, not exactly a tower. What we had here were two walls connected by a roof. One guy sat on a folding chair. He sat next to a folding table with a radio and soda on it. His headset and microphone were connected to a radio that had its antenna wire going from the table to both walls. There weren’t any doors or windows and he had a great view of the runway with no obstructions in his way.

The front-end loader stopped, and Dan and I jumped off with our bags. I asked Dan, “Now what?”

“We’ll just check to see if the helo is still scheduled to fly out to the supply ship. I so, we can get ourselves onboard.”

I realized how all this sounded simple enough, and I followed Dan up to the guy at the table. At least this time I could hear what he was asking.

“Man ole man, you have a nice view of the airfield,” Dan said, and I guessed that he was just trying to break the ice.

“Not so great when it’s raining, because I can’t close the doors or windows.”

"I can appreciate that my man," I said, wanting to fit in.

"What can I do for you guys," he asked.

"I understand that this cargo that just arrived, is going by helo to a supply ship."

He looked at his clipboard and said, "That's right, and it's scheduled to be loaded in about thirty minutes."

"That's what I was told. My buddy and I need to hitch a ride out to the ship with this cargo."

He responded by saying, "I don't know about that, there might be a problem."

Shit, this meant that we were out in the middle of nowhere with nowhere to go.

Dan quickly added, "If we load the cargo for you, can we just slip onboard for the ride out?"

This brought a smile to his face and he responded, "Not a problem with me. If you can get onboard and they don't mind, do it."

"Great," Dan said, "We really want to follow this cargo because it's going to our ship."

"What's the name of your ship?"

"SUMMIT."

With a puzzled look, he questioned, "The repair ship, SUMMIT?"

"Yeah, that's her."

"She's not out there."

I was thinking damn, here we go again, wrong place at the wrong time.

"Any idea where she might be?" I asked hoping he was not just pulling our leg.

"No, no idea. I just know that she's not where this cargo is going."

Dan asked, "We'll just follow the cargo anyway, if you don't mind. It's the latest information we have on finding her."

"No problem with me, man. Just make sure you're here when the helo lands. I can tell you right now that she will not wait for you."

"No sweat, we'll just camp out over there and wait. Thanks again."

Dan and I took a seat on the ground, just outside the terminal, and I asked him, "So why did you volunteer us for a working party? You have said many times that you always try and avoid them."

Giving the impression that I was asking another stupid question, he said to me, "No sweat, I'll load the cargo for my ride out, and you can work on your own plans to get there."

"Sorry, you know what I meant."

"Listen up. I volunteered us to load the cargo to get on his good side. I noticed that he had a pair of work gloves next to him, and the front-end loader is never used to load a helo. By doing him this favor of loading the helo ourselves, I believe that he felt the obligation to return the favor to us. Bottom line, we're getting our ride to our unit. Not exactly first-class, but we'll get there just the same."

"Yeah, not exactly first-class and she's not exactly there."

"Besides," Dan continued, "we don't have all that much to load and no where else to go anyway."

"He said that the SUMMIT was not out there. Now what?" I questioned.

"We'll check-it-out for ourselves. Besides, whom do you want to believe? Some officer in charge of supplies, or some clerk out here in the middle of nowhere?"

He was correct on both accounts. "Okay." I answered with approval.

The supply guy that we just spoke with, was now checking on the inventory. What he did was odd. He opened each box and checked out everything in each box. I said to Dan, "I guess he's doing a detail check for his inventory."

He looked over and said back to me, "Don't think so."

I may be new in the military and new in 'The-Nam,' but I could tell when someone was checking inventory. "You don't think so," I questioned.

"No. Now just watch what he's doing."

"I can see what he's doing, and I still think he's checking the inventory."

"Watch just a little bit longer, you'll see. Besides, what is he checking the inventory against?" He asked me that question and now this had my interest.

What happened next should not have surprised me. He took something out of one of the boxes and sat it aside. He did this two more times from different boxes.

"See, what did I tell you?"

It took me a second or two, but I finally got the fact that this guy was stealing. I told Dan, "Picking out a few items that he needs for himself, I see. How could you tell he was going to take stuff before he took anything?"

"He doesn't have a clip-board."

"Clip-board?"

"Yeah, if he was checking the inventory, what was he checking it against?"

"Okay, I got it. I guess he needs these items for himself."

"Not exactly."

"Now what do you mean by, 'not exactly?'" Damn, I could not even get that part right.

"There are probably some items that he doesn't need for himself. And he will sell those items," he explained.

Sure enough, this guy continued to take items and placed them under his desk. After a few trips from the cargo to his desk, he reorganized and closed the boxes to give them the appearance that nothing had been opened. He then looked over at us, and I just looked down at the ground as if I didn't see anything.

Of course, Dan had to go and say something smart to him. He said, "At least you left something for us to load."

His reply was a no reply. He just ignored Dan and returned to his desk.

I looked around for the guy that drove the front-end loader and noticed that he was in a hammock under some trees. I said to Dan trying to crack a joke, "Great duty station, with one guy stealing stuff, while the other naps all day."

Dan looked over at the guy at the desk, and then at the guy in the hammock and said, "Don't think so my friend."

"And why not?" I didn't think that he and I would ever agree on anything.

"Like you said, one guy is a thief, busy counting his inventory and the other is napping away. Don't you think that one of them should be on guard duty?"

Dan must have noticed my disappointed expression, and that I hadn't said anything, so he added, "Don't sweat it. When we get on the river, no one sleeps on guard duty because shit happens to us all the time."

Before I could respond to that, three little girls came up and were just standing there staring at us. They were acting just like little kids back home, and I didn't know why I find this odd, but I just did. They were talking and laughing amongst themselves. I smiled, waved, and said to them, "Hello."

They continued to stand there and kept on talking and laughing, apparently at us.

"What's up with them," I asked Dan.

"They're just being friendly because they must want a handout or something."

I questioned, "Like candy?"

"That's right, but money will be more valuable to them than candy."

"I thought they would like a candy bar or something like that."

Dan proceeded to give me a little history lesson, "Only kids in W.W.II movies liked candy. Over here, they only want money or cigarettes."

Wanting to do something nice for the kids, I asked, "I don't have any Vietnamese money to give them, do you?"

"No sweat, they'll take MPC, and if you really want to see them smile, give'm green backs."

I took a one-dollar MPC bill out of my wallet and gave it to the oldest of the three girls. She gave me a smile and said, "Thank you Joe."

She showed the dollar to the other two, and it made me feel kind of good, until the smallest one looked at me and said, "Only one dollar for three of us? You cheap Joe, you give more money."

I got a smile from the girl holding the dollar, a mean look from the other two and laughter from Dan. I didn't know how it happened; I thought I did a good thing, and two out of the three of the girls were unhappy with me. I figured the hell with them. One dollar to split three ways was not a bad deal. It was not as if they did anything for it. I was a little ticked off at this, so I told them to, "Go away."

They left and headed right toward the guy at the desk. As he saw them approach, he reached under his desk and gave each of them a small box of something. I believed that to be something that he had taken from the cargo earlier. All three seemed real happy, and proceeded to walk over to the guy in the hammock. I heard him tell them to go away, but to come back tomorrow.

With that, they headed away, and I felt like I did a good thing for the wrong group of kids. I looked over at Dan and said, "I guess these are bar girls of the future."

"Yeah, that's probably how most of them got started," and with nothing more for either of us to discuss, we both closed our eyes for a siesta.

A minute later, we could hear the sound of a helo coming in for a landing.

I had never seen a helo like this one, and it looked kind of old. There were no guns or rockets on her, and I could assume that she was not going to be flying, 'low and slow.' Well, maybe 'low and slow,' not to attract attention. Just 'low and slow' because it was old.

It only took us a few minutes to load the cargo, with one of the pilots giving us loading instructions.

Once loaded, Dan and I hopped onboard for our flight out. There were no seats for us to sit on, so we just made ourselves comfortable on top of some of the boxes. We could hear and feel the blades coming up to speed, and we rolled forward a few feet. I could see the pilot and co-pilot talking and making a few adjustments before they tried to lift-off again. On this kind of helo, the pilot and co-pilot sat up front above us, with their feet at our eye level.

We only rolled forward a few feet again, and we never got off the ground. The co-pilot looked at Dan and me, and told us to move toward the center of the aircraft. We did as told, and I thought that if we were too heavy to take off, I would be glad to get off and wait for the next ride. At any rate, another attempt was made, and we took off after a short roll. I always thought that helicopters took off straight-up, and that they never rolled anywhere. Oh well, this must be another one of those 'Nam' things. At least we stayed up and continued to climb. Dan then said to me, "I didn't think we were going to take-off without crashing."

I only smiled, because I could not think of anything clever to say in response.

It didn't take long to make cruising altitude for such an old helo. I enjoyed a great view with the door opened and as always, everything was green and brown.

We were above the clouds now, and the view just got better and better. We were over some river, and it was interesting how it twisted and turned through the countryside.

Dan said, "Maybe we don't know where we are going, but at least you seem to be enjoying the view."

"Yeah. Flying is great with the doors opened, and, it's better than getting those bags of peanuts on commercial flights. I could fly like this all day. I might even want to change my rate to work at something where I can fly. What do you think?"

Dan responded, "Come down to earth my friend, we're almost there."

"Where is there?"

"Look down there. See the LST?"

"LST?"

"Yeah. It's just a supply ship."

"Damn, already," I said, with disappointment that our flight was over. I was enjoying a once in a lifetime view of a foreign country.

"Sorry my friend, we got a war to try and win."

I didn't want to land now. We were flying high enough, that I didn't expect to be shot at, and I was enjoying the flight. "No sweat," I answered.

"We will get to fly again," Dan assured me.

"We will!" I answered, sounding like a kid that was going to get a second ride on the merry-go-round.

Oh well, I might as well sit back and enjoy the rest of the flight. It only took a minute, and we were down and getting off. Dan said to me, as we exited the aircraft, "Let's stay with the cargo as if we were assigned to take care of it."

"No sweat. Is there someone we could ask to see about when our next ride will be here?" I asked that question, because we just might get stuck out here.

"I'll check in a minute," Dan said, as we unloaded the cargo.

Dan said a few words to a crewmember that was unloading the cargo with us. They spoke for a minute before Dan came back over to me and said, "We are to store our cargo to this side of the flight deck, next to the railing."

We did this quickly; all the while, the chopper had its motor running. I did not enjoy the taste of jet fuel mixed in with the sweat that rolled down my face and into my mouth. I wanted to spit before I swallowed, but the breeze generated by the chopper blades caused the breeze to change direction every second or two. No need to spit in my own face, and this be not the time to throw up.

Whatever. After just a minute or two, our cargo was off-loaded and neatly stacked. We took a seat on top of the boxes and enjoyed a well-deserved break. Our helo took off, and everything got quiet and still.

"You look sick," Dan said.

"Nah, I will be all right," I answered, and hoped that I didn't throw up.

Dan moved over, sat on the other side of me, and said, "Just in case you do, I'm going to sit, down-wind from you."

"No sweat," I answered, and gave that comment no more thought.

Dan spoke up and said, "I guess we'll just sit here for a few minutes and wait for our ride."

"Will we be here long?"

"Don't think so because here it comes now."

Sure enough, another helo came in and landed right next to us. I assumed this was our next ride out. We quickly got up, and Dan made his way to the pilot, as I just stood by. Dan then looked over and signaled me to start loading up. I loaded the cargo, as Dan kept on talking to the pilots, and I was done before he was finished. At least it only took me a few minutes to load-up the helo. It might have taken me a minute or two longer, except at our last stop, some of the items were stolen. I hoped we were not held accountable for what was missing, because we were keeping an eye on it.

Dan then said to me, "You ready? Our ride is leaving now."

Again, we were heading out on another trip. No sooner did we settle in, we took off and, 'up, up and away' we went. This might be an odd thing to say, but flying on helicopters was becoming, 'old hat' to me. With flying over open water, there was nothing to see. Maybe this time I would get to see an aircraft carrier from the air.

After only a few minutes, I looked down and saw a large supply ship. I figured this out because it was not an aircraft carrier, and it was too big for a destroyer. I didn't see any big guns, so it could not be a battleship.

I said to Dan, "Look, I believe that's where we are headed. I don't see any other ships near her. So do we assume that we are at another dead-end?"

"Nah, lets wait and see."

We landed and unloaded the cargo. This was done quickly because there were two guys already there to pick up the cargo. The cargo was loaded on a pallet, covered up, and tied down.

I looked at Dan and asked, "What now?"

"Let's take a walk to the radio room and see what the story is this time."

I asked, "Should I stay here and watch our bags and the cargo while you find out?"

"Good idea, I'll be back in a minute."

Dan took off, and to kill some time, I looked over the side and noticed another small supply ship that was apparently taking on some cargo. This little country sure had a lot of cargo being moved around. At least I was not involved in that working party.

After about twenty minutes, I started to get concerned. I didn't know where I was or where to look for Dan. I knew that he could not get far. I always seemed to be waiting for him and watching our bags. I didn't know why I was complaining. I did have the easy part.

Before I could think of anything else to complain about, Dan returned and said, "I have good news and bad news."

I came back with, "Let me guess, the ship is not here and that's the bad news. The good news is that you have a plan."

"Okay. You're right."

"What about this cargo that we've been trailing for the last hour or so," I questioned because the One Star Colonel's instructions could not be wrong.

"Okay, here's how things are. The cargo is going to the SUMMIT, but it might take a week to ten days to get there," Dan explained. "No way are we going to follow it around for that long of a time. Not here on this ship anyway."

"Our plans are?" I questioned him and followed up with, "What do we do now? Do we check-in here? Do we get our orders stamped, and does anyone get a copy of our orders?"

"Not this time," he answered. "We don't really belong here, and it'll be easier to get off if we don't check in."

I had to ask about that, "We don't have insurance about getting off? We do have a place to go, a ship to report to, right?"

"It wouldn't surprise me if this ship needed one of us, or even both of us. It would be to their advantage to keep one or both of us right here and to have our orders changed."

"Look man. We are out here in the middle of nowhere, and the last thing I need from you is a joke. Now please, what are you talking about," I asked, thinking that I didn't need this kind of crap from him. Not now. Hell, not ever.

"No man, for real. It would be cheaper for the navy to keep us here rather than to transfer us to our unit. We could be added to the billet here. So with that thought, and I was not joking, we'll make an effort to keep a 'low profile' from everyone onboard."

"So, where do we go?"

"The radio guy I met told me that flights are going off this thing all day long. We'll relax a bit and catch the next flight out," Dan instructed me, but he didn't sound too reassuring.

I asked this question again for the hundredth time, "So where is our ship?"

"This same guy believes that she's at Cam-Ranh-Bay. So for now, we'll get something to eat. You hungry?"

"Yeah," I said, sounding as if I was out of breath, because all of this travel made me tired.

"No sweat. We'll lock our bags up here to the railing and find the chow hall."

With nothing else to do, I did just as he instructed. We locked our bags to the railing and followed the smell of cooking food until we found the chow hall.

Chapter 14

Nice chow hall they have here on this huge supply ship. I wondered how many items were taken out of each box, as the cargo made its way from the states, to the units where it belonged after first getting here.

Whatever, my ham sandwich and cold soda with chips, really hit the spot. Dan had the same, along with a bowl of soup.

Half way into his soup, Dan put his spoon down and told me, "Hang-on. I'll be back in a second."

With the way this guy liked to eat, what could be so important that he would be willing to leave his meal, half-eaten? I watched him as he walked past a few tables and sat next to a guy in a flight suit. They talked for a few minutes, and he returned looking as if he had good news.

Dan took his seat and continued to eat as if he had never left. Curiosity got to me, and I asked, "Who's that, a friend of yours?"

"No. First time I've met him," Dan responded with a mouth full of soup. I think it was black bean soup.

I had to know, "What were you guys talking about? It had to be important for you to interrupt your meal."

"Yep, important. Did you notice what he was wearing?"

Here we go again with his, question and answer time. "Flight suit. He was wearing a flight suit."

"Exactly."

"Exactly what?"

After another sip of soup, Dan continued, "Exactly what we need to get off this boat."

"A flight suit," I questioned.

"That is not it my friend."

"Then, how about a hint," I suggested, and thinking how this conversation would soon give me a headache.

"Simple, my inquisitive friend," he told me, as he gulped down the rest of his soda. "A person wearing a flight suit is a person that's part of a flight crew. We need a flight off this boat today, and I thought that he would have some knowledge about today's flight schedule."

"And," I asked after it appeared that he wasn't going to give me any more additional information.

"After we finish our meal, it'll be time for us to go. I do believe that I have us a ride off this boat."

"Do I need to ask what kind of ride we have, or should I be happy that we have one?"

Trying to make me feel that I should be grateful for all he had done for me so far, he said, "Let me rephrase my last statement. I have a ride for me off this ship, and it's heading for Cam-Ranh-Bay. You can come along if you like or you can find your own way off this South China Sea cruise."

Hoping I didn't make him mad with what I said, I responded with, "Now that wasn't the way I meant it. I'm excited that you have taken the time and effort to look out for me. Naturally, a way off this ship is truly appreciated."

"You are full of crap today my, need a ride to work friend."

At least he said this with a smile, and yes; I did need a ride to work.

"So tell me," I said, trying to stay on his good side. "What kind of ride will I enjoy today, and when are we leaving?"

"I'm surprised you didn't ask why we're heading back to Cam-Ranh-Bay."

He was right on this one. However, at this point in time, I didn't think that it really mattered. Besides, I didn't really care. How does he say it, 'it don't mean nothing,' or, 'don't sweat the small stuff.'

I submitted to Dan, and said, "You must have some master plan on how to get around. Hell, I don't even know where I am. Even if I did know where I am, I have no idea where to go. I'll just follow your lead."

"Okay, no problem," Dan replied. "I'll just fill you in with the details of our, first class travel itinerary."

For once, I was getting details before it happened. Maybe this was the first time he really knew what was going on, and he was not making any of his, 'lucky guesses.' "Are you telling me because you are being kind; or, is it because we might become split up and separated?"

"Listen up my man. A Chinook will be in soon to drop off some people, and is returning to Cam-Ranh-Bay. We need to be on the flight deck when she lands, because she'll only be down for a few minutes. And, if there's room for two, then we'll both make it to Cam-Ranh-Bay at the same time."

"So, how soon is soon?"

"Soon equals almost now," Dan answered, looking at his watch.

"Now, now?"

"Kind of."

"Kind of what?"

"I mean, soon after I eat."

It figured that he wanted to finish his meal first. I responded with, "No sweat, I'm there my man."

We were off again on another adventure, together I hoped.

After we finished our meal, we put our trays away, and headed toward the flight deck. Once there, we unlocked our bags and found the perfect spot that we thought would keep us close to the landing pad, and not in anyone's way.

Dan explained as he settled down for the wait, "We need to maintain the old, 'low profile, low visibility' routine while we are here."

"Low what?" It always appeared that we were doing something just a little bit wrong. We always had to keep out of sight to keep out of trouble. Not serious trouble, just enough for someone in authority to be pissed if we were caught.

"Remember, we shouldn't be here, which means we shouldn't be leaving. You see, the Navy tries to keep tabs on all its personnel, especially, with the huge amount of people, with their comings and goings between duty stations. The crap we are pulling right now makes it hard to maintain accurate records about our leaving, when we haven't been recorded as arriving. Know what I mean?"

"No sweat," I answered, even though I had no idea what he was saying. The clandestine things he had me involved in were never talked about in boot camp or in a good John Wayne war movie.

At least for now, we had a good view of the flight deck, and we would not miss anything from up here. Looking out to sea, I could see a smaller supply ship coming up along side. This was certainly a busy place, and the only thing odd about our location was that we were in a gun tub with a machine gun. There was no one around, just a loaded machine gun and the two of us.

Dan pointed out and away from the ship, and said with excitement, "There she is. We have us a ride on a Shit-Hook."

I didn't know if a Shit-Hook was a good thing or a bad thing. Dan, apparently knowing that I was again confused, explained to me, "It's called a Shit-Hook because of all the shit stirred up by having two sets of massive rotors."

Right then and before we could continue our helicopter class, an officer in a flight suit came over and told us that we could not stand where we were. We needed to go up a deck or two, if we wanted to watch the landing.

Dan attempted to convince the officer that we were waiting for this flight out, and that it would be here in just a minute.

He told Dan and I, "There is no one listed on the flight manifest for the outbound flight to Cam-Ranh-Bay. So the way I see it gentlemen, you two cannot be waiting for a flight that you are not scheduled to be on. Right? Now move on and away before I move you two down to the brig."

I assumed that Dan had taken notice that this guy was an officer, because he responded with, "Yes sir," and wasn't giving him a hard time.

With that, Dan and I saluted the officer and headed away.

"Now what?" I asked Dan after we were far enough away that the officer could not hear us talking.

"Just a slight deviation from our original travel plans. Let's just head up and out of sight until it lands, and he's gone."

Now, I sadly thought that we might get split up after all. I could envision my situation now, Dan taking off, jumping down a deck or two, running across the flight deck, and onboard the chopper, like a rat from a sinking ship. What choice would I have if he did all that? 'No choice,' was what I would have. Whatever. I will make the escape with him. My mom would be so proud of me, sneaking around the way I had been doing for the last few days.

By the time we made it one deck up, we could see that the chopper was almost here. I noticed that Dan was looking all around to see how we could make it down to the flight deck, and not be seen. Do we go left, or do we go right? I assumed that he had considered that he and I were still not to be noticed by that one officer in the flight suit.

The chopper was landing, and the officer that chased us away, was directing it down to land. The chopper came right down, and landed just as smooth as silk, as a sailor ran over and placed a set of chocks around the wheels. You could hear and feel the difference when the chopper had cut its power.

As people exited the aircraft, the officer that made us move, was leading another officer away and into a hatch. To our delight, he was temporarily off the flight deck and out of sight. With that, I boldly said, "Let's go."

"You have the right idea," Dan said, as we took off down the way we came.

I thought that this was like boarding a train at the train station. It was just there for a minute or two. You get onboard, and then the train was off again. With that in mind, I tried to make this run as quickly as possible. From behind me, I heard a yell from Dan, "A little faster, please. We got a flight to catch. "

"If I run any faster, my pants will fall down and we won't make it."

"What is this *we* crap?" Dan asked.

"If I fall down and we crash, then we won't make it." There, now I told him.

"Well, could you at least try to go a little faster?"

I answered with, "No sweat, not a problem. It's not that hard to do, as long as I am not looking out for buffalo shit or water puddles."

As we rushed onto the flight deck, I slowed down to let Dan pass me. I figured that he knew what to do next. He did, and I followed him onboard.

Entering from the rear of the aircraft, Dan headed to the front. I joined him and sat in a cargo seat across from him. The seats all faced the center of the aircraft just like our earlier flight on the DC 2 or DC 3, whatever. He placed his sea bag on the deck in front of him between his legs, and I did the same.

There was a crewmember sitting down, that we passed on our way in. He got up and handed us a pair of headsets. I assumed that we would be able to listen in on the pilot and stuff with these headsets. However, there were no cords attached, and it appeared that these were to drown out the noise. They really worked because the noise was extremely loud, and we were only sitting here in neutral. In a chopper this size, you could hear and feel the noise, and the vibrations were enough to shake your eyes loose. I could not wait until this thing started to run at full speed. Maybe the headset was really used to keep our brains from vibrating out our ears.

With our escape taking place so quickly, I did not have time to ask Dan if this was a short flight or a long one. Besides, it was just too loud for us to attempt to hold a, 'question and answer time' right now. So I realized that I should just sit back, relax, and enjoy the ride.

Dan was looking out the window behind me. He pointed and motioned for me to look. I did, only to see the officer that chased us away coming toward us. I did not think he knew we were in here, not yet anyway.

Dan took his sea bag, sat it up in his seat next to him, and sat low and behind the bag. He looked over and yelled, "Sit low as if you are sleeping. Keep your bag between you and the door. No need to have him see us."

Here we go again. If this works, this will be the start of another adventure, a great escape adventure. I did not want to get into trouble for being a stow-away and a run-a-way all at the same time. I did as Dan suggested and got myself as low in the seat as I could behind my bag. Damn, I was afraid that I was going to get into trouble.

The officer did peek inside the door and the airman across from us just waved and sat back in his seat, and closed his eyes. I assumed the officer did not see the two of us because he just disappeared.

I looked over at Dan. He was smiling like the Cheshire Cat and giving me the thumbs-up. Damn, we did it. We got onboard and we were getting away.

A minute later, the motor started to wind up faster and everything got much louder. The vibrations increased, and I believed we were getting ready to depart, or fall apart.

Without thinking, I turned around and looked out the window, to checkout what was happening on the flight deck. I wanted to watch as we took off. Naturally, the officer that chased us away was just outside my window. It figured, and with my luck, we made eye contact. He looked very angry along with a touch of surprise. He pointed at me and started to yell something that I knew wasn't very flattering. It appeared that he wanted to stop the chopper from leaving, so he could throw us off and jump in both our cases. Well, my case anyway. I mean, he did see me, and not Dan. However, before he could do anything, we were already, 'up, up, and away' slowly turning toward land.

With my heart stopped, I yelled over at Dan, "I think he saw me, I mean, I know he saw me. Are we in trouble?"

With a snicker, smile, and laughter, Dan yelled, "What is it with you and all this we crap? He saw you, he didn't see me."

With that, my heart went from a dead stop to beating in high gear. I did, however after a few minutes, start to calm down quickly, as I noticed Dan laughing at me, and showing no concern for my problem. He yelled, "Enjoy the ride my man," and he settled back and closed his eyes for the trip.

I might as well enjoy the ride, because we were not heading back toward the ship. Now that was what I would call a, 'narrow escape.' With nothing to do and only ocean to see outside my window, I followed Dan's example and tried to take a nap. I must have fallen asleep because thirty minutes later, we were descending and getting ready to land. The crewmember that was onboard with us, got up, walked over to the starboard side window, and stuck his head out. I bet that was a great view, and I wanted to look; however, I was going to sit still until we landed, because I didn't want to fall out of the aircraft like I did earlier. Nothing else happened on this flight, which made it rather boring. I was kind of hoping that I could have seen more than water and that maybe I could have seen an entire fleet out there. You know, with an aircraft carrier and all that.

We landed and started to roll a short way before coming to a complete stop. I noticed that Dan was not in any real hurry to get off, so I followed his example and just took my time. I took off my headset and hung them up behind me. It was hard to imagine that anyone would want to fly this type of aircraft for a living because of all the nose that it made.

"Let's head towards town and find ourselves an acceptable hotel," Dan finally said as he got up and started to depart the aircraft.

I wondered about all this and asked, because this sounded like a bad idea, "Are you sure that it's all right not to check into a BEQ this time?"

"Man, don't sweat it. Take it from the master, this is going to be just fine, and you might even have a good time."

"I don't even care if it's an Army or Navy BEQ."

I got this look from him, as if I again had two heads. He said, "You don't have to follow me, you know."

He was right about that. "Okay, we'll do it your way."

"Trust me on this one, because the next time you pass this town, you'll be doing same-same and enjoying it."

"It is a little hard to imagine passing anywhere a third time, since I haven't checked into the one place that I needed to, for the first time."

With a smile, Dan said, "Get over it."

Oh well. I figured I would just go with the flow. It seemed to be working fine so far. Besides, if there were a third time, I would have already experienced it both ways, BEQ and non-BEQ. "What about our unit," I asked.

Dan thought for a minute and answered, "Let's get checked in someplace and take it from there."

I said to him in response, "Fine."

Dan placed his bag on his shoulder, and I did the same with mine. Again, we were heading out on another adventure. At least we were still together, and I was not back on that ship by myself, and spending time with an unhappy officer.

Dan said, "Now that was an uneventful chopper ride."

"Yeah, now that I can hear again. That thing was really loud."

After a few minutes of walking down the tarmac, Dan pointed toward a bus parked near the main gate. "We'll take the bus downtown, and check out a few things," Dan suggested, as he walked to the bus and got on.

After getting a seat, I noticed that the bus also had the windows screened to keep things out and away from us. Then I asked Dan, "How far away is downtown?"

Dan pointed toward a radio tower about three or four miles away and said, "That tower is almost at the center of town. The bus has a few stops downtown and we can just pick a spot that looks good and get off."

Was he saying we would pick one out? I assumed that he had no idea where we were going, or that he knew about the choices, and that he would pick the best one when he saw it. Anyway, it was just a short ride into town. Except for the buildings not being very tall, it was just like downtown Saigon. There was lots of traffic, noise, and about a million motorcycles. Each motorcycle was carrying two or more people at a time and the drivers here were just as bad as the drivers in Saigon were.

I noticed that Dan was looking all around, as if he was trying to get his bearings. He finally said to me, "We'll be getting off soon."

Sure enough, we got off at the next stop. Even with lots of people and traffic, I still felt rather lost and really out of place. I picked up that almost everyone over here was so little, and I felt like a giant. Whatever, I had no idea where I was, or which way to go. I did know that I was in Can-Rah-Bay and Can-Rah-Bay was not where I needed to be. I belonged onboard my new assignment.

"Let's try this way," Dan suggested.

"Do you know where you're going?"

"I sort of remember going this way before. Besides, do you have any other place to be right now?"

"Yeah. I would like to be onboard the USS SUMMIT."

"We'll make it okay. So don't sweat it. We'll get there," Dan answered, dismissing me.

It was no easy task carrying around my sea bag with all these little people running around. Some of them made an effort to move out of my way, and others appeared to want to run into me.

This gave me a strange feeling, because it seemed so cut and dry, with half of them appearing to be normal, and were willing to move out of the way. The other half just wanted to make things difficult for me, and they seemed determined to make me stop and change direction to get around them. I wondered if that half were from North Vietnam, or at least wished that North Vietnam would win the war. No matter what I thought, I wished I had some place to put down this sea bag.

With an idea, I said to Dan, "How about we put some wheels on our bags? You know, to make it easier for us to tour this country. It always seems like we must walk for miles and miles."

"Creative idea, but just one thing."

"Now what can be wrong with my suggestion?"

"Check out the condition of the sidewalks around here. When were we lucky enough to have something solid to walk on?"

A quick look around showed me what little sidewalks they had here, were torn up and cracked. For the most part, it was just dirt. I responded with, "A good idea for another country."

"Yeah, another place and another time," Dan responded.

Chapter 15

All this walking around was getting me tired. I was going to say something to Dan about this when, to my surprise, and out of nowhere, someone yelled, "Dan! Dan!" This was so loud that it was easily heard above all the traffic noise. Girls, American-sounding girls, were yelling, "Dan! Dan!" More than one American-sounding girl were yelling.

At the same time, the both of us started to check out the other side of the street. This was not as easy as it might sound, because of the traffic crossing between the other side and us.

"Over here," shouted one of them.

Damn, they were American girls, and there were three of them.

"All right. This will most definitely make our day," Dan responded, with a huge smile on his face, as if this was Christmas.

I pointed toward them with excitement and asked, "Who are they?"

"They, my friend, they just might be our entertainment for tonight. Come on. Lets cross over and check'em out before someone else does."

"Do you know them?" After I said that, I realized that it wasn't very smart of me to ask.

"Now what do you think, Einstein? You think these girls just picked a name out of a hat and decided to yell, 'Dan' on a busy corner, to see if they had a confirm hit."

"Sorry, dumb question."

"Yes, dumb question and yes, I do know them. Every time I come to town, I always seem to meet up with these young ladies. Well, maybe not the last time we were here, but most of the time."

Where did these girls come from? They looked as if they were a bunch of college girls out doing some window-shopping. From what I could see from here, they were all rather cute.

As we crossed the street towards them, Dan suggested, "Don't step in any shit this time."

"I'll try not to, if you don't tell them about it." I wished he would forget about that incident, I already had.

"No sweat. Besides, if I do tell them, they might wonder why I continued to cross the street with you."

Oh well, I guessed I would not be able to live that one down for the next year.

As we met up with these young ladies, Dan spoke up and said, "Long time no see. What brings you ladies to beautiful, downtown Cam-Ranh-Bay? Or should I ask, what brings you beautiful ladies to downtown Cam-Ranh-Bay?"

The short one with brown hair gave him a big hug. She said, "We all finally have the same day off, and the beaches here are just what my pale white skin needs. I'm going to get a fine numba-one, South Pacific tan on this numba-one body of mine."

She stepped back, and with her hands on her hip, she asked, "What are you doing in town again? Are you doing one of your, Cam-Ranh-Bay, R&R, time extension deals?"

Turning a little red, Dan replied with, "Not really. Not this time. I'm trying very hard to get back to the unit this time. You see, I have this new guy here with me and I don't want to set a bad example."

"Since when have you started to worry about setting a bad example?" She jokingly asked, as the others joined in and laughed at what she said.

"How about a little slack here?" Dan responded incidentally, sounding as if he had done nothing wrong.

"It just might be that you have served one tour too many, and all you can set are bad examples." Now this girl was really cool, and gave Dan no slack at all.

Dan ignored that statement, turned and pointed to me and said, "This is Charles. He's fresh out of boot camp and new here, in-country."

One at a time, they responded to me. The short one with brown hair said, "Hi, my name is Denise from North Dakota."

"I'm Betty from New York. Not the city New York, but the state, New York. So please leave out the negative comments," she warned me. She had big, brown eyes and large breasts.

"Hello, I'm Rose. Where are you from Charles?" Rose had strawberry blond hair, and would be hard to miss in a crowd. Her red hair really stood out; it almost glowed.

I was so surprised from just meeting three American girls from the states, that I was slow to answer. I finally responded to Rose with, "Baltimore, Baltimore, Maryland."

Betty spoke up and asked, "So how are you doing, Charles from Baltimore, Baltimore Maryland?"

Wow, three very attractive girls were all focused on me, and I didn't have to buy them a drink. This was great. I could only come back with; "I'm all right. Are you all here on, 'Spring Break' or something?"

Everyone started to laugh at me; and again, I found myself the brunt end of some kind of joke, and I had no idea why. As they continued to laugh, it attracted some attention from everyone around us. And naturally, they were all looking at me.

"What's so amusing? So Dan, what is it this time? Did I miss something again?"

Trying to answer my question without laughing at me, he explained, "This is not the place to take a, 'Spring Break.' What we have here are Navy Waves. These ladies are doing a tour here in 'The-Nam,' just like you. They work at the airbase doing administration or something.

With everyone still laughing at me, Dan continued, "And if you're a good boy, someday you too, can ride a wave."

They didn't seem to appreciate his humor with that nasty joke. I assumed that, by the way they responded, that they were very nice girls.

A few minutes passed by with everyone but me talking small talk about almost everything. Finally, Betty spoke out and suggested, "We're heading down to the beach for most of the afternoon. Do you guys care to join us for a little sun?"

I was extremely delighted to hear Dan respond with, "Yeah. We have time for that today. Hell woman, we have the time to join you all, for the rest of the week."

Betty quickly responded with, "No, not all week. We only have time for today, and before you even think about it, there is no time for you and us for tonight."

"What? You have plans with some officers," Dan asked sadly.

"No, no, no. We are back on duty tonight," Rose answered with Denise and Betty in agreement.

Going to the beach seemed like a wonderful idea. However, deep down inside, I wanted to report to my unit. However, you know this might be fun. As Dan said the other day, my orders did state in writing to report, 'on or about,' and most certainly, not right now.

After giving this some thought, if we were to hit the beach today, I believed that there were a few issues to consider. I didn't have a bathing suit, and I didn't like the idea of carrying my sea bag to the beach, and leaving it out to bake in the hot sun. I turned toward Dan and asked, "What about . . ."

Quickly he cut me off and said, "No problem. Not a big deal, my man. Just don't sweat the small stuff. We can get anything we need, and everything will work out just fine."

Looking at the girls with his childlike smile, then back at me, he continued with, "We really want to go to the beach with these lovely ladies, and a small thing like swim wear is of little concern."

"Let me guess. You have an answer to the question that I have yet to ask?" I questioned.

"I am the answer man, so listen to me. We can leave our sea bags at the guard shack on the beach. I've done that before, and it will not be a problem. We can just step into a local shop and purchase some shorts. We don't need anything fancy to wear to the beach. Just a little something to keep the fish from taking our bait."

The one girl, Betty, spoke up and joked, "What are you concerned about? Fish here aren't that small, for you and your little bait, to worry about."

It took me a minute, but I got the joke. This Betty girl had a sense of humor and was rather cute.

"Then it's all set," said Rose. "We'll just help you two pick out something to wear, and then we'll just, di-di-mau on down the road."

Betty suggested, "Let's check out that store across the street."

So across the street we headed. Dan looked over at me, as if he was going to say something about my shit stepping thing. I returned a look, showing that now was not a good time to bring that up to the ladies. He apparently decided in my favor, and we all crossed with no problem or shitty stories.

I followed them inside the store, and I tried to sort out in my mind what had just taken place. We were in Vietnam, with dates, and going to the beach. I could envision my mail to my mother now, "Hi Mom. I'm doing okay in Vietnam, and I'm not close to the shooting right now. Today I'm going to the beach with a bunch of friends. The only danger that I can see is that I might get sunburned. Take care and I'll write later." Somehow, my mother might not believe any of that. I found it hard to believe myself.

Inside the store, I found it hard getting around, with my being tall, and carrying around my sea bag, in a place build for little people. This problem definitely had its challenges. It was impossible to carry my sea bag on my shoulder, because most of the advertising signs, hung down too low, for me to pass under easily. We had five people and two sea bags making our way around this little store with very narrow aisles. I didn't think that any one of us really knew which way to go. It was not as if we could read any of the signs. You know, like men's clothes or swim wear. I would just follow the flow for now. Come to think about it, I always seemed to be following the flow lately.

With some help from all three of the girls, Dan and I were able to find a cheap set of shorts. Each of the girls had tried to make our selection her choice, and I was having a very good time.

After our purchase, we headed toward the door, and I wondered which way we needed to go. I thought to myself, I would check to see which way everyone was heading. I could just check to see who was carrying beach towels, and which way they were going. Dry beach towels were heading toward the beach, and the wet towels away from the beach. However, outside, I didn't see anyone carrying anything that belonged on a beach. No towels, umbrellas, coolers, or lawn chairs. No problem, I would just follow the flow for now and I was getting good at it.

Denise looked at me and said, "We forgot to get you two some suntan lotion. I bet you guys don't have any, right?"

Damn, I did not want to get sunburned today. I was about to say something about that, when Dan butted in and said, "Only a small detail, not a problem. I was hoping that one of you young ladies would have some lotion and would assist me with the application. Now you don't have to fight over which one of you gets the pleasure to lotion down my body. I will allow each of you to select your favorite part, as long as there's no fighting."

I could not believe he said that. I wanted to laugh, but because the girls didn't find his comment funny, then neither would I.

"On second thought," he continued, "I might not mind the fighting?"

They all laughed, and Dan got a smart remark from Rose, "The only favorite spot for me on your body is your mouth. It's so big that I can almost clog it up with my beach towel."

Laughter all around, even Dan had to appreciate that cut.

Denise added in her two cents, "There might be fighting over you, but it would be the loser, that'll have the dis-pleasure to lotion you up."

Rose said, "I have plenty of lotion and I'll be happy to share with you two, but you two can lotion up all by yourselves. Or, you two can lotion up each other."

That was funny and everyone laughed at that one.

"Well, I do not speak for Dan, but I would greatly appreciate some lotion when we get there. And I'll have no problem lotioning myself."

Betty added, "Don't worry about that. No one has to speak for Dan, he said too much already as it is."

Well, this was starting to be fun. I was enjoying these new friends, and going to the beach with them seemed like a wonderful idea. Yet, I still could not comprehend that we were in Vietnam. This was not what I had seen on the nightly news. The news only showed jungles, not beaches. Never, ever, did they show any young pretty girls. The news only showed old mama-sans with their little babies, and the babies were always crying.

It was just a short walk to the beach, and what an impressive beach this was. The sand was pure white, and the water, clear blue. I could see that there was a guard shack off to one side, and the girls were already heading that way.

"They really need to guard the beach?" I asked.

"Yes, they most certainly do. Now think why that is," Dan questioned.

Before I could attempt to answer him, I should give this some thought first. No need to have these girls hear a dumb response from me. "I could assume that with everyone in the relax mode, that it was much easier for the VC to sneak up on us. You know, with our guard down and all that."

"You are most accurate, and if anything does happen, as you can see for yourself, there's nowhere to hide," Dan explained.

Denise spoke up and said, "Is he trying to scare you? If you would just consider the source, then you can justify ignoring him. It happens to be very safe here."

Well, so much for me totally enjoying a relaxing field trip today with my new friends. Now, do I lie in the sun with one eye open checking everything and everyone out as they approached us? I asked, "Is there something that I must sweat besides the sun?"

Dan expressed his opinion and told me, "Don't sweat it. These guys on watch are here to protect us and allow everyone to enjoy this little bit of heaven in the middle of this hell-hole."

With yet another joke, Dan continued with, "Yeah, if the world was to get an enema, they would just stick the hose right here, in 'The-Nam.'"

"We were here a number of times, and to date, there haven't been any issues. Trust me, if it wasn't safe, there's no way we would spend time here," Denise said to loosen things up for me.

As we approached the guard shack, one of the guards spoke up and asked, "How long are you guys planning to stay?"

We looked at each other, as if hoping someone had the answer. Finally, Dan spoke up and said, "Just a few hours. Is there a problem?"

"No. Not a problem. I was just trying to figure out how long we would be watching your things. I didn't want your things to be here, when we get off duty later on today."

Rose said to the guard, "I doubt we'll be here that long."

With little delay, after receiving the guard's permission to store our bags, we placed them in the guard shack and out of direct sunlight. We thanked the guards and headed to the beach.

Denise already had made her way toward the water and was laying out her blanket. Dan and I followed behind her and started to lay our things out, as the girls started taking their clothes off revealing their bikinis.

"Where are we going to change?" I asked to no one in particular.

"Right here, unless you have a problem," answered Dan.

"What do you mean, right here?"

Betty spoke up and said, "Will you feel better if we stood around with blankets so no one will see you?"

"Well, yeah," I answered thinking that this was a great idea.

"Come-on man, are you serious?" Dan snickered, questioning me as if I were a sissy.

"Give the man a break. He's new in-country and hasn't hardened up yet," added Betty.

Rose said, "The only reason that you change in public Dan is because that's the only time you can have your clothes off, and be around a girl at the same time."

I thought that was very funny, but I did not want to let Dan know that.

Dan responded with, "No sweat. As for me, I will just change right here, and you girls can work it out amongst yourselves. Oh, and no peeking. I can't handle three excited girls at one time.

As before, these girls ignored Dan. While he was changing, all three of these girls stood around me, with towels hanging down as they formed a circle. At least they were all facing out and away, giving me a little privacy.

"Come on Charles, do this change thing so we can all get in the water," snapped Denise.

I felt some trust in these girls, especially with Dan standing further away. I quickly took advantage of this, while I had the chance. Then I started to undress. Just as I had the last thing taken off, which was my underpants, all three of them turned toward me and dropped their towels.

Screams, yells, and laughter came from the girls, Dan, and almost everyone else on the beach. Even the guards, almost a hundred yards away were yelling and giving out cat whistles.

One guard yelled, "Target practice."

The other guard added, "No way man. That target is too small to hit from this distance."

This was most embarrassing, and I did not believe I would make it a full year in-country. Quickly, I dropped to the sand, face down while reaching for my shorts. Denise grabbed them and stepped back a few feet. My other clothes were quickly kicked away from my reach. Here I was, face down in the sand with my un-tanned butt sticking out for everyone to see.

"Over here, if you still need them," Denise teased me.

"Come on, give me a break," I said this with one hand reaching out toward her and the other hand covering myself. I had sand stuck to my body everywhere except my back and butt.

"All right, here you go. I thought you might be bold enough to try and take them from me," Denise sadly told me, as she threw me my shorts.

"Maybe some other time, but not today," was the only thing I could muster up to say.

"Well at least we all got to see your tan line," Betty joked.

"Yeah, all of them," laughed Rose.

To my surprise, this died down quickly, and everyone just continued with preparing to get into the water. I looked over and saw that the two guards were busy looking elsewhere. So much for my fifteen seconds of fame.

"Nice going," Dan said to me.

"Did you know this was going to happen?"

Controlling his laughter, Dan answered, "Yeah, and I really couldn't warn you. Hell, I didn't want to warn you."

"Some friend you are."

"At ease, my man. This was great entertainment and the entire beach enjoyed it."

With some embarrassment, I asked, "Did this ever happen to you?"

"No way man. I'm not that dumb or stupid to fall for that old trick."

"Thanks. I thought I felt bad before, now I really feel bad."

Overhearing what we were discussing, Denise said, "Sorry Charles. It was a mean trick to play, but it sure was funny, don't you think?"

No way could I get angry over a thing like that, especially with her. Therefore, I said, "Yeah. That was funny. I bet it'll be even funnier the next time it happens to someone else."

"It's funny each time," she said with a warm smile.

"So, will you let me hold the towel for you someday?" I could not believe I said that. Yet, that was a cool question and a possible good move on my part.

She gave me a wink as she headed toward the water. "Someday, maybe."

Now that little smile and wink made this entire incident seem like small stuff, and not a big deal. Hell, I even really got a little excited about the wink. Does she like me or was it just a tease?

We were all dressed or undressed now, depending on how you see it. As a small group, we headed toward the water. I needed to get into the water soon because the sand was on me everywhere and started to chafe my legs and crotch. It was sort of like having a sheet of sandpaper in your pants.

The water was not very crowded, and it was warm and clean. Not exactly the same as the ocean water on the East Coast back home.

So, here I was enjoying myself with some good-looking girls in the South China Sea. In some ways, this could have been a trip to Ocean City, Maryland with some friends. It was unbelievable, and hard to comprehend that I was in a war zone.

Dan spoke out to everyone and said, "Aren't we out of uniform?"

Betty asked, "So what scam are you trying to pull this time?"

I did not know what Dan was talking about, either. When I heard, 'scam and uniform' mentioned with Dan around, I got worried that something was up, and that a scam was about ready to happen. Either way, I did not want to get into any trouble or be embarrassed. I would keep my guard up and my mouth closed.

"Isn't this a nude beach? If so, we should get into the uniform of the day. Doesn't everyone agree?"

"In your dreams, in your dreams," answered Denise.

Too bad, I could have really enjoyed that. I figured that because they got to see my tan lines, that I should at least get to see theirs.

After a few minutes of dipping ourselves in the water and a little swim, Rose started to swim further out. Denise was already heading back to the beach, and Betty was spending some time with Dan. I had just about enough water for now, and I would just head back in and get myself a little sun.

Denise was applying sun tan lotion to herself as I sat down beside her. She said, "You can have some of this when I'm though, if you like."

"I'd appreciate that."

As she handed me the lotion, I asked her, "So how long have you been here?"

"I got to the beach when you did."

"No, I mean here, as in Vietnam."

Then I realized I had just asked a stupid question. That was probably why she answered the way she did. Not wanting to seem like I was putting a move on her, I continued with, "I was not trying to pick you up or anything. I've only been here for a few days and I was just curious. I wanted to make a little conversation."

"So you think I'm not pretty enough to even consider picking up."

Now how in the world could I have screwed up so quickly? "No, no, no. You are rather attractive and picking you up would be something I would enjoy." I was not doing well with this.

"So what are you saying?" She asked, knowing that I was digging myself into a hole.

"Look, I'm new here, and I don't know the rules?"

"I see, so there are rules here? What are these rules?"

I wanted to go back into the water and just swim on the bottom. "I don't know anything about any rules. It was a statement that just came out. I'm sorry. Give me a break."

"A break, why?"

"Dan is always busting my balls and now so are you. Why?"

"I was joking with you Charles. You seem like a pleasant enough person."

"Thanks. What do you say we start over and try this conversation again?"

"Yeah. I believe that you've had enough for one day."

With a look as if she were sincere, she asked, "I've been here over nine months now, and I've been ready to leave this hell-hole for nine months. So where are you off to?"

"Dan and I are trying to get to our unit, the USS SUMMIT. She's a repair ship that travels all over the Mekong Delta. Each time we arrive at her last known location, she seems to have already left, or was never there in the first place."

"Was it supposed to be here in Cam-Ranh-Bay?"

"A good question. No. We just arrived by helo from a supply ship out on Yankee station."

"Was it out there?"

"No."

"Then why were you out there?"

"Well," I answered, pleased not to find myself on the defensive end with her. "We had information that she might be out on Yankee station near this supply ship. With that, we found ourselves a ride out to the supply ship from Dong-Tam. We tried to; at least, get ourselves in the same area with her. Naturally, when we arrived, our ship was nowhere to be found."

"Was it at Dong-Tam?"

"No."

"So why were you in Dong-Tam?"

"Dan thought it was there."

"Sounds like Dan's private tour of Vietnam.""

"Well, yeah. We've been all around the country and this has been going on for a few days now. At any rate, we thought it would make sense to leave the ship out on Yankee station, because Dan said that there was no nightlife there. So, we found that we could hop another ride to here."

"So your ship is not here, like you said."

"No, it wasn't. As a matter of fact, this is our second time here."

"Was it to be here the first time you were here?"

"No. It was just that Dan said this was a cool town for a lay. I mean lay-over."

"Yeah, he did more than just the lay-over thing here in this town. I guess he'll try to do some laying as well." she responded.

"I don't know anything about that. The last time we were here, we were just passing through."

With a puzzled look, she continued with, "So, what are you two going to do now?"

"For now, we will just enjoy your company and try not to get sunburned," I said, feeling rather good about what I had just said.

"No, not now-now. I mean, after now. You know, after your day in the sun," she asked me, sort of sounding like Dan.

"I assume we'll try to make another attempt to find her. So for now, I guess we'll just enjoy the time with you ladies and try later on today or tomorrow."

"I am curious, how will you go about finding your ship. Is there a big board someplace with little boats on it?" She questioned, and I at least had an answer for her.

"Yes and no. There is a board with ship's locations that we found in Saigon, but the one we saw on my first day here, didn't have her listed." I continued, "To answer your first question, we just find us a Comm-Center and see if they have any information of her location."

"It appears that the Comm-Center is as reliable as the board," she told me.

"Yes, it seems that no one knows the location of anything around here. I can't understand not knowing where things are. I mean, this is a whole ship with a couple of hundred people onboard."

Now Dan, Rose, and Betty came back dripping and plopped themselves down beside us.

Dan looked over at Denise and me, and said, "So, are you two, 'an item' now?"

Everyone gave us a smile, Denise answered, "Are you jealous, assuming that it's true."

"No way man. I have these two beautiful babes with me right now. I'm good, but not good enough to handle three at a time. But I am most willing to give that a try."

I had to give him credit; at least he kept trying to hit on them. I mean, he kept striking out, but at least he kept coming up to bat.

"This guy is always dreaming," said Rose with Betty in agreement.

Denise added, "I heard you were giving Charles a tour of, 'The-Nam,' with a stop-over or two, to all the ships at sea."

"It appears to be working out that way," Dan explained, apparently feeling very proud of the way things have been going for us.

"It always appears to be working out that way when you're involved," Denise replied.

I believe that these girls had his number. I could see that he was thinking and trying to scam up something for a response. If it involved these ladies, I hoped that they would say, 'yes,' and that I would be able to be involved.

"Would any one of you care to join us for the next few days? I could handle the transportation and a hotel room for us. I believe that one room would be sufficient for the entertainment that I have planned," Dan explained, as he tried to hit on all three of them at the same time.

Nice come back, I thought that it would be a great idea if one, two, or all three of them would join us. We might have a difficult time with checking into the BEQ's, but somehow I believed that Dan would find those issues a challenge.

"No. Not this time. We have a job to do and unlike your job, we will be missed," Rose interjected.

With what Rose just said, everyone, including Dan had a good laugh. This guy had to have a comeback for that one. As expected, Dan came back with, "You see, my job is so important and demanding, that I get extra liberty and extra R&R days and because I work twice as hard as everyone else, I get twice the time off."

"No, no, no," said Denise. "They allow you the extra days off so they have more time to recover from what you do while you were doing whatever it was that you do."

I was kind of enjoying this roasting of Dan, but I had to be careful not to join in on their side, because he just might leave me here and I would never get to the ship. Yet, it might not be so bad to be left here, with these ladies. On the other hand, if I sided with Dan, then the ladies might leave me hanging. I would just keep my mouth shut, try not to laugh too loud, and hope to stay neutral

"Bottom line is," Dan continued, "I'm here for as long as I want, and you ladies must work tonight. Apparently, I have the best job."

Way to go Dan. Tick them off, and we might be spending the rest of the day by ourselves.

Rose spoke up and said, "I'm here to get some sun, and not to have either of you put a hit on me."

Dan came back with, "Yeah, she keeps looking for Mr. Right, or was it Mr. Phillips?"

"Mr. Phillips," Rose questioned, with everyone paying attention for this latest round of humor.

"I heard he was a good screw . . . driver."

Everyone seemed to enjoy that one. Rose came back with, "How many men does it take to screw in a light bulb?"

I kept quiet on this one, but Dan gave it some serious thought. He answered, "One. A man will screw anything."

Rose replied, "Shit, if anyone knew that answer, it had to be Dan."

Dan quickly came back with, "What's the difference between 'ooooooh,' and 'aaaaaaah?"

Denise came back with; "I give."

Instantly, Dan answered that with, "I know you do. Now, how about my question?"

Denise reached over and smacked Dan on top of his head. Not a mean hit, just one to show that she did not appreciate that one.

Rose spoke up and said, "Just give us the answer."

"Three inches!"

Well, I thought that was funny. As for the ladies, they smiled, as they tried to hold back their laughter. Denise came back with, "Then, if we're talking about you, then it's 'eeeeeeek,' as in, you only have, three inches!"

Well, that one brought the house down. I loved that one. Dan was taking a beating with theses ladies.

Dan didn't have a comeback for that one, and we just got into some small talk between each other. After a few minutes of this, it finally died down, and we all just laid back, and took in some rays.

Things cooled down somewhat for the next hour or so. Well, it cooled down as far as conversations go, but heated up as far as the tanning. Everyone was lotioned up, and the sun and breeze were perfect for our activities.

"Mr. Dan. Hey Mr. Dan." Now that sounded just like that retarded guy from a few days ago. What was his name? Bill Bob, Billy-Bob Joe Jim, Joe Bob, or something likes that.

"My man, Billy-Bob. So how's it hanging?" Dan said, with a smile, while the three ladies gave Dan the obvious facial expression, of, 'I hope he's just passing by and not wanting to join us.'

"It's a hanging between my legs man. Hanging any place else and I'd be walking in circles. Know what I mean?"

Denise told Dan in a low, secretive, but serious voice, "You're not going to ask him to stay, are you? Remember the last time he got around the opposite sex?"

Rose added in her comment, "The opposite sex? He was the opposite of both sexes."

Even a comment from Betty, "If he stays, we're out-of-here. Get my drift?"

I hoped Dan would handle this correctly. I had no desire to spend my day with Billy-Bob the Retard, especially with us already here with three beautiful young ladies.

Before Dan had a chance to say anything to Billy-Bob, he plopped his blanket right down next to us and started to unfold his raft. All of us, especially Dan, had an expression on our faces as if the world, as we knew it today, would soon end.

No one was saying anything right now and the only sounds you could hear were the waves coming in. Then to our luck, Billy-Bob told us, "I only want to leave my towel here. As soon as I blow up my raft, I will be in the water and out of your way."

Everyone, as if on cue, replied with comments such as, 'Yeah man, no sweat. No problem, you can keep you stuff here. We'll keep an eye on your stuff. Swim out as far as you want. Stay in the water until your whole body wrinkles up. Take your time.'

Dan said, just loud enough for everyone to hear but Billy, "Take your time, except for the blowing up your raft part."

He settled down and started blowing up his raft. It was a good size raft and it would take him some time to fill it up completely even as he was blowing as hard and fast as he could. I assumed that he wanted to impress the girls or something with his stamina. This went on for a while and I thought it was about time that he took a break before he passed out, face down in the sand.

Dan told him, "Take it easy my man. You might pass out or something."

Betty said in a low voice, "If he passes out and needs mouth-to-mouth, you must understand, that man will die."

Everyone but Billy-Bob laughed. All he did was look up to take another deep breath, and continued filling the raft. After a few minutes, the raft was completed, and he quickly stood up and said to us, "Sorry I can't stay. Got to go."

With that, he took off his shirt and dropped his pants. Everyone, and I do mean everyone, was pleased that he had on a set of swim trunks under his pants. Then it was off to the ocean for him and his raft, and we were all relieved, now that he was gone.

Dan said, “Want to see a neat trick?”

No one answered him. We had no idea what he was going to pull this time.

“Now, check out this camera,” he said as he held up a camera that was on top of Billy-Bob’s things.

Dan pulled his pants out, aimed the camera down, and snapped a photo of himself. Now that was funny. Then he placed the camera right back where he had found it and said, “So how many copies do you ladies want?”

Denise said, “If you can get it blown up to three times its normal size, then I might be able to fit it into my cigarette case without bending it. Or maybe I could put the photo in a picture frame on my Barbie doll’s desk.”

After being cut down like that, Dan came back with; “It’s not my fault. His camera does not have the wide angle lends for anything really big.”

“No,” Denise replied. “We’re not taking a picture of your ego.”

Dan didn’t have an answer for that one, which surprised me.

Looking around to see if anyone was watching us, I happened to notice that one of the guards at the guard shack was aiming at us through the scope on his rifle. I said to Dan, “What’s he gonna shoot?”

Dan looked over and said, “Nothing, he’s just checking out our girls with his scope. Not a bad idea, works pretty good I believe.”

Right then, I could hear the other guard whistling and yelling at someone in the water. This was nothing new because they had been doing this all day, like at most beaches. With that in mind, I had not paid them much attention until I heard them getting louder and another set of guards were yelling and whistling.

We all sat up and tried to pick out whom they were yelling at in the water. We could see one person out quite a ways, on a raft.

He was just floating there and looking back at the guards that were looking out at him. This looked like some kind of standoff. The guards kept yelling and this guy kept looking back at them. The guards were waving for him to come on back closer to the shore because it appeared as if he was just too far out.

I questioned, "Isn't that Billy-Bob?"

"Yeah. It's him," Dan replied. "I don't think he can swim."

Now everyone on the beach was watching this. All the guards were yelling, blowing whistles, and waving their hands at Billy-Bob. Still, Billy-Bob floated on the raft as if nothing was wrong; at least that was how it appeared from our point of view.

Dan stood up and started to hand motion Billy-Bob to come on in to shore. Billy-Bob put up his hands as if he was helpless or something. He still was not attempting to come back. He was just floating around watching everyone that was watching him. I imagined that this was quite a sight from where he was.

One of the guards made his way to the water and started to walk out toward him. It took him a few minutes and when he finally reached Billy-Bob, he grabbed the raft and started to toe Billy-Bob back to shore. The water wasn't very deep and the guard was only about chest high in the water.

A moment later, with Billy-Bob in tow and still on the raft, they made it to shore. When Billy-Bob stood up, he was about a foot taller than the guard was.

They talked for a few minutes; I meant the guard talked to Billy-Bob and Billy-Bob listened. The guard finally walked away and Billy-Bob made his way toward us. Great, that dumb ass, retard was going to be spending some time with us after all.

Dan asked, "Billy-Bob, why didn't you just get off the raft and come in when the guards told you to?"

"You know I can't swim, I didn't know how deep the water was. If I would have gotten off the raft and it was over my head, then I might not have been able to get back on. Don't you know?"

We all got a chuckle out of that one. He was right and that did make sense.

"So Billy-Bob, what are you going to do now?" Dan asked, suggesting that he didn't want him to hang around.

It was very obvious that we all wanted him to move on and to leave us alone.

"I got to go. I have a place to stay for tonight. I met a girl and she's going to fix me dinner and let me stay at her place."

Damn, he had a date for tonight. All I had today was a smile and a wink, and he was the retarded one. And to top if off, he can't even swim. Everybody knows how to swim.

"So Billy-Bob, how did you get this girl? What did it cost you?" Dan asked.

Okay, I get it now. Over here, you can buy anything. In that case, I am doing better. At least my smile and wink only cost me a little time. Maybe taking my clothes off and jumping face down in the sand helped a little. I guess I have a nice butt.

"Four cartons of cigarettes. If I would have had five cartons, I could have stayed two nights."

No one had a response as he quickly packed up his things and told Dan that he would see him at the unit in a few days.

I asked him as he started to walk away, "Do you know where she is right now?"

"Yeah, she's at her house fixing me my dinner."

"No, I mean the ship," I asked.

"Nope. I won't check on that until I'm ready to go. Usually I check on her location in the morning, so I can make it back by dinner time."

"How do you find out where she is?" I wondered how he knew and Dan did not.

His whole facial expression changed, as if he just became smarter. He said to me, "How come you can find a pile of buffalo shit in the middle of a busy road, and you can't find a ship with two hundred people onboard? Damn man, you'd think with that question that you're the retarded one."

Well, that was some answer and it completely caught me of guard. With that, I said, "I'm just the new guy here and I'm just asking."

"That's not your only problem," he said, as he continued to toy with me.

"I give up, what's my other problem?"

"You're following him around and you'll never get there," he said, as he pointed to Dan.

Dan's only reply was; "You got me on that one Billy-Bob. See you at the unit."

Billy-Bob said, "Bye," to everyone and then headed away without saying anything else.

Rose commented, "Go figure. The retarded guy is scoring better than you two put together."

Denise said, "Not to mention that he could find your ship and get there all in the same day."

With that comment, Dan and I did not laugh; however, everyone else did. I hoped Dan could come back with a smart remark because I could not think of anything to say about that.

"So, which one of your girls did he give the cigarettes to and what are you fixing him for dinner?" Now that was funny. I like that one, nice going Dan I thought.

Rose came back with, "It was me. I would have fixed you dinner and let you stay with me, but it would have cost you eight cartons of cigarettes."

Denise added in, "Remember, we saw you when you took that picture. I would have required twelve cartons of cigarettes to make up for your, 'short comings.'"

This was not like talking to the girls I knew back in high school. These girls had some great comebacks.

Dan attempted to make a good comeback of his own, "Yeah, but after a night with me, you would not only return all the cigarettes, you'd go out and buy me some more to show me your appreciation."

"Appreciation for what?" Denise questioned.

"You'd enjoy your tour with, 'Little Danny Boy and the Twins.'"

Rose added, "I'd rather do a double tour here than a single tour with, 'Little Danny,' with or without the twins."

Now that was funny.

She continued, “You did say little?”

Even Dan laughed at that one. Man ole man, these ladies were not giving him any slack. They were not being mean or anything, just giving him the same crap he was giving out.

Denise got up and jokingly said, “I’m all hot and bothered with all this talk. I have to get back in the water to cool off. You coming?”

Wow! She asked that, looking right at me. I was thinking, not right now, but with some luck, maybe I could later. “Yeah, I’ll join you,” I responded quickly and got right up. Maybe she liked me.

We both made our way back to the water, and we could hear them all talking and laughing. I hoped that it was not directed toward us. If so, why should I care? I was just here for the day, and then each of us would take off in a different direction. Well, with some luck, Dan and I would be off in the same direction. It was hard and unusual to met someone nice and know that by the end of the day, I would never see them again.

Anyway, in the water, nothing of importance happened between the two of us. We just swam around a little bit, talked about the weather, and what it was like being over here in, ‘The-Nam.’ After awhile, we headed back to join up with everyone.

Things were quiet while everyone tanned. I was hoping that Denise would ask me to lotion her down and vice-versa. She did not, and I was too shy to ask. I was thinking that her wink and smile earlier was just that, a wink, and a smile. Oh well, I might as well lotion-up and catch some rays.

Betty sat up and said, “I almost forgot,” as she started to go through her things. “A radio, I forgot I had this radio. What we need here is some music.”

I liked that idea, because it was too quiet. Whenever I made it to Ocean City, Maryland, we always had a radio. Sometimes, there were so many radios on the beach and everyone had a different station that it was difficult to hear.

She got it out; pulled up the antenna, and scanned for a station. Nothing came out except static at first. Then she found a few stations that were almost clear, but we could not make out what they were saying, or the music would sound as if it was coming from India. After only a few tries, she cursed out the radio, slammed down the antenna, and threw it aside. Well, so much for some music today.

Every now and then, some guys coming down to take in the sun and water, would walk by us. It appeared that they would purposely walk close to us to check out our girls and I could not blame them. These must be the only round-eyed girls on the beach, possibly in all of South Vietnam, and maybe the North Vietnam as well.

I did notice that a few guys here on the beach had the local girls with them. I did not know if they were boyfriend/girlfriend, or just rentals. I did feel kind of cool that I was with American girls, and they were not. And it did not cost me any cigarettes. However, a little reality check here for me. I was here, with them yes, but not exactly with them, as if I was their date.

Anyway, an hour or so went by with no comments, music, or interruptions, just plenty of sun and sweat.

Betty sat up and said, "You know, it's about that time."

Time for what, I wondered. I hoped it was not time for them to go.

Denise looked inside her purse for her watch and responded sadly, "Yeah you're right."

Damn. This could not be over already.

Dan asked, "Do you have a place where we can shower and stuff?"

That sounded like a great idea. With luck, that just might happen.

Rose said to Dan, "We, as in us girls, have a place to shower and get ready for work. As far as your shower and stuff goes, you guys are on your own. Sorry about that."

Denise joked, "You can always catch up with Billy-Bob. I bet he's in the shower right now with someone."

That would have been funny if it were meant for someone else.

"No sweat," Dan replied.

No sweat, no sweat! We had been here for a couple of hours sweating our asses off, with sand stuck to all parts of my body, and a shower was not only needed, but also required.

The girls started to gather their things and packed up to leave. I could not believe that I was feeling such a loss right now. Maybe it was because I was so far away from home and friends. These three girls meant a lot to me right now. Yeah, it was safe to say that because they were beautiful girls, it did have something to do with it.

I did not know whether Denise cared about me or that she could tell by the expression on my face, that I was saddened by their departure. With that, she said to me, "Don't look so sad Charles. We'll cross paths again."

"I hope so," I answered, doing my best to give her the, 'puppy dog' look, as if suggesting for her to take me home.

Dan butted in and said, "We have a whole year left, and passing through here again is very possible."

"Maybe so, but they are leaving in three months," I said sadly, and as if on cue, it produced a tear. Lucky for me, it blended in with my sweat, and no one noticed. It was not as if I could ask for her phone number and hope to take her out Saturday night. I couldn't even volunteer to give her a ride home.

The girls quickly placed their street clothes on over their bathing suits. With a few hand shakes and a hung from Denise, they were off and soon out of sight.

Dan asked me, "So how long do you want to stay here?"

"I'm ready to leave now. I was kind of hoping that we could have left with them."

"Me too, but with some luck, we'll see them again."

Sadly, I asked, "What do you say we find out where our unit is. Then we can either arrange for transportation out or find a place to crash for tonight?"

"We can do that. What would you say that we just find a place for tonight and check on our unit tomorrow morning?"

"Sure, sounds okay with me," I answered in total agreement.

With nothing to change into, we just put our clothes on over what we had on, even with our shorts soaked in sweat, sand, and seawater. We retrieved our sea bags from the guards, and stuffed our wet towels inside.

Dan thanked the two guards for watching our things, and the one guard thanked me for the 'show' earlier.

I almost forgot about my, getting undressed episode. Anyway, I answered, "No problem. Next time, I'll play that trick on some beautiful babe, and that way, we can both enjoy the show."

He responded, "Peace man. If we can't have a good piece, then I hope you can get a piece."

Throwing my sea bag on my shoulder was quite a shock. I could not believe that my sunburn was hurting this bad so quickly. With that, I decided just to drag my bag across the beach and hoped that I would not wear a hole in the bottom and have all my things fall out and all over the sand. I shouldn't complain because I had a fantastic time at the beach today.

Chapter 16

After a short walk, we were off the beach and in town. We came to a stop at a corner, and I began to realize just how tired I was. I was sun burnt, hungry, had sand in every crease and fold in my body, and to boot, the retard had a date for tonight, and I was here with Dan. Then again, I kept repeating to myself that I should not complain because I did have a nice time at the beach today.

I asked Dan, "Hungry?"

"Yes, I am. I am hungry. What would you like to eat this evening?" Dan responded, apparently giving me a choice.

I took a quick look around and spotted a restaurant with a sign in English, 'Vietnamese Cuisine.' "Now that place might be interesting," I said, as I pointed toward the sign giving Dan my suggestion.

"I'm not sure about that place, my quick to decide friend," Dan expressed, with disappointment.

"Now what could be wrong with a Vietnamese restaurant in the middle of Vietnam?" I needed an answer for this one.

"Would you expect to see a sign in Japan that read, 'Japanese food?' How about a carry-out restaurant next to the Great Wall of China that said, 'Chinese carry-out?'"

"What's your point? You can buy Kentucky Fried Chicken in Kentucky. There's the Boston cream pie, that you can buy in

Boston and you can buy a New York strip steak in New York, New York."

"Good point. If you would, just pick another place please," Dan suggested, and he appeared to be rather serious.

It didn't mean anything to me, so I did. "How about the place next door? Just to the left." Not that it made any difference. They both looked the same to me, and I had never been to either one before.

"Cool, let's do it," Dan responded, giving his approval.

After crossing the street without incident, we entered my second establishment choice and sat down in a booth. Lucky for me, I was able to select my meal by again pointing to the pictures. I felt safe ordering a hamburger, fries, and a Coke this time. "Interesting menu," I said to Dan.

"If you want to keep one this time, try asking first," he told me indicating that taking another one would not be a good idea.

"No sweat, I am not going to pull that stunt again. I may be stupid on some things but I do learn quickly," I assured him.

"Damn, I was kind of hoping for another situation where you get assaulted by another waitress," Dan jokingly told me.

"I should have figured you would enjoy something like that."

Before we could carry this conversation any further, our waitress came over and took our order. To my surprise, I did just fine, and Dan ordered the same as me. Our food came quickly, and it was great. In no time at all, we were finished and back outside.

"Let's find a place to stay for tonight. I'd like to put my bag down and get a shower," Dan said.

After a few minutes and a few blocks later, I suggested, "Now that looks like an acceptable hotel for us to spend the night. What do you think, my man?" I was tired of walking and it was about time we found a place to stay.

Dan came back with, "Sounds as if it's a good idea to me. Let's check-it-out and see what we have here."

As we crossed the street, Dan asked me, "So Charles, why did you pick this place?"

"Easy. It's got a big Hotel sign on it," I explained, pointing to the building.

He did look and nodded approval of my selection. Wow, two good choices, and all in one day. Well, one and a half. I had to make a second selection for our last meal.

At the registration desk, I noticed three young girls sitting on a couch, between the elevator and the check-in counter. Dan said in a whisper, "I see this fancy place has bell hops. And these ladies are real bell hops."

Now what in the world could he be talking about? I was just happy that one of them didn't run over and grab me. No need to have myself dragged and paraded all over the hotel lobby.

"They want to check out your ding-dong, and ring your bell. Know what I mean?" Dan explained, as he continued to tease me. That was a little more than I wanted to know. I didn't care about that, and I was just glad that they stayed on the couch.

Dan said to the clerk, "We'll need a single room with two beds for tonight, please."

"Okay Joe," responded the old guy from behind the counter.

Just like in the old western movies, the clerk turned around and picked a set of keys from one of the many small cubbyholes mounted on the wall. Some of these cubbyholes had mail and others had notes and keys in them. He turned back at us, set the keys on the counter, and said, "Ten dollars."

Dan responded with, "Here's ten, my good man."

As the clerk gave the money the, 'once over' as if it were counterfeit, Dan said to me, "It'll be my treat tonight."

The clerk noticed that I was keeping an eye on the girls on the couch, and he said to me, "You want, Joe? Numba-one girl take bag to room."

I continued watching them to insure that neither one decided to sneak up and grab me. However, before I could answer, Dan spoke up and said, "Maybe later, we call. Okay?"

"Okay Joe."

Dan whispered to me, "They'll do more than service your room."

He turned to the clerk and asked, "We'll need a wake-up call for 6 AM. You can do?"

"Okay, Joe," replied the clerk as the clerk reached under the counter, and pulled out an alarm clock. He wound it up, set the time on the alarm, and handed it to Dan.

"Okay Joe?" The old guy asked, as he left his hand out, suggesting a tip.

"Thanks," Dan quickly responded to the clerk. "No tip now. If clock work okay in morning, then I give you tip."

Dan turned to me, saw my surprised look, and said, "What? Did you think that we had a phone in our room for a wake-up call? Besides, this would be more reliable than Papa-san here."

"Yeah, I guess."

The clerk spoke up and said, "Want girl help carry?"

I looked over and told Dan, "I don't think the girls can get our bags off the floor."

"Dummy," Dan said, "It's not the bags they want to get-off, it's us."

With that remark from Dan, I turned to the clerk and said, "No thank you."

He smiled back at my refusal with a mouth filled with missing teeth.

Anyway, with my bag in hand, and without their help, we headed toward the elevator and stood aside as one local guy came into the lobby with his motorcycle. To yet another surprise for me, this guy took his cycle on the elevator with him.

I looked around toward the desk clerk to see how he would respond to this and saw that he was looking our way, but did not appear to care about this guy and his bike. With this a, 'no sweat' situation, we all got onboard as if the whole elevator ride was completely normal. Of course, that was except for standing close to the bike because it was still hot. In addition, let's not forget the smell of gasoline and exhaust.

This guy and his bike got off before us and I said to Dan, "Is there an extra charge to sleep with your bike?"

"Nah, it's considered a luggage carrier."

At any rate, the doors closed and we went up two more floors. As we were getting off, there was another guy with his bike getting on, and he did allow us to get off first. As we headed down the hall, I noticed that the walls appeared to have only one coat of paint on them. This was probably the original paint when the hotel was new about a hundred years ago. It just needed a fresh coat of paint everywhere and it would look like new. The only odors that I could smell in this hotel were gasoline and engine exhaust.

Now our room was rather nice. It was clean and had one dresser, two beds, and two ceiling fans. Dan leaned over and turned on the TV. After a long pause as the TV warmed up, the Beverly Hillbillies came on. Their voices were being dubbed in Vietnamese and I got a kick out of this. Dan clicked the channels all around using the pliers that had been locked in-place on the channel changer. With nothing else on, he ended up back at the Beverly Hillbillies.

"At least we have one TV station," Dan said, as he took out some rubber bands from his sea bag.

"Do you have any rubber bands?" He asked.

"No. Besides, the only thing in my bag is Navy issue stuff, other than my seawater soaked towel and a pound of sand. Why do you need one?"

"To hide our wallet, while we sleep at night."

Now this must be a good one, so I just had to ask, "How are rubber bands going to protect me from losing my wallet? Do I attach it to one of my legs or arms? No way was I going to attach it anyplace else on my body."

"No, not there. That'll be the first place they'll look."

"So how?"

"Watch me."

I didn't know if I wanted to watch him or not.

Dan took one rubber band and his wallet, and stood on the bed. He pulled the string to stop the fan. With the fan stopped, he placed his wallet on one blade and secured it with the rubber band.

"Hand me your wallet so I can balance out this thing. I don't need it to shake its way loose and fly across the room."

"Can I trust you with my wallet?" I said this only trying to make a joke.

"No problem," he said, as he was getting ready to turn the fan back onto full speed.

"Just joking my man, give me a break. Here's my wallet. You have to admit that it's a good idea, but a strange one."

With both wallets secured, he turned the fan back on at high speed and you could not tell anything was there. As Dan jumped down from the bed, we got a knock at the door. I walked over, and because there was no peephole, I asked, "Who's there?"

A response was given by a Vietnamese sounding girl, "I from Welcome Wagon. How we help you?"

"Let's see what we got here. Let'em in," Dan said with an inquisitive tone.

This was good and maybe we would get a couple of coupons for, 'two for one-dinner' deals and some free tickets to a movie or show. I opened the door and there stood two girls in go-go boots, hot pants, and nothing else on but smiles. These girls were like . . . topless. They were both very cute with bangs and long, straight, black hair and I believed this to be the national haircut for all women in Vietnam. No coupons or tickets to a show like I thought, but in some ways I was getting a private showing.

They both were wearing a lot of make-up. It appeared to me that they must have a day job at a cosmetic counter at some big department store. They had that, "One of every shade of color makeup on their faces." I meant, it was neat. It was just that there was too much of it. You could probably have made up another dozen or so girls with the excess makeup.

"What you want? Make good time for you," the one standing on the left asked.

With my mouth wide open and unable to talk, Dan spoke up for me and said, "Nothing right now, thank you, maybe we call later. Okay?"

"Okay Joe, but night early. You numba-one pick now, not later."

"We'll just have to take that chance," Dan replied.

After a short pause and because the two girls did not leave right away, Dan continued with, "So how much for good time? I don't want numba-ten price. Numba-one price, I only want numba-one price. How much for boom-boom."

The one on the right smiled and said, "How you pay Joe? Green back or MPC?"

"I pay Green Back."

"Twenty Green Back. You pay first."

I didn't want to be involved with any of this. I only wanted to get caught up on some much needed rest and sleep. I hoped that Dan would just send them off, and that they would go away.

Dan turned to me and asked, "You pay twenty-dollars? What you think?"

"Hey man, remember I'm new here. You decide what you want to do. As for me, I'll just skip it this time." I did not need this kind of thing right now, and I was not going to pay for it.

Giving this some thought, I wondered what if he wanted a girl. What would I do? Would I stand in the hall until he was done? On the other hand, maybe I would just watch TV and try not peek. Man, all I wanted to do was to relax, ignore my sunburn, and get the sand out of my ass.

The girl on the right said to me, "You cherry boy, Joe? You no want good time, twenty-dollar? I numba-one girl and twenty-dollar numba-one price. I go easy you. Break you in like new pair boots."

I didn't know how to handle this and I certainly did not want to be broken-in by either one of them. I hoped Dan would step in and find a nice way to send them away.

This made Dan smile and he responded, "Like I said, maybe later we do a boom-boom, good time thing."

With that, he just shut the door on the two girls and told them both, "Good night."

"So was that a good deal, not that I would be willing to pay for it?" I asked.

"In some ways, yes. At least this way, we didn't have to go out and pick them up after buying them a lot of Saigon Teas."

"They were both somewhat cute. Don't you think?" I asked.

"They were okay. Right now, you are still new in-country and almost every girl that you see with no top on will be attractive. After a while, you'll start to be more selective."

I found that a little hard to imagine. I still thought that they were both cute. I might not take them home to meet my parents, but I would have no problem going out with them in public. Whatever. I was not going to do anything anyway with them, cute or not.

I reached into my bag because I wanted to hang up my towel and let it dry. After shaking off the sand, I said to Dan, "No need to carry around this extra weight."

"Good idea," he responded and he did the same to his towel and shorts.

Dan plopped down on the bed after putting the alarm clock on top of the TV and said, "So do you want to rest a little before we check out the night life?"

"Won't we have time during the rest of the year that we're here to checkout the town? Do we need to do it all at one time?" I would not mind going out, but I was beat and burned.

"No, not really. You see my friend, while we're on the rivers with our unit, there'll be no nightlife. The few times that we get liberty will only be in the daytime. Remember that we have a job to do. We won't get much liberty on the rivers because of the type of war we fight there. It's not like the Army or Marines."

"What do you mean?"

"They, the Army guys and Marines, for the most part, live on a base. Some of the bases are big and some of the bases are small. Usually, it's near a town or city, and they can go out and off the base every now and then. For us, we are on the rivers and everything for us is on the ship."

After a few moments considering this, I responded with, "Okay, how about this? A shower and a short nap for now, and then, we'll go and do the town."

Dan's only response was, "Then you can set the clock for a few hours from now." With that said, he lay down and closed his eyes as if he were already asleep.

I reached over, turned off the TV, and set the clock. Within a few seconds, and without a shower, I was also fast asleep.

After only a short nap, I was woken by the sound of the TV. Dan was up and sitting on the side of his bed flicking the channel changer. As earlier, only one station came in clear and it was the Johnny Carson Tonight show on the tube. It was in English and by the style of his clothes and the jokes; this had to be an old show.

"What time is it?" I asked, hoping that maybe we slept through the entire night. I secretly hoped that it might have been too late to go out and do anything.

"Eight PM or 2000 hours. We only have time to hit one or two places before the MP's strongly suggest that we get off the streets."

In just ten minutes, we were up, showered, and ready to explore the nightlife. It was not as if I had to spend any time washing and drying my hair or picking out what to wear. My boot camp haircut made washing my hair as easy as washing my face, and all I had to do was wet up, soap up, rinse, and wipe dry.

Again, we locked up our sea bags. Only this time we locked them together to the pipes in the bathroom tub. Dan mentioned that if anyone did come into the room, they might not check the bathroom for our things. We made the beds and left the room as if no one were staying there. We even hid the alarm clock. Dan had said that if it appeared that no one was occupying the room, that they might not search it for something to steal.

Once outside, Dan asked me which way I wanted to go.

"Which way do you suggest?" I asked.

"It'll be cool, no matter which way we go."

I looked up and down the street, then up and down again. I was thinking that the drunks would be walking one way and those going to the bars sober, would be walking the other way. Whatever, both ways seemed the same-same to me. "I think if we are going to do it right, then we should head to the right," I suggested and headed that way.

"Grand idea my man, grand idea," said Dan, as if I somehow made the correct choice.

After a few blocks, Dan said, "I think you might want to get a shoeshine before you check into our unit. So what do you think?"

"Why do I want to shine my boots? I don't believe that I'll be standing any inspections with these any time soon. Besides, they still don't even fit."

"Come on. It'll be cool."

Where was this going, I wondered. "So what is the big deal anyway? It's just a shoeshine. What could be so cool about a shoeshine at this time at night?"

"Remember where you are."

"Yeah okay, we're in 'The-Nam.' So how can a shoeshine be a big deal? In 'The-Nam,' or not, a shoeshine is a shoeshine is a shoeshine."

This must be something stupid, or it was something that would make me look stupid I thought.

With a smile he said, "You'll see when we turn this corner."

I could not believe I was giving this much attention to a shoeshine. This just could not be all that big of a deal.

"While we are at it, how about we get a haircut?" I only brought this up because I might as well look good at both ends.

"Man, you do not want a hair cut from anyone other than a military issue barber," Dan instructed.

"Why? Can't Orientals cut anything other than straight-black-hair?" I did not know why I said that or even why I thought of such a rude remark. It was just that I could not ever recall seeing any Orientals that did not have straight black hair. Except, for maybe the old people, and then it was just straight, gray, and falling out.

"I never thought about that. Good point, however, while you are here in 'The-Nam,' you don't want a local standing behind you with a straight razor in his hand."

"And?"

"And, what?"

I asked, "Isn't that the way most people get their hair cut?"

"What if this guy was supporting the North? He might be getting a bounty for every ear that he turns over."

I would never have considered any of this for a simple haircut.

"Remember," he continued. "He can just slit your throat and drag you in the back. With that, you are history, AWOL, missing in action, and maybe even a little hard of hearing."

Now, I did agree with him. "But what if we go in at the same time? You know, we get our hair cuts together." Not a bad way to solve a bad situation I was thinking.

"Oh yeah, two chairs, no waiting. Two barbers could slit our throats as easy as one. Nah, for me, I can wait until we check into our unit and that, my friend, has its own set of rules."

"Sounds like a sensible idea. I can wait; I mean, I got my last hair cut only a few weeks ago the day I left boot camp."

Once around the corner, I looked up at the first of many signs. Not that I should have been surprised by what I saw, but I was caught off guard just the same. "Topless Shoeshine" read the sign.

"Care to invest a dollar or four bits per shoe? You can even think of it as, four bits per tit," Dan explained, but not too clearly, indicating that this sort of thing was done all the time over here.

I would normally have never checked out a place like this, but because I was here, I might as well pay it a visit. Hell, there was not a place like this anywhere back home, even if I wanted to pay one a visit.

"Yeah, I guess. This may be a dirty place, but at least my boots can come out looking clean," I answered.

Dan stepped aside, allowing me to enter first. Quickly, I stepped back and said, "You can go in first this time. I didn't know what to expect or whether they would grab me or not, but at least I could see it happen to you. So how does that grab you, my man?"

"No sweat," Dan said. "I'll be glad to go first and that will grab me just fine."

Now what did I do? He seemed fine to go in first. Does this mean that nothing would really happen to the first guy going in? On the other hand, maybe the second person was grabbed. Whatever, I would just go in second with my hands guarding myself.

Once inside, and a little disappointed that nothing happened, I could see that it was just like any normal shoeshine establishment. There was a row of six shoeshine chairs on a platform a little higher than the floor up against one wall. The other wall had an equal number of normal chairs with some old guy sitting down reading a paper.

Dan asked the old man, "How are they hanging today?"

I did not think this old man knew what Dan was asking. Yet to my surprise, he did. He answered, "Big hanging big, little, no hang. No hang at all."

Dan came back with, "Are you open for business?"

"Okay Joe, sit. Sit please."

This old guy seemed pleasant enough. I didn't know if he owned the place, or if he was just an employee. And if he were shining shoes, I certainly did not want to see his tits.

"How much?" Dan asked as he took a seat.

With a smile showing only two teeth in his entire mouth, he responded with, "One dollar little, two dollar big. What you want Joe? You want big? Big numba-one?"

Looking at me, Dan said, "I guess we must pay by the pound."

This got a chuckle out of me, as Dan turned to this old guy and asked, "How big is big and how small is small, papa-san?"

"Today, small is very small. Hard to tell someday. Big, numba-one big. You like. Two Dollar."

This started to sound like we were at a fish market. Pick a size, and we give you the price.

"Can we check them out before we decide?"

This question was not well received and he responded with, "Look Joe, One dollar, or two dollar. What you decide? No pick and no choose. No carry-out."

I did not want to pay two dollars for a shoeshine, big tits or not. I turned to Dan and said; "I'll go for the small tits. I only want to spend a dollar for a shine."

"I'll go for the big tits then. This way we can tell if little is little and if big is big."

The old man responded with, "Okay, one big, one little. Please wait. I go now get little and numba-one big tit. You like."

The old man stepped into the back behind a set of curtains, and Dan and I just smiled at each other.

"Have you done this before?" I asked.

"No, this'll be my first time. I've heard that it's quite an adventure and hard to forget."

"Do we tit, I mean tip?"

"You are cheap. You should always leave a tip for something like this. The bargirls don't count. You are already paying too much for their drinks."

About this time, two girls came out and both were topless. Both were young girls probably around 17 or 18 years old. To our surprise, both sets of tits were about the same size, small. They both reached down and with brushes in hand, started to buff our boots.

I said to Dan as I kept an eye on my girl, "I may not be an expert on tits, but I do know the difference between big and little tits. These are two sets of little ones. The four of them together didn't make up one good big tit."

Dan looked toward the doorway where the little old man went. Right then, the old guy came out and told the one girl doing Dan's shoes something. She stopped what she was doing and returned to the back room. A moment later, another girl that had a set of very big tits bounced in to take her place. They were so big for such a small body that they did not look natural, or even real. Of all things, she had stretch marks all over the top, and this was not attractive at all. With them being almost perfectly round and with the stretch marks, well, it looked like craters on the moon.

Dan said, "If she were to ever fall down face first, her face would never hit the ground."

"Now there's a pair of two dollar tits," I added.

"Yeah man, I guess I'll get my moneys worth here."

I knew that it was impolite to stare at someone, but I was paying for this view and I might as well look. I had just never been this close to two sets of tits at the same time before. Except for earlier in our room.

Dan joked, "I can't see my boots." Inferring that she was big enough to hide them from view.

"I can see mine all the way to the toes." Naturally, referring to her very small build.

The two girls never did look up at us as they just kept on doing our boots. After only a minute or two, they were finished, and they walked away into the back room.

With this style of boot, there were no sides to shine because the sides were made of canvas material. They only had the toe part and a little on the sides to shine. A dollar was a steep price for what we received. I really should not complain because my boots did shine and I did get a private showing.

Papa-san stepped over and said, "Good shine, good tits. Now you pay."

"Relax old man. This happened so fast that I didn't have time to reach for my money."

"That was rather quick," I agreed with Dan.

"I'll tell you what," Dan said to me. "I'll treat this one and only time."

"Thanks, that's big of you."

"Not big of me, they were big on her. So, what did you think?"

"They never cover this kind of stuff on the nightly news back home, nor did I ever see any of this in my travel catalog at the Navy recruitment center."

"So, you gonna come back to this place someday?"

With a quick answer, I said, "Nah, once is enough. I might tell others, that we will be in town to stop by and give it a shot, but no, once is plenty."

Dan paid the man, and I assumed he left a tip for the girls.

Once outside, I said, "Now, I'm grateful for this experience. I do appreciate the shoe shine, and I thank you for the treat. Times two."

"You're most welcome."

Dan pointed toward a place across the street to a club called the, 'Numba-One Club.' He suggested, "Let's check out that place. I had a great experience the last time I was there. Maybe they won't remember me, and I can stay a little longer this time."

I didn't like the sound of that but I followed him there anyway.

I could see two MP's standing right in front of the doorway and I asked, "Is this a good idea with the MP's out front?"

"It's the best idea. You see, with them out front, that means they aren't inside. In addition to that, no one is willing to go inside with them outside, and start any trouble."

"Are we allowed to go in with them in the doorway?" I asked.

"If not, they'll let us know. If okay, they'll just step aside and let us in. Come on and don't sweat it."

Crossing the street was no problem, and the two MP's did step aside and let us in without saying a word to us. I didn't believe they even gave us any notice. Like most clubs I had seen so far, it was dark inside, and the music was loud. Yet, this place appeared to be clean and did not give the impression of being a dump. Dan and I headed up to the bar, grabbed two stools, and made ourselves comfortable.

"You want a beer or glass of warm milk tonight?" Dan asked jokingly.

I didn't know why he was starting on me already, but I answered, "A beer will be just fine."

After a few minutes, the music stopped, and a spot light shined on one part of the bar. Then some music started again. This one girl got up on the bar and started to dance. She was the oldest stripper I had ever seen. Well, that was not entirely true. At eighteen, I had only been to a strip joint once, the one time that a few of us took off for Washington, DC, because the drinking age there was eighteen. Other than that, the only other dancers I had seen, had been on TV and at the movies. Anyway, her go-go boots, hot pants, and tube top did nothing to help attract me because she was very unattractive. Unattractive was too kind; she was very ugly. Even her body was ugly. She did not get hit with the ugly stick. She was the ugly stick.

I told Dan, "Now she's really a dog, and I don't mean that she's a fox."

Dan said, "Do you know the difference between a dog and a fox?"

"Yeah, six beers." I already heard that joke before.

It was at this time that Dan pointed to her and started to count out very loud. He was so loud, that everyone could easily hear it.

"Seven, eight, nine, ten," he continued, all the while he pointed at her. He got even louder now with, "Sixteen, seventeen, eighteen."

Other people started to look over at him and listen as he continued with this counting.

"Nineteen." Apparently, she had taken enough of this and had stopped dancing. With her hands on her hips she snapped, "What you count, GI?"

Everyone in the place was now paying, I believed, too much attention to this confrontation that was about ready to hit the fan. The good news was that my wallet was not attached to the fan here.

"What you count?" She said again to him.

"I'm counting stretch marks," as he continued to count out loud pointing to her waist.

"Twenty, twenty-one."

Without any warning, she jumped down off the bar and grabbed him around the neck. This really scared the crap out of me. I mean, she was quick about it like a lightening bolt.

Now she was yelling plenty of shit in Vietnamese. This was one very angry, ugly lady, and somehow, I was on her side. That was a very crude and rude thing to say to someone, bargirl, or no bargirl. I did not know whether to help him, help her, or get out of their way. Lucky for me, and especially for Dan, the bartender reached over and pulled her back across the bar. He had her by the back of her tube top as her arms and legs were still kicking and swinging as she continued cursing him out in many languages.

In a calm voice Dan said, "Lets find another place. I think I've outstayed my welcome this time. Now that I think about it, this is the second time I outstayed my welcome here."

"No shit ass-hole," I told him. "That was not a very kind thing to do. She should have broken your neck and scratched your eyes out for that mean comment."

"The last time I did that, she just laughed and everything seemed okay. I guess she was in a bad mood tonight or maybe I counted too high this time."

"Still, that was very mean."

As we strolled out the door, the two MP's we passed earlier, came rushing by us. Like an idiot, I stopped to look back to see what or whom they were after. I got a push from behind and Dan said, "Don't stop now."

"Oh yeah, it's you they want to talk to."

"No sweat, we'll just try the place next door," Dan instructed, as we continued to head out.

"Okay," I answered and I figured what the hell. I mean, this was only one bar, in a city, in a country, that I was only going to visit once, in my lifetime. We had only gone a couple of feet and already we were in another bar.

"Are you going to cause any trouble this time?" I asked.

"Nah, I promise I won't use the same joke again tonight."

Great, that must mean he had more insulting comments that I had not heard yet. I was hoping to make it through the next twelve months and now I hoped just to make it through the next twelve minutes.

Inside, we again took two seats at the bar. We got two more beers and just sat quietly for a few minutes.

"I hope we can finish our beers this time," I said to break the silence.

Some Army guy flopped down next to me and said, "Hi. How' ya doin?"

"Fine," I answered after I turned around. "How 'bout you?"

"My assignment for the next four days is to stay as drunk as I can get," he proceeded to inform me.

Who was this guy? I do not believe that I knew him. I questioned, "How did you get that assignment?"

He ordered two beers and a drink called a salty-dog. He turned to me and said, "I, myself, and me ordered that assignment. Do you want to know why?"

Not really. He's probably just a drunk, and I believed that drunks just wanted to stay drunk, cool assignment or not. Oh well, I might as well amuse myself. "So tell me," as I checked out the name on his shirt. "Johnson, why did you order yourself this pristine assignment?"

He downed the salty-dog and one of his beers in one swallow. He wiped his lips with the entire arm of his shirt and said, "I'm getting out-of-here in four days. I'm going home."

He thought for a minute as if he forgot the rest of his sentence. Then he said, "As long as I'm drunk, they can't order me out on any kind of operations, dangerous ones or not."

Not bad, not a bad assignment at all, and a good idea, if it worked. I wondered if I could get that kind of assignment for the next twelve months. Nah, I did not even like to drink all that much.

Dan said to me, "So, you found a new friend?"

"Just a guy that thinks like you," I answered jokingly.

I looked back at Johnson and he had just completed his second beer.

I asked him, "Won't you get into trouble for not following orders?" There had to be something wrong here with what he was doing.

"No man, ain't you been a listen' to me? I can't be disobeying any orders if I ain't been given any orders to disobey."

Now that did make sense. This guy and Dan must be cousins or something because they think alike.

"Even the stupid officers won't order me to do anything," he continued telling me as he ordered yet another round for himself.

"Can't you be in trouble for not being available to take orders?" I asked because I learned in boot camp that we needed to be available to receive orders.

"Yes I can but, I'll be home before anything can be written up against me."

Dan leaned over to me and said, "The way you two are talking, I would have thought you were the drunk one."

"What do you mean by that?"

Dan explained, "What he says makes sense. Don't you know?"

"Yeah, I guess," I answered as if I thought I knew what he was saying.

Johnson placed his hand on my shoulder and said, "At midnight, I'll only have three days." With that, he got up and made his way to a table in the corner.

No sooner did he have a seat, a girl stopped over and apparently was trying to get him to buy her a drink. I could hear him respond with, "No way. I only have enough money to keep me drunk for now. Go away and leave me alone."

She did, just as his drinks arrived. Nothing more happened, and we just finished off a few beers and left.

Back at our hotel room, we first checked to see if our things were still there. They were and we got ourselves relaxed and turned on the TV. The Lucy Show was on, and it was funnier than ever with their voices and sound effects dubbed.

Right then, we heard a knock on the door. Dan opened it, and there stood the two girls from earlier. This time their long straight hair was all messed up and their make up was all over their faces. All they had on now were their hot pants. Still no tops on, and now their boots were missing. This was definitely a turn-off.

Dan looked back at me and said in a low voice, "I wonder how much they are now?"

I didn't know and I didn't care. He can have them both, no matter what the price.

One girl said, "How you pay? You pay now. Ten dollars?"

Sounding and acting as if he were shocked, Dan replied, "Ten dollars? Now, is that ten dollars for each of you or ten for both?"

Damn, the price had come down 50% and he wanted to cut that down 50% more.

The two girls talked between themselves and the one that has been doing all the talking said, "Ten each."

"Too much."

The girls were again talking between themselves. "Okay Joe," the one said. "Ten for both."

I hoped that he was not doing the bidding for me. I wanted to go to bed, and I wanted to go to bed by myself.

"No thank you. Not now, maybe tomorrow. Good night," Dan said as he shut the door in their face and took a seat on his bed.

"I'm glad you didn't invite them to spend some time with us. I'm not interested in them."

Dan answered, "Nah, no need for that kind of used stuff tonight. I figured that if you wanted a girl, you could do your own bidding."

"Thanks," and I got comfortable on the bed and continued to watch the rest of the Lucy Show.

I had seen this one before and following the story was easy. This was the one where Lucy and Ethel buy a side of beef and hide it in the furnace from Ricky and Fred. The four of them were talking in Lucy's apartment, while Fred told Ricky that they were testing the furnace. The smell of the meat cooking was overwhelming, and off they went to the basement to throw a cookout.

Dan took the alarm clock that he had hid under the bed and said; "I'll set it for 0800. What do you think?"

"Fine with me. What's the plan tomorrow?"

"First, I'll turn off the alarm, get up, and then make it to the bath room for a shit, shave, and a shower."

"No man, I mean like tracking down our unit and finding a way to get to her."

"Don't know just yet. We'll find a Comm-Center and check things out. Maybe we can make it back on the air base and see if they have any information. Its not like we can find a phone booth and call information, you know."

"Yeah, I know what you mean."

"Look," Dan said. "For now, let's just get some sleep and we'll check-it-out tomorrow. No need for us to plan our whole day out right now, is there? Hell man, the war might be over in the morning."

He was right. There was nothing I could do, say, think, or worry about that would have any effect on my night's sleep. With that said, I turned off the TV and quickly fell sound asleep.

Chapter 17

The alarm woke me, and I quickly turned it off because it was rather loud. I didn't want to wake my parents up this early on a Saturday morning. As I lay still for a moment or two before getting up, I looked up and noticed that there was a ceiling fan above me. I didn't remember putting a fan up in my room. Hell, I didn't even remember painting my ceiling that ugly color. I looked over at the window and asked myself, "My mom bought those curtains, those ugly curtains, how could she."

I could hear some traffic outside, and with all the little horns blowing; I knew that I was not in my neighborhood. The noise sounded as if I were near a little kids' amusement park.

Then it finally hit me. "Damn, damn, damn," I repeated quietly to myself. I'm not in my room at my parent's home in Baltimore, and this was certainly not Kansas. I was in a hotel room in Vietnam, and I was in the U.S. Navy. I had a unit to report to, a war to fight, and the way things had been going for me lately, I might never get to do either one.

Dan, who was in the bed next to me, turned over, stuck his head out from under the covers, and asked, "Were you calling my name? You know, Dan, Dan, Dan."

"No, I just said 'damn.' Didn't mean to wake you. Sorry about that," I said with some embarrassment. Oh well, here I go again.

Welcome to 'The-Nam,' I told myself. "Sorry," I told him a second time.

"No sweat. Time to get moving anyway," he answered. Just as he had explained last night, he got up and made his way to the bathroom for a shit, shave, and a shower. I stayed where I was, and figured that I could at least grab a few extra minutes of sleep before I got myself up.

There was a knock at the door that messed up my extra sleep time. I got up quickly and opened the door and saw, not that I should have been surprised, the same two girls from last night. I thought they looked bad before, but today was another story, because they looked war torn. These ladies were a serious turn off. One of them could have caused a fuse to blow by appearance alone, and the other would definitely trip a circuit breaker. In fact, they were so much of a turn-off, that I wished they would just turn-around and go away.

Not only was their hair totally messed up, but it was very dirty as well, and I mean ugly-dirty. As far as their make-up goes, their make-up appeared to have been worn clean off their faces and, seeing them up close was truly horrifying. The one looked as if she tailgated a water buffalo a little too close, and once too often.

Their faces were so messed up that it was making it hard to make eye contact with them. I started to look down at their necks to get away from their faces and the only thing I could see missing was a date and time stamp next to each hickey for identification. There were so many hickeys on them, and each one a different shade of purple, that I assumed that this was because different guys made them on different days. And naturally with the possibility of a few farm animals mixed in.

If I ever woke up in the morning with one of them lying beside me, I would start the day off by getting drunk. Damn, going to bed with both of them would be justifiable ground for suicide.

Their breath smelled like a mixture of beer and whisky. Then to add to that, there were potato chips stuck between all their teeth. One girl even had a cheese ball stuck in her hair. I was willing to bet that it would have taken a stainless steel pick to comb it out and that was only if you could get the kinks out first. Their mascara was smeared from eye to eye, all the way back to each ear. Now this reminded me of someone wearing a Batman mask, or maybe, they wanted to look that way for Halloween and pass for a pair of raccoons.

The one girl's hot pants were not zipped up all the way. Apparently, she was advertising for a quick de-pants-ing. Well, there would be no, quick de-pants-ing here from me. Even if I wanted a hooker, and I did not, I would not want these two hand-me-downs. I asked them, as if I didn't already know why they were here, "What do you want?" Yep, that was a dumb question. I could not think of anything else to ask without laughing at them, and I didn't want to be rude.

"Show you good time, Joe?"

I was thinking, yeah, you could show me a good time by leaving Dodge. I didn't want to say all that because I didn't want to hurt their feelings.

I was about ready to tell them to, 'go away,' when I realized that, hell; I had a great idea. I would just send them both into the shower with Dan. I would do just that, because that was the kind of thing that he could and would do to me. Besides, I didn't think Dan would mind their visit. Yet, these girls might shy away from clean water. Whatever, I was going to do it.

"I no want good time. You go check friend. He in shower. You go shower. Do good time there," I told them.

Without delay, the both of them took off toward the bathroom. There was no hesitation as to which way to go because they probably had been in all the bathrooms in this hotel anyway, at one time or another. Maybe every one except this one last night, by they way they looked.

I took a quick check out in the hallway to see if anyone was watching. I didn't want anyone to see me or think that I wanted those two for myself.

Without warning, one of the girls screamed, followed quickly by the both of them running past me and out the door. As if nothing happened, I closed the door, turned on the TV, and lay back in bed, as Mighty Mouse came on, in black and white, to save the day. I was expecting Dan to come running out or something, but he did not. He continued with his shower and after a few minutes, he came out as if nothing happened. He pointed to the bathroom gesturing for me to take my turn.

Agreeing with him, I did not say anything about the two girls and went on to shave and shower. While in the shower with my eyes closed and letting the hot water beat down on my face, it occurred to me that he might want to get even. Somehow, some way, he would not let me get away with what I did. I quickly peeked out and saw nothing. I felt somewhat safer now, but I decided that I would hurry up, and get done. He might try to find those two girls, send them in, and let them have their way with me. I didn't know what made them scream, but if they came in on me, I would be the one screaming and running away.

After I completed my shower, we were soon packed and out the door. We flew down the hall, trying to catch the elevator that had just let off some local guy with his motorcycle. He still had the motor running and down the hallway he went, riding his bike.

Walking down to the lobby, I asked, "So, what are we going to do now?"

"We will continue down and make our way to the front desk to check out."

"And after we do that, what next?"

"What do you want to do?"

I thought for a moment and suggested that we get something for breakfast and he responded with, "Okay. That sounds good. You pick a place."

"No sweat. I'll pick us a good place." I answered as we stepped up to the front desk.

I asked the clerk, "Any messages for me?"

Dan looked at me, and questioned, "What are you doing?"

"Give me a break; I always wanted to do that. You know, ask if I had any messages," I explained with a smile on my face. I thought this to be funny.

Before Dan could put me down, the clerk handed me a slip of paper, or note, and said, "Yea, just one."

I turned to the clerk flabbergasted and retrieved my message. To my dissatisfaction, it was written in Vietnamese. I handed it back to the clerk and asked him to read it to me.

He read the note to himself and responded with, "Sorry Joe. No message. You wrong Joe." With that, he placed the note in another cubbyhole and that was one down and over from ours. Oh well, so much for that.

After Dan signed us out, he asked me, "You want to stay here again?"

I came back quickly with, "I hope not."

"Why not? Are you cheap and ungrateful?"

"No, that was not what I meant. I mean, I don't want to stay here again. Only because I want to find our ship today. If so, there would be no reason to check back here again. You know what I mean?" I hoped he knew that I was only joking.

I asked the desk clerk if he knew a good place for breakfast that was nearby. He told me to head out, turn right, and walk two blocks.

We followed his instructions and sure enough, we found a pleasant little restaurant for breakfast. The only thing I didn't like about this place was that the menu didn't have pictures for me to make my selection. I figured that I would just ask Dan what he was eating, and if I liked it, I would order, same-same.

"What's your pleasure, I'll treat," I informed Dan.

"I'm going for two eggs, two slices of bacon, and fresh milk with two pieces of toast."

"Sounds good, and I believe I'm going have the same thing."

Outstanding, I did not have to worry about ordering my meal. My own concern now was to explain that I wanted the same thing without ordering, same-same twice.

Dan commented, "You can order for me. I'm going to make a head call. Be back in a minute."

Shit, I didn't want to do this order thing by myself. However, I might luck out, and he would return before our waitress did. No luck for me today, because as he walked away, here she came. Oh well, it was time to get this ordering adventure a try.

"Yes," she said to me. "You order. You order now."

I pointed to Dan's seat and ordered, "Two eggs, two slices of bacon, two pieces of bread, and fresh milk."

She wrote this down and looked up at me. I told her, "Same-same. Me too," I ordered while holding up two fingers to indicate two orders.

She answered, "Same-same, two," as she held up two fingers.

"Yes."

She asked me, "Fresh?"

What does she mean, fresh? With that, I answered, "Fresh, yeah fresh, you know, fresh-fresh."

"Okay Joe, you want fresh."

She left, and Dan returned a moment later, sat down, and commented, "I feel lucky. I believe that we might make it to our unit by dinnertime today. What do you think?"

I wanted to continue along with this lucky feeling of his, because I scored a hit with ordering breakfast. I came back with, "No sweat, me too. I can agree that this should be our lucky day today."

Nothing more was communicated between us until our waitress showed up with our order. She gave Dan his order and gave me mine, except she had double what I ordered. Four eggs, four slices of bacon, a pile of bread and two glasses of milk with some kind of crap floating on top.

Smiling, Dan asked, "Let me guess, you told her, same-same, ordered two, and then held up two fingers."

"Yeah, I ordered two meals here. You know, one for you and one for me," I responded and thought, how could I have messed up that simple task? So much for this being my lucky day.

"Nice going," Dan told me, with a smile on his face and eggs in his mouth.

"No man. I was just reaffirming what I was ordering, one meal times two," I explained, because I had ordered that way before and never had a problem. Of course, that was back home and not over here.

Dan came back with a suggestion, "No sweat, we'll just divvy up the extra and skip lunch."

Still disappointed about my meal, I turned my attention to my milk. I commented, "What is that floating in my milk?"

"Cream."

"Look, I didn't order cream for anything. I didn't order coffee, and cream only comes with your coffee," I informed him letting him know that I didn't like the idea of someone putting cream in my milk. In 'The-Nam,' or not, you don't put cream in someone's milk.

"You must have ordered fresh milk, right?" Dan inquired.

"Well, yeah. I won't drink old or expired milk."

"What you have there is fresh milk and I bet it's just a few minutes old," he told me pointing to my glass.

"Oh shit. You mean like fresh from the cow and not out of the bottle?"

Laughing at me, Dan commented, "That's right. It came directly from the cow. I bet it was squirted right into your glass and never touched the inside of a milk bucket."

"Gross, my man. This is gross, and I can't drink it," I told him as I moved my glass away, and I made it a point to move both glasses away from me.

"Look my sissy friend. Drink your damn milk and stop your whining," he snapped as he took a big swig from his glass of fresh milk.

Whatever, I did remember getting milk like this when I was a kid, so I figured I might as well drink it. I was thirsty. And with that, I took a big swig only to discover that this thing was warm. I mean, like body temperature warm. If I didn't die from this, I would get so sick that I which I were dead.

I placed my glass of milk down on the table, and I almost knocked over my second glass of milk. Too bad, that I didn't just knock it over. Just what I needed, a second glass of warm, cream filled milk. I started to think about trying my eggs. I was not going to say anything more to Dan. He would just make fun of me and drinking the milk was bad enough. With fork in hand and positioned to attack my eggs, I noticed that there were some feathers in my plate. "What the hell is this?" I asked Dan in a low voice pointing to my plate.

As if I was a kid refusing to eat his vegetables, he responded, "Fresh eggs means that the eggs are probably as fresh as your milk."

"Okay, yeah, but, I guessed that, but . . . look at my plate," I told him excitingly using my fork to point to some chicken feathers. "It's dirty. I'm not eating in a barn here."

Dan butted in and told me, "Look, I don't see any reason for them to wash the eggs first."

"And why not?" I asked, because I could see no reason why someone would serve dirty eggs with feathers.

As if he wanted me to shut up, so he could finish his meal, he added. "Eggs are not the same as fruit. You don't eat the outside skin of an egg. You eat what's inside and that means that nobody should take the time to clean the outside. Man ole man, you haven't been out much, have you?"

I picked out some of the feathers and a piece of straw from my eggs as I muttered; "They can at least keep them in a clean place."

"What, the chickens," Dan questioned.

"No, not the chickens. I meant the eggs," I responded, making a face to indicate how disgusting this was to me.

"Look, there's no reason for them to take the eggs from the chickens and then store them someplace else. Your eggs could have been picked up from there as well as any other place. So, what are you going to do next, complain about your bacon?"

He was right. I should just shut up and enjoy my fresh milk and fresh eggs. Even if I had twice as much as I ordered.

I did however; finish my meal without further complaining. Dan took care of my extra glass of milk along with one of my four eggs. I didn't give my bacon any thought; I just ate it with my eyes closed. I like bread, but this time, I just left it alone. Besides, I didn't have any of those little jelly packets to pick from to dress up my bread.

Sitting there waiting for our check, I asked, "So what happened with the two girls earlier?"

With a gleam in his eye, he proceeded and told me, "Well my man. These two little ladies of the evening took a look at little Danny and the twins."

"And."

"And, they ran for their lives. They may have been with half the men in our hotel last night, but I believe that my little Danny and the boys was a lot more than they could handle."

"Yeah, right," I answered indicating that he was full of it this morning.

"You know, my man," he injected with pride, "You weren't even there to see for yourself. I just gave you the true story, believe it or not."

Realizing that I had a deserving come back to this, I boldly responded with, "Give me a break, my man. Breakfast did not make me sick this morning, but your story just might."

He returned a smile as if he told me the truth. Nah, I had to let that one go.

Luck was with me today, because our waitress came over, and, after paying our tab, we headed out and left that conversation behind. Outside, Dan came to a halt and placed his sea bag on his shoulder. I asked him, "You thinking on which way to go?"

"Yeah."

"I have an idea."

"And that is?"

I believed that this was a good idea. "Let's say we check in with a Comm-Center and do our routine with a search and find."

"And where is the Comm-Center."

"No sweat, that's the easy part."

"Okay, I'm listening," Dan answered, putting his bag down on the sidewalk.

I continued because I was on a roll here, "We catch a cab. Tell the cabby to take us to the nearest military base, US base that is. Once we get there, find the Comm-Center, and simply check in, and ask about our ship."

"Your plan just might work. Okay then. You take care of the cab part," he answered with approval and that made me feel good.

"Great," I answered and I looked around for a cab. Finding one was as easy as putting up my hand to hail one. Before my hand was all the way up, a couple of cabs pulled up to the curb. I jumped into the one with the biggest motor because I figured it world get us there quicker.

"Let's do it," Dan said, as he jumped into the back with me.

I was so busy trying to fit the two of us in the cab along with our sea bags, that I forgot to tell the driver where we wanted to go. This might be a problem because our driver had already pulled away and was flying down the road.

"And where is the driver taking us?" Dan questioned me.

I answered with; "I'll take care of it." I turned to the driver and said, "Military base. You know, American base."

"Okay Joe."

With that, he made a U-turn right in the middle of the block without even slowing. So much for me selecting a safe ride. We pulled in behind another taxi, and the one guy riding on the tailgate just smiled at us. I guessed we were some sight making a U-turn in the middle of the road the way we did.

In no time at all, we pulled up to a base, and our driver drove right on in without stopping for the sentry. Quickly, I told him, "Comm-Center."

"No sweat, Joe, I find," he answered, and he did.

We pulled right up to the front door, and for a couple of dollars, we were there. With that accomplishment, I thought to myself, I did good, damn good. My mom would be so proud.

Dan followed me inside and I felt bold enough to ask for myself. "Sir," I said to the first officer I saw, a Marine pilot, Captain, I think. "We are trying to find the location of the ship, USS SUMMIT. Do you have any information on her location?"

"Why are you two interested in the location of a ship?" He answered with a question.

Seemed like a logical question to ask, but I best think before I answer. "Sir, we are to report to her, and she's been somewhat hard to catch up with."

"I don't see the problem. She's here in town. Has been for a couple of days now."

"Here? In town, Sir?" I responded and looked at Dan as if maybe he knew that all along.

Dan stepped in and asked, "Thank you sir. We were not aware that she was here in town. We have been given the run-around by some Air force personnel."

"I see," he answered, as if he wanted to hear some more information about that.

I didn't know how to respond to this, so I would just let Dan take the lead on this one, and he did. "Sir, you know how those Air force guys can be. They can't get anything straight. Hell, if it weren't for the Air Force, those dropout Marine pilots wouldn't have anything to fly."

He came back with a smile and said, "I see and I agree. Is there anything else you guys need today?"

"No sir, thank you, sir," I answered just as Dan spoke up and asked, "Sir, we could use a ride to the pier where she is. Can you help us out with that? The two of us are kind of short on cab fair."

He thought for a moment and said, "Very well, wait one."

Dan and I responded with, "Yes sir. Thank you sir." However, Dan responded in a happy tone and my response was that of confusion.

"We're gonna get a ride?" I asked. "He's going to call us a cab?"

"What's your problem?" Dan responded with his shoulders up and hands out. "The man asked if we needed anything else and a ride is something that we need. I just threw in the part about being short of cab fair to save you a buck or two." Dan answered me as if I could have figured that out myself.

"Yeah, but," I came back suggesting that we might be doing something wrong, again.

"Listen up, my long lost friend. In the last few days, we have asked and gotten rides on helicopters, boats, planes, and this is only our second request for a jeep ride. Explain to me why this wrong here?"

Dan's point was reasonable and he was most correct. "Okay, no sweat. If we can get a ride to check in sooner, no problem with me."

This got a smile from him, and remembering what he said a minute ago, I asked him, "Are Marine pilots better than Air Force pilots?"

"No man, they both are equally talented. It just depends on whom you are talking with and what you need at the time," he explained to me.

"Oh."

"We needed a favor from a Marine this time, so I put the Air force down. Next time, I might have to change it around a bit. Besides, we got the ship's location and are able to get us a ride to boot."

Dan made it sound so simple and yet so effective. After about five minutes, the officer returned and told us, "I have a jeep outside waiting for you guys."

Before we could thank him, he was already gone. Whatever, Dan and I made our way out front for our ride. "We get to check in today." I excitingly announced.

"Calm down, my friend. Let's wait until we see her first. This guy could have been wrong, you know."

I hadn't thought about that. I'm starting to realize that offices were just people and not gods. I knew that I had to, 'sir' them and all that, but I always understood that I had to believe them simply because they were officers.

Sure enough, there was a jeep and driver outside waiting for us. Immediately, I excitedly threw my bag in the back and I grabbed the front seat. This time Dan could ride in the back. Feeling happy and bold, I told the driver, "To my ship James, and step on it."

I looked over and smiled at the driver to show him that I was only trying to be funny, only to see an angry face in return. Damn, this guy couldn't take a joke. A second look at him and then, oh shit, it was the little guard from Saigon. He apparently remembered me by the look I was getting. I looked back at Dan thinking on how we could smooth things out before we started out.

However, to my surprise and horror, Dan leaned up toward me and said, "Oh wow! How in the hell does this little guy reach the little pedals?"

Oh no, I thought. What was he doing? I happened to notice that the guard was armed with a handgun because he reached for it. Damn, we were going to miss our ship, and get shot.

Dan continued after he leaned far enough over to see that there were no blocks on the pedals. "Damn man, no blocks. Then how can he hit the little gas pedals, see over the steering wheel, and drive, all at the same time?"

I thought how there were times that you didn't need to be funny. Like right now, for example. We have a ride. Let's not lose it. The guard gave Dan a dirty look and then stared at me again. He placed both hands on the steering wheel at ten and two and floored it. At least we were heading towards the ship at a high rate of speed. Even if he was turning red with anger, he did ignore Dan and his comments and was no longer reaching for his side arm.

Dan leaned up from the back seat and said loud enough for everyone to hear "Look how angry he looks, I bet he has a short fuse."

I told Dan, "Give the guy a break, will you?"

"Okay," he responded, sitting back in his set. "But, only for a little while and it will be a little break."

I was sitting as still as I could. This was hard to do because we were making some mean and sharp turns. Dan, on the other hand, instead of maintaining silence, and allowing our driver to drive, sat up, and said, "Look, no car seat. I figured that he was at least sitting on phone books or something."

Even with that being funny, I kept my eyes front, all the while wanting just to get to the ship without seeing Dan shot.

The driver kept on driving as Dan added another insult, "I hope it's just a short ride."

Without warning, our driver pulled over to the side of the road with a screeching halt. Great, we are in the middle of nowhere and this was definitely not in our favor. Are we going to get shot?

The driver looked at Dan and I, and told Dan to, "Get the fuck out! Get out now!"

"No sweat, little man." Dan told him, not sounding the least bit worried. "You don't have to take us anywhere. I'll just take a *short* walk back and have a *little* conversation with my uncle. You remember, the Captain that got us this *little* ride. I will return *shortly* and see your *little* sissy ass get chewed out in *short* fashion."

The driver just stared back at Dan. At least he wasn't reaching for his gun.

Continuing to sound confident, Dan asked him, "What you say? You got a *little* problem with this?"

Now that was a good bluff that Dan was pulling. I hoped it would be enough to get us to the ship in time for dinner.

"No problem for me. The problem is with you," was the response from the driver, as if he was now in control.

"And my problem is?" Dan came back smartly, still expecting to one up on this guy.

"Your uncle, if he was your uncle, he's shipping out tonight. Going bye-bye, never to return, as in no longer in charge. Not to mention that he's not even my boss," the driver informed Dan.

The jig was up and we were in trouble. Not a little bit of trouble; but big trouble. Well, not me, because I never said that he was my uncle. But wait, I could not leave Dan with this. We were in this together. I only hoped we would get out of this clean and without getting shot.

Dan questioned him, “So, are you saying that this is as far as you are willing to go?”

“That’s right,” the driver responded knowing that he held the high ground. Dan’s smart-ass comments were no longer in our favor now.

Apparently knowing when to cut his loses, Dan told him, as he grabbed his bag on his way off the jeep, “No sweat, we’re out of here.”

The driver wanting to put Dan down one more time, added, “It’s been *short* and sweet.”

With that comment out of the way, he punched the gas and made a 180. I watched, as he flew on down the road and commented to Dan, “He sure remembered us.”

“I’m surprised at that,” Dan said, sounding bewildered.

I could not believe that he said that, I asked, “After what you said to him the other day, how could he forget us?”

“I had always assumed that short people had short memories,” he explained.

That was the most stupidest thing that I had heard him say so far. The only thing stupider than that, was that it appeared that he was serious.

I didn’t wait for any additional comments from him right now. I didn’t want to be *short* with him; so, I suggested, “What do you say we just get a cab and continue on?”

Dan smiled in agreement and, with no trouble at all, he hailed a cab and told the driver, “SUMMIT, big green sip. You take me now.”

“Okay Joe,” the driver responded as we got in. Our driver then made a 180° turn and headed back the way we came. I then realized that our driver was going the wrong way all along. I would not mention that to Dan, it would just tick him off even move.

Dan looked over and informed me, "That little shit was taking us the wrong way. Oh well, no problem. We'll see him again."

I looked over at Dan and questioned, to change the subject, because I still didn't like putting little people down, "All you had to do was to say the ship's name, and a cab driver knew where to go?"

"Yeah."

I would try not to sound too pissed off because he could have done this taxi thing a couple of days ago. So, I asked, "So much for the location of our ship being classified and all that. Our own military didn't know where she was. Damn, ask any cab driver, and he not only knows where she is, he'll take us to her."

"Look," Dan started to explain. "It's not all that easy. It was a simple fact that a cabdriver would have picked up and/or delivered a few people to the ship. With that, he would have known that she was in town."

"Okay, I got that. Now, why didn't we just ask cab driver every time we get into town? This could have saved us some time checking in with the Comm-Centers."

"Nah, if we would have done that, we would have ended up at some pier every time. The driver would then tell us after he collected the fair, 'Sorry Joe. She gone.'"

"Okay."

Dan continued with, "This time, we kind of knew that she was already here in town."

"Okay, I see," I admitted, indicating that I agreed with him. "And once we got to the pier, the cabby would have us for the return ride."

"You got it," Dan said, giving me some credit.

Our driver appeared to be headed out of town. I asked Dan, "Where are we going?"

"No sweat, if I recall correctly, it's just outside of town. Relax and enjoy the ride."

I did just that, relaxed and tried to enjoy myself. After about twenty minutes, we pulled into a little town. We drove through this small town and ended up at a pier. Again, not that I was surprised or disappointed, but there was no ship anywhere on the river.

"What now?" I asked Dan disappointedly.

Dan got out of the cab and told the driver and I to, "Wait one."

He made his way over to some Army looking guy, sitting by the pier, and started a conversation. He then waved for me to come on over as I assumed that this was the place. I got out, paid our driver, and dragged our bags over to Dan, since he made no effort to help me, because he just kept talking with the guy. For such a short walk from the cab, I was sweating to death. Man ole man, it sure was hot out here, and these bags just kept getting heavier and heavier.

As soon as I placed our bags down, Dan grabbed his, made his way over, and took a seat near the pier. I did the same, and asked, "What's up. Were is she this time?"

"Up river a little ways just beyond that turn. This guy told me that a boat comes in every few hours or so, to drop off and pick up supplies and people. We're in, my man. All we have to do right now is to sit tight and wait for our ride."

We did just that. We took a seat and got ourselves comfortable. Damn, I could not believe it. We were almost there.

After just a few minutes of sitting and waiting, we were both as hot and sweaty as could be. Dan suggested, "You fly and I'll buy."

"Buy what?"

"I'll buy us a soda."

"I'll go for that," I answered.

"That's what I mean. I pay, you fly, you go, and you can go now."

"Okay man, no sweat. Give me the money and I'll be back in a minute with cold sodas."

Dan gave me a dollar, and I said, "I'll make it a point to hurry back, and I won't take in any sight-seeing detours."

Dan looked at me as if I should just go away already because I was taking up his precious naptime. With that, and having gotten the hint, I turned and headed out. After a few blocks, it hit me that this was the first time I had been alone over here. I was not scared or anything, I just hoped that I could do this simple task without creating an incident. I didn't need to meet up with Bigfoot, the little guard again, or any officer that I had pissed off lately. In addition, I didn't need to be paying twice the amount for sodas, because I was ripped off. What I was going to do, and no mater what I paid for the two sodas, I was not going tell Dan how much I paid for them.

After checking out a number of small stores, I had no success with my simple task of finding cold sodas. In some stores, it was hard to tell what they sold because it was so dark inside and I thought that it was that they kept the light off just to save on their electric bills. In addition, part of my problem was that I could not tell what kind of stores some of these places were. Hell, back home, a 7-11 was a 7-11 and it said so. I was not trying to find a slurpee or something unusual. I just wanted a cold soda. I would have even settled for a 7UP or a root beer. I found one store that had sodas; but none of them were cold. The last thing I wanted to buy was a warm soda on a hot day.

Another store, same thing, only warm sodas. Then finally, I found a place that sold cold sodas and I assumed that one-dollar would be a good price. With that, I tried to hold a conversation with the store owner to determine a price. We were getting nowhere, because he didn't understand English, and I didn't understand what he was trying to tell me.

An idea then hit me; I would simply get out my little pamphlet and work my way to a good deal. I needed to find out how much for how many. I showed him the page for how much and pointed to the two sodas in the cooler next to the counter. He laughed at me and said in clear English, "One dollar. One American dollar."

Great I thought. Problem solved, almost. I didn't have any American dollars, only MPC. Damn.

"One American dollar," he repeated.

I might as well start out and see if I can get myself a good deal. "Two MPC, two soda."

"MPC. Three MPC, two soda," he snapped back at me as if I were doing something illegal here.

Damn, I just wasn't in the mood. "Okay. Three MPC, two soda."

Our deal was completed and I left remembering not to tell Dan what I paid for the sodas.

Once outside, I realized that I had forgotten which way was back. I had been in and out of so many stores on both sides of the street that I disoriented myself. Oh shit, by the time I get back, if I get back, these sodas will be warm.

I walked back into the store and asked the storekeeper, "Which way to water."

He looked at me again as if I was from Mars. No problem, I thought again that I could use my helpful pamphlet to get me through this. (APPENDIX A) I found the page with water and showed him.

"Water. We no got water. We got soda. Cold soda. You need more?" He asked and I could tell this was going nowhere fast.

I showed him the page again and moved my hand around trying to indicate water motion. I must have looked pretty stupid to him because the storekeeper responded with a blank look. His assistant, I think she was his wife, came over, and gave me the same look. This was not going to work, and my sodas already started to warm.

Again, I tried to ask, "Find ship, and find water."

This went on for a few minutes with no change in their expression. Finally, a young kid came in from the back of the store. He told me, "One dollar."

"One dollar?" What the hell is this, one-dollar? I already paid for the sodas. "I need find ship. Soda mine. Already paid."

This little shit for a kid said something to his parents, and that got everyone laughing at me, and right then, I didn't care why they were laughing. I just wanted to be heading toward the pier with my lukewarm sodas.

The kid said to me, "One dollar, find water."

"I do not want buy water. I have soda. Want find pier."

He said something else to his parents and again they started to laugh. I became pissed at the way they were treating me. Damn man, it's a simple request I thought.

The kid said to me, "Look Joe, your English is bad and so is your sense of direction. You want directions. I want a dollar. What you say, Joe?"

Damn, damn, damn, I just met another kid that I wanted to smack. Yet, what choice did I have? I gave him a dollar and he walked outside with me. He then told me to, "Go to corner, turn right."

The father came out and patted his kid on the shoulder as if saying, "Nice going, son. We just got three bucks for two sodas."

To make things worse for me and to rub it in, the father gave him a soda and he said in good, clear English to his son, "Drink it now while it's good and cold."

Pissed off, hot, and short four dollars, off I went, and the pier was just around the corner like he said. I could have thrown Dan his sodas from where I was standing. Well, I would never tell him about this little adventure, and if I ever get around to writing a book, I will leave this part out. Four dollars for two sodas, what a shame for someone who has finished high school.

Just outside the door, and before I got to the corner, another kid approached me and asked. "You want buy women's watch?"

He moved his right shirtsleeve up past his elbow and there were about a dozen women's watches on his arm.

"How much?" Now why did I ask him that? I didn't need to buy anything else from a kid today. Besides, what was I going to do with a woman's watch? I was an ass-hole, because instead of just walking on and ignoring this kid, I asked him, "No need woman watch. You got man watches?"

"No sweat Joe," he responded, as he lifted up his left shirtsleeve showing about a dozen men's watches.

As if I had yet to learn my lesson, I asked, "How much?"

"For you Joe, good deal. One watch, two-dollar. Two watch, five dollar."

I responded with, "No thank you," as I started to walk away. Damn, I can count. No way would I allow him to take me for a ride.

The little kid ran past me and said, "Okay Joe, better deal. Three watch, ten-dollar. What you say? Numba-one deal."

Did I look that stupid to him; no, I didn't think so. Damn, damn, damn. One watch, two dollars, and three watches for ten, yeah right. I was just gonna assume that all kids think that all Americans were stupid, and that it was not just me. A little pissed, I answered him with, "Go away."

"What matter Joe? You no can tell time? That why you no buy watch?"

I walked around him and continued on my way. This little shit passed me again and said, "Okay, you no tell time. I have watch that, no tell time. It always ten-ten. Or, if you like, it be two fifty. You buy this watch. One dollar. Numba-one deal. What you say now, Joe?"

I stopped for a second only to give him a dirty look, suggesting that I wanted to be left alone, because I was getting mad. Of course, he took my stop as if I could not tell time and that I wanted the watch that did not work. He reached into his pocket and pulled it out for me to see, and then buy. He said, "Here Joe. No work watch, one dollar. For you, numba-one deal."

Well, because the watch was already out for my inspection, I took the damn watch just to check-it-out. Sure enough, it could be ten-ten, or two fifty. Both hands were the same size, and it wasn't working. I handed it back and thought to myself, the next time I find a mirror, I must check to see if I had, 'sucker' tattooed on my forehead. I told him, "No," and to, "go away. I got watch, and I can tell time. And the next time you bug me, I will kick your little ass and take all your damn watches."

Only for a second, he seemed scared. Apparently, seeing that I was unarmed, he knew that at least he wasn't going to get shot. I started on my way and he did not follow or bug me again.

I only got a few feet, when a little boy stopped me and asked, "Joe, you want candy for girl friend?"

What was going on, I wondered? Here was yet another kid with something for me to buy, and he had nothing with him to sell me. I figured that I might as well have a little fun, before I lose it on one of these little brats. I asked him, "What you got, Charlie?"

"I no Charlie. No VC here," he responded looking pissed. But just as quick as he looked mad, he changed back into a salesman's smile, as if he had a Ford Pinto for me to buy at a numba-one price. And a full tank of gas.

The little shit then told me, "You buy candy. Numba-one candy. One dollar. You buy candy now. Okay Joe?"

I looked at his empty hands and asked, "What candy? You no got candy. No candy, no dollar."

He whistled and this little girl came over. I guessed this to be his little sister with the candy. On her head was a tray with something small wrapped in little newspaper strips. The little brat then told me, "You buy, you buy now. One dollar."

Now he was getting pushy, and I needed to get going. I told him, "No thank you. Maybe next time. I go now."

With that, I quickly turned and walked away and ignored anything else this kid was trying to tell or sell me. After a couple of steps, I guessed that he got the hint and he left me alone. Oh well, walking back and without any additional interruptions, I thought about how impossible it was that a cold soda could be such an item over here. I was going though a lot of crap just to get two cold sodas. Naturally, I wanted to forget about the money I paid for directions.

Back home, every gas station, and grocery store on each corner had sodas to sell. Over here, it took an effort to find a store that sold them and then it was a 50/50 shot if it was a cold soda or not. Anyway, I returned with two, almost cold, sodas for us to enjoy, and I thought I should have gotten myself an extra one for my trouble.

Approaching Dan, I saw that he was talking to five little kids between ten and twelve years old. They were all dressed alike and it appeared to be some kind of school uniform. I didn't think they were trying to sell anything, because they didn't have anything with them to sell. Maybe they were just trying to get something for nothing. On the other hand, maybe they were selling each other.

There was someone else with them, an Army guy I think, because of the way he was dressed. I didn't know who he was, and to add in more suspense, I thought I heard, of all things, singing. Dan saw me coming. He stood between the new guy and me and did the introductions, he said, "Tony, Charles, Charles, Tony."

So, this Army guy was Tony. Oops. Sorry. He was just another navy guy dressed up as if he were in the Army. We shook hands, and in my defense, I told him jokingly, "Sorry, didn't know you were going to be here or I would have gotten you a soda too."

"No sweat my man, I'm just glad to be here," he responded, with a strange look I his eye.

I thought for a second, and then asked, "Here? What the hell was it, 'here,' that you got to be glad about?"

Apparently, he picked up on my confusion and explained, "Here man. I like being here in, 'The-Nam,' and all that. You see, I happen to enjoy shooting up little gook guys. Know what I mean?" After a short pause, Tony continued, "Sort of like shooting wild turkeys back home cause they are both about the same size."

Now this guy really scared me a little. Wanting to further introduce Tony and I, Dan continued with, "Tony here was once a member of Jersey Joe's boat crew."

I questioned, "Oh, okay. I don't remember you from the last time I was on Joe's boat."

"Well yea, I've been off his crew for a few weeks now. You see, because of me, we kept running out of ammo," he informed me, with Dan shaking his head in agreement.

I didn't see any reason to discuss this with Tony right now. He might be in on a joke with Dan and that was reason enough to drop it, whatever it was. I just wanted to enjoy my soda before it got too warm. I gave Dan his soda and he responded, "Thanks. Oh good, you got'em cold."

"Not an easy task, my man. Not everyone sells them cold over here, you know. It was hard to find a store that did," I answered, thinking how glad I was that he thought they were cold.

After a swig from his soda, Dan asked, "You want to know an easy way to tell if a store sells cold sodas or not?"

"So now you're gonna tell me," I responded, giving the impression that he should had told me this before I went out on my cold soda hunt.

"Simple, my not too cool friend. First off, you should check to see if the store has any power," he informed me.

"Now how do you tell that? I mean, do I check along the wall for outlets," I explained, as if there was not an easy way to know this.

With a smile indicating that he had all the answers, he answered, "If they have ceiling fans and they're running, that'll be a good sign."

"Okay fine, and knowing that will tell me what?"

"It'll tell you that they have power. Moreover, power will allow them to have refrigeration. And refrigeration will allow them to have cold sodas."

Again, he was right, and I felt stupid.

Dan apparently was aware that I felt a little inadequate with this situation, and for some strange reason; he didn't put me down in front of this Tony guy. Dan continued, "No sweat, my man. I didn't learn that lesson until my second tour. One day, now that was a long time ago, I spent so much time hunting for a cold soda in the hot sun, that after a while, I forgot what I was looking for."

"I didn't do too bad. I did find us a cold soda, and if we need another one, it wouldn't take me as long the next time." I also knew how to get back here, I reminded myself.

Whatever, I downed half my soda, and noticed all these kids there were around us. They seemed like a likeable group of kids, because they were all clean looking. Now, I didn't know why I thought that, because being clean doesn't necessary make anyone likeable. Out of curiosity, I asked Dan as I pointed to the kids, "So, who are they, friends of yours?"

"I might want to adopt these kids," Dan responded, looking as if this was a great idea.

I knew he was joking about this, but if not, he had a scam brewing up somewhere with these kids. "All five of them? Or are you gonna be selective," I questioned.

"These are really cool kids. I met them once before when I was here with Tony a few weeks ago."

"Seeing them for the second time and being cool is your criteria for adopting kids?" I asked, hoping that there was more to learn about this.

"Yeah, that helps, but you see, I could make a musical group out of these kids based on their names."

"What's your scam?" Something was up with this. Even my guard was up on this one. It was not as if what he had here looked like a group of any kind. The Four Tops or Gladys Knight and the Pips had nothing to fear from this group of kids.

"I'm hurt that you would even consider that I would do something a little shady with minors," Dan responded to me. He seemed most serious with what he just said.

"Not necessarily a little shady my man, but shady just the same," I said being careful not to offend him or Tony.

Looking at the kids again and trying to make a joke of this, I came back with, "Besides, all five? Why not just two, or possibly three, but five? I mean, did you not stop that Billy-Bob guy from getting just one the other day to take home?"

"Never mind the details," Dan said defending himself. "Look, maybe I'll call them the, 'Danny-Five,' or 'Gooks-Galore;' or my favorite, 'The Five-Nams.'"

He just might be serious about this, but I could not believe that he really was. I would just play along for now until he finished with this. Besides, I had nothing else to do right now, except to enjoy my soda and wait for our boat ride.

"Let me introduce them to you," Dan explained as he pointed to the tallest one. "This is Ooo-eee and she's the oldest. The one with short hair is, Bing-Bang."

I smiled at them as he continued with the introductions. These were silly names and not very Vietnamese sounding, and this has got be a game he's playing with these kids. Now on the other hand, these kids seemed to be enjoying this individual attention they received and are apparently having fun with this.

Tony introduced the other ones to me. "Ting-tang is the short one here and she has the best voice. The twins here are Walla-walla and Ooo-ah-ah," he continued.

"Nice to meet you all," I responded before I realized that they might not even understand English or what I was saying.

Dan stood up and placed them into some kind of order. I didn't understand why he was doing all this but the kids seemed to want to go along with it. Dan was not doing this by height or anything that I could tell. After Dan arranged everyone, he instructed me, "Now pay attention to this because Tony and I want you to follow what's going on here."

"Okay," I answered, thinking that they were going to put on a show or something.

Tony sung out, "Ready, here we go."

These kids were all smiles now. They really seemed to enjoy whatever it was that was going on here. Yet, it still seemed a little odd to me that no one was buying or selling anything.

Standing back and admiring the order at which he and Tony had placed them, Dan tried to sound like Lawrence Welk, and sung out, "Okay, a one, and a two, and a . . ."

Then altogether, as Dan pointed to each one and called out their name as Tony joined in along with the girls. Out comes, "Ooo-eee, Ooo-ah-ah, Ting-tang, Walla-walla, Bing-bang, Ooo-eee, Ooo-ah-ah, Ting-tang, Walla-walla, Bing-bang."

Very funny, this was very funny. I remembered this song as Tony instructed everyone, "One more time everybody."

"Ooo-eee, Ooo-ah-ah, Ting-tang, Walla-walla, Bing-bang, Ooo-eee, Ooo-ah-ah, Ting-tang, Walla-walla, Bing-bang."

Now they were all dancing around singing and I had to join in with them, "Ooo-eee, Ooo-ah-ah, Ting-tang, Walla-walla, Bing-bang, Ooo-eee, Ooo-ah-ah, Ting-tang, Walla-walla, Bing-bang."

I was enjoying this frenzy and it was hard to imagine where we were right now. After a day at the beach, I was now at a free concert. After a few minutes of all this, it all came to a halt. I believe that the hot sun had gotten to everyone, or that was the only song that they knew.

"What do you think? They make a good group?" Dan asked, with a gleam in his eye, sounding as if he was sincere about the group's chances to make it big.

I jokingly came back with, "That sounded great, but don't give up your day job. These kids should finish school first."

Thinking I was serious, Dan answered, "You really thought I was for real about this? You know, taking them home and all that?"

Damn, damn, damn. I think I said the wrong thing and I quickly responded with, "I knew that you weren't serious about these kids. Nice group, but they were nothing to write home about. Know what I mean?"

Dan smiled at me and turned to the oldest kid. He told her something and then gave each of the five kids a hug and handed them, what appeared to be a dollar each. I assumed it was a dollar because all I saw was him giving them paper money and naturally, it was not green back. He then gave the oldest one a little extra and told her to, "Bring us three sodas, three cold sodas please."

She smiled and responded, "Okay Joe, three cold sodas."

Dan sat down and said in a way, as if his own children had won a singing contest, "Now that was fun and those kids enjoyed learning that song."

I got to admit, that was very entertaining, and I questioned, "How do you know these little kids?"

"They go to that school over there. They were on their way home from school the last time I was here with Tony. Tony had a transistor radio with him and that song came on. Well, the kids loved it when they heard him and I singing it. Because Tony and I had some time to kill, we thought that we would teach them that song for fun."

Tony explained, "Yeah, they caught on very fast, and it was a good thing for them."

I looked at Tony and believed in a strange way, that to him, it was a do or die thing for these kids.

Dan quickly spoke up and said, "No sweat Tony. You were having a bad day that day because you were out of your medication. Now you got to agree that singing with those kids did make you feel a little better."

"That true," he answered, as if he were a disappointed that it worked. Maybe he liked being miserable, I didn't know, and I didn't want to know. This guy continued to scare me. With caution, I asked him, "So, did you take your medication today?"

With spaced out eyes that appeared focused on the moon, he told me, "You don't need to worry about me. I only take it when I think I need it."

After a short pause, he added, "Today, today I needed it." Then under his breath, he continued, "Especially around kids. Yeah, man, I took it today."

Dan spoke up and asked, "Do you have enough to last until we get back onboard?"

"Yeah," he responded, sounding a little disappointed that he would not run out anytime soon.

Dan then told me, "No need to worry about Tony, you're okay in his book."

Here I am again with another stupid question. "So, how did I make it to his, 'good book?'"

"Round eyes, may man, just by having round eyes," Dan explained as if I should take this warning very seriously.

I believe that I knew what he meant, and I would a make a point not to ask any more questions about this Tony guy. He must really hate gooks.

With that, Dan and I took a comfortable seat against the wall and Tony took the spot on the other side of Dan. I was glad because I didn't want him anywhere next to me. Being tired and all that, I closed my eyes and hoped that I could fall asleep and take a nap.

Chapter 18

"Wake up, my man," Dan said to me, as he pushed on my shoulder. I must have fallen asleep. I could hear the telltale sound of a diesel boat off in the distance, and through unfocused eyes; I could almost make out a small boat coming our way. I pointed in that direction and questioned Dan, "Is that our ride?"

He and Tony may not have been excited about this, but I was. The two of them stared in that direction and Tony responded with, "Yeah, that's it."

Dan did not seem to be very happy at all, that we would soon be checking into our unit. He said, "I hope that Ooo-eee is back in time to give us our sodas."

"I don't care about the sodas. I just want to get checked in, and I can't wait," I told them both, trying not to sound too excited.

Off in the distance, I could hear singing, and it was the kids coming our way. I heard, "Ooo-eee, Ooo-ah-ah, Ting-tang, Walla-walla, Bing-bang, Ooo-eee, Ooo-ah-ah, Ting-tang, Walla-walla, Bing-bang."

Their singing was amusing the first time I heard it, and it was still entertaining, I thought to myself while singing the song in my head.

Our boat was still a very long way off, and it would be a little while before it got here. We had plenty of time for a song or two, and to finish off our drinks. I was a little embarrassed that they were gone for only a few minutes and that it took me almost an hour to find cold sodas. No sweat, I mean, this was their neighborhood and not mine, and they should know where to go.

When they got close, only the oldest girl came up to us with the sodas, as the other four waited a little ways off. I didn't know if they were afraid of us now or that they were just saving a few steps. We got our sodas, and the kids quickly headed off towards the school. I figured that they had a class or something to go to, and I gave it no further thought.

The girls were now walking rather fast and they kept suspiciously looking back at us. They were giving us a look as if they expected us to chase them or something. Now this seemed a little odd to me, but these were kids, and kids sometimes did weird things.

Tony looked at Dan and asked, "You thinking what I'm thinking?"

"Yeah, same-same."

"What's up guys?" I asked detecting fear in their voices that gave me some concern.

"Target practice," Dan explained to me in a soft voice as he started to look around.

I thought that maybe after we finished our sodas, that the two of them would throw their cans up in the air for a little skeet shooting or something. Then it occurred to me that neither one of them had a gun. What were they thinking, I wondered.

Tony questioned Dan, "See anything?"

"No, you?"

I asked that again, trying not to sound that worried, "What's up?"

Cautiously Dan answered, "Maybe nothing, but to be sure, we should sit someplace that's not so much out in the open."

"What's up?" I questioned again.

Tony explained to me, "I believe that it was just a little too odd the way the girls left us with our sodas."

"What was odd about that? I mean, we didn't take the sodas from them. Hell man, Dan not only paid for the sodas, he gave them a little extra money on the side. Besides, I thought we were having fun with them."

"Right," Dan responded, having agreed with me. "They had fun all right. They got some spending money and a soda. That was then, and now is now."

Tony added, "Someone may have given them even more money for information that the three of us are just sitting here, unarmed."

I hoped that these guys were just paranoid and not believing what they were thinking. However, I did follow them around to the other side of a little building that was on the pier; putting it between them, and who ever it was out there, that Dan and Tony were afraid of. We all took a seat with our backs to the wall and quietly sat there drinking our sodas, watching our ride approach.

After a few minutes with nothing happening, I spent my time looking out at the river, and it was hard not to notice how brown the water was. Off to my right, or up river, I saw a couple of women doing their laundry with some children playing nearby. Close to them were some oxen, or buffalo, drinking and messing in the water. Down from us, or down river, was an old man brushing his teeth and washing himself. If I were this guy, I would have moved up river from those animals and women doing their laundry. "I'm surprised that the old man doesn't get sick from washing where he is," I said aloud just making conversation.

"Yeah. Me to. I'm surprised we don't get sick like that also," Dan said, looking down at the old man that was now washing his hair.

"Why would we get sick? I certainly would not take a shower in that brown muck. I could handle a cold shower anytime compared to that water," I questioned him.

"Our ship draws its water from this river," Dan explained.

I came back quickly with, "And, you are saying?"

Dan continued with, "I'm saying that our ship draws its water from the river. It's cool, no sweat. It does go though a purification process to take out all the nasty stuff."

"Then it's always okay?" I questioned, because I must know about this.

"Sometimes, and only sometimes, they get the pipes confused on which direction the water is to flow."

After a smile and a little giggle, Dan continued with, "One day, they had our toilet water going into the showers."

Tony spoke up and added his comments, "Talk about the true meaning of taking a shit, shower, and a shave."

Dan came back with, "Yeah. They should have called it, taking a shitty shower and shave."

The way the two of them were laughing, I had to assume that they were just messing with me. I assured them, "I'll be careful to check the water before I shower."

With that discussion out of the way, the three of us took a break from talking and just rested. Nothing happened for a while, and after twenty minutes or so, our ride finally arrived. Dan walked over to the boat driver and started a conversation, as a few guys got off and headed toward town. There might be the possibility that this was not our boat, but I knew that Dan would make sure, before we boarded her. Hell, our ship might not even be here and we might end up back at square one.

Dan walked back to me and said as if he had good news, "Let's get our bags onboard, and locked."

"We got to lock them up while we're onboard?" I questioned, because we would be standing right next to them and it was not as if our ride had a cargo hold or anything.

"Look, my impatient friend, we have some time for a few drinks in town before we head back. Unless of course, you want to sit here for a while, guarding our bags, while Tony and I make a quick trip to town."

"No, I don't want to do that. I'll stick with you guys. I was expecting to be leaving now, that's all."

Tony had to add in his two cents, "No sweat man, this is not like boarding a train. You know, where it stops for a minute or two and then takes off again. It will be here for a while."

I looked at him and with my shoulders up, I confessed, "Hey, I'm the FNG here, what do I know?"

"No sweat," Tony answered.

Dan suggested that, "We can just head back into that little town nearby and enjoy a few beers. We got some time to kill."

I was still concerned about our ride and asked, "So how much time do we have before we have to head back?" I didn't want to miss it now. We were too close.

Dan yelled at the boat driver, "What time you shoving off?"

He looked at his watch and answered, "Forty-five minutes. Not forty-six or forty-seven, but forty-five minutes. You here on time, you get a ride. If not, you get a hotel."

Well that was clear enough. I was thinking what could we do, in just forty-five minutes. Trying not to sound like a wimp, I questioned Dan, "That's not very much time. We can't do all that much drinking if we have to walk to town and back."

Tony butted in, "Walk, shit, I ain't doing no walking. We'll just do the taxicab trick thing. Remember Dan? Go, park, drink, and return."

Dan responded with, "Yeah, I remember. No sweat my man, a taxi ride for three," and pointed to a group of taxies that had just arrived at the same time that our boat did.

I quickly reached for my pamphlet to find the page on cab-calling figuring that I could call for a cab; however, Tony called for a cab and a cab pulled right up. I turned and was going to load our bags on the boat, when I saw that Dan, had already done that. Oh well, all I could contribute to our adventure is my presence. I was standing there thinking to myself, what was my part? Dan had taken care of our bags, and Tony took care of our ride. Oh well, so let me see if I have things straight here, we were leaving our bags locked on a boat so we could do some taxi trick thing for forty-five minutes, not forty-six or forty-seven minutes, but for forty-five minutes.

After Dan had locked the bags together, he ran past me toward the cab and shouted to me, "You gonna joins us?"

I yelled back with, "Okay," and made my way quickly to the back seat of the cab. Damn, these cabs were little. Dan and I, in the back seat, had our knees up against our ears.

Tony, who was up front, told the driver, "Town, bar, park, two hoots, wait, bring back. Okay. Can do?"

The driver responded with, "Okay Joe, can do." And away we went to town.

I was not totally sure what was explained to the driver, but he understood better than I did. This must be in military code or something. So much to learn, and I only have a year left.

Into town we went, and the driver was driving fast and crazy. A little blue and yellow cab in front of us had some of the guys that had gotten off the boat when it pulled in. I assumed that they were also going to town. Their cab was kicking up dust and stones that came into the back seat with me. I would need a drink just to wash down the dirt that I was inhaling. The roads here are not paved, and dust kicked up all around us, and blew right in our faces.

Our cab pulled to a hard stop right in front of some bar. I assumed that it was a bar, because there was a Pabst Blue Ribbon Beer sign out front, and it was all lit up. I'll bet that our beers were cold, because I saw ceiling fans running inside.

I was about ready to get out of the cab when Dan held down my shoulder, and told me, "My man, we stay onboard for this one."

The driver tapped the horn twice, and out came two girls. I assumed that they were waitresses from the bar and not hookers, because they had menu pads with them. Well, I hoped that they were not hookers. I was not sure about this Tony guy, because he could have ordered them. If they were, I hoped he and Dan didn't want to bring these two girls into this toy cab for their entertainment.

To my relief, Dan told the one girl, "Three beers, three cold beers. PBR's to be exact."

Without asking or saying anything, the two of them headed back inside, and now I understood. We were just going to sit here in our ride and drink beer.

Tony told the driver something and then said to Dan, "He knows to pull out in thirty minutes and to, chop-chop, di-di-mau, back to the pier."

"Cool, everything is under control," Dan answered, with approval.

One of the girls returned and handed us our cold beers. I figured what the hell; I was just going to drink a beer, even though I was full of soda. No need to be a sissy boy and all that.

Tony was the first to finish his beer. He reached over and tapped the horn another two times. As before, two girls came out and he told them, "Three cold beers."

Damn, I like a cold beer and all that, but enough was enough. I informed Dan, "After this one, no more beers for me."

Dan belched, crushed his beer can against his forehead, threw the can out the window, and commented, "No sweat," and that was followed by another belch.

Tony was busy up front gesturing with his hands, as if he had a pistol. He started making sound effects to match with what his hands were doing.

"Click," he said for the hammer, as he pulled back his thumb. A few more quick, 'clicks,' as he spun his knuckles around like an old Colt-45. His left hand held his wrist showing how steady he could be.

He followed some gook guy crossing the street in front of us. That poor, unsuspecting guy was a target, and Tony was the sniper. A pretend sniper, but a sniper just the same.

Normally, I would have asked someone acting that way, "What's up?" However, this guy seemed a little weird. I would ignore him for now, at least he was not aiming at me, and it was not a real gun.

"Bang," Tony shouted as he fired a shot. He then followed that with a blow on his finger, clearing away the imaginary smoke from the barrel. Sorry, I meant finger.

"Between the eyes?" Dan asked.

"No man, side shot. In one ear and out the other."

As if he was admiring his shot, he continued with, "You know, with nothing between his ears, my shot continued on across the street and hit that dumb shit slope there on the bike."

Now both of these guys were looking and talking about this, as if he really did fire a shot. Damn, they were even discussing all kinds of ballistics stuff. Tony now took aim at someone else as Dan encouraged him on.

Well, before another shot was fired, our beers arrived, and that kind of changed the subject. Now we were just talking about getting back and checking onboard.

After a few minutes of drinking and sweating, Dan reached over and tapped the horn twice and again a girl came out. Dan paid the whole tab and said, "It's on me, guys."

Tony and I thanked him as our driver spun around and headed back to the pier.

Back on the boat, we unlocked our bags and found ourselves a good spot in the shade. I followed Dan's example and made myself cozy on top of my bag.

I heard two cabs pull up next to the pier, and before anyone got out, about a dozen or more beer cans and bottles were thrown out in all directions followed by loud laughter. Six guys got out, and all of them were dressed for war. Two guys were wearing flack jackets, another two were wearing helmets, and they were all equally drunk. I saw that we had more passengers to join us for our ride to the ship.

Two more cabs pulled up and it appeared that everyone getting out was fresh out of boot camp. Just like I was the other day, dress white uniforms on everyone. Wow, they really did stand out, and I could clearly see how obvious I must have looked.

Everyone got onboard, and I assumed that we would be departing soon.

Tony questioned Dan and I, "When did you guys see Jersey Joe last?"

I answered, "A couple of days ago, when were you there?"

"Your couple of days ago, plus a couple of days more."

Dan asked, "Are you still in trouble?"

"Don't think so. Well, maybe not as much as I was initially. I got the feeling that no one wanted to piss me off any more than they already had."

Dan saw my puzzled look and informed me," Tony shot and killed one too many VC."

I was afraid to ask about this, because I didn't know where this would take me, but I did anyway. "How can you shoot one too many VC? Isn't that why we are over here?"

Tony answered in a low voice; "I can't talk about that until after my Captain's Mast, you understand."

Again, I had a puzzled look as Dan continued and filled in the blanks for me, "Captain's Mast is like a small court, but it is not as big as a full blown court marshal."

"I know what a Captain's Mast is. I'm asking about the reason behind the Captain's Mast."

"Sort of like a small claims court," Tony added.

Laughing at that comment, Dan continued, "You think it be small claims, because you gave little value to the gooks."

"Almost right," Tony responded. "Small value to the VC that are alive and fighting. Now that's big value to the VC that are dead or dying. I sometimes help out with the dying to dead part."

Still not sure of what they were talking about, I said, "I'm a little confused. Isn't a dead VC a good thing no matter how he got dead?"

Dan thought for a minute and added, "True, very true. But you are missing some details."

"Details?"

A little chuckle from Dan, as he continued, "Yeah. Like what happened to a small village that's no longer a small village."

"Stop right there," Tony butted in. "I can't talk about it. I don't think that it's a good idea if you guys are discussing that situation around me."

"Point well taken," Dan responded, and said nothing more.

In a low voice and facing away from Tony, Dan explained, as if this was an issue of national security, "Now, this town you see . . . that he blew up. Well, it was blown up so completely that they even took it off all the maps."

"No shit?"

"No shit, he even killed all the vegetation that was there," Dan added looking at Tony to make sure he could not hear us.

I didn't know what to believe right now and no way was I going to ask any more questions about this. If this guy Tony, was what he appeared to be, I didn't want to be found talking to him, much less talking about any of this. Besides, I didn't want to be involved with any kind of Captains Mast stuff; especially with me being the new guy here and all that.

On the other hand, I did want to hear more about this village thing. However, I would just settle back and close my eyes for now. This could be just another thing to talk to Dan about later. I sure hoped that I could remember all these questions that kept adding up, for me to ask him.

Without any kind of send off, the driver kicked off the motor, and the one crewmember on the pier unhooked, or, untied the boat. I didn't know what they called it, but after we were cut loose from the pier, the crewmember jumped back onboard. It was not a very big jump and any girl could have made it. However, what surprised me was that the boat captain and he did the high-five thing, as if he just pulled a major stunt that was worthy of a Hollywood movie. Now that pissed me off a little, because of what I did a few days ago. Stepping off a pier was not a big deal compared to dropping out of an aircraft, and I did that twice. Maybe I should tell him so. Nah, I would just tell my grand children about that, or someday, maybe, I would write a book.

Our ride started out very slow because of all the river traffic. At least we were heading in the right direction and toward my new home. Well, not as in my, American home, but my new home away from home. A place to stow my stuff, and my extra stuff.

Dan pointed to my left and told me to, "Check out the river bus."

Sure enough, there was one very long, skinny boat filled with people. I bet that it was an interesting ride, and I wondered how they went to the bathroom on long trips.

My next interesting view was a group of boats that were tied together. Maybe that was the same thing over here as the row houses we have back home.

Once outside of town and into the open river, I thought how beautiful the countryside was. All the greens and browns seemed to blend into, and out of each other. The only thing that stood out was our American flag, with its bright red, white, and blue.

I asked Dan, "What's the story with the flag?"

Without opening his eyes from his catnap, he answered, "What's the matter? Is it flying upside down or something?"

I didn't check for that, but after I did, I saw that it was flying correctly. At any rate, I continued, "No, that was not it, I meant everything we have here is camouflaged. Our uniforms and all the boats are completely camouflaged. But it's our flag that stands out like a sore thumb."

"Yeah, I know. Sort of like having a bulls eye flying a few feet above your head and visible from anywhere on the river."

"Why is that?"

"Well, it's on a pole, and the pole is taller than you or me."

"I know that, not that part," I snapped back. "You know what I meant. The red, white, and blue part."

"I believe that it all started back with Betsy Ross in her little flag shop many years ago in Baltimore," he answered. "I can recall that an earlier model for the flag had a big snake in the center on a white background."

"No, not that part either. You know, why don't we fly a smaller flag, or something. How about a battle flag?" I suggested, knowing that I had a good idea.

"It's just the military way of doing things, I guess," was his uncomplicated response.

"I mean, I like and respect the flag and all that. I just can't understand why it's so big and colorful."

"I agree with your lack of understanding. The American military have always been that way. They want everyone to know where we are."

"Agreed," I answered. "Maybe you can write in a suggestion to the Chief of Navy Operations to make a change."

"Nah, if I'm going to write to the CNO about making a change, I'll begin by telling him to let us cross over into Cambodia."

"Cambodia?"

"Yeah, if we're going to have a war, then let's fight to get it finished and win."

I didn't know what he was talking about, so I might as well ask him. We did have some time to kill. "What about Cambodia? What's this about finishing off a fight?"

"Simple, the VC gets their act together, in broad daylight, I might add, and form up inside Cambodia, like just across the border. When assembled, they would cross over, kick ass and kill. Then it would just be a little stroll back across the border, while our U.S. and ARVN allies must stop, and not cross over, to complete the chase."

"Can't we just go over and get them? I mean, we're at war with them and all that, right?"

"No, we are not at war because this is a military conflict, as the Korean War was a police action. This is political and not military doctrine. For the most part, rules for this war are controlled by the lawyers that are back home holding elected office."

I shook my head in disgust from hearing that. I recognized from what he told me, that no matter what we did, we really could not do the things needed to win this war. (Our conflict, as he called it.) I knew that I was not trained in military doctrine, but I did know that we could not win any war, if the other side had a safe place to go and regroup. I remembered that in other wars, there was always, 'behind the enemy lines;' but we could always fly over and at least drop a few bombs on them.

Dan added, after he saw my apparent confused state, "Your appearance and mannerism show that you don't care about this military situation. Am I correct?"

"I just got here a few days ago, but that's an affirmative," I answered, being careful not to have anyone hear me.

"I believe that's why we must only do a year tour over here. Anything longer than that, and it would give you time to think about other alternatives."

"You're right. I'll just keep it to myself and do my best to get out of here alive," I answered.

Dan suggested, "Maybe someday, Nixon will allow us to cross over into Cambodia to take care of some unfinished business, or at the very least, finish off a few things."

"Think that will be easy for us?"

"Not really. It might even be a little more dangerous."

"Like what?" I asked, because he seemed to be sincere about this, and not joking with me for a change.

"On the other side of the border, because it's safe from us, some of the VC has their families with them."

"Okay," I did not know that, but I assumed that he was telling me the truth.

"Now, one thing about this," he continued. "You already have some idea how well they fight for their ideas of a united Vietnam. Imagine for a moment, how hard they will fight when we're taking shots at their wives and kids."

"I can definitely appreciate that, and I can see where the VC would feel the same way," I said. In a way, I wanted to hear more about that, but for now, the combination of too many beers and the hot sun had made me sleepy. Tony was asleep, and Dan was trying to sleep, if I would just leave him alone.

I took one last look out at the river and saw a single house on the shore all by itself. At least they had running water in front of their home.

I looked on the other side and saw a row of homes. I hoped that no one there would take a shot at any of us. At least everyone from those houses was waving at us.

In addition, just before I tried to take a nap, another one of the buses we saw earlier went by. This one had some flags on it that indicated to me that it just might be a first class boat. I would bet this one had a bathroom on it. Whatever. Naptime for me, and if anything happened, Dan would keep me informed. That was something I could count on.

Before I did fall asleep, I heard a couple of guys talking about another boat on the other side of the river.

I looked up, and sure enough, there was another boat, hopefully one of ours, going in our direction, but a little slower. It did not look like a man-of-war or patrol type of boat, just a boat that carried supplies.

Dan said to Tony after looking out at the other boat, "I hope we get in behind him."

"Me too. I'll be a slower ride, but I won't mind," Tony responded.

"What are you guys talking about," I asked. I would have thought that getting there fast and first, that it would be a good thing. Certainly better than going slow.

Tony looked at Dan and asked, "Should I tell him, or do you want to explain it?"

"You can do it. I am always explaining stuff to him, "Dan answered, as he sat back down and closed his eyes.

Great, now I had both of them thinking that I was a dummy. Oh well, I added, "Okay, I give. Tell me."

"You know, war zone, river, boat, mines. You put them altogether, and you have explosions," he explained, as he and Dan had a good laugh.

Whatever, so I assumed that we would get in behind the one boat, and if anyone was going to go, 'booms,' it would be the boat up front, and not us. I responded, "No sweat, I got it."

Almost at the same time that I came to a realization of this issue, our boat changed course, moved over, and got in behind the other boat. I felt a little more secure tailing behind the other boat. I then figured that we might be a bigger target that was going much slower, and easier to hit and all that. Giving this a little more thought, I figured that it was best to just take a nap and let our driver work out the details about our trip. With little difficulty, plus a little help from my beers, I was able to take a nap.

"Wake up. Wake up," Dan said as he pushed on my shoulder to wake me up from a sound sleep.

"What's up," I asked without opening my eyes.

"Check-it-out man. Check-it-out. You can check-in now."

"What?" I was both excited and confused. Were we there? Now?

I looked up and could see a big green ship. Wow, I was here. After days of hitchhiking all around South Vietnam on all types of transportation, I could finally see the light at the end of the tunnel, the USS SUMMIT. I am here. I had made it. And now . . . the adventure will begin for me.

TO BE CONTINUED:

Brown Water II, The adventure begins . . .

Review by Joni Bour

Here we are again, you, me, Dan and Charles. BrownWater II picks up where BrownWater I leaves off. After finishing this book, I can't help but wonder if the author has some of the quirks as the characters. My guess is that these characters are much like him, and maybe this is how he writes so well about their antics. True, the characters are night and day different from each other, but then aren't we all that way at some point in our lives? Given the proper test and circumstance, any young man might surprise himself or his mother as to what he might do when the chips are down. I would imagine further that Mr. Crawford has a few hair-raising stories he chose not to tell, whether they were about himself, Dan or Charles.

The author keeps you chuckling through most of the book, but here is an odd anomaly—you actually cry at the same time. How do I explain that? I am not sure I can explain why, but many times through the 425 pages of actual story, I laughed, then I shook my head and felt very sad, all the while with a smile on my face. That isn't very easy to understand I guess, but I think it is because, the events he wrote about would be funny if written about young men sitting around out behind the school, and not in the middle of the Mekong Delta. If would be hysterical, if not for the fact that these boys were throwing percussion grenades in the water around their ship to keep the VC away, instead of working on their muscle cars and smooching with their high school sweetheart. Except for the inescapable reality of war, this is a very funny book.

Sometimes you may worry about Charles and whether he will ever grow a thicker skin, ever find a way to blend and not be the butt of so many jokes. You will also puzzle over Dan, and how he became so indifferent, so disillusioned with life. These two seem to be polar opposites and yet they seem drawn to each other. I think as you read the book, you begin to see why. They need each other, the way flowers need dirt, and coffee needs a cup. They balance each other. Perhaps Dan sees something of himself in Charles, the way he had been before the wages of war left its mark. Maybe Charles saw a survivor instinct in Dan, that he knew he needed to learn. However or why ever it was, it makes a good story.

The book is refreshing, because it is different. I would stake all the money in my pocket that you will never find another book series like this. The world should breath a thankful sigh that there are veterans like Sam Crawford around to tell a good story, whether it is all fact or not. The world should also be glad that there is only one Sam Crawford with which to contend. I doubt that we could handle more.

It isn't often that an author who has experienced what he is writing about finds a way to take the focus off himself, and place it on others. Mr. Crawford wanted to be the storyteller and not the story, though I do believe he is the story all the same. Have you ever believed something so strongly in your heart that you did not need someone else to tell you whether it was true or not? Have you ever known something was real even though you had no proof? Of course you have. That is the same feeling I had about this series of books. These little war stories, like snapshots into fictitious lives, are not so fictitious at all. They happened. Maybe not all of them and maybe not even in the same order as you will read them, but they are real.

I find this series of books precious like an old photo of a great-grandfather in his WWI uniform or a letter written by a sailor to his loving wife. They are history, not the sort you will find in the 8th grade American studies, but personal history, the kind that lives in the heart and minds of those who have survived war. It won't probably win a Pulitzer or even be on the New York Times bestseller list, but I don't care. Dan and Charles story is far more important than that.

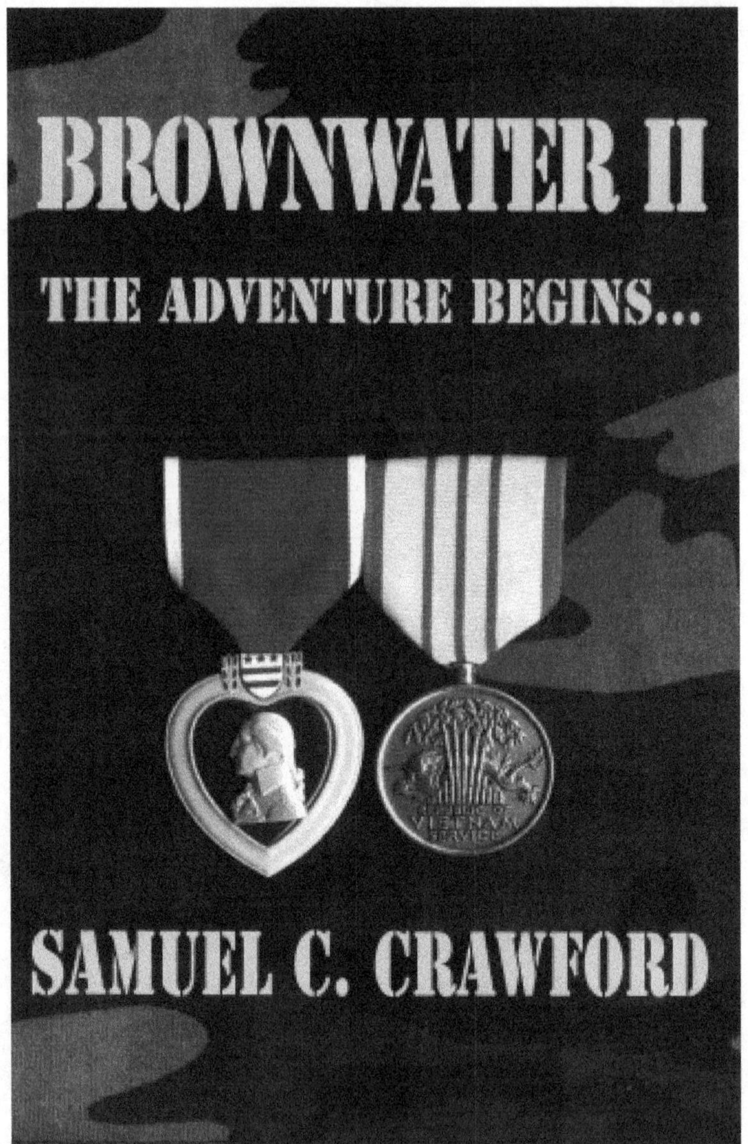

BrownWater II—COMING SOON

GLOSSARY

A TEAMS	12-man Green Beret unit.
AFB	Air Force Base.
AFT	directional—in, at, toward, or close to the back or STERN of a BOAT or SHIP.
AFTERDECK	the STERN or AFT open area of a SHIP, also called the FANTAIL.
AGENT ORANGE	one of several defoliants (herbicides) containing trace amounts of a toxic contaminant, TCDD (dioxin). Defoliants were used to kill vast areas of jungle growth.
AHC	Assault Helicopter Company (HUEYS).
AHOY	traditional greeting for hailing other vessels, originally a Viking battle cry.
AK-47	basic infantry weapon of the NVA and VC
ALPHA BOAT	Assault Support Patrol Boat (ASBP). A light, fast, shallow draft boat designed specifically to provide close support to Riverine infantry. Armament consisted of machine guns (M-60 and .50 cal.), plus whatever the boat crew could scrounge.

AMF	literally, "Adios, Mother Fucker."
AMMO	ammunition.
AMNESTY BOX	a bright blue box made of solid steel shaped like a freestanding US Postal box but about half again as high, twice as deep, and maybe four times as wide. It stood in front of the customs line so you could dump any contraband (drugs, weapons, porno magazines, whatever) no questions asked, before going through customs.
AO DAI	traditional slit skirt and trousers worn by Vietnamese women.
ARL	Repair Ship Light.
ARVN	Army of the Republic of Vietnam.
ASAP	(A-sap) As Soon As Possible.
ASBP	Assault Support Patrol Boat—see ALPHA BOAT.
ATC	Armored Troop Carrier—see TANGO BOAT.
ATCH	Armored Troop Carrier Helicopter—see TANGO BOAT.
AWOL	Absent Without Official Leave.
BAHT	Thai unit of currency.
BEQ	Bachelor Enlisted Quarters.
BID BOAT	any boat patrolling around an anchored ship on the rivers.
BILGES	the rounded portion of a ship's hull, forming a transition between the bottom and the sides. The lowest inner part of a ship's hull.
BITTS	tie-down points on a SHIP or BOAT that provide places for mooring lines to attach the SHIP or BOAT to the pier.
BLUE LINE	a river on a map.
BOAT	a relatively small; usually open craft of a

size that might be carried aboard a ship. An inland vessel of any size.

BOAT CAPTAIN usually a First Class or Chief Petty Officer in command of a BOAT. i.e. TANGO or ALPHA BOATS, etc.

BOATSWAIN an enlisted rating, running from Boatswain's striker (E-2) through Master Chief and then into Warrant Officers. A deck crewmember.

BODY BAGS plastic bags used for retrieval of bodies on the battlefield.

BODY COUNT number of enemy killed, wounded or captured during an operation. Used by Saigon and Washington as a means of measuring progress of the war.

BOHICA short for "Bend Over, Here It Comes Again." Usually describing another undesirable assignment.

BOOBY TRAP explosive charge hidden in a harmless object, which explodes on contact.

BOOKOO Vietnamese/French term for "many," or "lots of . . ."

BOOM-BOOM term used by Vietnamese prostitutes in selling their product.

BOONDOCKS expression for the jungle, or any remote area away from a base camp or city, some times used to refer to any area in Vietnam. Also knows as BOONIES and BRUSH

BOONDOGGLE any military operation that has not been completely thought out. An operation that is considered ridiculous.

BOONIES expression for the jungle, or any remote area away from a base camp or city, some times used to refer to any area in Vietnam. Also knows as BOONDOCKS and BRUSH.

BOOT	negative common name for anyone recently out of BOOT CAMP.
BOOT CAMP	initial training for anyone in the military.
BOQ	Bachelor Officer's Quarters.
BOUNCING BETTY	explosive propelled upward about four feet into the air and then detonates.
BOW	directional—in, at, toward, or close to the front of a BOAT or SHIP.
BREAK SQUELCH	to send a "click-hiss" signal on a radio by depressing the push-to-talk button without speaking.
BRUSH	expression for the jungle, or any remote area away from a base camp or city, sometimes used to refer to any area in Vietnam. Also knows as BOONIES and BOONDOCKS.
BUAER	Bureau of Aeronautics.
BULKHEAD	one of the upright partitions dividing a ship into compartments and serving to add structural rigidity and to prevent the spread of leakage or fire. A partition or wall serving a similar purpose in a vehicle, such as an aircraft or spacecraft.
BUNAV	Bureau of Navigation.
BUNO	Bureau of Numbers.
BUOY	a floating object moored to the bottom, to mark a channel or to point out the position of something beneath the water, as an anchor, shoal, rock, etc.
BUPERS	Bureau of Naval Personnel in Washington, DC.
BUWEPS	Bureau of Naval Weapons.
C-130's	C-130 Lockheed Hercules 4 engine, high wing cargo plane with a rear loading door.
CAO BOIS	(COWBOYS) term referred to criminals of SAIGON who rode motorcycles.

CAPTAIN'S MAST	military trial usually tried on naval ships by the CO.
CCB	Command & Control Boat. A converted landing craft of the MONITOR class Riverine boat, packed with radios, designed for forward command and communications.
CHARLIE	Vietcong—short for the phonetic representation Victor Charlie.
CHARLIE BOAT	see CCB.
CHECK-IT-OUT	a common slang as ubiquitous as "okay," meaning to have a close look at something or someone.
CHERRY	a new troop replacement. Someone fresh out of BOOT CAMP.
CHERRY BOY	term given to anybody still a virgin.
CHEWING THE FAT	"God made the vittles but the devil made the cook," was a popular saying used by seafaring men in the 19th century when salted beef was staple diet aboard ship. This tough cured beef, suitable only for long voyages when nothing else was cheap or would keep as well (remember, there was no refrigeration), required prolonged chewing to make it edible. Men often chewed one chunk for hours, just as it were chewing gum and referred to this practice as "chewing the fat."
CHICKEN PLATE	chest protector (body armor) worn by helicopter gunners.
CHIEF	Chief Petty Office in the Navy. E7, E8, and E9. An enlisted rank that is above Petty Officer First Class.
CHINOOK	the CH-47 cargo helicopter, also called "SHIT-HOOK."

CHIT	a signed voucher, short letter, note; a written message or memorandum; a certificate given as a pass, permission, or the like.
CHOKE	peanut butter.
CHOPPER	helicopter.
CHURCH KEY	bottle opener.
CIB	Combat Infantry Badge is awarded for actual time in combat.
CINC	Commander in Chief
CINCLANTFLT	Commander in Chief, U.S. Atlantic Fleet
CINCPACFLT	Commander in Chief, U.S. Pacific Fleet
CLAYMORE	a popular fan-shaped antipersonnel land mine. An unorthodox use—the explosive burned with intense heat, and a small amount of explosive could quickly heat a can of C-RATIONS. The method became one of the most popular field stoves in the war.
CNO	Chief of Navy Operations.
CO	Commanding Officer.
COASTIES	nickname used to identify the US Coast Guard servicemen.
COBRA	the AH-1G "attack helicopter." Nicknamed by some the "Shark" or "Snake." Most of the COBRAS were painted with eyes and big, scary teeth like a shark for psychological impact.
CO-CONG	female Vietcong.
COMIC BOOKS	military maps or COMIC BOOKS.
COMM	Communications.
CONCUSSION GRENADE	—an explosive device thrown in the water to keep away swimmer or SAPPERS.
CONTACT	condition of being in CONTACT with the enemy, a FIREFIGHT, also "IN THE SHIT."

CONUS	continental US
COOK-OFF	a situation where an automatic weapon has fired so many rounds that the heat has built up enough in the weapon to set off the remaining rounds without using the trigger mechanism.
COXSWAIN	generally a BOATSWAIN'S MATE in charge of steering and/or directing the crew of a BOAT. A boat is defined as a vessel smaller than a SHIP.
CP	Command Post.
C-RATIONS	canned meals used in military operations. Also, know as C-RATS.
CREW CHIEF	crewmember that maintains an aircraft.
CUP OF JOE	Josephus Daniels was appointed Secretary of the Navy by President Woodrow Wilson in 1913. Among his reforms of the Navy was the abolishment of the officers' wine mess. From that time on, the strongest drink aboard Navy ships could only be coffee and over the years, a cup of coffee became known as "a CUP OF JOE."
CYA	Cover Your Ass.
CYCLICAL RATE	in machine guns, the number of rounds fired in one minute.
CYCLO	a three-wheel passenger vehicle powered by a human on a bicycle.
DAP	a stylized, ritualized manner of shaking hands, started by colored American troops consisting of knuckle-knocking and finger-grabbing.
DCNO	Deputy Chief of Naval Operations.
DEEP-SHIT	the worst possible position, such as being nearly overrun. See SHIT.

DEROS — Date Eligible for Return from OverSeas, a person's tour was to end.

DEVIL TO PAY — today the expression "DEVIL TO PAY" was used primarily to describe having an unpleasant result from some action that has been taken, as in someone has done something they should not have, and, as a result, "there will be the DEVIL TO PAY." Originally, this expression described one of the unpleasant tasks aboard a wooden ship. The "devil" was the wooden ship's longest seam in the hull. Caulking was done with "pay" or pitch (a kind of tar). The task of "paying the devil" (caulking the longest seam) by squatting in the BILGES was despised by every seaman.

DI-DI-MAU — move quickly, also shortened to just "DI-DI."

DINKY-DAU — Vietnamese term for "crazy" or "You're crazy."

DMZ — demilitarized zone. An area from which military forces, operations, and installations are prohibited

DOC — affectionate title for enlisted medical aidman/corpsmen.

DOD — Department of Defense.

DON'T MEAN NOTHIN'—term meaning nothing to worry or SWEAT about.

DONUT DOLLY — American Red Cross volunteer—female.

DOUBTFULS — indigenous personnel who cannot be categorized as either VC or civil offenders. It also can mean suspect personnel spotted from ground or aircraft.

DRESS WHITES	summer uniform.
DUFFEL BAG	oblong, unwieldy bag that troops stored all their gear. See SEA BAG.
DUSTOFF	nickname for medical evacuation helicopter or mission. See MEDEVAC.
E & E	Escape & Evasion.
E1, E2, ETC	enlisted men's grades, E1-Seaman Recruit, E2-Seaman Apprentice, E3-Seaman, E4-3rd Class Petty Officer, E5 2nd Class Petty Officer, etc.
EIGHT BELLS	aboard Navy ships, bells are struck to designate the hours of being on watch. Each watch is four hours. One bell is struck after the first half-hour has passed, two bells after one hour has passed, three bells after an hour and a half, four bells after two hours, and so forth up to EIGHT BELLS are struck at the completion of the four hours. Completing a watch with no incidents to report was "EIGHT BELLS and all is well." The practice of using bells stems from the days of the sailing ships. Sailors could not afford to have their own timepieces and relied on the ship's bells to tell time. The ship's boy kept time by using a half-hour glass. Each time the sand ran out, he would turn the glass over and ring the appropriate number of bells.
ELEPHANT GRASS	tall, sharp-edge grass
EM	Enlisted Man.
EM CLUB	Military club for enlisted personnel only. Officers and Chief Petty Officers are not allowed.

ENSIGN — entry-level officer (US Navy).

EQUAL TURNING POINT—a point determined by the "HOW GOES IT CURVE" beyond which it would not be possible for an aircraft to return to the point of origin. A plot of speed, distance, engine settings, remaining fuel, etc., that assisted the crews in determining the crucial, "POINT OF NO RETURN."

ET — Electronics Technicians.

EVAC — see MEDEVAC.

F-4 PHANTOM — a twin-engine, all weather, tactical fighter-jet.

FAM — Federal Air Marshal.

FANTAIL — the STERN or AFT open area of a ship, also called the AFTERDECK.

FAST MOVER — usually a jet

FATIGUES — standard combat uniform, green in color. Sometimes called GREENS.

FEELING BLUE — if you are sad and describe yourself as "FEELING BLUE," you are using a phrase coined from a custom among many old deepwater sailing ships. If the ship lost the captain or any of the officers during its voyage, she would fly blue flags and have a blue band painted along her entire hull when returning to homeport.

FIELD OF FIRE — area that a weapon or group of weapons can cover effectively with fire from a given position.

FIGMO — state of blissful abandon, achieved after receiving orders out of Vietnam. Literally "Fuckit, I Got My Orders."

FIREFIGHT — exchange of small arms fire between opposing units.

FLACK JACKET	heavy fiberglass-filled vest worn for protection from shrapnel.
FLAG OFFICERS	an officer in the navy or coast guard holding a rank higher than captain, such as rear admiral, vice admiral, or admiral.
FLARE	illumination projectile.
FNG	most common name for newly arrive person in Vietnam. It was literally translated as "Fuckin' New Guy."
FOM (short)	French River Patrol Boat.
FORWARD	directional—in, at, toward, or near the BOW of a SHIP or BOAT.
FREE FIRE ZONE	any area in which permission was not required to fire on targets.
FREEDOM BIRD	name given to any aircraft that took troops out of Vietnam. Usually the commercial jet flight that took men back to the WORLD.
FREQ	radio Frequency.
FRIENDLIES	US troops, allies, or anyone not on the other side.
FRIENDLY FIRE	a euphemism used to describe air, artillery, or small-arms fire from American forces mistakenly directed at American positions.
FUBAR	"Fucked Up Beyond All Repair" or "Recognition." Impossible situations, equipment, or persons as in, "It is (or they are) totally FUBAR!"
FUNNY BOOKS	military maps or COMIC BOOKS.
GALLEY	the kitchen of the ship. The best explanation as to its origin is that it is a corruption of "GALLEY." Ancient sailors cooked their meals on a brick or stone gallery laid amidships.

GANGPLANK — a board or ramp used as a removable footway between a ship and a pier. Also called gangway.

GCT — Greenwich Civil Time

GERONIMO — an expression used when doing something exciting in combat.

GOOKS — slang expression brought to Vietnam by Korean War Veterans. The term refers to anyone of Asian origin.

GQ GENERAL QUARTERS—battle stations where military personnel are assigned to go ASAP when alarm sounds.

GREENS — same as FATIGUES, standard combat uniform, green in color.

GREEN BACKS — term used to describe American money.

GREEN BERETS — members of the Special Forces of the U.S. Army. Awarded the Green Beret headgear as a mark of distinction.

GREENWICH MEAN TIME—zero degrees of longitude runs through Greenwich; time is measured relative to GREENWICH MEAN TIME. It is used in airplane and ship navigation, where it also sometimes known by the military name, "ZULU TIME." "ZULU" in the phonetic alphabet stands for "Z" which stands for longitude zero.

GROSSCHECK — everyone checks everyone else for things that are lose, make noise, light up, smell bad, etc.

GRUNT — a popular nickname for an infantryman in Vietnam, supposedly derived from the sound one made from lifting up heavy items.

GSW-TTH — casualty report term meaning "gunshot wound, thru and thru."

GUARD THE RADIO — term meaning to stand by and listen for messages.

GUERRILLA — soldiers of a resistance movement, organized on a military or paramilitary basic. GUERRILLA warfare military operations conducted in enemy-held or hostile territory by irregular, predominantly indigenous force.

GUN SALUTE — guns were first fired as an act of good faith. In the days when it took so long to reload a gun, it was a proof of friendly intention when the ship's cannon were discharged upon entering port.

GUNG HO — very enthusiastic and committed.

GVN — Government of South Vietnam.

HANOI HANNA — Propaganda radio announcer representing North Vietnam. She was known for having "good music, but lousy commercials."

HANOI HILTON — nickname American prisoners of war used to describe the Hoa-Loa Prison in Hanoi.

HATCH — another name for doorway onboard ships.

HE KNOWS THE ROPES—in the very early days, this phrase was written on a seaman's discharge to indicate that he was still a novice. All he knew about being a sailor was just the names and uses of the principal ropes (lines). Today, this same phrase means the opposite and that the person fully knows and understands the operation (usually of the organization).

HEAD — a bathroom aboard Navy ships. Term comes from the days of sailing ships when the place for the crew to relieve themselves was all the way forward on

	either side of the bowsprit, the integral part of the hull to which the figurehead was fastened.
HOOTCH	house or living quarters or a native hut.
HOT	dangerous, such as HOT LZ.
HOW GOES IT CURVE—see EQUAL TURNING POINT.	
HUEY	nickname for the UH-series utility helicopter.
HUNKY-DORY	everything is "O.K." was coined from a street named "Honki-Dori" in Yokohama, Japan. Since the inhabitants of this street catered to the pleasures of sailors, it is easy to understand why the street's name became synonymous for anything that is enjoyable or at least satisfactory and, the logical follow-on is "Okey-dokey."
INCOMING	receiving enemy mortar or rocket fire.
IN-COUNTRY	term used to refer to American troops operating in South Vietnam. They were all IN-COUNTRY.
IN THE SHIT	see SHIT.
JCS	Joint Chiefs of Staff.
JESUS NUT	main rotor retaining nut that holds the main rotor onto the rest of the helicopter. If it came off, only JESUS could help you.
JOHN WAYNE	can opener for canned C-RATIONS, also called the P-38.
KA-BAR	type of military combat knife.
KIA	Killed In Action.
KLICK	short for kilometer.
KP	Kitchen Patrol or kitchen duty.
LAUGH A MINUTE	translated as a "Walk in the Park," but it meant going up a river.
LAY-CHILLY	lie motionless.

LBGB	little bitty gook boat, (small watercraft for one or two people).
LCM	Landing Craft Mechanized.
LCPL	Landing Craft, Personnel (Large).
LIBERTY	permission given to a sailor to go ashore.
LIFER	career sailor.
LOGBOOK	in the early days of sailing ships, the ship's records were written on shingles cut from logs. These shingles were hinged and opened like a book. The record was called the "LOG BOOK." Later on, when paper was readily available and bound into books, the record maintained it name.
LSIL	Infantry Landing ship (Large).
LST	Landing Ship, Tank.
LT	Lieutenant, US Navy (O-3).
LT (JG)	Lieutenant (junior grade) US Navy (O-2).
LURPS	lightweight food packet consisting of a dehydrated meal and named after the soldiers it was most often issued.
LZ	Landing Zone.
MAA	see Master-AT-Arms.
MAAD MINUTE	concentrated fire of all weapons for a brief period of time.
MAGS	magazines where ammunition kept/stored until placed in a weapon. The magazines is where the ammo is placed and then it is the magazine that is placed into the weapon.
MAKE A HOLE	term spoken when you wanted people to move out of the way.
MAIL BUOY	fictitious location for collecting the mail. This trick is same-same as sending someone Snipe hunting.

MAMA-SAN	mature Vietnamese woman.
MARKET TIME	Coastal patrol operations off the coast of South Vietnam, 1968-71.
MARS	Military Affiliate Radio System. Licensed ham radio operators (sometimes known as radio geeks) in civilian life, were given civilian amateur radio equipment and told to use their ham radio skills to run phone patches, or telephone calls home for their fellow Marines. Their counterparts in the United States placed collect telephone calls to the families and friends of the Marines in the field and patched the calls through on frequencies near the ham bands.
MASTER-AT-ARMS	usually a senior Navy Chief Petty Officer on a navy ship. The MAA holds the position of police officer.
MAYDAY	the internationally recognized voice radio signal for ships and people in serious trouble at sea. Made official in 1948, it is an anglicizing of the French m'aidez, "help me."
MEDEVAC	medical evacuation by HUEY, also called an EVAC or DUSTOFF.
MIA	Missing In Action.
MONITOR BOAT	A converted landing craft packed with radios, designed for forward command and communications. See CCB.
MOO-MOO DRESS	one-piece dress worn by Vietnamese woman.
MP	Military Police.
MPC	Military Payment Certificate, used instead of US dollars (Green Backs), was also used to replace US coins.

MRF	Mobile Riverine Force.
MSB	Minesweeping Boat.
MSM	Minesweeper (medium).
MUC	Meritorious Unit Commendation.
MUZZLE VELOCITY	The speed at which a projectile leaves the muzzle of a weapon, generally measured in feet per second.
MWOK	Married WithOut Kids.
M-16	nickname, the widow-maker, the standard American rifle used after 1966.
M-60	American-made machine-gun.
NDSM	National Defense Service Medal. Awarded to US military personnel who enlisted in peacetime.
NEWBIE	any person with less time in Vietnam than the speaker.
NEXT	person who had been in Vietnam for nearly a year and who would be rotated back to the WORLD soon. When the DEROS was the shortest in the unit, this person was said to be NEXT.
NO SWEAT	can do—easily done or accomplished—nothing to worry about.
NON-LA	conical hat, part of traditional Vietnamese costume.
NUC	Naval Unit Commendation.
NUMBA	slang for number.
NUMBA-ONE	good.
NUMBA-TEN	bad.
NUMBA-TEN-THOUSAND—very bad.	
OCS	Officer Candidate School.
OJT	On the Job Training.
OOD	Officer of the Day.
OPNAV	Office of the Chief of Naval Operations.
OSD	Office of the Secretary of Defense.

P-38	can opener for canned C-RATS, also called JOHN WAYNE.
PACV	Patrol Air Cushion Vehicle.
PAPA-SAN	an elderly Vietnamese man.
PBR	Patrol Boat River. Another name for Pabst Blue Ribbon beer, the only beer a PBR sailor would drink.
PCF	Patrol Craft Fast—Swift boat.
PCF MK1	Patrol Craft, Inshore—Swift boat.
PEA COAT	sailors who have to endure pea-soup weather often don their pea coats but the coat's name is not derived from the weather. The heavy topcoat worn in cold, miserable weather by seafaring men was once tailored from pilot cloth and a heavy, course, stout kind of twilled blue cloth with the nap on one side. The cloth was sometimes called P-cloth for the initial letter of "pilot" and the garment made from it was called a p-jacket and later, a pea coat. The term used since 1723 to denote coats made from that cloth.
PETER PILOT	the less experienced co-PILOT in a HUEY

PETTY OFFICER U.S.—Navy enlisted higher than SEAMEN.

PFC	Private First Class (US ARMY).
PGM	Patrol Motor Gunboat.
PH	Purple Heart. Medal issued to anyone wounded.
POD	Plan of the Day. Daily newsletter published onboard U.S. Navy ships. Will list watch schedules and ships schedule.

POINT OF NO RETURN—see EQUAL TURNING POINT.

POP SMOKE	to mark a target, or Landing Zone (LZ) with a smoke grenade.

PORT	directional—left side of the ship or boat when facing forward.
PORTHOLES	originated during the reign of Henry VI of England (1485). King Henry insisted on mounting guns too large for his ship and the traditional methods of securing these weapons on the forecastle and aftcastle could not be used. A French shipbuilder named James Baker was commissioned to solve the problem. He put small doors in the side of the ship and mounted the cannon inside the ship. These doors protected the cannon from weather and were opened when the cannon were to be used. The French word for "door" is "porte" which was later Anglicized to "port" and later went on to mean any opening in the ship's side, whether for cannon or not.
POW	Prisoner Of War. Also known as Petty Officer of the Watch.
PRC	River Patrol Craft.
PRC-25	nicknamed PRICK, lightweight infantry field radio.
PRESSURE WAVE	Damage inflicted by ordnance dropped into the water next to a ship. Transmission of explosive force is conducted through hydraulic effect to crush the hull of the target.
PRICK	lightweight infantry field radio, PRC-25.
PUC	Presidential Unit Citation.
PUCKER FACTOR	assessment of the "fear factor," as in the difficulty/risk of an upcoming mission.
R & R	Rest & Recreation. One-week of free-leave awarded to military personnel

serving In-Country during a one-year tour of duty. Married personnel would mostly select Hawaii where they would meet up with their spouses. Single personnel usually selected Tokyo, Hong Kong, Sydney Austria, or Bangkok Thailand.

RAG	Vietnamese River Assault Group boat.
RECON	reconnaissance.
REVETMENTS	A barricade against explosives.
ROACH COACH	something like the lunch wagons found around construction sites.
ROCK 'N' ROLL	to put an M16 on full automatic fire.
RON	Remain OverNight.
ROUND EYE	slang term to describe Americans.
RTO	Radio/Telephone Operator who carried the PRC-25.
RVN	Republic of Vietnam (South Vietnam).
SAIGON TEA	high-cost drink that one would buy the bargirls that would have little or no alcohol content.
SAME-SAME	same as.
SAPPERS	North Vietnamese Army or Vietcong demolition commandos.
SAR	Search And Rescue.
SCUTTLEBUTT	a nautical parlance for a rumor, comes from a combination of "scuttle" and to make a hole in the ship's hull and thereby causing her to sink—and "butt" and a cask or hogshead used in the days of wooden ships to hold drinking water. The cask from which the ship's crew took their drinking water and like a water fountain and was the "SCUTTLEBUTT." Even in today's Navy, a drinking fountain is referred to as such. But, since the crew used

	to congregate around the "SCUTTLE-BUTT," that is where the rumors about the ship or voyage would begin. Thus, then and now, rumors are talk from the "SCUTTLEBUTT" or just "SCUTTLE-BUTT."
SEA BAG	oblong, unwieldy bag that sailors stored all their gear. See DUFFEL BAG
SEAL	Navy special-warfare force members—Seal Air Land team.
SEAMAN	Low ranking U.S. navy enlisted personnel.
SECDEF	Secretary of Defense.
SECNAV	Secretary of the Navy.
SERETTE	little disposable needles with morphine.
SHAKEN-BAKE	an officer straight out of OCS without any combat experience.
SHIP	a vessel of considerable size for deep-water navigation.
SHIT	a catchall multipurpose term, i.e., a FIREFIGHT was "IN THE SHIT," a bad situation was "DEEP SHIT," to be well prepared and alert was to have your "SHIT WIRED TIGHT."
SHIT-HOOK	name applied to Chinook helicopter because of all the "SHIT" stirred up by its massive rotors.
SHIT WIRED TIGHT	see SHIT.
SHORT	someone whose tour IN-COUNTRY was almost over. Also called SHORT-TIMER.
SHORT-TIMER	see SHORT.
SHOTGUN	armed guard on or in a vehicle who watches for enemy activity and returns fire if attacked. A door gunner on a helicopter.

SICK BAY	mini hospital onboard ship.
SIT-REP	situation report.
SIX	from aviation jargon, 'My 6 o'clock.' Directly behind me, hence my back—cover my back or rear of operation.
SKATE	goof off.
SKY PILOT	another name for the Chaplain.
SLOPE	a derogatory term used to refer to any Asian.
SMALL STUFF	not a big deal, nothing to worry about.
SNAFU	Situation Normal—All Fucked Up.
SOP	Standard Operating Procedure.
SOS	"Shit On A Shingle." Creamed meat on toast.
S.O.S.	contrary to popular notion, the letters S.O.S. do not stand for "Save Our Ship" or "Save Our Souls." They were selected to indicate a distress because, in Morse code, these letters and their combination create an unmistakable sound pattern. Three short, three long, three short.
SPORKS	combination of a spoon and fork.
STAB BOAT	SEAL Team Strike Assault Boat.
STAND DOWN	term used to indicate that a naval ship, squadron, or other military unit will stop all operations and do a safety review. Also, period of rest and refitting in which all-operational activities except for security is stopped.
STARBOARD	the Vikings called the side of their ship its board, and they placed the steering oar, the "star" on the right side of the ship, thus that side became known as the "star board." It's been that way ever

since. Moreover, because the oar was in the right side, the ship was tied to the dock at the left side. This was known as the loading side or "larboard." Later, it was decided that "larboard" and "starboard" were too similar, especially when trying to be heard over the roar of a heavy sea, so the phrase became the "side at which you tied up to in port" or the "port" side.

STARLIGHT — Scope. Light amplifying telescope, used to see at night.

STEEL POT — standard US Army helmet. The outer metal cover.

STERN — the AFTERDECK or aft open area of a ship, also FANTAIL.

SWIFT BOAT — U.S. Navy patrol boat, designated PCF (Patrol Craft Fast).

SYNCHRONIZED FIRE—firing through the propeller an airplane that coupled the machine gun sear mechanism with a cam on the engine crankshaft. Shots were timed to miss the propeller.

TAD — Temporary Additional Duty.

TAKEN ABACK — One hazards faced in days of sailing ships is incorporated into English to describe someone who has been jolted by unpleasant news. We say that person has been "TAKEN ABACK." The person is at a momentary loss, unable to act or even to speak. A danger faced by sailing ships was for a sudden shift in wind to come up (from a sudden squall), blowing the sails back against the masts, putting the ship in grave danger of having the masts break off and rendering the ship totally helpless. The ship was TAKEN ABACK.

TANGO BOAT — Armored Troop Carrier. Nine seats for troops and a canvas top. Each tango could carry a fully equipped rifle platoon.

TDY — Temporary Duty.

TEE-TEE — Vietnamese term for, "A little bit."

TET — Vietnamese Lunar New Year holiday period.

TF — Task Force

TG — Task Group

THE-NAM — slang term for Vietnam.

THREE-MILE LIMIT — a recognized distance from a nation's shore over which that nation had jurisdiction. This border of inter-national waters or the "high seas" was established because, at the time this international law was established, 3 miles was the longest range of any nation's most powerful guns and there-fore the limit from shore batteries at which they could enforce their laws. International law and the 1988 Territorial Sea Proclamation established the "high seas" border at 12-miles.

THREE SHEETS TO THE WIND—describes someone who has too much to drink. As such, they are often bedraggled with perhaps shirttails out, clothes a mess. The reference is to a sailing ship in disarray, that is with sheets (lines, not "ropes" that adjust the angle at which a sail is set in relation to the wind) flapping loosely in the breeze.

THUMPER (THUMP-GUN): M-79 grenade launcher.

TIGER BALM — foul-smelling oil used by many Vietnamese to ward off evil spirits.

TOUR	a one year tour was equal to 365 days.
TRIP-WIRE	thin wire used by both sides strung across an area where someone may walk through. Usually attached to a mine, flare, or booby-trap.
TURRET	On ships, a rotatable armored enclosure-protecting heavy rifled ordnance.
UA	Unauthorized Absence.
USO	United Service Organization.
USS	United States Ship.
VC	VIETCONG, called Victor Charlie (phonetic alphabet) or just CHARLIE
VCNO	Vice Chief of Naval Operations.
VERY	the name of the inventor of an extensive production series of bright flares for illumination at night, either dropped from the air or fired from a hand-held pistol.
VIETCONG	communist forces fighting the South Vietnamese Government.
VN	VIETNAM.
VNSM	Vietnam Service Medal.
WAKE-UP	term to indicate that being in THE-NAM was a bad dream, a nightmare, and that when you leave, you will WAKE-UP from your nightmare.
WAKEY	the last day in country before going home.
WATCHES	traditionally, a 24-hour day is divided into seven watches. These are: midnight to 4 a.m. [0000-0400], the mid-watch; 4 to 8 a.m. [0400-0800], morning watch; 8 a.m. to noon [0800-1200], forenoon watch; noon to 4 p.m. [1200-1600], afternoon watch; 4 to 6 p.m. [1600-1800] first dog watch; 6 to 8 p.m. [1800-2000],

	second dog watch; and, 8 p.m. to midnight [2000-2400], evening watch. The half-hours of the watch are marked by the striking the bell an appropriate number of times.
WATER-COOLED	water circulating within a jacket surrounding a machine-gun barrel that transfers heat away from the surface of the metal.
WHITE MICE	South Vietnamese police. The nickname came from their uniform white helmets and gloves.
WIA	Wounded In Action.
WORLD	the WORLD, the United States.
XO	Executive Officer onboard Navy ships, second in command.
YANKEE STATION	operational staging area at 16N-110E in the South China Sea off the coast of Vietnam.
ZIPPO	flame-thrower, also refers to the popular cigarette lighter.
ZIPPO BOAT	LCMs with flame-throwers.
ZULU TIME	SAME-SAME as GREENWICH MEAN TIME. It is used in airplane and ship navigation. Zero degrees of longitude runs through Greenwich; time is measured relative to GREENWICH MEAN TIME. "ZULU" in the phonetic alphabet stands for "Z" which stands for longitude zero.
1MC	PA system onboard Navy ships.
365	the actual number of days in a one year tour. See TOUR.

APPENDIX A

MILITARY PAY CERTIFICATES (MPC)

APPENDIX B

This Vietnamese Language Phrase Book is produced by the Navy Personal Response Project Office. Learning a few Vietnamese phrases contained herein is the first step in a suggested Individual Action Program for Navymen.

1 - Learn thirty Vietnamese Phrases.
2 - Meet one Vietnamese as a Person.
3 - Discuss Problems.
4 - Teach English.

CHÀO
HELLO

XIN LỔI
EXCUSE ME

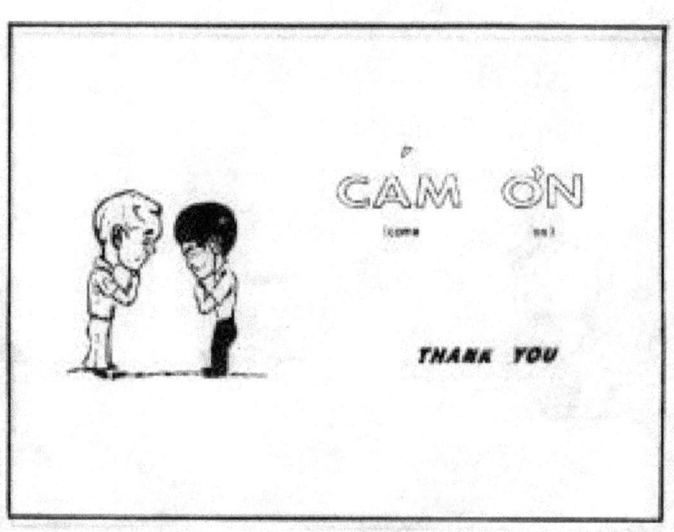
CẢM ƠN
THANK YOU

BAO NHIÊU ?
HOW MUCH ? : HOW MANY ?

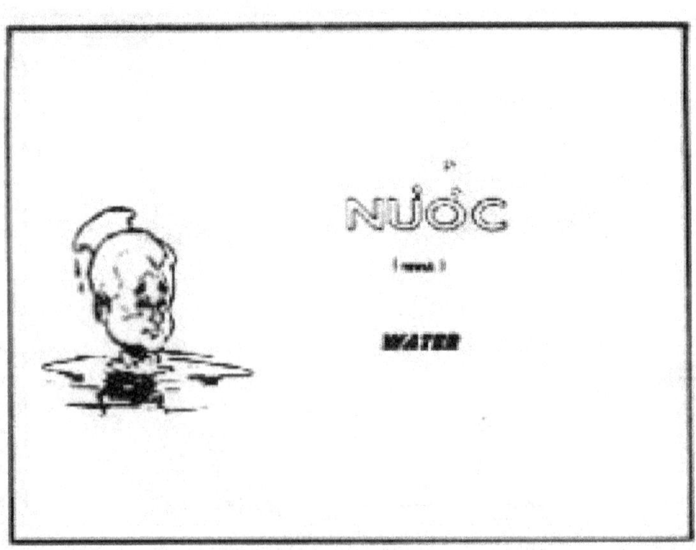
NƯỚC
WATER

XIN LẠI ĐÂY
PLEASE COME HERE

CÁI NÀY LÀ
CÁI GÌ ?
THING THIS IS THING WHAT ?
WHAT IS THIS ?

KHÔNG TỐT
(kum thote)
NO GOOD
NOT GOOD

VIETNAMESE COURTESY PHRASES

APPENDIX C

WELCOME TO

THE REPUBLIC OF VIETNAM

and the

ANNAPOLIS BOQ/BEQ

'Saigon's Innkeeper'

A COMPONENT OF

NAVAL SUPPORT ACTIVITY SAIGON

ALL HANDS INFORMATION

Welcome aboard the Annapolis BOQ/BEQ and the Republic of Vietnam. Depending upon which unit you are assigned to, you can expect to remain here approximately three days. During that time, with the exception of shipboard, HAL-3, VAL-4, RIVFLOT ONE, and TAD personnel, you will participate in an administrative briefing at which time you will complete your travel claims, Dislocation Allowance/Family Separation Allowance, Postal Locator forms, Ration Card, and Currency Control Card applications. Enlisted members will be counseled on their duty preferences for their next tour (VEY Interview). One of the members of the Master-at-Arms force will conduct an in-country security briefing and marijuana lecture to be attended by all new arrivals. Later, depending upon your assignment, you will either draw a weapon or field gear, or both. Finally, you are required to take part in the Personal Response Discussion, conducted in Saigon.

While you are at the Annapolis, you are under the command of COMNAVSUPPACT, Saigon. In addition, there are a few rules, which must be adhered to as well as some pertinent items important to you, namely:

1. Water

    a. All water is non-potable with the exception of that in the coolers.

2. Head Facilities

    a. A sewage problem exists. All the sewage, as well as the shower water and the water from the sinks is pumped into a 5,000-gallon tank. This is pumped out at various times, so use water sparingly and adhere to the posted Head Regulations.

3. Berthing Areas

a. Lying on bunks during working hours is prohibited. The one exception is from 1100-1300, but one must be in underwear only.

b. Personnel utilizing lockers will attach a card to their locker, showing their name and bunk number. This will be done on arrival and cards may be picked up in the Master-at-Arms office.

c. All lockers found untagged are subject to having locks cut and contents placed in the lucky bag.

d. There are women in this billet. Be courteous to them and use your heads with regard to dress while utilizing the head facilities.

4. Departing Billet

a. Before departing the Annapolis for any reason, you must log out with the Master-at-Arms. Upon returning, you will log back in with the MAA.

b. E-6 and below who find it necessary to leave the Annapolis for any reason other than going to chow must have a signed chit.

c. Before departing for your ultimate duty station, make certain you have cleaned our locker.

5. Musters

a. Musters are held at 0730, 1300, and1700. Attendance is mandatory. Officers and E-7and above are required to attend the 0730 musters only, in order to pass on necessary information.

b. Approximately 30 minutes after checking into the Annapolis you will be required to at-tend your first lecture, held in Bay 8. At this time, all personnel will be given a security brief—informed of their next lecture.

6. Watches

a. In order to defend the Annapolis in event of enemy attack and to ensure your safety, various watches have been established and men in grades E-1 thru E-6 may expect to be placed on the watch bill.

7. Watch Bill and Flight List

a. Be certain & check lists once announcement has been made that they are posted.

8. Daily Charge

a. You will be charged 25 piasters per day while at this billet. This fee is used for linen service and to pay the maids for services rendered. You are reminded that this fee is to be paid in piasters only.

9. Uniforms

a. Civilian clothing, mixed uniforms, and camouflaged greens are not authorized in the Saigon area.

10. Personal appearance

    a. Long hair, sideburns, and uncleanliness are not tolerated.

11. Lounge area (Bay 8)

    a. This is a reading and TV viewing area only. Do not sleep there, nor put your feet on the furniture or the bulkheads.

12. Movies

    a. Movies are shown five out of seven evenings from 1900-2000 in the Muster Bay.

13. Lobby and Quarterdeck

    a. Pass quickly through this area. Do not congregate.

14. Outside area

    a. Tables, chairs and trash cans have been put there for your convenience. Keep this area clean by putting waste and cigarette butts in the cans provided.

15. Annapolis Master-at-Arms Force

    a. The purpose of the MAA is to enforce rules and regulations and to maintain security throughout the building.

b. Strict discipline will be adhered to while you are on board and rowdiness and unruly conduct will not be tolerated.

c. We solicit your cooperation doing your part in order to make your stay enjoyable.

(1) Willingly follow commands and regulations.

(2) Relate all problems such as lack of supplies, water pressure, uncleanliness, etc. to the duty MAA.

(3) Conduct yourself in a courteous manner at all times.

16. Security and Theft

a. All gear adrift will be confiscated and placed in the lucky bag.

b. At no time should valuables such as watches, wallets, radios, etc., be left adrift.

c. Personnel are reminded that it is unwise to carry or possess large sums of money.

17. Messing

a. Officers will mess at the Idaho BOQ, which is located directly behind the Annapolis

b. Enlisted personnel will mess at the Montana BEQ, which is located about three blocks down the street from the Annapolis.

18. Liberty

a. There is no authorized liberty for transients in the Saigon/Cholon area; however, you are allowed to utilize the facilities at Idaho BOQ and Montana BEQ.

19. RIVFLOT ONE and Naval Advisory Personnel Assigned to DaNang

a. RIVFLOT ONE personnel do not draw field gear or weapons from the Annapolis.

b. Naval Advisory personnel being assigned to DaNang will not draw a weapon from the Annapolis armory, but will draw field gear from the Annapolis.

20. DON'T CONGREGATE!

a. At no time will anyone congregate around the entrance to the building and the front bunker. Standing outside the protected area and gathering groups is extremely dangerous—Charlie is watching! ! !

OFFICERS' IN-PROCESSING INFORMATION

All NAVSUPPACT and other officers administratively supported by COMNAVSUPPACT, Saigon will report immediately upon arrival in-country to the Annapolis BOQ/BEQ in Saigon for In-processing. All officers assigned to Naval Advisory Group, COMNAVFORV, MACV and other commands will proceed to their respective commands upon completion of In-processing at the Annapolis. RIVPATFLOT FIVE officers designated as Squadron Commanders and Division Commanders will proceed to Binh-Thuy for briefing when released by the Annapolis. All others will proceed to their respective units.

NAVSUPPACT officers will generally spend one night in the Annapolis and will attend a Personal Response briefing prior to going to Nha-Be to check in with Headquarters. All NAVSUPPACT Supply Corps Officers will report to NAVSUPPACT Saigon Supply Department where they will meet with the Assistant to the Supply & Fiscal Officer and the Supply & Fiscal Officer, at which time they will be informed of their ultimate assignment.

NSA and COMNAVFORV officers will draw greens and weapons while here at the Annapolis. MAC officers will draw greens and weapons from MACV. NSA officers will take all gear with them to Nha-Be, unless otherwise advised.

NAVSUPPACT OFFICERS

Upon arrival at Nha-Be, you will report to the Officer Personnel Office, Headquarters, Building C. You will turn in your records to the Officer Records Yeoman, and then have your picture taken. From there you will meet the Admin Officer who will then set up an appointment for you to meet the Chief Staff Officer and the Commander.

After meeting with the Chief Staff Officer and the Commander, you will be briefed by appropriate departments and transportation will be arranged to your ultimate duty station if located outside the Nah Be area.

DO'S AND DON'T'S

A few DO's:

1. Conduct yourself as gentlemen.
2. Remain in a complete, clean, and neat uniform.
3. Pay all bills.
4. Treat all persons with due respect.

A few DON'Ts:

1. Don't become intoxicated.
2. Don' t become involved in political discussions.
3. Don't "talk shop" or discuss classified matters ashore.
4. Don't make tactless comparisons between conditions in Vietnam and the United States.

APPENDIX D

CHRISTMAS CARDS

CHAPTER ONE

Looking out the bus window at a family of four.

Passing by the Presidential Palace.

Lots of young girls dressed in American clothes.

CHAPTER ONE

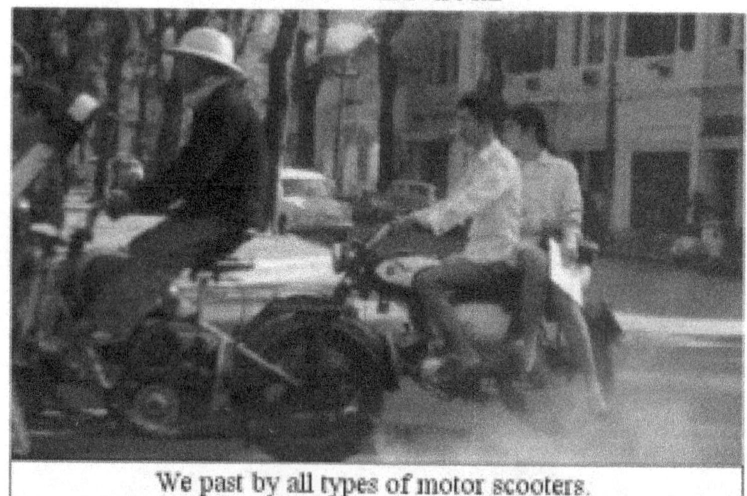

We past by all types of motor scooters.

The Annapolis BEQ.

CHAPTER TWO

An armed escort trailing behind a military bus.

The Tailor's sign.

Going on guard duty.

With shots fired, the other side of the street was vacant.

CHAPTER THREE

Money exchanging.

Every kid I saw had something to sell me.

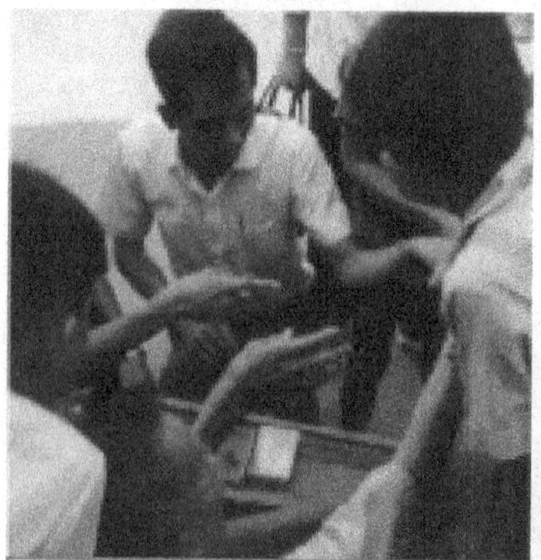

A good old cock roach fight. Not many dogs around for a dog fight.

Some ladies trying to cross a busy street

CHAPTER FOUR

Machine guns and rocket launchers on both sides

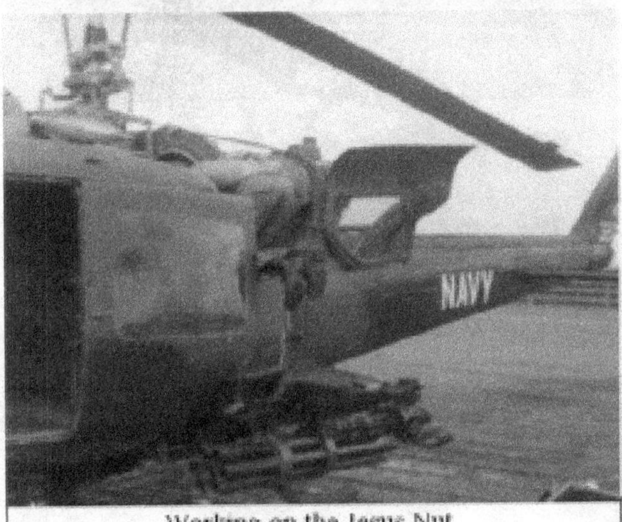

Working on the Jesus Nut.

CHAPTER FOUR

Backing out.

Easy does it.

The helo can now proceed to the runway.

CHAPTER FOUR

A-4 Fighter Jet trailing a parachute.

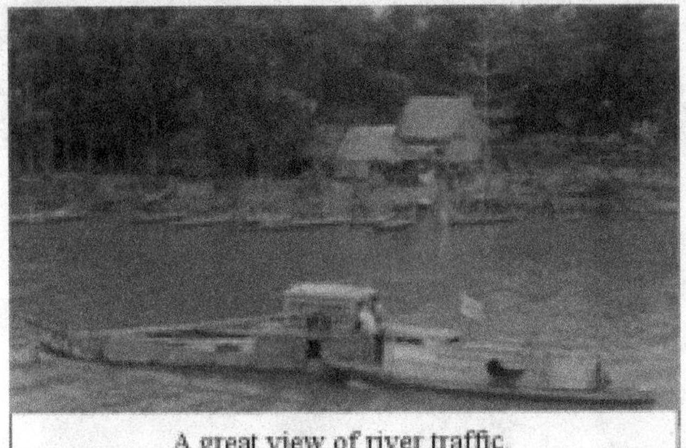

A great view of river traffic.

The girl in white, bottom right half, was giving me the finger.

CHAPTER FOUR

The further from Saigon we flew,the larger the homes.

Jersey Joe's PBR.

Getting out on the skid for my departure.

CHAPTER FIVE

We were going to follow suspected VC up this river. Not necessarily a good idea.

A COBRA Gun ship flew just over our heads.

Nice house.

CHAPTER FIVE

They loved what I did and wanted an encore.

I saw this little kid making his way toward us. I didn't know what he wanted and I had nothing to give him.

CHAPTER SIX

The USS Behawah(APB35)

An ARMY, radio controlled, mine sweeper?

Our ride out to the USS Behawah to call home.

Nothing more than a concussion grenade going off in the water near a Tango Boat

CHAPTER SIX

Our ride off the USS Behawah approaching the flight deck.

Coming in for a landing.

Loaded up and ready to take off.

And we're off.

CHAPTER EIGHT

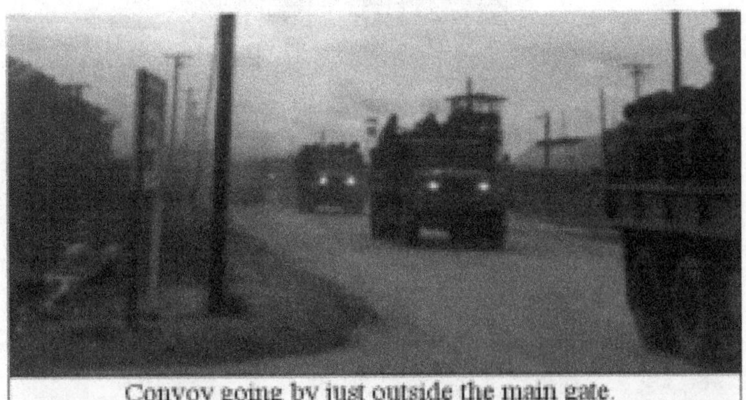

Convoy going by just outside the main gate.

Personnel carriers.

Riding on the back fender of a jeep looking at the two guys riding on the hood.

CHAPTER EIGHT

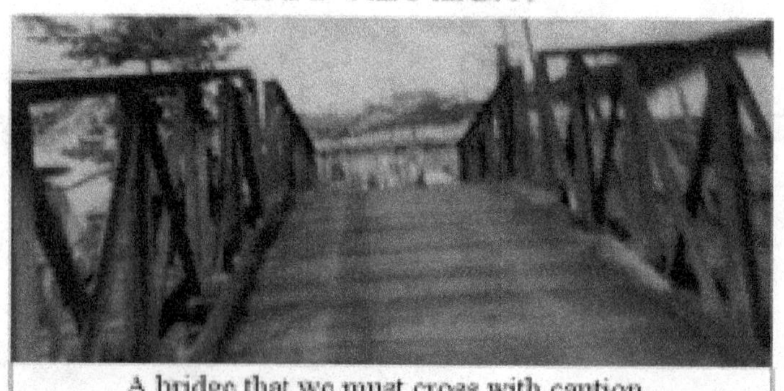

A bridge that we must cross with caution.

A packed local bus pulling up for gas.

Young gas station attendant filling the tank.

Everyone must pull over and out of the way for this fast moving convoy.

CHAPTER EIGHT

A group of kids checking us out as we checked them out.

This aircraft was older than any of us that were going to fly her.

CHAPTER NINE

Two drunk guys going to a party.

Drinking beer on a Richshaw ride.

Young girls on motor scooters.

CHAPTER NINE

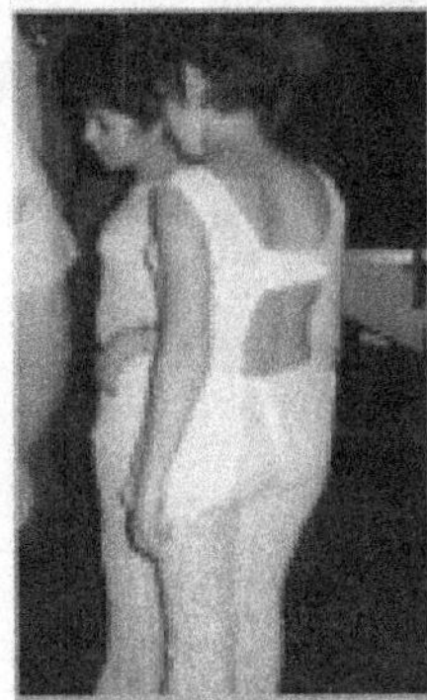

Nice outfits.

Pretty smile and round eyes.

The girls at the party.

Our view from the window ledge as we escaped from the party and Bertha-Butt.

CHAPTER THIRTEEN

Airport control tower and terminal.

Cute little kids.

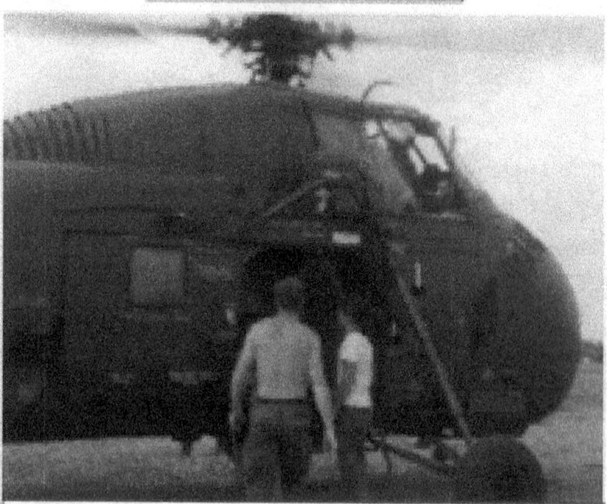

She flew low and slow because she was old.

CHAPTER THIRTEEN

I had a 'door' seat.

An LST ship below us.

Nice view.

CHAPTER THIRTEEN

Landing on an LST.

Our next ride out to the supply ship as we followed the cargo.

A large supply ship, the next leg of our trip.

Off loading supplies to a smaller supply ship.

CHAPTER FOURTEEN

Another, even smaller supply boat coming alongside.

Another one of our rides is coming in.

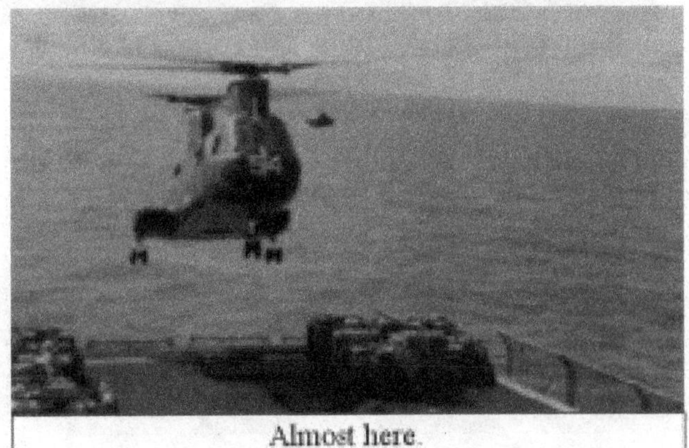

Almost here.

CHAPTER FOURTEEN

Down, safe and sound.

Crewmember with his head out the starboard door.

We're back on solid ground.

CHAPTER FOURTEEN

This town had few, if any, sidewalks.

Our hotel for the night.

We pulled in behind a taxi.

Unable to read the store signs and finding a place that sold cold sodas was difficult.

CHAPTER SEVENTEEN

This little shit for a kid said something to his parents and that got everyone laughing at me. I didn't care why they were laughing, I just wanted to be heading back to the pier with my lukewarm sodas.

A little boy and his sister with a tray of candy.

Taxi riding in the right lane with bikes passing on the sidewalks.

In a taxi drinking beers enjoying the view.

CHAPTER EIGHTEEN

A taxi boat full of people.

Our American flag really stood out in a place of browns and greens.

A single house on the shore all by itself. At least it had running water out front.

CHAPTER EIGHTEEN

A row of small homes. I hoped that no one there was going to take a shot at us. At least everyone was waving and smiling.

Another taxi bus and this one was fancy with flags.

Someone for us to follow was on the other side of the river.

CHAPTER EIGHTEEN

We pulled in behind the other boat.

Finally, I have arrived.

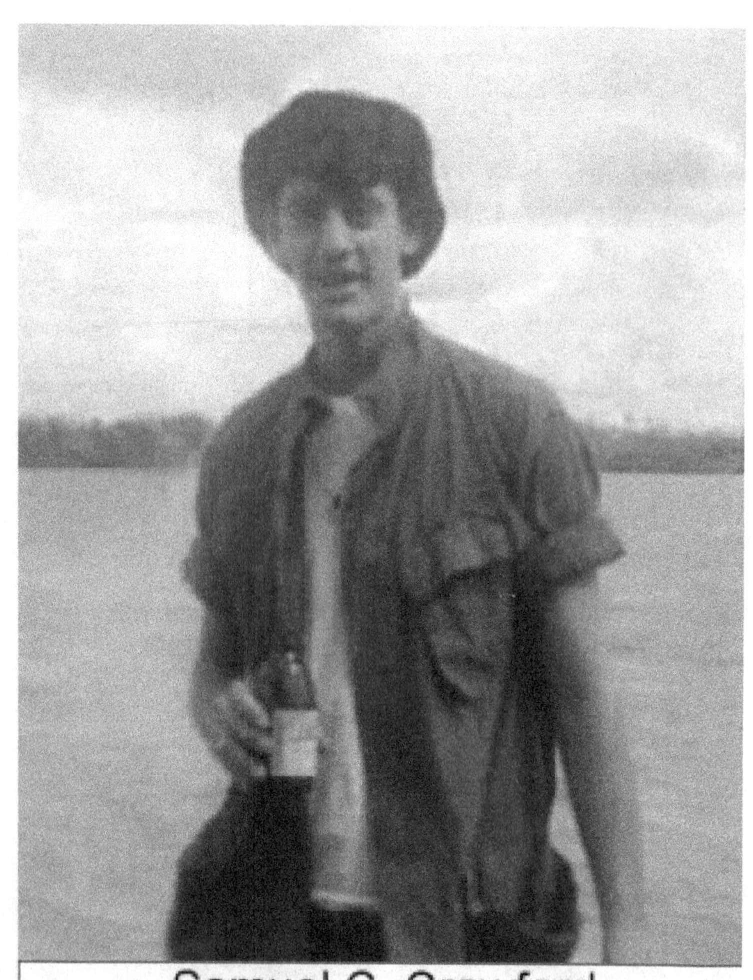

Samuel C. Crawford
Mekong Delta, Vietnam 1969